Stephen Hyde

Nick Hornby is the author of the novels *A Long Way Down, How to Be Good, High Fidelity*, and *About a Boy*, and the memoir *Fever Pitch*. He is also the author of *Songbook*, a finalist for a National Book Critics Circle Award, and *The Polysyllabic Spree*, and editor of the short-story collection *Speaking with the Angel*. Recipient of the American Academy of Arts and Letters' E. M. Forster Award, and the Orange Word International Writers' London Award 2003, he lives in North London.

Praise for *A Long Way Down*
A *New York Times* Bestseller

"Sparkling . . . That comic set piece—four people wind up on top of a building with the same mission but get distracted by a quarrel over who has the best reason to end it all—is a brilliant opening to another irresistible comic novel by the author of *About a Boy*. . . . Hornby's humor is so cutting that you can cuddle up with his (ultimately) warm view of humanity and not hate yourself in the morning."   —*People* (four stars)

"If Camus had written a grown-up version of *The Breakfast Club*, the results might have had more than a little in common with Hornby's grimly comic, oddly moving novel. It's a thrill to watch a writer as talented as Hornby take on the grimmest of subjects without flinching, and somehow make it funny and surprising at the same time. This is a brave and absorbing book."

—Tom Perrotta, *Publishers Weekly* (starred review)

continued . . .

Praise for *About a Boy*
A *New York Times* Bestseller

"Mr. Hornby's wonderful antic sense of humor is employed here . . . [His] sharp observations and his quirky comedic instincts ensure that our journey . . . is entertaining, funny—and occasionally affecting."
—*The New York Times*

"With any luck, we'll soon be having lots of fab and funny writers emulating Nick Hornby, and his kind of accomplishment won't seem quite so foreign."
—*The New York Times Book Review*

"Acerbic, hip wit."
—*Elle*

"Horby is a fine writer, swift and pointed, with a lighter, more mischievous heart than he lets on, and more sympathy for the devil than he admits to."
—*New York* magazine

"You should read [*About a Boy*] for its depictions of the trials of motherhood, the drawbacks of self-imposed detachment, the ache of childhood need, the elastic confines of what constitutes a family, and how it may never be too late to grow up."
—*The Washington Post*

"Horby's *About a Boy* is that rare thing—a second novel that is better, richer, and more rounded than its author's successful debut."
—*The Weekly Standard*

"His *point,* lads, is that there's more to life than shagging!"
—*Newsweek*

"No one- or two-hit wonder, Hornby once again shows his deftness at plucking the heartstrings of lost, frozen souls in '90s London."
—*Paper*

"*About a Boy* is the sort of writing you laugh over even when you read it for the second time—and it's well worth that second read. . . . Fresh and original . . . What does Hornby give the man who has everything? A life."
—*The Hamilton Spectator* (Ontario)

continued . . .

Praise for *High Fidelity*
A *New York Times* Notable Book

"One of the top ten books of the year."   *—Entertainment Weekly*

"It is rare that a book so hilarious is also so sharp about sex and manliness, memory and music. Many men—and certainly, all addictive personalities—will find these pages shadows of themselves. And most of us will hear, in Hornby's acoustic prose, the obsessive chords of the past that more often lock up than liberate our hearts."   *—The New Yorker*

"As funny, compulsive and contemporary a first novel as you could wish for."   *—GQ*

"Mr. Hornby captures the loneliness and childishness of adult life with such precision and wit that you'll find yourself nodding and smiling. *High Fidelity* fills you with the same sensation you get from hearing a debut record album that has more charm and verve and depth than anything you can recall."

—The New York Times Book Review

"A true original . . . Hornby is as fine an analyst as he is a funny man."
—Time

"Hornby's seamless prose and offhand humor make for one hilarious set piece after another, as suffering, self-centered Rob ruminates on women, sex, and *Abbey Road*. But then he's forced to consider loneliness, fitting-in, death, and failure—and *that* is what lingers."   *—Spin*

"Keep this book away from your girlfriend—it contains too many of your secrets to let it fall into the wrong hands."   *—Details*

ALSO BY NICK HORNBY

FICTION

HIGH FIDELITY

ABOUT A BOY

HOW TO BE GOOD

NONFICTION

FEVER PITCH

SONGBOOK

THE POLYSYLLABIC SPREE

ANTHOLOGY

SPEAKING WITH THE ANGEL

RIVERHEAD BOOKS

NEW YORK

A

L
O
N
G

W A Y

NICK HORNBY

D
O
W
N

THE BERKLEY PUBLISHING GROUP
Published by the Penguin Group
Penguin Group (USA) Inc.
375 Hudson Street, New York, New York 10014, USA
Penguin Group (Canada), 90 Eglinton Avenue East, Toronto, Ontario M4P 2Y3, Canada
(a division of Pearson Penguin Canada Inc.)
Penguin Books Ltd., 80 Strand, London WC2R 0RL, England
Penguin Group Ireland, 25 St. Stephen's Green, Dublin 2, Ireland (a division of Penguin
Books Ltd.)
Penguin Group (Australia), 250 Camberwell Road, Camberwell, Victoria 3124, Australia (a division of Pearson Australia Group Pty. Ltd.)
Penguin Books India Pvt. Ltd., 11 Community Centre, Panchsheel Park, New Delhi–110 017,
India
Penguin Group (NZ), cnr Airborne and Rosedale Roads, Albany, Auckland 1310, New Zealand
(a division of Pearson New Zealand Ltd.)
Penguin Books (South Africa) (Pty.) Ltd., 24 Sturdee Avenue, Rosebank, Johannesburg 2196,
South Africa

Penguin Books Ltd., Registered Offices: 80 Strand, London WC2R 0RL, England

First Riverhead hardcover edition: June 2005
First Riverhead trade paperback edition: May 2006
Riverhead trade paperback ISBN: 1-59448-193-8

The Library of Congress has catalogued the Riverhead hardcover edition as follows:

Hornby, Nick.
    A long way down / Nick Hornby.
      p. cm.
    ISBN 1-57322-302-6
    I. Title.
    PR6058.O689L66   2005   2004058837
    823'.914—dc22

PRINTED IN THE UNITED STATES OF AMERICA

10

Thanks to: Tony Lacey, Wendy Carlton,

Helen Fraser, Susan Petersen, Joanna Prior,

Zelda Turner, Eli Horowitz, Mary Cranitch,

Caroline Dawnay, Alex Elam, John Hamilton

To Amanda

The cure for unhappiness is happiness,
I don't care what anyone says.

ELIZABETH McCRACKEN,
Niagara Falls All Over Again

PART ONE

MARTIN

Can I explain why I wanted to jump off the top of a tower block? Of course I can explain why I wanted to jump off the top of a tower block. I'm not a bloody idiot. I can explain it because it wasn't inexplicable: It was a logical decision, the product of proper thought. It wasn't even very serious thought, either. I don't mean it was whimsical—I just mean that it wasn't terribly complicated, or agonized. Put it this way: Say you were, I don't know, an assistant bank manager in Guildford. And you'd been thinking of emigrating, and then you were offered the job of managing a bank in Sydney. Well, even though it's a pretty straightforward decision, you'd still have to think for a bit, wouldn't you? You'd at least have to work out whether you could bear to move, whether you could leave your friends and colleagues behind, whether you could uproot your wife and kids. You might sit down with a bit of paper and draw up a list of pros and cons. You know:

CONS: aged parents, friends, golf club

PROS: more money, better quality of life (house with pool, barbecue, etc.), sea, sunshine, no left-wing councils banning "Baa, Baa Black Sheep," no EEC directives banning British sausages, etc.

It's no contest, is it? The golf club! Give me a break. Obviously your aged parents give you pause for thought, but that's all it is—a pause, and a brief one, too. You'd be on the phone to the travel agent's within ten minutes.

Well, that was me. There simply weren't enough regrets, and lots and lots of reasons to jump. The only things on my "cons" list were the kids, but I couldn't imagine Cindy letting me see them again anyway. I haven't got any aged parents, and I don't play golf. Suicide was my Sydney. And I say that with no offense to the good people of Sydney intended.

MAUREEN

I told him I was going to a New Year's Eve party. I told him in October. I don't know whether people send out invitations to New Year's Eve parties in October or not. Probably not. (How would I know? I haven't been to one since 1984. June and Brian across the road had one, just before they moved. And even then I only nipped in for an hour or so, after he'd gone to sleep.) But I couldn't wait any longer. I'd been thinking about it since May or June, and I was itching to tell him. Stupid, really. He doesn't understand, I'm sure he doesn't. They tell me to keep talking to him, but you can see that nothing goes in. And what a thing to be itching about anyway! It just goes to show what I had to look forward to, doesn't it?

The moment I told him, I wanted to go straight to confession. Well, I'd lied, hadn't I? I'd lied to my own son. Oh, it was only a tiny, silly lie: I'd told him months in advance that I was going to a party, a party I'd made up. I'd made it up properly, too. I told him whose party it was, and why I'd been invited, and why I wanted to go, and who else would be there. (It was Bridgid's party, Bridgid from the church. And I'd been invited because her sister was coming over from Cork, and her sister had asked after me in a couple of letters. And I wanted to go because Bridgid's sister had taken her mother-in-law to Lourdes, and I wanted to find out all about it, with a view to taking Matty one day.) But confession wasn't possible, because I knew I would have to repeat the sin, the lie, over and over as the year came to an end. Not only to Matty, but to the people at the nursing home, and . . . Well, there isn't anyone else, really. Maybe someone at the church, or someone in a shop. It's almost comical, when you think about it. If you spend day and night looking after a sick child, there's very little room for sin, and I hadn't done anything worth confessing for donkey's years. And I went from that, to sinning so terribly that I couldn't even talk to the priest, because I was going to go on sinning and sinning until the day I died, when I would commit the biggest sin of all. (And why is it the biggest sin of all? All your life you're told that you'll be going to this marvelous place when you pass on. And the one thing you can do to get you there a bit quicker is something that stops you getting there at all. Oh, I can see that it's a kind of queue-jumping. But if someone jumps the queue at the Post Office, people tut. Or sometimes they say, Excuse me, I was here first. They don't say, You will be consumed by hellfire for all eternity. That would be a bit strong.) It didn't stop me from going to the church. But I only kept going because people would think there was something wrong if I stopped.

As we got closer and closer to the date, I kept passing on little tidbits of information that I told him I'd picked up. Every Sunday I pretended as though I'd learned something new, because Sundays were when I saw Bridgid. "Bridgid says there'll be dancing." "Bridgid's worried that not everyone likes wine and beer, so she'll be providing spirits." "Bridgid doesn't know how many people will have eaten already." If Matty had been able to understand anything, he'd have decided that this Bridgid woman was a lunatic, worrying like that about a little get-together. I blushed every time I saw her at the church. And of course I wanted to know what she actually was doing on New Year's Eve, but I never asked. If she was planning to have a party, she might've felt that she had to invite me.

I'm ashamed, thinking back. Not about the lies—I'm used to lying now. No, I'm ashamed of how pathetic it all was. One Sunday I found myself telling Matty about where Bridgid was going to buy the ham for the sandwiches. But it was on my mind, New Year's Eve, of course it was, and it was a way of talking about it, without actually saying anything. And I suppose I came to believe in the party a little bit myself, in the way that you come to believe the story in a book. Every now and again I imagined what I'd wear, how much I'd drink, what time I'd leave. Whether I'd come home in a taxi. That sort of thing. In the end it was as if I'd actually been. Even in my imagination, though, I couldn't see myself talking to anyone at the party. I was always quite happy to leave it.

JESS

I was at a party downstairs in the squat. It was a shit party, full of all these ancient crusties sitting on the floor drinking cider and smoking huge spliffs and listening to weirdo space-out reggae. At midnight, one of them clapped sarcastically, and a couple of others laughed, and that was it—Happy New Year to you, too. You could have turned up to that party as the happiest person in London, and you'd still have wanted to jump off the roof by five past twelve. And I wasn't the happiest person in London anyway. Obviously.

I only went because someone at college told me Chas would be there, but he wasn't. I tried his mobile for the one zillionth time, but it wasn't on. When we first split up, he called me a stalker, but that's like an emotive word, "stalker," isn't it? I don't think you can call it stalking when it's just phone calls and letters and e-mails and knocking on the door. And I only turned up at his work twice. Three times, if you count his Christmas party, which I don't, because he said he was going to take me to that anyway. Stalking is when you follow them to the shops and on holiday and all that, isn't it?

Well, I never went near any shops. And anyway I didn't think it was stalking when someone owed you an explanation. Being owed an explanation is like being owed money, and not just a fiver, either. Five or six hundred quid, minimum, more like. If you're owed five or six hundred quid, minimum, and the person who owes it to you is avoiding you, then you're bound to knock on his door late at night, when you know he's going to be in. People get serious about that sort of money. They call in debt collectors, and break people's legs, but I never went that far. I showed some restraint.

So even though I could see straightaway that he wasn't at this party, I stayed for a while. Where else was I going to go? I was feeling sorry for myself. How can you be eighteen and not have anywhere to go on New Year's Eve, apart from some shit party in some shit squat where you don't know anybody? Well, I managed it. I seem to manage it every year. I make friends easily enough, but then I piss them off, I know that much, even if I'm not sure why or how. And so people and parties disappear.

I pissed Jen off, I'm sure of that. She disappeared, like everyone else.

MARTIN

I'd spent the previous couple of months looking up suicide inquests on the Internet, just out of curiosity. And nearly every single time, the coroner says the same thing: "He took his own life while the balance of his mind was disturbed." And then you read the story about the poor bastard: His wife was sleeping with his best friend, he'd lost his job, his daughter had been killed in a road accident some months before . . . Hello, Mr. Coroner? Anyone at home? I'm sorry, but there's no disturbed mental balance here, my friend. I'd say he got it just right. Bad thing upon bad thing upon bad thing until you can't take any more, and then it's off to the nearest multistory car park in the family hatchback with a length of rubber tubing. Surely that's fair enough? Surely the coroner's report should read, "He took his own life after sober and careful contemplation of the fucking shambles it had become."

Not once did I read a newspaper report that convinced me that the deceased was off the old trolley. You know: "The Manchester United forward, who was engaged to the current Miss Sweden, had recently achieved a unique Double: He is the only man ever to have won the FA Cup and an Oscar for Best Actor in the same year. The rights to his first novel had just been bought for an undisclosed sum by Steven Spielberg. He was found hanging from a beam in his stables by a member of his staff." Now, I've never seen a coroner's report like that, but if there were cases in which happy, successful, talented people took their own lives, one could safely come to the conclusion that the old balance was indeed wonky. And I'm not saying that being engaged to Miss Sweden, playing for Manchester United, and winning Oscars inoculates you against depression—I'm sure it doesn't. I'm just saying that these things help. Look at the statistics. You're more likely to top yourself if you've just gone through a divorce. Or if you're anorexic. Or if you're unemployed. Or if you're a prostitute. Or if you've fought in a war, or if you've been raped, or if you've lost somebody . . . There are lots and lots of factors that push people over the edge; none of these factors are likely to make you feel anything but fucking miserable.

Two years ago Martin Sharp would not have found himself sitting on a tiny concrete ledge in the middle of the night, looking a hundred feet down at a concrete walkway and wondering whether he'd hear the noise that his bones made when they shattered into tiny pieces. But two years ago Martin Sharp was a different person. I still had my job. I still had a wife. I hadn't slept with a fifteen-year-old. I hadn't been to prison. I hadn't had to talk to my young daughters about a front-page tabloid newspaper article, an article headlined with the word SLEAZEBAG! and illustrated with a picture of me lying on the pavement outside a well-known London nightspot. (What would the headline have been if I had gone over? SLEAZY DOES IT! perhaps. Or maybe SHARP END!) There was, it is fair to say, less reason for ledge-sitting before all that happened. So don't tell me that the balance of my mind was disturbed, because it really didn't feel that way. (What does it mean, anyway, that stuff about "the balance of the mind"? Is it strictly scientific? Does the mind really wobble up and down in the head like some sort of fish scale, according to how loopy you are?) Wanting to kill myself was an appropriate and reasonable response to a whole series of unfortunate events that had rendered life unlivable. Oh, yes, I know the shrinks would say that they could have helped, but that's half the trouble with this bloody country, isn't it? No one's willing to face their responsibilities. It's always someone else's fault. Boo hoo hoo. Well, I happen to be one of those rare individuals who believe that what went on with Mummy and Daddy had nothing to do with me screwing a fifteen-year-old. I happen to believe that I would have slept with her regardless of whether I'd been breast-fed or not, and it was time to face up to what I'd done.

And what I'd done is, I'd pissed my life away. Literally. Well, OK, not *literally* literally. I hadn't, you know, turned my life into urine and stored it in my bladder and so on and so forth. But I felt as if I'd pissed my life away in the same way that you can piss money away. I'd had a life, full of kids and wives and jobs and all the usual stuff, and I'd somehow managed to mislay it. No, you see, that's not right. I knew where my life was, just as you know where money goes when you piss it away. I hadn't mislaid it at all. I'd spent it. I'd spent my kids and my job and my wife on teenaged girls and nightclubs: These things all come at a price, and I'd happily paid it, and suddenly my life wasn't there anymore. What would I be leaving behind? On New Year's Eve, it felt as though I'd be saying goodbye to a dim form of consciousness and a semi-functioning digestive system—all the indications of a life, certainly, but none of the content. I didn't even feel sad, particularly. I just felt very stupid, and very angry.

I'm not sitting here now because I suddenly saw sense. The reason I'm sitting here now is because that night turned into as much of a mess as everything else. I couldn't even jump off a fucking tower block without fucking it up.

MAUREEN

On New Year's Eve the nursing home sent their ambulance round for him. You had to pay extra for that, but I didn't mind. How could I? In the end, Matty was going to cost them a lot more than they were costing me. I was only paying for a night, and they were going to pay for the rest of his life.

I thought about hiding some of Matty's stuff, in case they thought it was odd, but no one had to know it was his. I could have had loads of kids, as far as they knew, so I left it there. They came around six, and these two young fellas wheeled him out. I couldn't cry when he went, because then the young fellas would guess something was wrong; as far as they knew, I was coming to fetch him at eleven the next morning. I just kissed him on the top of his head and told him to be good at the home, and I held it all in until I'd seen them leave. Then I wept and wept, for about an hour. He'd ruined my life, but he was still my son, and I was never going to see him again, and I couldn't even say goodbye properly. I watched the television for a while, and I did have one or two glasses of sherry, because I knew it would be cold out.

I waited at the bus stop for ten minutes, but then I decided to walk. Knowing that you want to die makes you less scared. I wouldn't have dreamed of walking all that way late at night, especially when the streets are full of drunks, but what did it matter now? Although then, of course, I found myself worrying about being attacked but not murdered—left for dead without actually dying. Because then I'd be taken to hospital, and they'd find out who I was, and they'd find out about Matty, and all those months of planning would have been a complete waste of time, and I'd come out of hospital owing the home thousands of pounds, and where was I going to find that? But no one attacked me. A couple of people wished me a happy New Year, but that was about all. There isn't so much to be afraid of, out there. I can remember thinking it was funny to find that out, on the last night of my life; I'd spent the rest of it being afraid of everything.

I'd never been to Toppers' House before. I'd just been past it on the bus once or twice. I didn't even know for sure that you could get onto the roof anymore, but the door was open, and I just walked up the stairs until I couldn't walk any farther. I don't know why it didn't occur to me that you couldn't just jump off whenever you felt like it, but the moment I saw it I realized that they wouldn't let you do that. They'd put this wire up, way up high, and there were curved railings with spikes on the top . . . Well, that's when I began to panic. I'm not tall, and I'm not very strong, and I'm not as young as I was. I couldn't see how I was going to get over the top of it all, and it had to be that night, because of Matty being in the home and everything. And I started to go through all the other options, but none of them were any good. I didn't want to do it in my own front room, where someone I knew would find me.

I wanted to be found by a stranger. And I didn't want to jump in front of a train, because I'd seen a program on the television about the poor drivers and how suicides upset them. And I didn't have a car, so I couldn't drive off to a quiet spot and breathe in the exhaust fumes . . .

And then I saw Martin, right over on the other side of the roof. I hid in the shadows and watched him. I could see he'd done things properly: He'd brought a little stepladder and some wire cutters, and he'd managed to climb over the top like that. And he was just sitting on the ledge, dangling his feet, looking down, taking nips out of a little hip flask, smoking, and thinking, while I waited. And he smoked and he smoked and I waited and waited until in the end I couldn't wait anymore. I know it was his stepladder, but I needed it. It wasn't going to be much use to him.

I never tried to push him. I'm not beefy enough to push a grown man off a ledge. And I wouldn't have tried anyway. It wouldn't have been right; it was up to him whether he jumped or not. I just went up to him and put my hand through the wire and tapped him on the shoulder. I only wanted to ask him if he was going to be long.

JESS

Before I got to the squat, I never had any intention of going onto the roof. Honestly. I'd forgotten about the whole Toppers' House thing until I started speaking to this guy. I think he fancied me, which isn't really saying much, seeing as I was about the only female under thirty who could still stand up. He gave me a fag, and he told me his name was Bong, and when I asked him why he was called Bong he said it was because he always smoked his weed out of a bong. And I went, Does that mean everyone else here is called Spliff? But he was just like, No, that bloke over there is called Mental Mike. And that one over there is called Puddle. And that one over there is Nicky Turd. And so on, until he'd been through everyone in the room he knew.

But the ten minutes I spent talking to Bong made history. Well, not history like 55 BC or 1939. Not historical history, unless one of us goes on to invent a time machine or stops Britain from being invaded by Al Qaeda or something. But who knows what would have happened to us if Bong hadn't fancied me? Because before he started chatting me up I was just about to go home, and Maureen and Martin would be dead now, probably, and . . . Well, everything would have been different.

When Bong had finished going through his list, he looked at me and he went, You're not thinking of going up on the roof, are you? And I thought, Not with you, stoner-brain. And he went, Because I can see the pain and desperation in your eyes. I was well pissed by that time, so looking back on it, I'm pretty sure that what he could see in my eyes were seven Bacardi Breezers and two cans of Special Brew. I just went, Oh, really? And he went, Yeah, see, I've been put on suicide watch, to look out for people who've only come here because they want to go upstairs. And I was like, What happens upstairs? And he laughed, and went, You're joking, aren't you? This is

Toppers' House, man. This is where people kill themselves. And I would never have thought of it if he hadn't said that.

Everything suddenly made sense. Because even though I'd been about to go home, I couldn't imagine what I'd do when I got there, and I couldn't imagine waking up in the morning. I wanted Chas, and he didn't want me, and I suddenly realized that easily the best thing to do was make my life as short as I possibly could. I almost laughed, it was so neat: I wanted to make my life short, and I was at a party in Toppers' House, and the coincidence was too much. It was like a message from God. OK, it was disappointing that all God had to say to me was, like, Jump off a roof, but I didn't blame him. What else was he supposed to tell me?

I could feel the weight of everything then—the weight of loneliness, of everything that had gone wrong. I felt heroic, going up those last few flights to the top of the building, dragging that weight along with me. Jumping felt like the only way to get rid of it, the only way to make it work for me instead of against me; I felt so heavy that I knew I'd hit the street in no time. I'd beat the world record for falling off a tower block.

MARTIN

If she hadn't tried to kill me, I'd be dead, no question. But we've all got a preservation instinct, haven't we? Even if we're trying to kill ourselves when it kicks in. All I know is that I felt this thump on my back, and I turned round and grabbed the railings behind me, and I started yelling. I was drunk by then. I'd been taking nips out of the old hip flask for a while, and I'd had a skinful before I came out, as well. (I know, I know, I shouldn't have driven. But I wasn't going to take the fucking stepladder on the bus.) So, yes, I probably did let rip with a bit of vocabulary. If I'd known it was Maureen, if I'd known what Maureen was like, then I would have toned it down a bit, probably, but I didn't; I think I might even have used the "c" word, for which I've apologized. But you'd have to admit it was a unique situation.

I stood up and turned round carefully, because I didn't want to fall off until I chose to, and I started yelling at her, and she just stared.

"I know you," she said.

"How?" I was being slow. People come up to me in restaurants and shops and theaters and garages and urinals all over Britain and say, "I know you," and they invariably mean precisely the opposite; they mean, "I don't know you. But I've seen you on the telly." And they want an autograph, or a chat about what Penny Chambers is really like, in real life. But that night, I just wasn't expecting it. It all seemed a bit beside the point, that side of life.

"From the television."

"Oh, for Christ's sake. I was about to kill myself, but never mind, there's always time for an autograph. Have you got a pen? Or a bit of paper? And before you ask, she's a right bitch who will snort anything and fuck anybody. What are you doing up here anyway?"

"I was . . . I was going to jump, too. I wanted to borrow your ladder."

That's what everything comes down to: ladders. Well, not ladders literally; the Middle East peace process doesn't come down to ladders, and nor do the money markets. But one thing I know from interviewing people on the show is that you can reduce the most enormous topics down to the tiniest parts, as if life were an Airfix model. I've heard a religious leader attribute his faith to a faulty catch on a garden shed (he got locked in for a night when he was a kid, and God guided him through the darkness); I've heard a hostage describe how he survived because one of his captors was fascinated by the London Zoo family discount card he kept in his wallet. You want to talk about big things, but it's the catches on the garden sheds and the London Zoo cards that give you the footholds; without them you wouldn't know where to start. Not if you're hosting *Rise and Shine with Penny and Martin* you don't anyway. Maureen and I couldn't talk about why we were so unhappy that we wanted our brains to spill out onto the concrete like a McDonald's milk shake, so we talked about the ladder instead.

"Be my guest."

"I'll wait until . . . Well, I'll wait."

"So you're just going to stand there and watch?"

"No. Of course not. You'll be wanting to do it on your own, I'd imagine."

"You'd imagine right."

"I'll go over there." She gestured to the other side of the roof.

"I'll give you a shout on the way down."

I laughed, but she didn't.

"Come on. That wasn't a bad gag. In the circumstances."

"I suppose I'm not in the mood, Mr. Sharp."

I don't think she was trying to be funny, but what she said made me laugh even more. Maureen went to the other side of the roof and sat down with her back against the far wall. I turned around and lowered myself back onto the ledge. But I couldn't concentrate. The moment had gone. You're probably thinking, How much concentration does a man need to throw himself off the top of a high building? Well, you'd be surprised. Before Maureen arrived I'd been in the zone; I was in a place where it would have been easy to push myself off. I was entirely focused on all the reasons I was up there in the first place; I understood with a horrible clarity the impossibility of attempting to resume life down on the ground. But the conversation with her had distracted me, pulled me back out into the world, into the cold and the wind and the noise of the thumping bass seven floors below. I couldn't get the mood back; it was as if one of the kids had woken up just as Cindy and I were starting to make love. I hadn't changed my mind, and I still knew that I'd have to do it sometime. It's just that I knew I wasn't going to be able to do it in the next five minutes.

I shouted at Maureen.

"Oi! Do you want to swap places? See how you get on?" And I laughed again. I was, I felt, on a comedy roll, drunk enough—and, I suppose, deranged enough—to feel that just about anything I said would be hilarious.

Maureen came out of the shadows and approached the breach in the wire fence cautiously.

"I want to be on my own, too," she said.

"You will be. You've got twenty minutes. Then I want my spot back."

"How are you going to get back over this side?"

I hadn't thought of that. The stepladder really only worked one way: There wasn't enough room on my side of the railings to open it out.

"You'll have to hold it."

"What do you mean?"

"You hand it over the top to me. I'll put it flush against the railings. You hold it steady from that side."

"I'd never be able to keep it in place. You're too heavy."

And she was too light. She was small, but she carried no weight at all. I wondered whether she wanted to kill herself because she didn't want to die a long and painful death from some disease or other.

"So you'll have to put up with me being here."

I wasn't sure that I wanted to climb over to the other side anyway. The railings marked out a boundary now: You could get to the stairs from the roof, and to the street from the stairs, and from the street you could get to Cindy, and the kids, and Danielle, and her dad, and everything else that had blown me up here as if I were a crisp packet in a gale. The ledge felt safe. There was no humiliation and shame there—beyond the humiliation and shame you'd expect to feel if you were sitting on a ledge, on your own, on New Year's Eve.

"Why can't you shuffle round to the other side of the roof?"

"Why can't you? It's my ladder."

"You're not much of a gentleman."

"No, I'm fucking not. That's one of the reasons I'm up here, in fact. Don't you read the papers?"

"I look at the local one sometimes."

"So what do you know about me?"

"You used to be on the TV."

"That's it?"

"I think so." She thought for a moment. "Were you married to someone in ABBA?"

"No."

"Or another singer?"

"No."

"Oh. And you like mushrooms, I know that."

"Mushrooms?"

"You said. I remember. There was one of those chef fellas in the studio, and he gave you something to taste, and you said, 'Mmmm, I love mushrooms. I could eat them all day.' Was that you?"

"It might have been. But that's all you can dredge up?"

"Yes."

"So why do you think I want to kill myself?"

"I've no idea."

"You're pissing me around."

"Would you mind watching your language? I find it offensive."

"I'm sorry."

But I couldn't believe it. I couldn't believe I'd found someone who didn't know. Before I went to prison, I used to wake up in the morning and the tabloid scum were waiting outside the front door. I had crisis meetings with agents and managers and TV executives. It seemed impossible that there was anyone in Britain uninterested in what I had done, mostly because I lived in a world where it was the only thing that seemed to matter. Maybe Maureen lived on the roof, I thought. It would be easy to lose touch up there.

"What about your belt?" She nodded at my waist. As far as Maureen was concerned, these were her last few moments on earth. She didn't want to spend them talking about my passion for mushrooms (a passion which, I fear, may have been manufactured for the camera anyway). She wanted to get on with things.

"What about it?"

"Take your belt off and put it round the ladder. Buckle it your side of the railings."

I saw what she meant, and saw that it would work, and for the next couple of minutes we worked in a companionable silence; she passed the ladder over the fence, and I took my belt off, passed it round both ladder and railings, pulled it tight, buckled it up, and gave it a shake to check it would hold. I really didn't want to die falling backward. I climbed back over; we unbuckled the belt and placed the ladder in its original position.

And I was just about to let Maureen jump in peace when this fucking lunatic came roaring at us.

JESS

I shouldn't have made the noise. That was my mistake. I mean, that was my mistake if the idea was to kill myself. I could have just walked, quickly and quietly and calmly, to the place where Martin had cut through the wire, climbed the ladder, and then jumped. But I didn't. I yelled something like "Out of the way, losers!" and made this Red Indian war-whoop noise, as if it were all a game—which it was at that point, to me anyway—and Martin rugby-tackled me before I got halfway

A
L
O
N
G
W
A
Y

there. And then he sort of kneeled on me and ground my face into that sort of gritty fake tarmac stuff they put on the tops of buildings. Then I really did want to be dead.

I didn't know it was Martin. I never saw anything, really, until he was rubbing my nose in the grit, and then I just saw grit. But I knew what the two of them were doing up there the moment I got to the roof. You didn't have to be, like, a genius to work that out. So when he was sitting on me I went, So how come you two are allowed to kill yourselves and I'm not? And he goes, You're too young. We've fucked our lives up. You haven't yet. And I said, How do you know that? And he goes, No one's fucked their lives up at your age. And I was like, What if I've murdered ten people? Including my parents and, I don't know, my baby twins? And he went, Well, have you? And I said, Yeah, I have. (Even though I hadn't. I just wanted to see what he'd say.) And he went, Well, if you're up here, you've got away with it, haven't you? I'd get on a plane to Brazil if I were you. And I said, What if I want to pay for what I've done with my life? And he said, Shut up.

MARTIN

My first thought, after I'd brought Jess crashing to the ground, was that I didn't want Maureen sneaking off on her own. It was nothing to do with trying to save her life; it would simply have pissed me off if she'd taken advantage of my distraction and jumped. Oh, none of it makes much sense; two minutes before, I'd been practically ushering her over. But I didn't see why Jess should be my responsibility and not hers, and I didn't see why she should be the one to use the ladder when I'd carted it all the way up there. So my motives were essentially selfish; nothing new there, as Cindy would tell you.

After Jess and I had had our idiotic conversation about how she'd killed lots of people, I shouted at Maureen to come and help me. She looked frightened, and then dawdled her way over to us.

"Get a bloody move on."

"What do you want me to do?"

"Sit on her."

Maureen sat on Jess's arse, and I knelt on her arms.

"Just let me go, you old bastard pervert. You're getting a thrill out of this, aren't you?"

Well, obviously that stung a bit, given recent events. I thought for a moment Jess might have known who I was, but even I'm not that paranoid. If you were rugby-tackled in the middle of the night just as you were about to hurl yourself off the top of a tower block, you probably wouldn't be thinking about breakfast television presenters. (This would come as a shock to breakfast television presenters, of course, most of whom firmly believe that people think about nothing else but, breakfast, lunch, and dinner.) I was mature enough to rise above Jess's taunts, even though I felt like breaking her arms.

"If we let go, are you going to behave?"

"Yes."

So Maureen stood up, and with wearying predictability Jess scrambled for the ladder, and I had to bring her crashing down again.

"Now what?" said Maureen, as if I were a veteran of count-less similar situations and would therefore know the ropes.

"I don't bloody know."

Why it didn't occur to any of us that a well-known suicide spot would be like Piccadilly Circus on New Year's Eve I have no idea, but at that point in the proceedings I had accepted the reality of our situation: We were in the process of turning a solemn and private moment into a farce with a cast of thousands.

And at that precise moment of acceptance, we three became four. There was a polite cough, and when we turned round to look, we saw a tall, good-looking, long-haired man, maybe ten years younger than me, holding a crash helmet under one arm and one of those big insulated bags in the other.

"Any of you guys order a pizza?" he said.

MAUREEN

I'd never met an American before, I don't think. I wasn't at all sure he was one, either, until the others said something. You don't expect Americans to be delivering pizzas, do you? Well, I don't, but perhaps I'm just out of touch. I don't order pizzas very often, but every time I have, they've been delivered by someone who doesn't speak English. Americans don't deliver things, do they? Or serve you in shops, or take your money on the bus. I suppose they must do in America, but they don't here. Indians and West Indians, lots of Australians in the hospital where they see Matty, but no Americans. So we probably thought he was a bit mad at first. That was the only explanation for him. He looked a bit mad, with that hair. And he thought that we'd ordered pizzas while we were standing on the roof of Toppers' House.

"How would we have ordered pizzas?" Jess asked him. We were still sitting on her, so her voice sounded funny.

"On a cell," he said.

"What's a cell?" Jess asked.

"OK, a mobile, whatever."

Fair play to him, we could have done that.

"Are you American?" Jess asked him.

"Yeah."

"What are you doing delivering pizzas?"

"What are you guys doing sitting on her head?"

"They're sitting on my head because this isn't a free country," Jess said. "You can't do what you want to."

"What did you wanna do?"

She didn't say anything.

"She was going to jump," Martin said.

"So were you!"

He ignored her.

"You were all gonna jump?" the pizza man asked us.

We didn't say anything.

"The f——?" he said.

"The f——?" said Jess. "The f—— what?"

"It's an American abbreviation," said Martin. "'The f——?' means 'What the f——?' In America, they're so busy that they don't have time to say the 'what.'"

"Would you watch your language, please?" I said to them. "We weren't all brought up in a pigsty."

The pizza man just sat down on the roof and shook his

head. I thought he was feeling sorry for us, but later he told us it wasn't that at all.

"OK," he said after a while. "Let her go."

We didn't move.

"Hey, you. You f——ing listening to me? Am I gonna have to come over and make you listen?" He stood up and walked toward us.

"I think she's OK now, Maureen," Martin said, as if he was deciding to stand up of his own accord, and not because the American man might punch him. He stood up, and I stood up, and Jess stood up and brushed herself down and swore a lot. Then she stared at Martin.

"You're that bloke," she said. "The breakfast TV bloke. The one who slept with the fifteen-year-old. Martin Sharp. F——! Martin Sharp was sitting on my head. You old pervert."

Well, of course I didn't have a clue about any fifteen-year-old. I don't look at that sort of newspaper unless I'm in the hairdresser's, or someone's left one on the bus.

"You kidding me?" said the pizza man. "The guy who went to prison? I read about him."

Martin made a groaning noise. "Does everyone in America know, too?" he said.

"Sure," the pizza man said. "I read about it in the *New York Times*."

"Oh, God," said Martin, but you could tell he was pleased.

"I was just kidding," said the pizza man. "You used to host a morning talk show here. No one in the U.S. has ever heard of you. Get real."

"Give us some pizza, then," said Jess. "What flavors have you got?"

"I don't know," said the pizza man.

"Let me have a look, then," said Jess.

"No, I mean . . . They're not my pizzas, you know?"

"Oh, don't be such a pussy," said Jess. (Really. That's what she said. I don't know why.) She leaned over, grabbed his bag, and took out the pizza boxes. Then she opened the boxes and started poking the pizzas.

"This one's pepperoni. I don't know what that is, though. Vegetables."

"Vegetarian," said the pizza man.

"Whatever," said Jess. "Who wants what?"

I asked for vegetarian. The pepperoni sounded like something that wouldn't agree with me.

J J

I told a couple people about that night, and the weird thing is that they get the suicide part, but they don't get the pizza part. Most people get suicide, I guess; most people, even if it's hidden deep down inside somewhere, can remember a time in their lives when they thought about whether they really wanted to wake up the next day. Wanting to die seems like it might be a part of being alive. So anyway, I tell people the story of that New Year's Eve, and none of them are like, Whaaaaat? You were gonna kill yourself? It's more, you know, Oh, OK, your band was fucked up, you were at the end of the line with your music, which was all you wanted to do your whole life, *plus* you broke up with your girlfriend, who was the only reason you were in this fuckin' country in the first place . . . Sure, I can see why you were up there. But then like the very next second, they want to know what a guy like me was doing delivering fucking *pizzas*.

OK, you don't know me, so you'll have to take my word for it that I'm not stupid. I read the fuck out of every book I can get my hands on. I like Faulkner and Dickens and Vonnegut and Brendan Behan and Dylan Thomas. Earlier that week—Christmas Day, to be precise—I'd finished *Revolutionary Road* by Richard Yates, which is a totally awesome novel. I was actually going to jump with a copy, not only because it would have been kinda cool, and would've added a little mystique to my death, but because it might have been a good way of getting more people to read it. But the way things worked out, I didn't have any preparation time, and I left it at home. I have to say, though, that I wouldn't recommend finishing it on Christmas Day, in, like, a cold-water bedsit, in a city where you don't really know anybody. It probably didn't help my general sense of well-being, if you know what I mean, because the ending is a real downer.

Anyway, the point is, people jump to the conclusion that anyone driving around North London on a shitty little moped on New Year's Eve for minimum wage is clearly a loser, and almost certainly one *stagione* short of the full *quattro*. Well, OK, we are losers by definition, because delivering pizzas is a job for losers. But we're not all dumb assholes. In fact, even with the Faulkner and Dickens, I was probably the dumbest out of all the guys at work, or at least the worst educated. We got

African doctors, Albanian lawyers, Iraqi chemists . . . I was the only one who didn't have a college degree. (I don't understand how there isn't more pizza-related violence in our society. Just imagine: You're, like, the top whatever in Zimbabwe, brain surgeon or whatever, and then you have to come to England because the fascist regime wants to nail your ass to a tree, and you end up being patronized at three in the morning by some stoned teenaged motherfucker with the munchies . . . I mean, shouldn't you be legally entitled to break his fucking jaw?) Anyway. There's more than one way to be a loser. There's sure more than one way of losing.

So I could say that I was delivering pizzas because England sucks and, more specifically, English girls suck, and I couldn't work legit because I'm not an English guy. Or an Italian guy, or a Spanish guy, or even like a fucking Finnish guy or whatever. So I was doing the only work I could find; Ivan, the Lithuanian proprietor of Casa Luigi on Holloway Road, didn't care that I was from Chicago, not Helsinki. And another way of explaining it is to say that shit happens, and there's no space too small, too dark and airless and fucking hopeless, for people to crawl into.

The trouble with my generation is that we all think we're fucking geniuses. Making something isn't good enough for us, and neither is selling something, or teaching something, or even just doing something; we have to *be* something. It's our inalienable right, as citizens of the twenty-first century. If Christina Aguilera or Britney or some *American Idol* jerk can be something, then why can't I? Where's mine, huh? OK, so my band, we put on the best live shows you could ever see in a bar, and we made two albums, which a lot of critics and not many real people liked. But having talent is never enough to make us happy, is it? I mean, it should be, because a talent is a gift, and you should thank God for it, but I didn't. It just pissed me off because I wasn't being paid for it, and it didn't get me on the cover of *Rolling Stone*.

Oscar Wilde once said, "One's real life is so often the life that one does not lead." Well, fucking right on, Oscar. My real life was full of headlining shows at Wembley and Madison Square Garden and platinum records, and Grammys, and that wasn't the life I was leading, which is maybe why it felt like I could throw it away. The life I was leading didn't let me be, I don't know . . . be who I thought I was. It didn't even let me stand up properly. It felt like I'd been walking down a tunnel that was getting narrower and narrower, and darker and darker, and had started shipping water, and I was all hunched up, and there was a wall of rock in front of me and the only tools I had were my fingernails. And maybe everyone feels that way, but that's no reason to stick with it. Anyway, that New Year's Eve, I'd gotten sick of it, finally. My fingernails were all worn away, and the tips of my fingers were shredded up. I couldn't dig anymore. With the band gone, the only room I had left for self-expression was in checking out of my unreal life: I was going to fly off that fucking roof like Superman. Except, of course, it didn't work out like that.

Some dead people, people who were too sensitive to live: Sylvia Plath, van Gogh, Virginia Woolf, Jackson Pollock, Primo Levi, Kurt Cobain, of course. Some alive people: George W. Bush, Arnold Schwarzenegger, Osama bin Laden. Put a cross next to the people you might want to have a drink with, and then see whether they're on the dead side or the alive side. And, yeah, you could point out that I have stacked the deck, that there are a couple people missing from my "alive" list who might fuck up my argument, a few poets and musicians and so on. And you could also point out that Stalin and Hitler weren't so great, and they're no longer with us. But indulge me anyway: You know what I'm talking about. Sensitive people find it harder to stick around.

So it was real shocking to discover that Maureen, Jess, and Martin Sharp were about to take the Vincent van Gogh route out of this world. (And yeah, thank you, I know Vincent didn't jump off the top of a North London apartment building.) A middle-aged woman who looked like someone's cleaning lady, a shrieking adolescent lunatic, and a talk-show host with an orange face . . . It didn't add up. Suicide wasn't invented for people like this. It was invented for people like Virginia Woolf and Nick Drake. And me. Suicide was supposed to be cool.

New Year's Eve was a night for sentimental losers. It was my own stupid fault. Of course there'd be a low-rent crowd up there. I should have picked a classier date—like March 28, when Virginia Woolf took her walk into the river, or Nick Drake's November 25. If anybody had been on the roof on either of those nights, the chances are they would have been like-minded souls, rather than hopeless fuck-ups who had somehow persuaded themselves that the end of a calendar year is in any way significant. It was just that when I got the order to deliver the pizzas to the squat in Toppers' House, the opportunity seemed too good to turn down. My plan was to wander to the top, take a look around to get my bearings, go back down to deliver the pizzas, and then Do It.

And suddenly there I was with three potential suicides munching the pizzas I was supposed to deliver and staring at me. They were apparently expecting some kind of Gettysburg Address about why their damaged and pointless lives were worth living. It was ironic, really, seeing as I didn't give a fuck whether they jumped or not. I didn't know them from Adam, and none of them looked like they were going to add much to the sum total of human achievement.

"So," I said. "Great. Pizza. A small, good thing on a night like this." Raymond Carver, as you probably know, but it was wasted on these guys.

"Now what?" said Jess.

"We eat our pizza."

"Then?"

"Just give it half an hour, OK? Then we'll see where we're at." I don't know where that came from. Why half an hour? And what was supposed to happen then?

"Everyone needs a little time-out. Looks to me like things were getting undignified up here. Thirty minutes? Is that agreed?"

One by one they shrugged and then nodded, and we went back to chewing our pizza in silence. This was the first time I had tried one of Ivan's. It was inedible, maybe even poisonous.

"I'm not fucking sitting here for half an hour looking at your fucking miserable faces," said Jess.

"That's what you've just this minute agreed to do," Martin reminded her.

"So what?"

"What's the point of agreeing to do something and then not doing it?"

"No point." Jess was apparently untroubled by the concession.

"'Consistency is the last refuge of the unimaginative,'" I said. Wilde again. I couldn't resist.

Jess glared at me.

"He's being nice to you," said Martin.

"There's no point in anything, though, is there?" Jess said. "That's why we're up here."

See, now this was a pretty interesting philosophical argument. Jess was saying that as long as we were on the rooftop, we were all anarchists. No agreements were binding, no rules applied. We could rape and murder each other and no one would pay any attention.

"'To live outside the law, you must be honest,'" I said.

"What the fucking hell does that mean?" said Jess.

You know, I've never really known what the fuck it means, to tell you the truth. Bob Dylan said it, not me, and I'd always thought it sounded good. But this was the first situation I'd ever been in where I was able to put the idea to the test, and I could see that it didn't work. We were living outside the law, and we could lie through our teeth anytime we wanted, and I wasn't sure why we shouldn't.

"Nothing," I said.

"Shut up, then, Yankee boy."

And I did. There were approximately twenty-eight minutes of our time-out remaining.

JESS

A long time ago, when I was eight or nine, I saw this program on telly about the history of the Beatles. Jen liked the Beatles, so she was the one who made me watch it, but I didn't mind.

(I probably told her I did mind, though. I probably made a fuss and pissed her off.) Anyway, when Ringo joined you sort of felt this little shiver, because that was it, then, that was the four of them, and they were ready to go off and be the most famous group in history. Well, that's how I felt when JJ turned up on the roof with his pizzas. I know you'll think, Oh, she's just saying that because it sounds good, but I'm not. I knew, honestly. It helped that he looked like a rock star, with his hair and his leather jacket and all that, but my feeling wasn't anything to do with music; I just mean that I could tell we needed JJ, and so when he appeared it felt right. He wasn't Ringo, though. He was more like Paul. Maureen was Ringo, except she wasn't very funny. I was George, except I wasn't shy or spiritual. Martin was John, except he wasn't talented or cool. Thinking about it, maybe we were more like another group with four people in it.

Anyway, it just felt like something might happen, something interesting, and so I couldn't understand why we were just sitting there eating pizza slices. So I was like, Maybe we should talk, and Martin goes, What, share our pain? And then he made a face, like I'd said something stupid, so I called him a wanker, and then Maureen tutted and asked me whether I said things like that at home (which I do), so I called her a bag lady, and Martin called me a stupid, mean little girl, so I spat at him, which I shouldn't have done and which also, by the way, I don't do anywhere near as much nowadays, and so he made out like he was going to throttle me, and JJ jumped between us, which was just as well for Martin, because I don't think he would have hit me, whereas I most definitely would have hit and bitten and scratched him. And after that little fluffle of activity we sat there puffing and blowing and hating each other for a bit.

And then when we were all calming down, JJ said something like, I'm not sure what harm would be done by sharing our experiences, except he said it more American even than that. And Martin was like, Well, who's interested in your experiences? Your experiences are delivering pizzas. And JJ goes, Well, your experiences, then, not mine. But it was too late, and I could tell from what he'd said about sharing our experiences that he was up here for the same reasons we were. So I went, You came up here to jump, didn't you? And he didn't say anything, and Martin and Maureen looked at him. And Martin just goes, Were you going to jump with the pizzas? Because someone ordered those. Even though Martin was joking, it was like JJ's professional pride had been dented, because he told us that he was only here on a recce, and he was going downstairs to deliver before coming back up again. And I said, Well, we've eaten them now. And Martin goes, Gosh, you don't seem like the jumping type, and JJ said, If you guys are the jumping type then I can't say I'm sorry. There was, as you can tell, a lot of, like, badness in the air.

So I tried again. Oh, go on, let's talk, I said. No need for pain-sharing. Just, you know, our names and why we're up here. Because it might be interesting. We might learn something. We might see a way out, kind of thing. And I have to admit I had a sort of plan. My plan was that they'd help me find Chas, and Chas and I would get back together, and I'd feel better.

But they made me wait, because they wanted Maureen to go first.

MAUREEN

I think they picked me because I hadn't really said anything, and I hadn't rubbed anyone up the wrong way yet. And also, maybe, because I was more mysterious than the others. Martin everyone seemed to know about from the newspapers. And Jess, God love her . . . We'd only known her for half an hour, but you could tell that this was a girl who had problems. My own feeling about JJ, without knowing anything about him, was that he might have been a gay person, because he had long hair and spoke American. A lot of Americans are gay people, aren't they? I know they didn't invent gayness, because they say that was the Greeks. But they helped bring it back into fashion. Being gay was a bit like the Olympics: It disappeared in ancient times, and then they brought it back in the twentieth century. Anyway, I didn't know anything about gays, so I just presumed they were all unhappy and wanted to kill themselves. But me . . . You couldn't really tell anything about me from looking at me, so I think they were curious.

I didn't mind talking, because I knew I didn't need to say very much. None of these people would have wanted my life.

I doubted whether they'd understand how I'd put up with it for as long as I had. It's always the toilet bit that upsets people. Whenever I've had to moan before—when I need another prescription for my antidepressants, for example—I always mention the toilet bit, the cleaning up that needs doing most days. It's funny, because it's the bit I've got used to. I can't get used to the idea that my life is finished, pointless, too hard, completely without hope or color; but the mopping up doesn't really worry me anymore. That's always what gets the doctor reaching for his pen, though.

"Oh, yeah," Jess said when I'd finished. "That's a no-brainer. Don't change your mind. You'd only regret it."

"Some people cope," said Martin.

"Who?" said Jess.

"We had a woman on the show whose husband had been in a coma for twenty-five years."

"And that was her reward, was it? Going on a breakfast TV show?"

"No. I'm just saying."

"What are you just saying?"

"I'm just saying it can be done."

"You're not saying why, though, are you?"

"Maybe she loved him."

They spoke quickly, Martin and Jess and JJ. Like people in a soap opera: bang, bang, bang. Like people who know what to say. I could never have spoken that quickly, not then anyway; it made me realize that I'd hardly spoken at all for twenty-odd years. And the person I spoke to most couldn't speak back.

"What was there to love?" Jess was saying. "He was a vegetable. Not even an awake vegetable. A vegetable in a coma."

"He wouldn't be a vegetable if he wasn't in a coma, would he?" said Martin.

"I love my son," I said. I didn't want them to think I didn't.

"Yes," said Martin. "Of course you do. We didn't mean to imply otherwise."

"Do you want us to kill him for you?" said Jess. "I'll go down there tonight if you want. Before I kill myself. I don't mind. No skin off my nose. And it's not like he's got much to live for, is it? If he could speak, he'd probably thank me for it, poor sod."

My eyes filled with tears, and JJ noticed.

"What are you, a f——ing idiot?" he said to Jess. "Look what you've done."

"Sor-ry," said Jess. "Just an idea."

But that wasn't why I was crying. I was crying because all I wanted in the world, the only thing that would make me want to live, was for Matty to die. And knowing why I was crying just made me cry more.

MARTIN

Everyone bloody knew everything about me, so I didn't see the point of this lark, and I told them that.

"Oh, come on, man," said JJ in his irritating American way. It doesn't take long, I find, to be irritated by Yanks. I know they're our friends and everything, and they respect success over there, unlike the ungrateful natives of this bloody chippy dump, but all that cool daddy-o stuff gets on my wick. I mean, you should have seen him. You'd have thought he was on the roof to promote his latest movie. You certainly wouldn't think he'd been puttering around Archway delivering pizzas.

"We just want to hear your side of it," said Jess.

"There isn't a 'my side.' I was a bloody idiot and I'm paying the price."

"So you don't want to defend yourself? Because you're among friends here," said JJ.

"She just spat at me," I pointed out. "What kind of a friend is that?"

"Oh, don't be such a baby," said Jess. "My friends are always spitting at me. I never take it personally."

"Maybe you should. Perhaps that's how your friends intend it to be taken."

Jess snorted. "If I took it personally, I wouldn't have any friends left."

We let that one hang in the air.

"So what do you want to know that you don't know already?"

"There are two sides to every story," said Jess. "We only know the bad side."

"I didn't know she was fifteen," I said. "She told me she was eighteen. She looked eighteen." That was it. That was the good side of the story.

"So if she'd been, like, six months older you wouldn't be up here?"

"I don't suppose I would, no. Because I wouldn't have broken the law. Wouldn't have gone to prison. Wouldn't have lost my job, my wife wouldn't have found out . . ."

"So you're saying it was just bad luck."

"I'd say there was a certain degree of culpability involved." This was, I need hardly tell you, an attempt at dry understatement; I didn't know then that Jess is at her happiest wallowing in the marshland of the bleeding obvious.

"Just because you've swallowed a fucking dictionary, it doesn't mean you've done nothing wrong," said Jess.

"That's what 'culpability' . . ."

"Because some married men wouldn't have shagged her no matter how old she was. And you've got kids and all, haven't you?"

"I have indeed."

"So bad luck's got nothing to do with it."

"Oh, for fuck's sake. Why d'you think I've been dangling my feet over the ledge, you moron? I screwed up. I'm not trying to make excuses for myself. I feel so wretched I want to die."

"I should hope so."

"Thanks. And thanks for introducing this exercise, too. Very helpful. Very . . . curative."

Another polysyllabic word, another dirty look.

"I'm interested in something," said JJ.

"Go on."

"Why is it easier to, like, leap into the void than to face up to what you've done?"

"This is facing up to what I've done."

"People are always fucking young girls and leaving their wives and kids. They don't all jump off buildings, man."

"No. But like Jess says, maybe they should."

"Really? You think anyone who makes a mistake of this kind should die? Whoa. That's some heavy shit," said JJ.

Did I really think that? Maybe I did. Or maybe I had done. As some of you might know, I'd written things in newspapers which said exactly that, more or less. This was before my fall from grace, naturally. I'd called for the restoration of the death penalty, for example. I'd called for resignations and chemical castrations and prison sentences and public humiliations and penances of every kind. And maybe I had meant it when I'd said that men who couldn't keep their things in their trousers should be . . . Actually, I can't remember what I thought the appropriate punishment was now for philanderers and serial adulterers. I shall have to look up the column in question. But the point is that I was practicing what I preached. I hadn't been able to keep my thing in my trousers, so now I had to jump. I was a slave to my own logic. That was the price you had to pay if you were a tabloid columnist who crossed the line you'd drawn.

"Not every mistake, no. But maybe this one."

"Jesus," said JJ. "You're real tough on yourself."

"It's not just that, anyway. It's the public thing. The humil-iation. The enjoyment of the humiliation. The TV show on ca-ble that's watched by three people. Everything. I've . . . I've run out of room. I can't see any way forward or back."

There was a thoughtful silence for about ten seconds.

"Right," said Jess. "My turn."

JESS

I launched in. I just went, My name's Jess and I'm eighteen years old and, see, I'm here because I had some family prob-lems that I don't need to go into. And then I split up with this guy, Chas. And he owes me an explanation. Because he didn't say anything. He just went. But if he gave me an explanation I'd feel better, I think, because he broke my heart. Except I can't find him. I was at the party downstairs looking for him, and he wasn't there. So I came up here.

And Martin goes, all sarcastic, You're going to kill yourself because Chas didn't turn up at a party? Jesus.

Well, I never said that, and I told him. So then he was like, OK, you're up here because you're owed an explanation, then. Is that it?

He was trying to make me sound stupid and that wasn't fair, because we could all do that to each other. Like for example say, Oh, boo hoo hoo, they won't let me be on breakfast television anymore. Oh, boo hoo hoo, my son's a vegetable and I don't talk to anyone and I have to clean up his . . . Well, OK, you couldn't make Maureen sound stupid. But it seemed to me that taking the piss wasn't on. You could have taken the piss out of all four of us; you can take the piss out of anyone who's unhappy if you're cruel enough.

So I go, That wasn't what I said, either. I said an explanation might stop me. I didn't say it was why I was up here in the first place, did I? See, we could handcuff you to those railings and that would stop you. But you're not up here because no one's handcuffed you to the railings, are you?

That shut him up. I was pleased with that.

JJ was nicer. He could see that I wanted to find Chas, so I was like, Duh, yeah, except I wished I hadn't done the Duh bit because he was being sympathetic and Duh is taking the piss, really, isn't it? But he ignored the Duh and he asked me where Chas was and I said I didn't know, some party or another, and he said, Well, why don't you go looking for him instead of fucking around up here and I said I'd run out of energy and hope and when I said that I knew it was true.

I don't know you. The only thing I know about you is, you're reading this. I don't know whether you're happy or not; I don't know whether you're young or not. I sort of hope you're young and sad. If you're old and happy, I can imagine that you'll maybe smile to yourself when you hear me going, He broke my heart. You'll remember someone who broke your heart, and you'll think to yourself, Oh, yes, I can remember how that feels. But you can't, you smug old git. Oh, you might remember feeling sort of pleasantly sad. You might remember listening to music and eating chocolates in your room, or walking along the Embankment on your own, wrapped up in a winter coat and feeling lonely and brave. But can you remember how with every mouthful of food it felt like you were biting into your own stomach? Can you remember the taste of red wine as it came back up and into the toilet bowl? Can you remember dreaming every night that you were still together, that he was talking to you gently and touching you, so that every morning when you woke up you had to go through it all over again? Can you remember carving his initials in your arm with a kitchen knife? Can you remember standing too close to the edge of an Underground platform? No? Well, fucking shut up, then. Stick your smile up your saggy old arse.

JJ

I was going to just like splurge, tell 'em everything they needed to know—Big Yellow, Lizzie, the works. There was no need to lie. I guess I felt a little queasy listening to the other guys, because their reasons for being up there seemed pretty solid. Jesus, everyone understood why Maureen's life wasn't worth living. And, sure, Martin had kind of dug his own grave, but even so, that level of humiliation and shame . . . If I'd been him, I doubt if I'd have stuck around as long as he had. And Jess was very unhappy and very nuts. So it wasn't like people were being competitive exactly, but there was a certain amount of, I don't know what you'd call it . . . marking our territory? And maybe I felt a little insecure because Martin had pissed all over my patch. I was going to be the shame and humiliation guy, but my shame and humiliation were beginning to look a little pale. He'd been locked up for sleeping with a fifteen-year-old, and fucked over in the tabloids; I'd been dumped by a girl, and my band wasn't going anywhere. Big fucking deal.

Still, I didn't think of lying until I had the trouble with my name. Jess was so fucking aggressive, and I just lost my nerve.

"So," I said. "OK. I'm JJ, and—"

"Woss that stand for?"

People always want to know what my initials are for and I never tell them. I hate my name. What happened was, my dad was one of those self-educated guys, and he had a real, like, reverence for the BBC, so he spent too much time listening to the World Service on his big old shortwave radio in the den, and he was real hung up on this dude who was always on the radio in the '60s, John Julius Norwich, who was like a Lord or something, and wrote millions of books about churches and stuff. And that's me. John fucking Julius. Did I become a Lord or a radio anchor or even an Englishman? No. Did I drop out of school and form a band? Yep. Is John Julius a good name for a high school dropout? Nope. JJ is OK, though. JJ's cool enough.

"That's my business. Anyway, I'm JJ, and I'm here because—"

"I'll find out what your name is."

"How?"

"I'll come round your house and ransack it until I find something that tells me. Your passport or bank book or something. And if I can't find anything then I'll just steal something you love and I won't give it back until you've coughed up."

Jesus Christ. What gives with this girl?

"You'd rather do that than call me by my initials?"

"Yeah. Course. I hate not knowing things."

"I don't know you very well," said Martin. "But if you're

really troubled by your own ignorance, I'd have thought there should be one or two things higher up the list than JJ's name."

"What's that supposed to mean?"

"Do you know who the chancellor of the exchequer is? Or who wrote *Moby-Dick*?"

"No," said Jess. "Course not." As if anyone who knew stuff like that was a dork. "But they're not *secrets,* are they? I don't like not knowing *secrets.* I could find that other stuff out anytime I felt like it, and I don't feel like it."

"If he doesn't want to tell us, he doesn't want to tell us. Do your friends call you JJ?"

"Yeah."

"Then that's good enough for us."

"S'not good enough for me," said Jess.

"Just belt up and let him talk," said Martin.

But for me, the moment had gone. The moment of truth anyway, ha-ha. I could tell I wasn't going to get a fair hearing; there were waves of hostility coming off Jess and Martin, and these waves were breaking everywhere.

I stared at them all for a minute.

"So?" said Jess. "You forgotten why you were going to kill yourself, or what?"

"Of course I haven't forgotten," I said.

"Well, fucking spit it out then."

"I'm dying," I said.

See, I never thought I'd run into them again. I was pretty sure that sooner or later we'd shake hands, wish each other a happy whatever, and then either trudge back down the stairs or jump off the fucking roof, depending on mood, character, scale of problem, et cetera. It really never occurred to me that this was going to come back and repeat on me like the pickle in a Big Mac.

"Yeah, well, you don't look great," said Jess. "What you got? AIDS?"

AIDS fitted the bill. Everyone knew you could wander around with it for months; everyone knew it was incurable. And yet . . . I'd had a couple friends who died from it, and it's not the kind of thing you joke about. AIDS I knew I should leave the fuck alone. But then—and this all ran through my head in the thirty seconds after Jess's question—which fatal disease was more appropriate? Leukemia? The Ebola virus? None of them really says, "No, go on, man, be my guest. I'm only a joke killer disease. I'm not serious enough to offend anyone."

"I got like this brain thing. It's called CCR." Which, of course, is Creedence Clearwater Revival, one of my all-time favorite bands, and a big inspiration to me. I didn't think any of them looked like big Creedence fans. Jess was too young, I really didn't need to worry about Maureen, and Martin was the kind of guy who'd only have smelled a rat if I'd told him I was dying of incurable ABBA.

"It's like cranial corno-something." I was pleased with the "cranial" part. That sounded about right. The "corno" was weak, though, I admit.

"Is there no cure for that?" Maureen asked.

"Oh, yeah," said Jess. "There's a cure. You can take a pill. It's just that he couldn't be arsed. Der."

"They figure it's from drug abuse. Drugs and alcohol. So it's all my own fuckin' fault."

"You must feel a bit of a berk, then," said Jess.

"I do," I said. "If 'berk' means asshole."

"Yeah. Anyway, you win."

Which confirmed to me once and for all that a competitive edge had snuck in.

"Really?" I was pleased.

"Oh, yeah. Dying? Fuck. That's, you know . . . like diamonds or spades or those . . . trumps! You've got trumps, man."

"I'd say that having a fatal disease was only any good in this game," said Martin. "The who's-the-most-miserable-bastard game. Not much use anywhere else."

"How long have you got?" Jess asked.

"I don't know."

"Roughly. Just like off the top of your head."

"Shut up, Jess," said Martin.

"What have I said now? I wanted to know what we were dealing with."

"*We're* not dealing with anything," I said. "*I'm* dealing with it."

"Not very well," Jess said.

"Oh, is that right? And this from the girl who can't deal with being dumped."

We fell into a hostile silence.

"Well," said Martin. "So. Here we all are, then."

"Now what?" said Jess.

"You're going home, for a start," said Martin.

"Like fuck I am. Why should I?"

"Because we're going to march you there."

"I'll go home on one condition."

"Go on."

"You help me find Chas first."

"All of us?"

"Yeah. Or I really will kill myself. And I'm too young to do that. You said."

"I'm not sure I was right about that, looking back," said Martin. "You're wise beyond your years. I can see that now."

"So it's OK if I go over?" She started to walk toward the edge of the roof.

"Come back here," I said.

"I don't give a fuck, you know," she said. "I can jump, or we can look for Chas. Same thing to me."

And that's the whole thing, right there, because we believed her. Maybe other people on other nights wouldn't have, but the three of us, that night, we had no doubts. It wasn't that we thought she was really suicidal, either; it was just that it felt like she might do whatever she wanted to do at any given moment, and if she wanted to jump off a building to see what it felt like, then she'd try it. And once you'd worked that out, then it was just a question of how much you cared.

"But you don't need our help," I said. "We don't know how to start looking for Chas. You're the only one who can find him."

"Yeah, but I get weird on my own. Confused. That's sort of how I ended up here."

"What do you think?" said Martin to the rest of us.

"I'm not going anywhere," said Maureen. "I'm not leaving the roof, and I won't change my mind."

"Fine. We wouldn't ask you to."

"Because they'll come looking for me."

"Who will?"

"The people in the respite home."

"So what?" said Jess. "What are they going to do if they can't find you?"

"They'll put Matty somewhere terrible."

"This is the Matty who's a vegetable? Does he give a shit where he goes?"

Maureen looked at Martin helplessly.

"Is it the money?" said Martin. "Is that why you have to be dead by the morning?"

Jess snorted, but I could see why he had asked the question.

"I only paid for one night," said Maureen.

"Have you got the money for more than one night?"

"Yes, of course." The suggestion that she might not seemed to make her a little pissed. Pissed off. Whatever.

"So phone them up and tell them he'll be staying two."

Maureen looked at him helplessly again. "Why?"

"Because," said Jess. "Anyway, there's fuck all to do up here, is there?"

Martin laughed, kind of.

"Well, is there?" said Jess.

"Nothing I can think of," said Martin. "Apart from the obvious."

"Oh, that," said Jess. "Forget it. The moment's gone. I can tell. So we've got to find something else to do."

"So even if you're right, and the moment has passed," I said, "why do we have to do anything together? Why don't we go home and watch TV?"

"'Cause I get weird on my own. I told you."

"Why should we care? We didn't know you half an hour ago. I don't give much of a fuck about how weird you get on your own."

"So you don't feel like a bond kind of thing because of what we've been through?"

"Nope."

"You will. I can see us still being friends when we're old."

There was a silence. This was clearly not a vision shared by all.

MAUREEN

I didn't like it that they were making me sound tight. It wasn't anything to do with money. I needed one night so I paid for one night. And then someone else would have to pay, but I wouldn't be around to know.

They didn't understand, I could tell. I mean, they could understand that I was unhappy. But they couldn't understand the logic of it. The way they looked at it was this: If I died, Matty would be put in a home somewhere. So why didn't I just put him in a home and not die? What would the difference be? But that just goes to show that they didn't understand me, or Matty, or Father Anthony, or anyone at the church. No one I know thinks that way.

These people, though, Martin and JJ and Jess, they're different from anyone I know. They're more like the people on television, the people in *EastEnders* and the other programs where people know what to say straightaway. I'm not saying they're bad. I'm saying they're different. They wouldn't worry so much about Matty if he was their son. They don't have the same sense of duty. They don't have the church. They'd just say, "What's the difference?" and leave it at that, and maybe they're right, but they're not me, and I didn't know how to tell them that.

They're not me, but I wish I was them. Maybe not them, exactly, because they're not so happy either. But I wish I was one of those people, the people who know what to say, the people who can't see the difference. Because it seems to me that you have more chance of being able to live a life you can stand if you're like that.

So I didn't know what to say when Martin asked me if I really wanted to die. The obvious answer was, Yes, yes, of course I do, you fool, that's why I've climbed all these stairs, that's why I've been telling a boy—dear God, a man—who can't hear me all about a New Year's Eve party that I made up. But there's another answer, too, isn't there? And the other answer is, No, of course I don't, you fool. Please stop me. Please help me. Please make me into the kind of person who wants to live, the kind of person who has a bit missing, maybe. The kind of person who would be able to say, I am entitled to something more than this. Not much more; just something that would have been enough, instead of not quite enough. Because that's why I was up there—there wasn't quite enough to stop me.

"Well?" said Martin. "Are you prepared to wait until to-morrow night?"

"What will I tell the people in the home?"

"Have you got the phone number?"

"It's too late to call them."

"There'll be somebody on duty. Give me the number." He pulled one of those tiny little mobile telephones out of his pocket and turned it on. It started ringing, and he pressed a button and put the phone to his ear. He was listening to a message, I suppose.

"Someone loves you," said Jess, but he ignored her.

I had the address and phone number written down on my little note. I fished it out of my pocket, but I couldn't read it in the dark.

"Give it here," said Martin.

Well, I was embarrassed. It was my little note, my letter, and I didn't want anyone reading it while I was watching them, but I didn't know how to say that, and before I knew it, Martin had reached over and snatched it from me.

"Oh, Christ," he said when he saw it. I could feel myself blushing. "Is this your suicide note?"

"Cool. Read it out," said Jess. "Mine are crap, but I bet hers is worse."

"Yours *are* crap?" said JJ. "Meaning, there are, like, what, hundreds of them?"

"I'm always writing them," said Jess. She seemed quite cheerful about it. The two boys looked at her, but they didn't say anything. You could see what they were thinking, though.

"What?" said Jess.

"I imagine that most of us have just written the one," said Martin.

"I keep changing my mind," Jess said. "Nothing wrong with that. It's a big decision."

"One of the biggest," Martin said. "Certainly in the top ten." He was one of those people who sometimes seemed to be joking when he wasn't, or not joking when he was. "Anyway. No, I won't be reading this one out." He was squinting at it to read the number, and then he tapped the number out. And a few seconds later it was all done. He apologized for ringing so late, and then told them something had come up and Matty would be staying for another day, and that was it.

The way he said it, it was like he knew they weren't going to be asking any more questions. If I'd phoned I would have come up with this great long explanation for why I was phoning at four in the morning, something I'd have had to have thought up months ago, and then they would have seen through me and I'd have confessed and ended up going to get Matty out a few hours earlier rather than a day later.

"So," said JJ. "Maureen's OK. That just leaves you, Martin. You wanna join in?"

"Well, where is this Chas?" Martin said.

"I dunno," said Jess. "Some party somewhere. Is that what it depends on? Where he is?"

"Yes. I'd rather f——ing kill myself than try and get a cab to go somewhere in South London at four in the morning," said Martin.

"He doesn't know anyone in South London," Jess said.

"Good," said Martin. And when he said that, you could tell that instead of killing ourselves, we were all going to come down from the roof and look for Jess's boyfriend, or whatever he was. It wasn't much of a plan, really. But it was the only plan we had, so all we could do was try and make it work.

"Give me your mobile and I'll make some calls," said Jess.

So Martin gave her the phone, and she went to the other side of the roof where no one could hear her, and we waited to be told where we were going.

MARTIN

I know what you're thinking, all you clever, clever people who read the *Guardian* and shop in Waterstones and would no more think of watching breakfast television than you would of buying your children cigarettes. You're thinking, Oh, this guy wasn't serious. He wanted a tabloid photographer to capture his quote unquote cry for help so that he could sign a "My Suicide Hell" exclusive for the *Sun*. SHARP TAKES THE SLEAZY WAY OUT. And I can understand why you might be thinking that, my friends. I climb a staircase, have a couple of nips of Scotch from a hip flask while dangling my feet over the edge, and then when some dippy girl asks me to help find her ex-boyfriend at some party, I shrug and wander off with her. And how suicidal is that?

First of all, I'll have you know that I scored very highly on Aaron T. Beck's Suicide Intent Scale. I'll bet you didn't even know there was such a scale, did you? Well, there is, and I reckon I got something like twenty-one out of thirty points, which I was pretty pleased with, as you can imagine. Yes, suicide had been contemplated for more than three hours prior to the attempt. Yes, I was certain of death even if I received medical attention: It's fifteen stories high, Toppers' House, and they reckon that anything over ten will do it for you pretty well every time. Yes, there was active preparation for the attempt: ladder, wire cutters, and so on. He shoots, he scores. The only questions where I might not have received maximum points are the first two, which deal with what Aaron T. Beck calls isolation and timing. "No one nearby in visual or vocal contact" gets you top marks, as does "Intervention highly unlikely." You might argue that as we chose the most popular suicide spot in North London on one of the most popular suicide nights of the year, intervention was almost inevitable; I would counter by saying that we were just being dim. Dim or grotesquely self-absorbed, take your pick.

And yet, of course, if it hadn't been for the teeming throng up there, I wouldn't be around today, so maybe old Beck is bang on the money. We may not have been counting on anyone to rescue us, but once we started bumping into each other, there was certainly a collective desire—a desire born, more than anything, out of embarrassment—to shelve the whole idea, at least for the night. Not one of us descended those stairs having come to the conclusion that life was a beautiful and precious thing; if anything, we were slightly more miserable on the way down than on the way up, because the only solution we had found for our various predicaments was not available to us, at least for the moment. And there had been a sort of weird nervous excitement up on the roof; for a couple of hours we had been living in a sort of independent state, where street-level laws no longer applied. Even though our problems had driven us up there, it was as if they had somehow, like Daleks, been unable to climb the stairs. And now we had to go back down and face them again. But it didn't feel like we had any choice. Even though we had nothing in common beyond that one thing, that one thing was enough to make us feel that there wasn't anything else—not money, or class, or education, or age, or cultural interests—that was worth a damn; we'd formed a nation, suddenly, in those few hours, and for the time being we wanted only to be with our new compatriots. I had hardly exchanged a word with Maureen, and I didn't even know her surname, but she understood more about me than my wife had done in the last five years of our marriage. Maureen knew that I was unhappy, because of where she'd met me, and that meant she knew the most important thing about me; Cindy always professed herself baffled by everything I did or said.

It would have been neat if I'd fallen in love with Maureen, wouldn't it? I can even see the newspaper headline: SHARP TURNED! And then there'd be some story about how Old Sleazebag had seen the error of his ways and decided to settle down with a nice, homely older woman rather than chase around after schoolgirls and C-list actresses with breast enlargements. Yeah, right. Dream on.

JJ

While Jess called everyone she knew to find out where this guy Chas was at, I was leaning on the wall, looking through the wire at the city, and trying to figure out what I'd listen to at that exact moment if I owned an iPod or a Discman. The first thing that came to mind was Jonathan Richman's "Abominable Snowman in the Market," maybe because it was sweet and silly, and reminded me of a time in life when I could afford to be that way. And then I started humming the Cure's "In Between Days," which made a little more sense. It wasn't today and it wasn't tomorrow, and it wasn't last year and it wasn't next year, and anyway the whole roof thing was an in-between, kind of a limbo, seeing as we hadn't yet made up our minds where our immortal souls were headed.

Jess spent ten minutes talking to sources close to Chas, and came back with a best guess that he was at a party in Shoreditch. We walked down fifteen flights of stairs, through the thud of dub and the stink of piss, and then emerged back onto the street, where we stood shivering in the cold while waiting for a black cab to show. Nobody said much, besides Jess, who talked enough for all of us. She told us whose party it was, and who would probably be there.

"It will be all Tessa and that lot."

"Ah," said Martin. "That lot."

"And Alfie and Tabitha and the posse who go down Ocean on Saturdays. And Acid-Head Pete and the rest of the whole graphic design crew."

Martin groaned; Maureen looked seasick.

A young African guy driving a shitty old Ford pulled up alongside us. He wound down the passenger window and leaned over.

"Where you wanna go?"

"Shoreditch."

"Thirty pounds."

"Fuck off," said Jess.

"Shut up," said Martin, and got in the front seat. "My treat," he said.

The rest of us got in the back.

"Happy New Year," said the driver.

None of us said anything.

"Party?" said the driver.

"Do you know Acid-Head Pete at all?" Martin asked him. "Well, we're hoping to run into him. Should be jolly."

"'Jolly'," Jess snorted. "Why are you such a tosser?" If you were going to joke around with Jess, and use words ironically, then you'd have to give her plenty of advance warning.

It was maybe four-thirty in the morning by now, but there were tons of people around, in cars and cabs and on foot. Everyone seemed to be in a group. Sometimes people waved to us; Jess always waved back.

"How about you?" Jess said to the driver. "You working all night? Or are you gonna go and have a few somewhere?"

"Work *toute la nuit*," said the driver. "All the night."

"Bad luck," said Jess.

The driver laughed mirthlessly.

"Yes. Bad luck."

"Does your missus mind?"

"Sorry?"

"Your missus. *La femme.* Does she care? About you working all night?"

"No, she don't care. Not now. Not in the place where she is."

Anyone with an emotional antenna could have felt the mood in the cab turn real dark. Anyone with any life experience could have figured out that this was a man with a story, and that this story, whatever it was, was unlikely to get us into the party mood. Anyone with any sense would have stopped right there.

"Oh," said Jess. "Bad woman, eh?"

I winced, and I'm sure the others did, too. *Bigmouth strikes again.*

"Not bad. Dead." He said this flat, like he was just correcting her on a point of fact—as if in his line of work, "bad" and "dead" were two addresses that people got confused.

"Oh."

"Yes. Bad men kill her. Kill her, kill her mother, kill her father."

"Oh."

"Yes. In my country."

"Right."

And right there was the place Jess chose to stop: exactly at the point where her silence would show her up. So we drove on, thinking our thoughts. And I would bet a million bucks that our thoughts all contained, somewhere in their tangle and swirl, versions of the same questions: Why hadn't we seen him up there? Or had he been up and come down, like us? Would he sneer if we told him our troubles? How come he turned out to be so fucking . . . *dogged*?

When we got to where we were going, Martin gave him a very large tip, and he was pleased and grateful, and called us his friends. We would have liked to be his friends, but he probably wouldn't have cared for us much if he got to know us.

Maureen didn't want to come in with us, but we led her through the door and up the stairs into a room that was the closest thing I've seen to a New York loft since I've been here.

It would have cost a fortune in NYC, which means it would have cost a fortune plus another 30 percent in London. It was still packed, even at four in the morning, and it was full of my least favorite people: fucking art students. I mean, Jess had already warned us, but it still came as a shock. All those woolly hats, and mustaches with parts of them missing, all those new tattoos and plastic shoes . . . I mean, I'm a liberal guy, and I didn't want Bush to bomb Iraq, and I like a toke as much as the next guy, but these people still fill my heart with fear and loathing, mostly because I know they wouldn't have liked my band. When we played a college town, and we walked out in front of a crowd like this, I knew we were going to have a hard time. They don't like real music, these people. They don't like the Ramones or the Temptations or the 'Mats; they like DJ Bleepy and his stupid fucking bleeps. Or else they all pretend that they're fucking gangstas, and listen to hip-hop about hos and guns.

So I was in a bad mood from the get-go. I was worried that I was going to get into a fight, and I'd even decided what that fight would be about: I'd be defending either Martin or Maureen from the sneers of some motherfucker with a goatee, or some woman with a mustache. But it never happened. The weird thing was that Martin in his suit and his fake tan, and Maureen in her raincoat and sensible shoes, they somehow blended right in. They looked so straight that they looked, you know, *out there*. Martin and his TV hair could have been in Kraftwerk, and Maureen could have been, like, a real weird version of Moe Tucker from the Velvet Underground. Me, I was wearing a pair of faded black pants, a leather jacket, and an old Gitanes T-shirt, and I felt like a fucking freak.

There was only one incident that made me think I might

have to break someone's nose. Martin was standing there drinking wine straight out of a bottle, and these two guys started staring at him.

"Martin Sharp! You know, off of breakfast telly!"

I winced. I have never really hung out with a celebrity, and it hadn't occurred to me that walking into a party with Martin's face is like walking into a party naked: Even art students tend to take notice. But this was more complicated than straightforward recognition.

"Oh, yeah! Good call!" his buddy said.

"Oi, Sharpy!"

Martin smiled at them pleasantly.

"People must say that to you all the time," one of them said.

"What?"

"You know. 'Oi, Sharpy' and all that."

"Well, yes," said Martin. "They do."

"Bad luck, though. Of all the people on TV, you end up looking like that cunt."

Martin gave them a cheerful, what-can-you-do shrug and turned back to me.

"You OK?"

"That's life," he said, and looked at me. He'd somehow managed to give an old cliché new depth.

Maureen, meanwhile, was plainly petrified. She jumped every time anyone laughed or swore or broke something; she stared at the partygoers as if she were looking at Diane Arbus photos projected fifty feet wide on an Imax screen.

"You want a drink?"

"Where's Jess?"

"Looking for Chas."

"And then can we go?"

"Sure."

"Good. I'm not enjoying myself here."

"Me neither."

"Where do you think we'll go next?"

"I don't know."

"But we'll all go together, do you think?"

"I guess. That's the deal, right? Until we find this guy."

"I hope we don't find him," said Maureen. "Not for a while. I'd like a sherry, please, if you can find one."

"You know what? I'm not sure there's going to be too much sherry around. These guys don't look like sherry drinkers to me."

"White wine? Would they have that?"

I found a couple paper cups and a bottle with something left in it.

"Cheers."

"Cheers."

"Every New Year's is the same, huh?"

"How do you mean?"

"You know. Warm white wine, a bad party full of jerks. And this year I'd promised myself things would be different."

"Where were you this time last year?"

"I was at a party at home. With Lizzie, my ex."

"Nice?"

"It was OK, yeah. You?"

"I was at home. With Matty."

"Right. And did you think, a year ago . . ."

"Yes," she said quickly. "Oh, yes."

"Right." And I didn't really know how to follow up, so we sipped our drinks and watched the jerks.

MAUREEN

It can't be hygienic, living in a place without rooms. Even
people who live in bedsits usually have access to a proper
bathroom, with doors and walls and a window. This place, the
place where the party was being held, didn't even have that. It
was like a railway station toilet, except there wasn't even a
separate gents'. There was just a little wall separating the bath
and toilet from the rest of it, so even though I needed to go, I
couldn't; anyone might have walked around the wall and seen
what I was doing. And I don't need to spell out how unhealthy
it all was. Mother used to say that a bad smell is just a germ
gas; well, whoever owned this flat must have had germs everywhere. Not that anyone could use the toilet anyway. When I
went to find it, someone was kneeling on the floor and sniffing the lid. I have no idea why anyone would want to smell the
lid of a toilet. (While someone else watched! Can you imagine!) But I suppose people are perverted in all sorts of different ways. It was sort of what I expected when I walked into
that party and heard the noise, and saw what kind of people
they were; if someone had asked me what I thought people

like that would do in a toilet, I might have said that they'd sniff the lid.

When I came back, Jess was standing there in tears, and the rest of the party had cleared a little space around us. Some boy had told her that Chas had been and gone, and he'd gone with somebody he met at the party, some girl. Jess wanted us all to go round to this girl's house, and JJ was trying to persuade her that it wasn't a good idea.

"It's OK," Jess said. "I know her. There's probably been some sort of misunderstanding. She probably just didn't know about me and Chas."

"What if she did know?" said JJ.

"Well," said Jess. "In that case I couldn't let it go, could I?"

"What does that mean?"

"I wouldn't kill her. I'm not that mad. But I would have to hurt her. Maybe cut her a little."

When Frank broke off our engagement I didn't think I'd ever get over it. I felt almost as sorry for him as I did for myself, because I didn't make it easy for him. We were in the Ambler Arms, except it's not called that anymore, over in the corner by the fruit machine, and the landlord came over to our table and asked Frank to take me home, because nobody wanted to put any money in the machine while I was there howling and bawling my eyes out, and they used to make a fair bit of money from the fruit machine on quiet nights.

I nearly did away with myself then—I certainly considered it. But I thought I could ride it out; I thought things might get better. Imagine the trouble I could have saved if I had done! I would have killed the both of us, me and Matty, but of course I didn't know that then.

I didn't take any notice of the silly things Jess said about cutting people. I came up with a lot of utter nonsense when Frank and I broke up; I told people that Frank had been forced to move away, that he was sick in the head, that he was a drunk and he'd hit me. None of it was true. Frank was a sweet man whose crime was that he didn't love me quite enough, and because this wasn't much of a crime I had to make up some bigger ones.

"Were you engaged?" I asked Jess, and then wished I hadn't.

"Engaged?" Jess said. "Engaged? What is this? *Pride and f——ing Prejudice*? 'Oooh, Mr. Arsey Darcy. May I plight my troth? Oh, yes, Miss Snooty Knobhead, I'd be charmed, I'm sure.'" She said this last part in a silly voice, but you could probably have guessed that.

"People do still get engaged," Martin said. "It's not a stupid question."

"Which people get engaged?"

"I did," I said. But I said it too quietly, because I was scared of her, and so she made me say it again.

"You did? Really? OK, but what living people get engaged? I'm not interested in people out of the Ark. I'm not interested in people with, with like shoes and raincoats and whatever." I wanted to ask what she thought we should wear instead of shoes, but I was learning my lesson.

"Anyway, who the f—— did you get engaged to?"

I didn't want any of this. It didn't seem fair that this is what happened when you tried to help.

"Did you shag him? I'll bet you did. How did he like it? Doggy style? So he didn't have to look at you?"

And then Martin grabbed her and dragged her into the street.

JESS

When Martin pulled me outside, I did that thing where you decide to become a different person. It's something I could do whenever I felt like it. Doesn't everybody, when they feel themselves getting out of control? You know: You say to yourself, OK, I'm a booky person, so then you go and get some books from the library and carry them around for a while. Or, OK, I'm a druggy person, and smoke a lot of weed. Whatever. And it makes you feel different. If you borrow someone else's clothes or their interests or their words, what they say, then it can give you a bit of a rest from yourself, I find.

It was time to feel different. I don't know why I said that stuff to Maureen; I don't know why I say half the things I say. I knew I'd overstepped the mark, but I couldn't stop myself. I get angry, and when it starts it's like being sick. I puke and puke over someone and I can't stop until I'm empty. I'm glad Martin pulled me outside. I needed stopping. I need stopping a lot. So I told myself that from that point on I was going to be more a person out of the olden days kind of thing. I swore not to swear, ha-ha, or to spit; I swore not to ask harmless old ladies who are clearly more or less virgins whether they shagged doggy style.

Martin went spare at me, told me I was a bitch, and an idiot, and asked me what Maureen had ever done to me. And I just said, Yes, sir, and No, sir, and Very sorry, sir, and I looked at the pavement, not at him, just to show him I really was sorry. And then I curtsied, which I thought was a nice touch. And he said, What the fuck's this, now? What's the Yes, sir, No, sir, business? So I told him that I was going to stop being me, and that no one would ever see the old me again, and he didn't know what to say to that.

I didn't want them to get sick of me. People do get sick of me, I've noticed. Chas got sick of me, for example. And I really need that not to happen anymore, otherwise I'll be left with nobody. With Chas, I think everything was just too much; I came on too strong too quickly, and he got scared. Like that thing in the Tate Modern? That was definitely a mistake. Because the vibe in there . . . OK, some of the stuff is all weird and intense and so on, but just because the stuff is all weird and intense, that shouldn't have meant that I went all weird and intense. That was inappropriate behavior, as Jen would have said. I should have waited until we'd got outside and finished looking at the pictures and installations before I went off on one.

I think Jen got sick of me, too.

Also, the business in the cinema, which, looking back on it, might have been the final straw. That was inappropriate behavior, too. Or maybe the behavior wasn't inappropriate, because we had to have that conversation sometime, but the place (the Holloway Odeon) wasn't right, and nor was the time (halfway through the film) or the volume (loud). One of the points Chas made that night was that I wasn't really mature enough to be a mother, and I can see now that by yelling my head off about having a baby halfway through *Moulin Rouge* I sort of proved it for him.

So anyway. Martin went mental at me for a while, and then he just seemed to shrink, as if he was a balloon and he'd been punctured. "What's wrong, kind sir?" I said, but he just shook his head, and I could understand enough from that. What I understood was that it was the middle of the night and he was standing outside a party full of people he didn't know, shouting at someone else he didn't know, a couple of hours after sitting on a roof thinking about killing himself. Oh yeah, and his wife and children hated him. In any other situation I would have said that he'd suddenly lost the will to live. I went over and put my hand on his shoulder, and he looked at me as if I were a person rather than an irritation and we almost had a Moment of some description—not a romantic Ross-and-Rachel-type moment (as if), but a Moment of Shared Understanding. But then we were interrupted, and the Moment passed.

JJ

I want to tell you about my old band—I guess because I'd started to think about these guys as my new one. There were four of us, and we were called Big Yellow. We started out being called Big Pink, as a tribute to the Band album, but then everyone thought we were a gay band, so we changed colors.

Me and Eddie started the band in high school, and we wrote together, and we were like brothers, right up until the day that we weren't like that anymore. And Billy was the drummer, and Jesse was the bassist, and . . . Shit, you could care less, right? All you need to know is this: We had something that no one else ever had. Maybe some people used to have it, before my time—the Stones, the Clash, the Who. But no one I've ever seen had it. I wish you'd come to one of our shows, because then you'd know that I'm not bullshitting you, but you'll have to take my word for it: on our good nights we could suck people up and spit 'em out twenty miles away. I still like our albums, but it was the shows that people remember; some bands just go out and play their songs a little louder and faster, but we found a way of doing something else; we used to speed 'em up and slow 'em down, and we used to play covers of things we loved, and that we knew the people who came to hear us would love, too, and our shows came to *mean* something to people, in a way that shows don't anymore. When Big Yellow played live, it was like some kind of Pentecostal service; instead of applause and whistles and hoots, there'd be tears and teeth-grinding and speaking in tongues. We saved souls. If you love rock 'n' roll, all of it, from, I don't know, Elvis right through James Brown and up to the White Stripes, then you'd have wanted to quit your job and come and live inside our amps until your ears fell off. Those shows were my reason for living, and I now know that this is not a figure of speech.

I wish I was deluding myself. Really. It would help. But we used to have these message boards up on our Web site, and I'd read them every now and again, and I could tell that people felt the same way we did; and I looked at other people's boards, too, and they didn't have the same kind of fans. I mean, everyone has fans who love what they do, otherwise they wouldn't be fans, right? But I could tell from reading the other boards that our guys walked out of our shows feeling something special. We could feel it, and they could feel it. It's just that there weren't enough of them, I guess. Anyway.

Maureen felt faint after Jess cut loose on her, and who could blame her? Jesus. I would have needed to sit down, too, if Jess ever cut loose on me, and I've been around the block a few times. I took her outside onto a little roof terrace that looked like it never got the sun at any time of the day or year, but there was a picnic table and a grill out there anyway. Those little grills are everywhere in England, right? To me they've come to represent the triumph of hope over circumstance, seeing as all you can do is peer at them out the window through the pissing rain. There were a couple of people sitting at the picnic table, but when they saw that Maureen wasn't feeling too good they got up and went back inside, and we sat down. I offered to get her a glass of water, but she didn't want anything, so we just sat there for a while. And then we both heard like this hissing noise, coming from the shadows next to the grill in the far corner, and eventually we figured out that there was a guy back there. He was young, with long hair and a sorry-ass mustache, hunkered down in the dark, trying to attract our attention.

"Excuse me," he whispered as loudly as he dared.

"You wanna talk to us, you come here."

"I can't come into the light."

"What would happen to you if you did?"

"A nutter might try to kill me."

"There's only Maureen and me out here."

"This nutter's everywhere."

"Like God," I said.

I walked over to the other side of the terrace and crouched down next to him.

"How can I help you?"

"You American?"

"Yes."

"Oh. Howdy, pardner." If I tell you that this amused him, you'll know all you need to know about this guy. "Listen, can you check the party and see if the nutter's gone?"

"What does he look like?"

"She. I know, I know, but she's really scary. A mate saw her first and told me to hide out here. I went out with her once. Not like 'once upon a time.' Just once. But I stopped because she's off her head, and . . ."

This was perfect.

"You're Chas, aren't you?"

"How did you know that?"

"I'm a friend of Jess's."

Oh, man, I wish you could have seen the look on his face. He scrambled to his feet and started looking for ways to escape over the back wall. At one point I thought he was going to try running up it, like a squirrel.

"Shit," he said. "Fuck. I'm sorry. Shit. Will you help me climb over?"

"No. I want you to come and talk to her. She's had, she's had, like, a rough evening, and maybe a little chat would help calm her down."

Chas laughed. It was the hollow, desperate laugh of a man who knew that, when it came to calming Jess down, several elephant tranquilizers would be much more useful than a little chat.

"You know I haven't had sex since that night we went out, don't you?"

"I didn't know that, Chas, no. How would I know? Where would I have read that?"

"I've been too scared. I can't make that mistake again. I can't have another woman shouting at me in the cinema. I don't mind, you know, never having sex again. It's better that way. I'm twenty-two. I mean, by the time you're sixty, you don't feel like it anyway, right? So we're only talking forty years. Less. I can live with that. Women are fucking maniacs, man."

"You don't want to think shit like that, man. You've just had some bad luck."

I said this because I knew it was the right thing to say, not because my experience told me anything different. It wasn't true that women were fucking maniacs, of course it wasn't—just the ones that I had slept with and Chas had slept with.

"Listen. If you came outside and had a little chat, what's the worst that could happen?"

"She's tried to kill me twice and she got me arrested once. Plus, I'm banned from three pubs, two galleries, and a cinema. Plus, I've had an official warning from—"

"OK, OK. So you're saying the worst that could happen is, you die a painful and violent death. And I say to you, my friend, that it's better to die like a man than hide underneath grills like a mouse."

Maureen had stood up and come to join us in our dark barbecue corner.

"I'd try to kill you if I were Jess," she said quietly—so quietly that it was hard to square the violence of the words with the timidity in the voice.

"There you go. You're in trouble wherever you look."

"Who the fuck's this now?"

"I'm Maureen," said Maureen. "Why should you get away with it?"

"Get away with what? I didn't do anything."

"I thought you said you had sex with her," Maureen said. "Or maybe you didn't say that in so many words. But you said you hadn't had sex since. So I'm thinking that you slept with her."

"Well, we had sex that once. But I didn't know she was a fucking maniac then."

"So once you find out that the poor girl is confused and vulnerable, that's when you run away."

"I had to run away. She was chasing me. With a knife, half the time."

"And why was she chasing you?"

"What is this? Why is it your business?"

"I don't like to see people upset."

"What about me? I'm upset. My life is a shambles."

Now, see, Chas couldn't know, but that wasn't such a good line of argument to use with any of our crowd, the Toppers' House Four. We were, by definition, the Kings and Queens of Shambles. Chas had given up on sex, whereas we were trying to decide whether to give up on fucking life.

"You have to talk to her," said Maureen.

"Fuck off," said Chas. And then, *whomp!* Maureen popped him as hard as she could.

I can't tell you how many times I'd watched Eddie pop

someone at a party or after a show. And he'd probably say the same thing about me, although in my memory I was the Man of Peace, with only the occasional lapse into violence, and he was the Man of War, with only the occasional moment of calm and clarity. And OK, Maureen was, like, this little old lady, but watching her take a swing really brought it all back home.

Here's the thing about Maureen: She had a lot more guts than I had. She'd stuck around to find out what it would feel like, never to live the life she had planned for herself. I didn't know what those plans were, but she had them, same as everybody, and when Matty came along, she'd waited around for twenty years to see what she'd be offered as a replacement, and she was offered nothing at all. There was a lot of feeling in that slap, and I could imagine hitting someone pretty hard when I was her age, too. That was one of the reasons I didn't intend ever to be her age.

MAUREEN

Frank is Matty's father. It's funny to think that might not be immediately obvious to someone, because it's so obvious to me. I only ever had intercourse with one man, and I only had intercourse with that one man once, and the one time in my entire life I had intercourse produced Matty. What are the chances, eh? One in a million? One in ten million? I don't know. But of course even one in ten million means that there are a lot of women like me in the world. That's not what you think of, when you think of one in ten million. You don't think, That's a lot of people.

What I've come to realize over the years is that we're less protected from bad luck than you could possibly imagine. Because though it doesn't seem fair—having intercourse only the once and ending up with a child who can't walk or talk or even recognize me—well, fairness doesn't really have much to do with it, does it? You only have to have intercourse the once to produce a child, any child. There are no laws that say, You can only have a child like Matty if you're married, or if you have lots of other children, or if you sleep with lots of different men. There are no laws like that, even though you and I might think there should be. And once you have a child like Matty, you can't help but feel, That's it! That's all my bad luck, a whole lifetime's worth, in one bundle. But I'm not sure luck works like that. Matty wouldn't stop me from getting breast cancer, or from being mugged. You'd think he should, but he can't. In a way, I'm glad I never had another child, a normal one. I'd have needed more guarantees from God than He could have provided.

And anyway, I'm Catholic, so I don't believe in luck as much as I believe in punishment. We're good at believing in punishment; we're the best in the world. I sinned against the Church, and the price you pay for that is Matty. It might seem like a high price to pay, but then, these sins are supposed to mean something, aren't they? So in one way it's hardly surprising that this is what I got. For a long time I was even grateful, because it felt to me as though I were going to be able to redeem myself here on earth, and there'd be no reckoning to be made afterward. But now I'm not so sure. If the price you have to pay for a sin is so high that you end up wanting to kill yourself and committing an even worse sin, then Someone's done His sums wrong. Someone's overcharging.

I had never hit anyone before, not in the whole of my life, although I'd often wanted to. But that night was different. I was in limbo, somewhere between living and dying, and it felt as if it didn't matter what I did until I went back to the top of Toppers' House again. And that was the first time I realized that I was on a sort of holiday from myself. It made me want to slap him again, just because I could, but I didn't. The once was enough: Chas fell over—more from the shock, I think, than from the force, because I'm not so strong—and then knelt on all fours covering his head with his hands.

"I'm sorry," Chas said.

"For what?" JJ asked him.

"I'm not sure," he said. "Whatever."

"I had a boyfriend like you once," I told him.

"I'm sorry," he said again.

"It hurts. It's a horrible thing to do, to have intercourse with someone and then disappear."

"I can see that now."

"Can you?"

"I think so."

"You can't see anything from down there," said JJ. "Why don't you get up?"

"I don't really want to be thumped again."

"Is it fair to say that you're not the bravest man in the world?" JJ asked him.

"There are lots of different ways of showing courage," said Chas. "If what you're saying is that I don't set much store by physical bravery . . . then yes, that's fair. It's overrated, I think."

"Well, you know, Chas, I think that's kinda brave of you, to show you're so afraid of a small lady like Maureen. I respect your honesty, man. You won't thump him again, will you, Maureen?"

I promised I wouldn't, and Chas got to his feet. It was a strange feeling, watching a man do something because of me.

"Not much of a life, hiding underneath people's grills, is it?" said JJ.

"No. But I don't really see the alternatives."

"Howsabout talking to Jess?"

"Oh, no. I'd rather live out here all the time. Seriously. I'm already thinking of relocating, you know."

"What, to someone else's backyard? Maybe somewhere with some grass?"

"No," Chas said. "To Manchester."

"Listen," JJ said. "I know she's scary. That's why you should talk to her now. With us around. We can, you know. Mediate. Wouldn't you rather do that than move to another city?"

"But what is there to say?"

"Maybe we could work something out. Together. Something that might get her off your back."

"Like what?"

"I know for a fact she'd marry you if you asked her."

"Ah, no, you see that's just—"

"I was just kidding around, Chas. Lighten up, man."

"These aren't, like, lightening-up times. These are dark times."

"Dark times indeed. What with Jess, and going to Manchester, and living under a grill, and the Twin Towers, and everything."

"Yeah."

JJ shook his head.

"OK. So what can you tell her that's going to get you out of this f——ing mess?"

And JJ gave him some things to say, as if he were an actor and we were in a soap.

MARTIN

I'm not averse to having a go at DIY every now and again. I decorated the girls' bedrooms myself, with stencils and everything. (And yes, there were TV cameras there, and the production company paid for every last drop of Day-Glo paint, but that doesn't make it any less of an achievement.) Anyway, if you're a fellow enthusiast then you'll know that sometimes you come across holes that are too big for plaster, especially in the bathroom. And when that happens, the sloppy way to do it is to bung the holes up with anything you can find—broken matches, bits of sponge, whatever is to hand. Well, that was Chas's function that night: He was a bit of sponge that plugged a gap. The whole Jess-and-Chas thing was ludicrous, of course, a waste of time and energy, a banal little sideshow; but it absorbed us, got us down off the roof, and even as I was listening to his preposterous speech I could see its value. I could also see that we were going to need a lot more bits of sponge over the coming weeks and months. Maybe that's what we all need, whether we're suicidal or not. Maybe life is just too big a gap to be plugged by plaster, so we need anything we can get our hands on—sanders and planers, fifteen-year-olds, whatever—to fill it up.

"Hi, Jess," said Chas when he was shoved out of the party and onto the street. He was trying to sound cheery and friendly and casual, as if he'd been hoping to bump into Jess at some point during the evening, but his general lack of volition undid him; cheeriness is hard to convey when you are too scared to make eye contact. He reminded me of a petty gangster caught thieving from the local godfather in a movie, out of his depth and desperately trying to suck up in order to save his skin.

"Why wouldn't you talk to me?"

"Yeah. Right. I knew you'd want to know that. And I've been thinking about it. I've been thinking about it very hard, actually, because, you know, it's . . . I'm not happy about it. It's weak. It's a weakness in me."

"Don't overdo it, man," said JJ. There seemed no attempt on anyone's part to pretend that this was going to bear any resemblance to a real conversation.

"No. Right. So. First of all, I should say sorry, and it won't happen again. And second of all, I find you very attractive, and stimulating company, and—"

This time JJ just coughed ostentatiously.

"And, well. It's not me, it's you." He winced. "Sorry. Sorry. It's not you, it's me."

At that point, just as he was trying to remember his lines, he caught my eye.

"Hey. You look like that wanker off the telly. Martin Thing."

"It is him," said Jess.

"How the fuck do you know him?"

"It's a long story," I said.

"We were both just up on the roof of Toppers' House. We was going to throw ourselves off," Jess said, thus making the long story considerably shorter, and, to be fair, leaving out very few of the salient points.

Chas swallowed this information almost visibly, like snakes swallow eggs: You could see the slow march to the brain. Chas, I'm sure, had many attractive aspects to his personality, but quickness of intelligence was not one of them. "Because of that girl you shagged? And your wife and kids throwing you out and everything?" he asked finally.

"Why don't you ask Jess why she was going to jump? Isn't that more relevant?"

"Shut up," said Jess. "That's private."

"Oh, and my stuff isn't?"

"No," she said. "Not anymore. Everyone knows about it."

"What's Penny Chambers like? In real life?"

"Is that what we came out here to talk about, Chas?" JJ said quietly.

"No. Right. Sorry. It's just a bit distracting, having someone off the telly standing there."

"Do you want me to leave?"

"No," said Jess quickly. "I want you here."

"I wouldn't have thought you'd be his type," said Chas. "Too old. Plus he's a cunt." He chuckled, and then looked around for someone to share the chuckle with, but none of us—none of them, I should say, because even Chas didn't expect me to laugh at my own age or cunthood—was even remotely amused.

"Oh, right. It's like that, is it?"

And suddenly, yes, it was exactly like that: We were more serious than him, in every way. And even Jess saw it.

"You're the tosser," she said. "None of this is anything to do with you. Fuck off out of my sight." And then she kicked him, an old-fashioned, straight-legged toe into the meatiest part of the arse, as if the two of them were cartoon characters.

And that was the end of Chas.

JESS

When you're sad—like, really sad, Toppers' House sad—you only want to be with other people who are sad. I didn't know this until that night, but I suddenly realized it just by looking at Chas's face. There was nothing in it. It was just the face of a twenty-two-year-old boy who'd never done anything, apart from dropped a few Es, or thought anything, apart from where to get the next E from, or felt anything, apart from off his face. It was the eyes that gave him away: When he made that stupid joke about Martin and expected us to laugh, the eyes were completely lost in the joke, and there was nothing else left of them. They were just laughing eyes, not frightened eyes or troubled eyes—they were the eyes a baby has when you tickle it. I'd noticed with the others that when they made jokes, if they did (Maureen wasn't a big comedian), you could still see why they'd been up on the roof even while they were laughing—there was something else in there, something that stopped them giving themselves over to the moment. And you can say that we shouldn't have been up there, because wanting to kill yourself is a coward's way out, and you can say that none of us had enough reason to want to do it. But you can't say that we didn't feel it, because we all did, and that was more important than anything. Chas would never know what that was like unless he crossed the line, too.

Because that's what the four of us had done—crossed a line. I don't mean we'd done anything bad. I just mean that something had happened to us which separated us from lots of other people. We had nothing in common apart from where we'd ended up, on that square of concrete high up in the air, and that was the biggest thing you could possibly have in common with anyone. To say that Maureen and I had nothing in common because she wore raincoats and listened to brass bands or whatever was like saying, I don't know, the only thing I've got in common with that girl is that we have the same parents. And I didn't know any of that until Chas said that thing about Martin being a cunt.

The other thing I worked out was that Chas could have told me anything—that he loved me, he hated me, he'd been possessed by aliens and the Chas I knew was now on a different planet—and it wouldn't have made any difference. I was still owed an explanation, I thought, but so what? What good was it going to do me? It wouldn't have made me any happier. It was like scratching when you have chicken pox. You think it's going to help, but the itch moves over, and then moves over again. My itch suddenly felt miles away, and I couldn't have reached it with the longest arms in the world. Realizing that made me scared that I was going to be itchy forever, and I didn't want that.

I knew all the things that Martin had done, but when Chas had gone I still wanted him to hug me. I wouldn't even have cared if he'd tried anything on, but he didn't. He sort of did the opposite; he held me all funny, as if I was covered in barbed wire.

I'm sorry, I went. I'm sorry that little shitbag called you names. And he said it wasn't my fault, but I told him that of course it was, because if he hadn't met me he wouldn't have had to experience the trauma of being called a cunt on New Year's Eve. And he said he got called a cunt a lot.

(This is actually true. I've known him for a while now, and I'd say I've heard people, complete strangers, call him a cunt about fifteen times, a prick about ten times, a wanker maybe about the same, and an arsehole approximately half a dozen times. Also: tosser, berk, wally, git, shithead, and pillock.) Nobody likes him, which is weird, because he's famous. How can you be famous if nobody likes you?

Martin says it's nothing to do with the fifteen-year-old thing; he reckons that if anything it got slightly better after that, because the people who called him a cunt were exactly the sort of people who didn't see anything wrong with under-age sex. So instead of shouting out names, they shouted out things like, Go on, my son, Get in there, Wallop, et cetera. In terms of personal abuse, although not in terms of his marriage or his relationship with his children or his career or his sanity, going to prison actually did him some good.

But all sorts of people seem to be famous even though they have no fans. Tony Blair is a good example. And all the other people who present breakfast TV programs and quiz shows. The reason they're paid a lot of money, it seems to me, is because strangers yell terrible words at them in the street. Even a traffic warden doesn't get called a cunt when he's out shopping with his family. So the only real advantage to being Martin

D

O

W

N

85

is the money, and also the invitations to film premieres and dodgy nightclubs. And that's where you get yourself into trouble.

These were just some thoughts I had when Martin and I hugged. But they didn't get us anywhere. Outside my head it was five o'clock in the morning and we were all unhappy and we didn't have anywhere to go.

I was like, So now what? And I rubbed my hands together, as if we were all enjoying ourselves too much to let the night end—as if we'd been giving it large in Ocean, and we were all off for bagels and coffee in Bethnal Green, or back to someone's flat for spliffs and a chill. So I went, Whose gaff? I'll bet yours is tasty, Martin. I'll bet you've got Jacuzzis and all sorts. That'll do. And Martin said, No, we can't go there. And, by the way, my Jacuzzi days are long gone. Which I think meant that he was broke, not that he was too fat to go in one or anything. Because he's not fat, Martin. He's too vain to be fat.

So I said, Well, never mind, as long as you've got a kettle and some cornflakes. And he went, I haven't, so I was like, What have you got to hide? And he said, Nothing, but he said it in a funny way, an embarrassed, hiding sort of a way. And then I remembered something from before which I thought might be relevant and I said, Who was leaving messages for you on your mobile? And he went, Nobody. And I said, Is that Mr. Nobody or maybe Miss Nobody? And he said, Just Nobody. So I wanted to know why he didn't want to invite us back, and he went, Because I don't know you. And I said, Yeah, like you didn't know that fifteen-year-old.

And then he said, as if he was angry, OK. Yeah. Let's go to mine. Why not?

And so we did.

JJ

I know I'd had that bonding moment with Maureen when she'd smacked Chas, but to tell you the truth I was working on the assumption that if we all made it through to break-fast time, then my new band would split up due to musical differences. Breakfast time would mean that we'd made it through to a new dawn, new hope, a new year, tra la la. And no offense intended, but I really didn't want to be seen in daylight with these people, if you know what I mean—especially with . . . some of 'em. But breakfast and daylight were still a couple of hours away, so it felt to me like I had no real choice but to go with them back to Martin's place. To do anything else would have been mean and unfriendly, and I still didn't trust myself to spend too much time on my own.

Martin lived in a little villagey part of Islington, right around the corner from Tony Blair's old house, and really not the kind of hood you'd choose if you'd fallen on hard times, as Martin was supposed to have done. He paid the cab fare, and we followed him up the front steps to his house. I could see three or four front doorbells, so I could tell it wasn't all his, but I couldn't have afforded to live there.

Before he put his key in the lock, he paused and turned around.

"Listen," he said, and then he didn't say anything, so we listened.

"I don't hear anything," said Jess.

"No, I didn't mean that sort of listen. I meant, 'Listen, I'm going to tell you something.'"

"Go on, then," said Jess. "Spit it out."

"It's very late. So just . . . be respectful of the neighbors."

"That's it?"

"No." He took a deep breath. "There'll probably be someone in there."

"In your flat?"

"Yes."

"Who?"

"I don't know what you'd call her. My date. Whatever."

"You had a date for the evening?" I tried to keep my voice in neutral, but, you know, Jesus . . . What kind of evening had she had? One moment you're sitting in a club or whatever, the next he's disappeared because he wants to jump off a building.

"Yes. What of it?"

"Nothing. Just . . ." There was no need to say any more. We could leave the rest to the imagination.

"Fucking hell," said Jess. "What kind of date ends up with you sitting on the fucking ledge of a tower block?"

"An unsuccessful one," said Martin.

"I should think it was fucking unsuccessful," said Jess.

"Yes," said Martin. "That's why I described it as such."

He opened the door to his flat and ushered us in ahead of him; so we saw the girl sitting on the sofa a moment before he did. She was maybe ten or fifteen years younger than him, and pretty, in a kind of bimbo TV weathergirl way; she was wearing an expensive-looking black dress, and she'd been crying a whole lot. She stared at us, and then at him.

"Where have you been?" She was trying to keep it light, but she couldn't quite pull it off.

"Just out. Met some . . ." He gestured at us.

"Met some who?"

"You know. People."

"And that's why you left in the middle of the evening?"

"No. I didn't know I was going to run into this crowd when I left."

"And which crowd are they?" said the girl.

I wanted to hear Martin answer the question, because it might have been funny, but Jess interrupted.

"You're Penny Chambers," said Jess.

She didn't say anything, probably because she knew that already. We stared at her.

"Penny Chambers," said Maureen. She was gaping like a fish.

Penny Chambers still didn't say anything, for the same reasons as before.

"*Rise and Shine with Penny and Martin,*" said Maureen.

No response for a third time. I don't know much about English television stars, but I got it. If Martin was Regis, then Penny was Kathy Lee. The English Regis had been nailing the English Kathy Lee, and then disappeared to kill himself. That was pretty fucking hilarious, you have to admit.

"Are you two going out?" Jess asked her.

"You'd better ask him," said Penny. "He's the one who vanished in the middle of a dinner party."

"Are you two going out?" Jess asked him.

"I'm sorry," said Martin.

"Answer the question," said Penny. "I'm interested."

"This isn't really the time to talk about it," said Martin.

"So there's clearly some doubt," Penny said. "Which is news to me."

"It's complicated," said Martin. "You knew that."

"Nope."

"You knew I wasn't happy."

"Yes, I knew you weren't happy. But I didn't know you were unhappy about me."

"I wasn't . . . It's not . . . Can we talk later? In private?"

He stopped, and gestured around the room again at the three staring faces. I think I can speak for everyone when I say that, as a rule, potential suicides tend to be pretty self-absorbed: Those last few weeks, it's pretty much all me me me. So we were gulping this shit down (a) because it was not about us, and (b) because it was not a conversation likely to depress the hell out of us. It was, for the moment, just a fight between a boyfriend and a girlfriend, and it was taking us out of ourselves.

"And when will we be in private?"

"Soon. But probably not immediately."

"Right. And what do we talk about in the meantime? With your three friends here?"

No one knew what to say to that. Martin was the host, so it was up to him to find the common ground. And good luck to him.

"I think you should call Tom and Christine," said Penny.

"Yeah, I will. Tomorrow."

"They must think you're so rude."

"Who are Tom and Christine? The people you were having dinner with?"

"Yes."

"What did you tell them?"

"He told them he was going to the toilet," said Penny.

Jess burst out laughing. Martin glanced at her, replayed in his head the lame excuse he'd used, and then smirked, very briefly, at his shoes. It was a weirdly familiar moment. You know when you're being torn a new asshole by your dad for some crime you've committed, while a pal watches and tries not to laugh? And you try not to catch his eye, because then you'll laugh, too? Well, that's what it was like. Anyway, Penny spotted the little-boy smirk and flew across the room at the little boy in question. He grabbed her wrists to prevent her from hitting him.

"How dare you find it funny."

"I'm sorry. Really. I know it's not funny in any way." He tried to hug her, but she pushed herself away from him and sat down again.

"We need a drink," said Martin. "Would you mind if they stayed for one?"

I'll take a drink off just about anybody in any situation, but even I wasn't sure whether to take this one. In the end, though, I was just too thirsty.

MARTIN

It was only when we got back to the flat that I had any recollection of describing Penny as a right bitch who would fuck anybody and snort anything. But when had I said that? I spent the next thirty minutes or so praying that it had been before Jess's arrival, when Maureen and I were on our own; if Jess had heard, then I had no doubt that my opinion of Penny would be passed on.

And, needless to say, it was hardly a considered opinion anyway. Penny and I don't live together, but we'd been seeing each other for a few months, more or less ever since I got out of prison, and as you can imagine she had to endure a fair amount of difficulty in that time. We didn't want the press to know that we'd been seeing each other, so we never went out anywhere, and we wore hats and sunglasses more often than was strictly necessary. I had—still have, will always have—an ex-wife and children. I was only partially employed, on a dismal cable channel. And as I may have mentioned before, I wasn't terribly cheerful.

And we had a history. There was a brief affair when we were copresenting, but we were both married to other people, and so the affair ended, painfully and sadly. And then, finally, after much bad timing and many recriminations, we got together, but we'd missed the moment. I had become soiled goods. I was broken, finished, a wreck, scraping the bottom of my own barrel; she was still at the top of her game, beautiful and young and famous, broadcasting to millions every morning. I couldn't believe that she wanted to be with me for any reason other than nostalgia and pity, and she couldn't persuade me otherwise. A few years ago, Cindy joined one of those dreadful reading groups, where unhappy, repressed middle-class lesbians talk for five minutes about some novel they don't understand, and then spend the rest of the evening moaning about how dreadful men are. Anyway, she read a book about this couple who were in love but couldn't get together for donkey's years and then finally managed it, aged about one hundred. She adored it and made me read it, and it took me about as long to get through as it took the characters to pair off. Well, our relationship felt like that, except the old biddies in the book had a better time than Penny and I were having. A few weeks before Christmas, in a fit of self-disgust and despair, I told her to bugger off, and so she went out that night with some guest on the show, a TV chef, and he gave her her first-ever line of coke, and they ended up in bed, and she came round to see me the next morning in floods of tears. That's why I told Maureen she was a right bitch who would snort anything and fuck anybody. I can see now that this was a bit on the harsh side.

So that, give or take a few hundred heart-to-hearts and

tantrums, a couple of dozen other split-ups, and the odd punch thrown—by her, I hasten to add—is how Penny came to be sitting on my sofa waiting up for me. She would have been waiting a long time if it hadn't been for our impromptu roof party. I hadn't even bothered writing her a note, an omission which only now is beginning to cause me any remorse. Why did we persist in the pathetic delusion that this relationship was in any way viable? I'm not sure. When I asked Penny what the big idea was, she said merely that she loved me, which struck me as an answer more likely to confuse and obscure than to illuminate. As for me . . . Well, I associated Penny, perhaps understandably, with a time before things had started to go awry: before Cindy, before fifteen-year-olds, before prison. I had managed to convince myself that if I could make things work with Penny, then I could make them work elsewhere—I could somehow haul myself back, as if one's youth were a place you could visit whenever you felt like it. I bring you momentous news: It's not. Who'd have thought?

My immediate problem was how to explain my connection with Maureen, JJ, and Jess. She would find the truth hurtful and upsetting, and it was hard to think of a lie that would even get off the ground. What could we possibly be to one another? We didn't look like colleagues, or poetry enthusiasts, or clubbers, or substance abusers; the problem, it has to be said, was Maureen, on more or less every count, if failing to look like a substance abuser could ever be described as a problem. And even if they were colleagues or substance abusers, I would still find it hard to explain the apparent desperation of my desire to see them. I had told Penny and my hosts that I was going to the toilet; why would I then shoot out the front door

A
L
O
N
G

W
A
Y

half an hour before midnight on New Year's Eve in order to at-
tend the annual meeting of some nameless society?

So I decided simply to carry on as if there was nothing to
explain.

"Sorry. Penny, this is JJ, Maureen, Jess. JJ, Maureen, Jess,
this is Penny."

Penny seemed unconvinced even by the introductions, as
if I had started lying already.

"But you still haven't told me who they are."

"As in . . . ?"

"As in, How do you know them and where did you meet
them?"

"It's a long story."

"Good."

"Maureen I know from . . . Where did we meet, Maureen?
First of all?"

Maureen stared at me.

"It's a long time ago now, isn't it? We'll remember in a
minute. And JJ used to be part of the old Channel 5 crowd,
and Jess is his girlfriend."

Jess put her arm around JJ, with a touch more satire than
I might have wished.

"And where were they all tonight?"

"They're not deaf, you know. Or idiots. They're not . . .
deaf idiots."

"Where were you all tonight?"

"At . . . like . . . a party," said JJ tentatively.

"Where?"

"In Shoreditch."

"Whose?"

"Whose was it, Jess?"

Jess shrugged carelessly, as if it had been that sort of crazy night.

"And why did you want to go? At eleven thirty? In the middle of a dinner party? Without me?"

"That I can't explain." And I attempted to look simultaneously helpless and apologetic. We had, I hoped, crossed the border into the land of psychological complexity and unpredictability, a country where ignorance and bafflement were permitted.

"You're seeing someone else, aren't you?"

Seeing someone else? How on earth could that explain any of this? Why would seeing someone else necessitate bringing home a middle-aged woman, a teenaged punk, and an American with a leather jacket and a Rod Stewart haircut? What would the story have been? But then, after reflection, I realized that Penny had probably been here before, and therefore knew that infidelity can usually provide the answer to any domestic mystery. If I had walked in with Sheena Easton and Donald Rumsfeld, Penny would probably have scratched her head for a few seconds before saying exactly the same thing.

In other circumstances, on other evenings, it would have been the right conclusion, too; I used to be pretty resourceful when I was being unfaithful to Cindy, even if I do say so myself. I once drove a new BMW into a wall, simply because I needed to explain a four-hour delay in getting home from work. Cindy came out into the street to inspect the crumpled bonnet, looked at me, and said, "You're seeing someone else, aren't you?" I denied it, of course. But then, anything— smashing up a new car, persuading Donald Rumsfeld to come to an Islington flat in the early hours of New Year's Day—is easier than actually telling the truth. That look you get, the look which lets you see right through the eyes and down into the place where she keeps all the hurt and the rage and the loathing . . . Who wouldn't go that extra yard to avoid it?

"Well?"

My delay in replying was a result of some pretty complicated mental arithmetic; I was trying to work out which of the two different sums gave me the smallest minus number. But, inevitably, the delay was interpreted as an admission of guilt.

"You fucking bastard."

I was briefly tempted to point out that I was owed one, after the unfortunate incident with the line of coke and the TV chef, but that would only have served to delay her departure; more than anything I wanted to get drunk in my own home with my new friends. So I said nothing. Everyone else jumped when she slammed the door on the way out, but I knew it was coming.

MAUREEN

I was sick on the carpet outside the bathroom. Well, I say "carpet"—I was actually sick where the carpet should have been, but he didn't have one. Which was just as well, because it was much easier to clean up afterward. I've seen lots of those programs where they decorate your house for you, and I've never understood why they always make you throw your carpets away, even good ones which still have a nice thick pile. But now I'm wondering whether they first of all decide whether the people who live in the house are sicker-uppers or not. A lot of younger people have the bare floorboards, I've noticed, and of course they tend to be sick on the floor more than older people, what with all the beer they drink and so on. And the drugs they take, too, nowadays, I suppose. (Do drugs make you sick? I'd think so, wouldn't you?) And some of the young families in Islington don't seem to go in for the carpets much, either. But you see, that might be because babies are always being sick all over the place as well. So maybe Martin is a sicker-upper. Or maybe he just has a lot of friends who are sicker-uppers. Like me.

I was sick because I'm not used to drinking, and also because I hadn't had a thing to eat for more than a day. I was too nervous on New Year's Eve to eat anything, and there didn't seem to be an awful lot of point anyway. I didn't even have any of Matty's mush. What's food for? It's fuel, isn't it? It keeps you going. And I didn't really want to be kept going. Jumping off Toppers' House with a full stomach would have seemed wasteful, like selling a car with a full tank of petrol. So I was dizzy even before we started drinking the whiskey, because of the white wine at the party, and after I'd had a couple the room started spinning round and round.

We were quiet for a little while after Penny had gone. We didn't know whether we were supposed to be sad or not. Jess offered to chase after her and tell her that Martin hadn't been with anyone else, but Martin asked her how she was going to explain what we were doing there, and Jess said she thought that the truth wasn't so bad, and Martin said that he'd rather Penny thought badly of him than be told that he'd been thinking of killing himself.

"You're mad," said Jess. "She'd feel all sorry for you if she found out how we'd met. You'd probably get a sympathy shag."

Martin laughed. "I don't think that's how it works, Jess," he said.

"Why not?"

"Because if she found out how we met, it would really upset her. She'd think she was responsible in some way. It's a terrible thing, finding out that your lover is so unhappy he wants to die. It's a time for self-reflection."

"Yeah. And."

"And I'd have to spend hours holding her hand. I don't feel like holding her hand."

"You'd still end up with a sympathy shag. I didn't say it would be easy."

Sometimes it was hard to remember that Jess was unhappy, too. The rest of us, we were still shell-shocked. I didn't know how I'd ended up drinking whiskey in the lounge of a well-known TV personality when I'd actually left the house to kill myself, and you could tell that JJ and Martin were confused about the evening, too. But with Jess, it was like the whole how's-your-father on the roof was like a minor accident, the sort of thing where you rub your head and sit down and have a cup of sweet tea, and then you get on with the rest of your day. When she was talking about sympathy intercourse and whatever other nonsense came into her head, you couldn't see what could possibly have made her want to climb those stairs up to the roof—her eyes were twinkling, and she was full of energy, and you could tell that she was having fun. We weren't having fun. We weren't killing ourselves, but we weren't having fun either. We'd come too close to jumping.

And yet, Jess had come the closest of all of us to going over. JJ had only just come out of the stairwell. Martin had sat with his feet dangling over the edge but hadn't actually nerved himself to do it; I'd never even got as far as the other side of the fence. But if Martin hadn't sat on Jess's head, she'd have done it, I'm sure of that.

"Let's play a game," said Jess.

"F—— off," said Martin.

It was impossible to go on being shocked by the bad language. I didn't want to get to the stage where I was swearing myself, so I was quite glad that the night was drawing to an end. But the getting used to it made me realize something. It made me realize that nothing had ever changed for me. In Martin's flat, I could look back on myself—the me from only a few hours before—and think, "Ooh, I was different then. Fancy being upset by a little bit of bad language!" I'd got older even during the night. You get used to that, the feeling that you're suddenly different, when you're younger. You wake up in the morning and you can't believe that you had a crush on this person, or used to like that sort of music, even if it was only a few weeks ago. But when I had Matty everything stopped and nothing ever moved on. It's the one single thing that makes you die inside, and eventually wants to make you die on the outside, too. People have children for all sorts of reasons, I know, but one of those reasons must be that children growing up make you feel that life has a sense of momentum—kids send you on a journey. Matty and I got stuck at the bus stop, though. He didn't learn to walk or talk, let alone read or write: He stayed the same every single day, and life stayed the same every single day, and I stayed the same, too.

I know it's not much, but hearing the word "f——" hundreds of times in an evening, well, even that was something different for me, something new. When I first met Martin on the roof, I physically flinched from the words he used, and now they just bounced off me, as if I had a helmet on. Well, they would, wouldn't they? You'd be a proper eejit if you flinched three hundred times in an evening. It made me wonder what else would change if I lived like this for just a few more days. Already I'd hit someone, and now there I was drinking whiskey and Coca-Cola. You know when people on the TV say "You should get out more"? Now I saw what they meant.

"Miserable bastard," said Jess.

"Well, yes," said Martin. "Exactly. Der, as you would say."

"What have I said now?"

"You accused me of being a miserable bastard. I was merely pointing out that, at this particular stage of my life, and indeed on this particular night, 'miserable' is a very appropriate adjective. I am a very miserable bastard indeed, as I thought you would have worked out by now."

"What, still?"

Martin laughed. "Yes. Still. Even after all the fun we've had tonight. What would you say has changed in the last few hours? Have I still been to prison? I believe I still have. Did I sleep with a fifteen-year-old? Regrettably, nothing much seems to have changed on that score. Is my career still in pieces, and am I still estranged from my children? Unhappily, yes and yes. Despite attending a party with your amusing friends in Shoreditch and being called a c——? What kind of malcontent must I be, eh?"

"I thought we'd cheered each other up."

"Really? Is that really and truly what you thought?"

"Yeah."

"I see. A trouble shared is a trouble halved, and because there are four of us, it's actually been quartered? That sort of thing?"

"Well, you've all made me feel better."

"Yes. Well."

"What's that supposed to mean?"

"Nothing. I'm glad we've made you feel better. Your depression was clearly more . . . amenable than ours. Less intractable. You're very lucky. Unfortunately, JJ is still going to die, Maureen still has a profoundly disabled son, and my life is still a complete and utter f——ing shambles. To be honest with you, Jess, I don't see how a couple of drinks and a game of Monopoly are going to help. Fancy a game of Monopoly, JJ? Will that help the old CCR? Or not really?"

I was shocked, but JJ didn't seem to mind. He just smiled and said, "I guess not."

"I wasn't thinking of Monopoly," said Jess. "Monopoly takes too long."

And then Martin shouted something at her but I didn't hear what it was because I was starting to retch, so I put my hand over my mouth and ran for the bathroom. But as I said, I didn't make it.

"Jesus f——ing Christ," Martin said when he saw the mess I'd made. I couldn't get used to that sort of swearing, though, the sort that involves Him. I don't think that will ever seem right.

JJ

I was beginning to regret the whole CCR scam, so I wasn't sorry when Maureen puked her whiskey and Coke all over Martin's ash-blond wooden floor. I'd been experiencing an impulse to own up, and owning up would have got my year off to a pretty bad start. That's on top of the bad start it had already got off to, what with thinking of jumping off a high building, and lying about having CCR in the first place. Anyway, I was glad that suddenly we all crowded around Maureen and were patting her on the back and offering her glasses of water, because the owning-up moment passed.

The truth was that I didn't feel like a dying man; I felt like a man who every now and again wanted to die, and there's a difference. A man who wants to die feels angry and full of life and desperate and bored and exhausted, all at the same time; he wants to fight everyone, and he wants to curl up in a ball and hide in a cupboard somewhere. He wants to say sorry to everyone, and he wants everyone to know just how badly they've all let him down. I can't believe that dying people feel that way, unless dying is worse than I'd thought. (And why shouldn't it be? Every other fucking thing is worse than I thought, so why should dying be any different?)

"I'd like one of my Polo mints," she said. "I've got one in my handbag."

"Where's your handbag?"

She didn't say anything for a little while, and then she groaned softly.

"If you're going to be sick again, would you do me a favor and crawl the last couple of yards to the bog?" Martin said.

"It's not that," said Maureen. "It's my handbag. It's on the roof. In the corner, right by the hole Martin made in the fence. It's only got my keys and the Polos and a couple of pound coins in it."

"We can find you a mint, if that's what you're worried about."

"I've got some chewing gum," said Jess.

"I'm not much of a one for chewing gum," said Maureen. "Anyway, I've got a bridge that's a bit loose. And I didn't bother getting it fixed because . . ."

She didn't finish the sentence. She didn't need to. I think we all had a few things we hadn't got around to fixing, for obvious reasons.

"So we'll find you a mint," said Martin. "Or you can clean your teeth if you want. You can use Penny's toothbrush."

"Thank you."

She got to her feet and then sat down again on the floor.

"What am I going to do? About the bag?"

It was a question for all of us, but Martin and I looked at Jess for the answer. Or rather, we knew the answer, but the answer would have to come in the form of another question,

and we had both learned, over the course of the night, that Jess would be the one who would be tactless enough to ask it.

"The thing is," said Jess, right on cue, "do you need it?"

"Oh," said Maureen, as the bag implications started to penetrate.

"Do you see what I mean?"

"Yes. Yes, I do."

"If you don't know whether you're gonna need it, just say so. 'Cause, you know. It's a big question, and we wouldn't want to rush you. But if you know for sure you won't be needing it, then probably best say so now. That'd save us all a trip, see."

"I wouldn't ask you to come with me."

"We'd want to," said Jess. "Wouldn't we?"

"And if you know you don't want your keys, you can stay here for the day," said Martin. "Don't worry about them."

"I see," Maureen said. "Right. I hadn't really . . . I thought, I don't know. I was going to put off thinking about it for a few hours."

"OK," Martin said. "Fair enough. So let's go back."

"Do you mind?"

"Not at all. It would be silly to kill yourself just because you didn't have your handbag."

When we got to Toppers' House, I realized that I'd left Ivan's moped there the night before. It wasn't there anymore, and I felt bad, because he's not such a bad guy, Ivan, and it's not like he's some fucking Rolls-Royce-drivin', cigar-smokin' capitalist. He's too poor. In fact, he drives one of his own mopeds around. Anyway, now I can never face him again, although one of the beauties of a minimum wage, cash-in-hand job is that you can clean windshields at traffic lights and make pretty much the same money.

"I left my car here, too," said Martin.

"And that's gone as well?"

"The door was unlocked and the keys were in the ignition. It was supposed to be an act of charity. There won't be any more of those."

The bag was where Maureen had left it, though, right in the corner of the roof. It wasn't until we got up there that we could see we'd made it through to dawn, just about. It was a proper dawn, too, with a sun and a blue sky. We walked around the roof to see what we could see, and the others gave me an American-in-London sightseeing tour: St. Paul's, the Ferris wheel down by the river, Jess's house.

"It's not scary anymore," said Martin.

"You reckon?" said Jess. "Have you looked over the edge? Fucking hell. It's a fuck sight better in the dark, if you ask me."

"I didn't mean the drop," said Martin. "I meant London. It looks all right."

"It looks beautiful," said Maureen. "I can't remember the last time I could see so much."

"I didn't mean that either. I meant . . . I don't know. There were all those fireworks, and people walking around, and we were squeezed up here because there was nowhere else for us to go."

"Yeah. Unless you'd been invited to a dinner party," I said. "Like you had."

"I didn't know anyone there. I'd been invited out of pity. I didn't belong."

"And you feel included now?"

"There's nothing down there to feel excluded from. It's just a big city again. Look. He's on his own. And she's on her own."

"She's a fucking traffic warden," said Jess.

"Yes, and she's on her own, and today she's got fewer friends than me even. But last night she was probably dancing on a table somewhere."

"With other traffic wardens, probably," said Jess.

"And I wasn't with other TV presenters."

"Or perverts," said Jess.

"No. Agreed. I was on my own."

"Apart from the other people at the dinner party," I said. "But yeah. We hear where you're coming from. That's why New Year's Eve is such a popular night for suicides."

"When's the next one?" Jess asked.

"December 31," said Martin.

"Yeah, yeah. Ha-ha. The next popular night."

"That would be Valentine's Day," said Martin.

"What's that? Six weeks?" said Jess. "So let's give it another six weeks, then. What about that? We'll probably all feel terrible on Valentine's Day."

We all stared thoughtfully at the view. Six weeks seemed all right. Six weeks didn't seem too long. Life could change in six weeks—unless you had a severely disabled child to care for. Or your career had gone up in fucking smoke. Or unless you were a national laughingstock.

"D'you know how you'll be feeling in six weeks?" Maureen asked me.

Oh, yes—and unless you had a terminal disease. Life wouldn't change much then, either.

I shrugged. How the fuck did I know how I'd be feeling? This disease was brand-new. No one was able to predict its course—not even me, and I invented it.

"So are we going to meet again before the six weeks is up?"

"I'm sorry, but . . . When did we become 'we'?" said Martin. "Why do we even have to meet in six weeks? Why can't we just kill ourselves wherever and whenever we want?"

"No one's stopping you," said Jess.

"Surely the whole purpose of this exercise is that someone is stopping me. We're all stopping each other."

"Until the six weeks is up, yeah."

"So when you said 'No one's stopping you,' then you meant the opposite."

"Listen," said Jess. "If you go home now and put your head in the gas oven, what am I going to do about it?"

"Exactly. So the purpose of the exercise is?"

"I'm asking, aren't I? Because if we're a gang, then we'll all try and live by the rules. And there's only one anyway. Rule 1: We don't kill ourselves for six weeks. And if we're not a gang, then, you know. Whatever. So are we a gang, or not a gang?"

"Not a gang," said Martin.

"Why aren't we?"

"No offense, but—" Martin clearly hoped these three words and a wave of the hand in our general direction would save him from having to explain himself. I wasn't going to let him off the hook, though.

I hadn't felt like I was in this gang either, until that moment. And now I belonged to the gang that Martin didn't like much, and I felt real committed to it.

"But what?" I said.

"Well. You're not, you know. My Kind Of People." He said it like that, I swear. I heard the capitals as clearly as I heard the lowercase.

"Fuck you," I said. "Like I usually hang out with assholes like you."

"Well, there we are, then. We should all shake hands, thank one another for a most instructive evening, and then go our separate ways."

"And die," said Jess.

"Possibly," said Martin.

"And that's what you want?" I said.

"Well, it's not a long-held ambition, I grant you. But I'm not giving away any secrets when I say it's come to look more attractive recently. I'm conflicted, as you people say. Anyway, why do you care?" he said to Jess. "I'd got the impression that you didn't care for anyone or anything. I thought that was your thing."

Jess thought for a moment. "You know those films where people fight up the top of the Empire State Building or up a mountain or whatever? And there's always that bit when the baddie slips off and the hero tries to save him, but, like, the sleeve of his jacket tears off and he goes over and you hear him all the way down. Aaaaaaaagh. That's what I want to do."

"You want to watch me plunge to my doom."

"I'd like to know that I've made the effort. I want to show people the torn sleeve."

"I didn't know you were a fully trained Samaritan," said Martin.

"I'm not. This is just my own personal philosophy."

"I'd find it easier if we saw each other on a regular basis," said Maureen quietly. "All of us. No one really knows how I feel about anything, apart from you three. And Matty. I tell Matty."

"Oh, for Christ's sake," said Martin. He was using profanity because he knew then he was beaten: Telling Maureen to go fuck herself required more moral courage than any of us possessed.

"It's only six weeks," said Jess. "We'll throw you off the top ourselves on Valentine's, if it helps."

Martin shook his head, but it was to indicate defeat rather than refusal.

"We'll all live to regret it," he said.

"Good," said Jess. "So is everyone all right with that?"

I shrugged. It wasn't like I had a better plan.

"I'm not going on beyond six weeks," said Maureen.

"No one will make you," said Martin.

"As long as we know that from the start," said Maureen.

"Noted," said Martin.

"Excellent," said Jess. "So it's a deal."

We shook hands, Maureen picked up her handbag, and we all went out for breakfast. We couldn't think of anything to say to one another, but we didn't seem to mind much.

P A R T

T W O

JESS

It didn't take long for the papers to find out. A couple of days, maybe. I was in my room, and Dad called me downstairs and asked me what I'd been up to on New Year's Eve. And I went, Nothing much, and he went, Well, that isn't what the newspapers seem to think. And I was like, Newspapers? And he said, Yeah, there's apparently going to be a story about you and Martin Sharp. Do you know Martin Sharp? And I was, you know, Yeah, sort of, only met him that night at a party, don't know him very well. And so Dad goes, What the hell kind of party is it where you meet someone like Martin Sharp? And I couldn't think what kind of party that would be, so I didn't say anything. And then Dad was like, And was there . . . Did anything . . . All tenterhooks or whatever, kind of thing, so I just dived in. Did I fuck him? No I did not! Thanks a bunch! Bloody hell! Martin Sharp! Eeeeuch! And so on and so on until he got the idea.

It was fucking Chas, of course, who phoned up the newspapers. He'd probably tried before, the little shit, but he never had much to go on then, when it was just me. The Jess

Crichton/Martin Sharp combo, though—unresistible. How much do you think you get for something like that? A couple of hundred quid? More? To be honest, I'd have done it if I were him. He's always skint. And I'm always skint. If he'd been anyone worth selling up the river, he'd be halfway out to sea by now.

Dad pulled back the curtain to sneak a look, and there was someone out there. I wanted to go out and have a go at him, but Dad wouldn't let me; he said that they'd take a mad picture of me, and I'd look stupid and regret it. And he said it was undignified to do that, and in our position we had to rise above it all and ignore them. And I was like, In *whose* position? I'm not in a position. And he went, Well, you are whether you like it or not, you are in a position, and I go, You're in a position, not me, and he said, You're in a position, too, and we went on like that for a while. But of course going on about it never changes anything, and I know he's right, really. If I wasn't in a position, then the papers wouldn't be interested. In fact, the more I act as though I'm not in a position, then the more I'm in a position, if you see what I mean. If I just sat in my room and read, or got a steady boyfriend, there'd be no interest. But if I went to bed with Martin Sharp, or threw myself off a roof, then there would be the opposite of no interest. There'd be interest.

When I was in the papers a couple of years ago, just after the Jen thing, I think the feeling was I was Troubled rather than Bad. Anyway, shoplifting isn't murder, is it? Everyone goes through a shoplifting phase, don't they? By which I mean *proper* shoplifting: boosting Winona-style, bags and clothes and shit, not pens and sweets. It comes just after ponies and boy bands, and right before spliff and sex. But I could tell that it was different this time, and that was when I started to think things through. Yeah, yeah, I know. But better late than never, eh? What I thought was this: If it was going to be all over the papers, it was better for Mum and Dad to think that I'd slept with Martin than to know the real reason we were together. The real reason would kill them. Maybe literally. Which would make me the only family member left alive, possibly, and even I'm making up my mind which way to go. So if the papers had got hold of the wrong end of the stick, it wouldn't be such a bad thing. Obviously it would be pretty humiliating at college, everyone thinking I'd fucked the sleaziest man in Britain, but it would be for the greater good, i.e., two alive parents.

The thing was, even though I'd started to think things through, I didn't think them through properly. I could have saved myself a lot of trouble if I'd just given it another two minutes before I'd opened my mouth, but I didn't. I just went, Da-ad. And he was like, Oh, no. And I just looked at him and he goes, You'd better tell me everything, and I said, Well, there isn't much to tell, really. I just went to this party and he was there and I had too much to drink and we went back to his place and that's it. And he was like, That's it as in end of story? And I went, Well, no, that's it as in dot, dot, dot, you don't need to know the details. So he went, Jesus Christ, and he sat down in a chair.

But here's the thing: I didn't need to say I'd slept with him, did I? I could have said we'd snogged, or he tried it on, or anything at all like that, but I wasn't quick enough. I was like, well, if it's a choice between suicide and sex, better go with sex, but those didn't have to be the choices. Sex was only a serving suggestion sort of thing, but you don't have to do exactly what it says on the packet, do you? You can miss the garnish out if you want, and that's what I should have done.

("Garnish"—that's a weird word, isn't it? I don't think I've ever used it before.) But I didn't, did I? And the other thing I should have done but didn't: Before I told him anything, I should have got Dad to find out what the story in the newspaper was. I just thought, Tabloids, sex . . . I don't know what I thought, to tell you the truth. Not much, as usual.

So Dad got straight on the phone and talked to his office and told them what I'd told him, and then when he'd finished, he said he was going out and I wasn't to answer the phone or go anywhere or do anything. So I watched TV for a few minutes, and then I looked out the window to see if I could see that bloke, and I could, and he wasn't on his own anymore.

And then Dad came back with a newspaper—he'd been out to get an early edition. He looked about ten years older than he had before he left. And he held up the paper for me to see, and the headline said, MARTIN SHARP AND JUNIOR MINISTER'S DAUGHTER IN SUICIDE PACT.

So the whole sex confession bit had been a complete and utter fucking waste of time.

JJ

That was the first time we knew anything about Jess's background, and I have to say that my first reaction was that it was pretty fucking hilarious. I was in my local store buying some smokes, and Jess and Martin were staring at me from the counter, and I read the headline and whooped. Which, seeing as the headline was about their supposed suicide pact, got me some strange looks. An education minister! Holy shit! You've got to understand, this girl talked like she'd been brought up by a penniless, junkie welfare mother who was younger than her. And she acted like education was a form of prostitution, something that only the weird or the desperate would resort to.

But then when I read the story, it wasn't quite so funny. I didn't know anything about Jess's older sister, Jennifer. None of us did. She disappeared a few years ago, when Jess was fifteen and she was eighteen; she'd borrowed her mother's car and they found it abandoned near a well-known suicide spot down on the coast. Jennifer had passed her road test three days before, as if that had been the point of learning to drive. They never found a body. I don't know what that would have done to Jess—nothing good, I guess. And her old man . . . Jesus. Parents who only beget suicidal daughters are likely to end up feeling pretty dark about the whole child-raising scene.

And then, the next day, it became a whole lot less funny. There was another headline, and it read, THERE WERE FOUR OF THEM!, and in the article underneath it there was a description of these two freaks that I eventually realized were supposed to be Maureen and me. And at the end of the article, there was an appeal for further information and a phone number. There was even, like, a cash reward. Maureen and I had prices on our heads, man!

The information had clearly come from that asshole Chas; you could hear the whine in his voice right through the weird British tabloid prose. You had to give the guy a little credit, though, I guess. To me, the evening had consisted of four miserable people failing dismally to do something they had set out to do—something that is not, let's be honest, real hard to achieve. But Chas had seen something else: He'd seen that it was a story, something he might make a few bucks off of. OK, he must have known about Jess's dad, but, you know, props to the guy. He still needed to put it together.

I'll tell you the honest truth here: I got off on the story a little. It was kind of gratifying, in an ironic way, reading about myself, and that makes sense if you think about it. See, one of the things that had brought me down was my inability to leave my mark on the world through my music—which is another way of saying that I was suicidal because I wasn't famous. Maybe I'm being hard on myself, because I know there was a little more to it than that, but that was sure a part of it. Anyway, recognizing that I was all washed up had got me onto the front page of the newspaper, and maybe there's a lesson there somewhere.

So I was sort of enjoying myself, sitting in my flat, drinking coffee and smoking, taking pleasure from knowing that I was sort of famous and completely anonymous, all at the same time. And then the fucking buzzer went, and I jumped out of my skin.

"Who is it?"

"Is that JJ?" A young woman's voice.

"Who is it?"

"I wondered if I could have a few words with you? About the other night?"

"How did you get this address?"

"I understand you were one of the people with Jess Crichton and Martin Sharp on New Year's Eve? When they tried to kill themselves?"

"You understand wrong, ma'am." This was the first sentence from either of us that didn't have a question mark at the end. The low note at the end of mine was a relief, like a sneeze.

"Which *bit* have I got wrong?"

"All of it. You pressed the wrong buzzer."

"I don't think I did."

"How do you know?"

"Because you didn't deny you were JJ. And you asked how I'd got this address."

Good point. They were professional, these people.

"I didn't say it was *my* address, though, did I?"

There was a pause, while we both allowed the complete stupidity of this observation to float around.

She didn't say anything. I imagined her standing out there in the street, shaking her head sadly at my pathetic attempts. I vowed not to say another word until she went away.

"Listen," she said, "was there a reason you came down?"

"What kind of reason?"

"I don't know. Something that might cheer our readers up. Maybe, I don't know, you gave each other the will to go on."

"I don't know about that."

"The four of you looked down over London and saw the beauty of the world. Anything like that? Anything that might inspire our readers?"

Was there anything inspirational in our quest to find Chas? If there was, I couldn't see it.

"Did Martin Sharp say anything that gave you a reason to live, for example? People would want to know, if he did."

I tried to think if Martin had offered us any words of comfort she could use. He'd called Jess a fucking idiot, but that was more of a spirit-lifting rather than lifesaving moment. And he'd told us that a guest on his show had been married to someone who'd been in a coma for twenty-five years, but that hadn't helped us out much, either.

"I can't think of anything, no."

"I'm going to leave a card with my numbers on it, OK? Ring me when you feel ready to talk about this."

I nearly ran out after her—I was, as we say, missing her already. I liked being the temporary center of her world. Shit, I liked being the temporary center of my own, because there hadn't been too much there recently, and there wasn't much there after she'd gone, either.

MAUREEN

So I went home, and I put the television on, and made a cup of tea, and I phoned the center, and the two young fellas delivered Matty to the house, and I put him in front of the TV, and it all started again. It was hard to see how I'd last another six weeks. I know we had an agreement, but I never thought I'd see any of them again anyway. Oh, we exchanged telephone numbers and addresses and so forth. (Martin had to explain to me that if I didn't have a computer, then I wouldn't have an e-mail address. I wasn't sure whether I'd have one or not. I thought it might have come in one of those envelopes you throw away.) But I didn't think we'd actually be using them. I'll tell you God's honest truth, even though it'll make me sound as if I was feeling sorry for myself: I thought they might see each other, but they'd keep me out of it. I was too old for them, and too old-fashioned, with my shoes and all. I'd had an interesting time going to parties and seeing all the strange people there, but it hadn't changed anything. I was still going back to pick Matty up, and I still had no life to live beyond the life I was already sick and tired of. You might be thinking, Well, why isn't she angry? But of course I am angry. I don't know why I ever pretend I'm not. The church had something to do with it, I suppose. And maybe my age, because we were taught not to grumble, weren't we? But some days—most days—I want to scream and shout and break things and kill people. Oh, there's anger, right enough. You can't be stuck with a life like this one and not get angry.

Anyway. A couple of days later the phone rang, and this woman with a posh voice said, "Is that Maureen?"

"It is."

"This is the Metropolitan Police."

"Oh, hello," I said.

"Hello. We've had reports that your son was causing trouble in the shopping center on New Year's Eve. Shoplifting and sniffing glue and mugging people and so on."

"I'm afraid it couldn't have been my son," I said, like an eejit. "He has a disability."

"And you're sure he's not putting the disability on?"

I even thought about this for half a second. Well, you do, don't you, when it's the police? You want to make absolutely sure that you're telling the absolute truth, just in case you get into trouble later on.

"He'd be a very good actor if he was."

"And you're sure he's not a very good actor?"

"Oh, positive. You see, he's too disabled to act."

"But how about if *that's* an act? Only, the, er, the wossname fits his description. The suspect."

"What's the description?" I don't know why I said that. To be helpful, I suppose.

"We'll come to that, madam. Can you account for his whereabouts on New Year's Eve? Were you with him?"

I felt a chill run through me then. The date hadn't registered at first. They'd got me. I didn't know whether to lie or not. Supposing someone from the home had taken him out and used him as a cover, sort of thing? One of those young fellas, say? They looked nice enough, but you don't know, do you? Supposing they had gone shoplifting, and hidden something under Matty's blanket? Supposing they all went out drinking, and they took Matty with them, and they got into a fight, and they pushed the wheelchair hard toward someone they were fighting with? And the police saw him careering into someone, and they didn't know that he couldn't have pushed himself, so they thought he was joining in? And afterward he was just playing dumb because he didn't want to get into trouble? Well, you could hurt someone, crashing into them with a wheelchair. You could break someone's leg. And supposing . . . Actually, even in the middle of my little panic I couldn't really see how he'd manage the glue sniffing. But even so! These were all the things that went through my mind. It was all guilt, I suppose. I hadn't been with him, and I should have been, and the reason I hadn't been with him was because I wanted to leave him forever.

"I wasn't with him, no. He was being looked after."

"Ah. I see."

"He was perfectly safe."

"I'm sure he was, madam. But we're not talking about *his* safety, are we? We're talking about the safety of people in the Wood Green shopping center."

Wood Green! He was all the way up in Wood Green!

"No. Yes. Sorry."

"Are you really sorry? Are you really, really, really f——ing sorry?"

I couldn't believe my ears. I knew the police used bad language, of course. But I thought it would come out more when they were under stress, with terrorists and such like, not on the phone to members of the public in the course of a routine inquiry. Unless, of course, she really was under stress. Could Matty, or whoever pushed him, have actually killed someone? A child, maybe?

"Maureen."

"Yes, I'm still here."

"Maureen, I'm not really a policewoman. I'm Jess."

"Oh." I could feel myself blushing at my own stupidity.

"You believed me, didn't you, you silly old bag."

"Yes, I believed you."

She could hear in my voice that she'd upset me, so she didn't try to make any more of it.

"Have you seen the papers?"

"No. I don't look at them."

"We're in them."

"Who's in them?"

"We are. Well, Martin and I are in them by name. What a laugh, eh?"

"What does it say?"

"It says that me and Martin and two other mystery, you know, people had a suicide pact."

"That's not true."

"Der. And it says I'm the junior minister for education's daughter."

D
O
W
N

123

"Why does it say that?"

"Because I am."

"Oh."

"I'm just telling you so you know what's in the papers. Are you surprised?"

"Well, you do swear a lot, for a politician's daughter."

"And a woman reporter came round to JJ's flat and asked him whether we came down for an inspirational reason."

"What does that mean?"

"We don't know. Anyway, we're going to have a crisis meeting."

"Who is?"

"The four of us. Big reunion. Maybe in the place where we had breakfast."

"I can't go anywhere."

"Why not?"

"Because of Matty. That's one of the reasons I was up on the roof. Because I can never go anywhere."

"We could come to you."

I began to flush again. I didn't want them here.

"No, no. I'll think of something. When are you thinking of meeting up?"

"Later on today."

"Oh, I won't be able to sort anything out for today."

"So we'll come to you."

"Please don't. I haven't tidied up."

"So tidy up."

"I've never had anyone from the television in my house. Or a politician's daughter."

"I won't put on any airs or graces. We'll see you at five."

And that gave me three hours to sort everything out, put

everything away. It does drive you a little bit mad, a life like mine, I think. You have to be a little mad to want to jump off the top of a building. You have to be a little mad to come down again. You have to be more than a little mad to put up with Matty, and the staying in all the time, and the loneliness. But I do think I'm only a little mad. If I were really mad, I wouldn't have worried about the tidying up. And if I were really, properly mad, I wouldn't have minded what they found.

MARTIN

I suppose it crossed my mind that my visit to Toppers' House might be of interest to our friends in the tabloid press. I was on the front page of the paper for falling down drunk in the street, for Christ's sake, and some would argue that attempting to fall off a high building is even more interesting than that. When Jess told Chas where we'd met, I did wonder whether he'd have the wit to sell the knowledge on, but as Chas seemed to me a particularly witless individual, I dismissed the fear as paranoia. If I'd known that Jess was newsworthy in her own right, then I could have prepared myself.

My agent called first thing, and read the story out to me— I only bother with the *Telegraph* at home now.

"Is any of this true?" he said.

"Between you and me?"

"If you want."

"I was going to jump from the top of a tower block."

"Gosh."

My agent is young, posh, and green. I came out of prison to find that there had been a quote unquote reorganization at the agency, and Theo, who used to make the coffee for my previous agent, is now all that stands between me and professional oblivion. It was Theo who found me my current job at FeetUp!TV, the world's worst cable channel. He has a degree in Comparative Religion, and he's a published poet. I suspect that he plays his football for Allboys United, if you get my drift, although that's neither here nor there. He's at the chocolate teapot end of the competency scale.

"I met her up there. Her and a couple of others. We came back down again. And here I am, in the land of the living."

"Why were you going to jump off the top of a tower block?"

"It was purely whimsical."

"I'm sure you must have had a reason."

"I did. I was joking. Read my file. Acquaint yourself with recent events."

"We thought we'd turned a corner." It's always very touching, his insistence on the first person plural. I've heard them all: "Since we came out of prison," "Since we had that spot of bother with the teenaged girl." If there was one cause for regret after a successful suicide attempt, it would be that I'd never get to hear Theo say, "Since we killed ourselves," or, "Since our funeral."

"We thought wrong."

There was a ruminative silence.

"Well. Gosh. Now what?"

"You're the agent. I'd have thought this gave you no end of creative opportunities."

"I'll have a little think and call you back. By the way, Jess's father has been trying to get hold of you. He called here, and

I said we didn't give out personal numbers. Did I do the right thing?"

"You did the right thing. But give him my mobile number anyway. I suppose there's no avoiding him."

"Do you want to call him? He left his number."

"Go on, then."

While I was on the phone to Theo, both my ex-wife and my ex-girlfriend left messages. I had thought of neither of them when Theo was reading out that story; now I felt sick. I was beginning to realize an important truth about suicide: Failure is as hurtful as success, and is likely to provoke even more anger, because there's no grief with which to water it down. I was, I could hear from the tone of the messages, in very deep shit.

I called Cindy first.

"You fucking selfish idiot," she said.

"You don't know anything, apart from what you read in the paper."

"You seem to be the only person in the world that the papers get bang to rights. If they say you've slept with a fifteen-year-old, you have. If they say you've fallen over drunk in the street, you have. They don't need to invent stuff for you."

This was actually quite an acute observation. She was right: Not once have I been the victim of misrepresentation or distortion. If you think about it, that was one of the most humiliating aspects of the last few years. The papers have been full of shit about me, and every word of the shit was true.

"So I'm presuming," she went on, "that they've got it right again. You were up the top of a tower block with the intention of hurling yourself off. And instead you came back down again with a girl."

"That's about the long and the short of it."

"And what about your daughters?"

"Do they know?"

"Not yet. But someone at school will tell them. They always do. What do you want me to say to them?"

"Maybe I should talk to them."

Cindy barked once. The bark was, I suspected, intended to be a satirical laugh.

"Tell them what you want," I said. "Tell them Daddy was sad, but then he cheered up again."

"Brilliant. If we had a pair of two-year-olds, that would be perfect."

"I don't know, Cindy. I mean, if I can't see them, then it's not really my problem, is it? It's something you've got to deal with."

"You bastard."

And that was the end of the first phone call. Pointing out that her refusal to let me participate in my daughters' upbringing left me out in the cold struck me as a restatement of the bleeding obvious, but never mind. It got her off the phone.

I don't know what I owe my daughters anymore. I gave up smoking years ago because I knew then that I owed them that much. But when you make the sort of mess I've made, smoking seems like the least of your worries—which is why I started again. Now *there's* a journey: from giving up smoking—giving up smoking because you want to protect your kids from loss for as long as possible—to arguing with their mother about the best way to tell them of your attempted suicide. They never said anything about that conversation in antenatal classes. It's the distance that does it, of course. I got further and further away, and the girls got smaller and smaller until they were just tiny dots, and I could no longer see them, literally or metaphorically. You can't make out their faces, can you, when they're just tiny dots, so you don't need to worry about whether they're happy or sad. It's why we can kill ants. And so after a while, suicide becomes imaginable, in a way that wouldn't be possible if they looked into your eyes every day.

Penny was still crying when I called her.

"At least that makes more sense," she said after a while.

"What?"

"You leaving the party to go up there. And then coming back with those people. I couldn't work out what they had to do with anything."

"All you knew was that somehow they'd helped me to have sex with someone else."

"Exactly." She gave a little rueful snort. She's OK, Penny. She's not a bitch at all. She's sweet-natured, self-deprecating, loving . . . She'd make someone a lovely partner.

"I'm sorry."

"I'm the one who's failed, aren't I?"

"I think my failures preceded yours. Which, by the way, don't amount to anything. I mean, anything at all. I mean, there weren't any failures. You've been fantastic to me."

"How do you feel today?"

I hadn't asked myself that question. I'd woken up with a hangover and the phone ringing, and since then, life seemed to have a momentum. I hadn't thought about killing myself once all morning.

"OK. I won't be going up there again just yet, if that's what you mean."

"Will you talk to me before you do?"

"About all that?"

"Yes. About all that."

"I don't know. It doesn't seem like something talking can fix."

"Oh, I know I can't fix it. I just don't want to have to read about it in the papers."

"You can do better than this, Penny. Better than me."

"I don't want to."

"Ah. So you don't disagree with the premise."

"I've got enough self-respect to think that there might be a man somewhere who'd rather spend New Year's Eve with me than leap to his death, yes."

"So why don't you try and find him?"

"Would you care one way or the other?"

"Well. Caring about stuff like that . . . It's sort of not where I'm at, is it?"

"Wow. That's honest."

"Is it? I would have thought it was merely self-evident."

"So what do you want me to do?"

"I'm not sure there's much you can do."

"Will you call me later?"

"Yes, of course."

I could promise that much, anyway.

Everyone—everyone apart from Chris Crichton, obviously—knows where I live. They all have my home phone number, my mobile number, my e-mail address. When I came out of prison, I gave all my coordinates to anyone who showed any interest at all: I needed work, and I needed a profile. I never heard back from any of the bastards, of course, but now here they all were, gathered outside my front door. When I say "all," I mean three or four rather squalid-looking hacks, mostly the young ones, those puffy-faced boys and girls who used to report on school fetes for a local paper and now can't believe their luck.

I pushed through the middle of them, even though I could have walked around them quite comfortably—four people shivering on a pavement and sipping coffee from Styrofoam cups doesn't constitute a media scrum. We all enjoyed the pushing, though. It made me feel important, and it made them feel as though they were at the center of a story. I smiled a lot, said "Good morning" to no one in particular, and batted one of them out of the way with a briefcase.

"Is it true you tried to kill yourself?" asked one particularly unattractive woman in a beige mac.

I gestured at myself, in order to draw their attention to my superb physical condition.

"Well, if I did, I clearly made quite a mess of it," I said.

"Do you know Jess Crichton?"

"Who?"

"Jess Crichton, the wossit minister's daughter. Education."

"I've been a friend of the family for many years. We all spent New Year's Eve together. Perhaps that's how this rather silly misunderstanding arose. It wasn't a suicide pact. It was a drinks party. Two entirely different things."

I was beginning to enjoy myself a little. I was almost sorry when I reached the Peugeot I was renting, at enormous expense, to replace the BMW I had given away. And it wasn't as if I knew where I was going anyway. But within minutes, the rest of my day was mapped out: Chris Crichton called on my mobile to invite me over for a chat; and then, shortly afterward, from the same telephone number, Jess called to inform me that we were all going to visit Maureen. I didn't mind. I had nothing else to do.

Before I knocked on Jess's door, I sat in the car for a couple of minutes and examined my conscience. The last confrontation I'd had with an angry father came shortly after my ill-advised and, as it turned out, illegal sexual encounter with Danielle (5'9", 36DD, fifteen years and 250 days old, and, let me tell you, those 115 days make quite a difference). The venue for this previous confrontation was my flat, the old, big flat in Gibson Square—not, needless to say, because Danielle's father responded to a warm invitation, but because he was outside waiting for me as I tried to sneak home one night. It wasn't a particularly fruitful meeting, not least because I tried to raise the issue of parental responsibility with him, and he tried to hit me. I still think I had a point. What was a fifteen-year-old doing snorting cocaine in the gents' toilets of Melons nightclub at one o'clock on a Tuesday morning? But there is a possibility that if I hadn't been so forceful in the expression of my view he wouldn't have marched round the corner to the police station and made a complaint about my relationship with his daughter.

This time, I thought I'd try to avoid that particular line of argument. I could see that the subject of parental responsibility was an altogether touchy one in the Crichton household, what with one teenaged girl missing, possibly dead, and the other suicidal, possibly nuts. And anyway, my conscience was entirely clear. The only physical contact I had had with Jess

was when I sat on her head, and that was for entirely nonsexual reasons. In fact, they were not only nonsexual but selfless.
Heroic, even.

Chris Crichton, unfortunately, was not prepared to greet
me as a hero. I wasn't offered a handshake or a cup of coffee;
I was ushered into his living room and given a dressing-down,
as if I were some hapless parliamentary researcher. I had
shown a lack of judgment, apparently—I should have found
out Jess's surname and phone number and called him. And I
had somehow shown "a lack of taste"—Mr. Crichton seemed
under the impression that his daughter's appearance in the
tabloids was something to do with me, simply because I'm the
kind of person who appears in the cheaper newspapers. When
I tried to point out the various flaws in his logic, he claimed
that I was likely to do very well out of it all. I'd just stood up to
go when Jess appeared.

"I told you to stay upstairs."

"Yeah, I know. It's just that I stopped being seven a while
ago. Has anyone ever told you you're an idiot?"

He was terrified of her; you could see that straightaway.
He had just enough self-respect to hide the fear behind a dry
world-weariness.

"I'm a politician. No one ever tells me anything but."

"What's it got to do with you where I spend New
Year's Eve?"

"You seem to have spent it together."

"Yeah, by accident, you stupid old bastard."

"This is how she talks to me," he said, looking at me
mournfully, as if my long relationship with the two of them
would somehow allow me to intercede on his behalf.

"I'll bet you're regretting the decision not to go private, aren't you?"

"I'm sorry?"

"Very admirable and all, sending her to the local comprehensive. But, you know. You get what you pay for. And you even got a bit less than that."

"Jess's school does a very good job under very difficult circumstances," said Crichton. "Fifty-one percent of Jess's year got grade C or above at GCSE, up 11 percent on the year before."

"Excellent. That must be a great consolation to you." We both looked at Jess, who gave us the finger.

"The point is, you were in loco parentis," said the proud father. I had forgotten that Jess felt about long words the way that racists feel about black people: She hated them, and wanted to send them back where they came from. She threw him a filthy look.

"Firstly, she's eighteen. And secondly, I sat on her head in order to stop her from jumping. Which might not have been parental, but it was at least practical. I'm sorry I didn't write you a full report at the end of the evening."

"Did you sleep with her?"

"Why is that your business, Dad?"

I wasn't having that. I wasn't going to get involved in an argument about Jess's right to a private sex life.

"Absolutely not."

"Oi," said Jess, "you don't have to say it like that."

"Like what?"

"Like you're relieved or something. You should be so lucky."

"I value our friendship too much to complicate it."

"Ha-ha."

"Are you going to maintain a relationship with Jess?"

"Define your terms."

"I think you should define yours first."

"Listen, pal. I came here because I knew how worried you must be. But if you're going to talk to me like that, I'll fuck off home." The word racist brightened a little: The Anglo-Saxon was striking back against the Roman invader.

"I'm sorry. But you know the family history now. It doesn't make things easy for me."

"Ha! Like it makes things easy for me," said Jess.

"It's hard for all of us." Crichton had clearly decided to make an effort.

"Yeah, I can see that."

"So what can we do? Please? If you've got any ideas . . ."

"The thing is," I said, "I've got problems of my own."

"Der," said Jess. "We were wondering why you were up there."

"I appreciate that, Martin." Like the rest of Blair's robots, he had clearly been media-trained to use first names wherever possible, to show that he was my mate. "I have a hunch about you. I can see you've made some, some *wrong turns* in your life—"

Jess snorted.

"But I don't think you're a bad man."

"Thank you."

"We're in a gang," said Jess. "Aren't we, Martin?"

"We are, Jess," I said, with what I hoped her father would recognize as a weary lack of enthusiasm. "We're friends forever."

"What sort of gang?" said Crichton.

"We're going to watch out for each other. Aren't we, Martin?"

"We are, Jess." If my words became any wearier, they would no longer have the energy to crawl up my throat and out of my mouth. I could imagine them slithering back down to where they'd come from.

"So you will be in loco parentis after all?"

"I'm not sure it's that sort of gang," I said. "The 'In Loco Parentis Gang' . . . Doesn't sound very tough, does it? What are we going to do? Beat up the Paterfamiliases?"

"You fucking shut up and you fucking shut up," Jess said to Crichton and me respectively.

"My point is," said Crichton, "that you're going to be around."

"He's promised," Jess said.

"And I'm supposed to feel reassured by that."

"You can feel what you like," I said. "But I'm not reassuring anyone about anything."

"You have children of your own, I understand?"

"Sort of," said Jess.

"I don't need to spell out how worried I've been about Jess, and what a difference it would make to know that there was a sensible adult looking out for her."

Jess sniggered unhelpfully.

"I know you wouldn't be . . . You're not exactly . . . Some of the tabloids would . . ."

"He's worried about you sleeping with fifteen-year-olds," said Jess.

"I'm not being interviewed for this job," I said. "I don't want it, and if you choose to give it to me, that's your lookout."

"All I want you to say is that if you see Jess getting herself into serious trouble, then you'll either try to prevent it, or you'll tell me about it."

"He'd love to," said Jess. "But he's flat broke."

"Why is money relevant?"

"Because say he had to keep an eye on me and I'd gone into some club or something, and they wouldn't let him in because he's skint . . . Well."

"Well what?"

"I could go in there and OD on smack. I'd be dead, just because you were too mean to stump up."

I suddenly saw Jess's point: A weekly wage of £250 from Britain's lowest-rated cable TV station not only focuses the mind but stimulates empathy and imagination. Jess slumped lifeless in a toilet, all for the sake of twenty quid . . . It was too ghastly to contemplate, if you contemplated in the right spirit.

"How much do you want?" Crichton let out a sigh, as if everything—the conversation we were having, New Year's Eve, my prison sentence—had been carefully plotted to lead to this moment.

"I don't want anything," I said.

"Yes you do," said Jess. "Yes he does."

"How much does it cost to get into a club these days?" Crichton asked.

"You can get through a hundred quid, easy," said Jess.

A hundred quid? We were humiliating ourselves for the price of a decent dinner for two?

"I don't doubt you can 'get through' a hundred quid without trying. But he wouldn't need to 'get through' anything, would he? He'd only need the price of admission, if you'd overdosed on drugs. I'm presuming that he wouldn't be stopping at the bar if you were hovering between life and death in the toilet."

"So what you're saying is, my life isn't worth a hundred

quid to you. That's nice, after what happened to Jen. I wouldn't have thought you had enough daughters to spare."

"Jess, that's not fair."

The front door slammed somewhere between the "not" and the "fair," and Crichton and I were left staring at each other.

"I handled that badly," he said. "Didn't I?"

I shrugged. "She was extorting money with menaces. Either you give her as much as she wants every time she asks for it, or she storms out. And I can see that might be a little . . . you know. Disconcerting. Given the family history."

"I'll give her as much as she wants, every time she asks for it," he said. "Please go and find her."

I left the house £250 richer; Jess was waiting for me at the end of the drive.

"I'll bet you got double what we were asking for," she said. "Always works, when you mention Jen."

JESS

You won't believe this—I don't think I do now—but in my head, what happened to Jen had fuck all to do with New Year's Eve. I could tell, from talking to the others and reading the papers, that no one else saw it that way, though. They were like, Ooooh, I get it: Your sister disappeared, so you want to jump off a building. But it isn't like that. I'm sure it must have been an ingredient sort of thing, but it wasn't the whole recipe. Say I'm a Spaghetti Bolognese: Well, I reckon Jen is the tomatoes.

Maybe the onions. Or even just the garlic. But she's not the meat or the pasta.

Everyone reacts to something like that in different ways, don't they? Some people would start support groups and all that; I know they would, because Mum and Dad are always trying to introduce me to some fucking group or another, mostly because the group was set up by someone who ended up getting a CSE or whatever off of the Queen. And some people would sit down, turn the TV on, and watch for the next twenty years. Me, I just started messing around. Or rather, messing around became more like a full-time job, whereas previously it had been a hobby: Some messing around had already been done before Jen went. I'll be honest about that.

Before I go on, I'll answer the questions that everyone always asks, just so's you don't sit there wondering and not concentrating on what I'm saying. No, I don't know where she is. Yes, I think she's alive. Why I think she's alive: because that whole thing with the car in the car park looked phony to me. What does it feel like, having a missing sister? I can tell you. You know how if you lose something valuable, a wallet or a piece of jewelry, you can't concentrate on anything else? Well, it feels like that all the time, every day.

There's something else people ask: Where do you think she is? Which is different from, Do you know where she is? At first I didn't understand that the two questions were different. And then when I did understand, I thought that the Where do you think she is? question was stupid. Like, well, if I knew that I'd go and look for her. But now I understand it as being a more poetic question. 'Cause, really, it's a way of asking what she was like. Do I think she's in Africa, helping people? Or do

I think she's on one long permanent rave, or writing poems on a Scottish island, or traveling through the bush in Australia? So here's what I think: I think she has a baby, maybe in America, and she's in a little town somewhere sunny, Texas, say, or California, and she's living with a man who works hard with his hands and looks after her and loves her. So that's what I tell people, except of course I don't know whether I'm telling them about Jen or about me.

Oh, and one more thing—especially if you're reading this in the future, when everyone's forgotten about us and how things turned out for us: Don't sit around hoping for her to pop up later on to rescue me. She doesn't come back, OK? And we don't find out she's dead, either. Nothing happens, so forget about it. Well, don't forget about her, because she's important. But forget about that sort of ending. It's not that sort of story.

Maureen lives halfway between Toppers' House and Kentish Town, in one of those little poky streets full of old ladies and teachers. I don't know for sure they're teachers, but there are an awful lot of bikes around—bikes and recycling bins. It's shit, recycling, isn't it? I said to Martin, and he was like, If you say so. He sounded a bit tired. And I asked him if he wanted to know why it was shit, but he didn't. Just like he hadn't wanted to know why France was shit, either. He wasn't in a chatty mood, I suppose.

It was just me and Martin in the car because JJ didn't want a lift with us, even though we nearly went past his flat. JJ probably would have helped smooth the conversation along a bit, I think. I wanted to talk because I was nervous, and that probably made me say stupid things. Or maybe "stupid" is the wrong word, because it's not stupid to say France is shit. It's just a bit abrupt or whatever. JJ could have put a sort of ramp up to my sentences to help people skateboard down from them.

I was nervous because I knew that we were going to meet Matty, and I'm sort of not good with disabled people. It's nothing personal, and I don't think I'm disablist, because I know they've got rights to an education and bus passes and that; it's just that they turn my stomach a bit. It's all that having to pretend they're just like you and me when they're not, really, are they? I'm not talking "disabled" like people who have only got one leg, say. They're all right. I'm talking about the ones who aren't right up top, and shout, and make funny faces. How can you say they're like you and me? OK, I shout and make funny faces, but I know when I'm doing it. Most of the time I do anyway. With them there's no predicting, is there? They're all over the place.

To be fair to him, though, Matty's pretty quiet. He's sort of *so* disabled that it's OK, if you know what I mean. He just sits there. From my point of view, that's probably better, although I can see that from his, it's probably not much good. Except who knows whether he's got a point of view? And if he hasn't got one, then it's got to be mine that counts, hasn't it? He's quite tall, and he's in a wheelchair, and he's got cushions and what-have-you stuffed up behind his neck to stop his head lolling about. He doesn't look at you or anything, so you don't get too freaked out. You forget he's there after a while, so I coped better than I thought I would. Fucking hell, though.

Poor old Maureen. I'll tell you, you wouldn't have persuaded me down from that roof. No way.

JJ was already there when we arrived, so when we walked in it was like a family reunion, except no one looked like each other, and no one pretended to be pleased to see each other. Maureen made us a cup of tea, and Martin and JJ asked her some polite questions about Matty. I just looked around a bit, because I didn't want to listen. She really had tidied up, like she said she was going to. There was almost nothing in the place, apart from the telly and things to sit on. It was like she'd just moved in. In fact, I got the impression that she'd moved things out and taken things down, because you could just make out marks on the wall. But then Martin was going, What do you think, Jess? so I had to stop looking around and start joining in. We had plans to make.

JJ

I didn't want to go to Maureen's place with Martin and Jess because I needed time to think. I'd done a couple interviews with music journalists in the past, but they were fans of the band, sweet guys who went away totally psyched if you gave them a demo CD and let them buy you a drink. But these people, people like the knock-on-the-door inspirational lady—man, I didn't know anything about them. All I knew was that they'd somehow found out my address in twenty-four hours, and if they could do that, then what couldn't they do? It was like they had the names and addresses of every single person living in Britain, just in case one day any of them did anything that might be interesting.

Anyway, she made me totally paranoid. If she wanted to, she could find out about the band in five minutes. And then she'd get ahold of Eddie and Lizzie, and then she'd find out that I wasn't dying of anything—or that if I was, I'd kept the news to myself. Plus, she'd find out that the disease I wasn't dying of was nonexistent.

In other words, I was freaked out enough to think I was in trouble. I took a bus up to Maureen's, and on the way I decided I was going to come clean, tell them all about everything, and if they didn't like it, fuck 'em. But I didn't want them reading about it in the papers.

It took us a while to get used to the sound of poor Matty's breathing, which was loud and sounded as if it took a lot of effort. We were all thinking the same thing, I guess: we were all wondering whether we could have coped if we were Maureen; we were all trying to figure out whether anything could have persuaded us to come back down off that roof.

"Jess," said Martin. "You wanted us to meet. Why don't you call us to order?"

"OK," she said, and she cleared her throat. "We are gathered here today—"

Martin laughed.

"Fucking hell," she said. "I've only done half a sentence. What's funny about that?"

Martin shook his head.

"No, come on. If I'm so fucking funny, I want to know why."

"It's perhaps because it's something more usually said in church."

There was a long pause.

"Yeah. I knew that. That was the vibe I was after."

"Why?" Martin asked.

"Maureen, you go to church, don't you?" Jess said.

"I used to," said Maureen.

"Yeah, see. I was trying to make Maureen feel comfortable."

"Very thoughtful of you."

"Why do you have to fuck up everything I do?"

"Gosh," said Martin. "I can almost smell the incense."

"Right, you can start it off, then, you fucking—"

"That's enough," said Maureen. "In my house. In front of my son."

Martin and I looked at each other, screwed up our faces, held our breath, crossed our fingers, but it was no use. Jess was going to point out the obvious anyway.

"In front of your son? But he's—"

"I haven't got CCR," I said. It was the only thing I could think of. I mean, obviously it needed saying, but I had intended to give myself a little more preparation time.

There was a silence. I was waiting for them to dump on me.

"Oh, JJ!" Jess said. "That's fantastic!"

It took me a minute to realize that in the weird world of Jess, they had not only found a cure for CCR during the Christmas holidays but delivered it to my front door in the Angel sometime between New Year's Eve and January the second.

"I'm not sure that's quite what JJ is saying," said Martin.

"No," I said. "The thing is, I never had it."

"No! Bastards."

"Who?"

"The fuck-bloody doctors." At Maureen's house, "fuckbloody" became Jess's curse of choice. "You should sue them. Supposing you'd jumped? And they'd got it wrong?"

Mother*fucker*. Did it really have to be this hard?

"I'm not sure he's quite saying that, either," said Martin.

"No," I said. "I'll try and be as clear as possible: There ain't no such thing as CCR, and even if there was, I'm not dying of it. I made it up, 'cause . . . I don't know. Partly 'cause I wanted your sympathy, and partly because I didn't think you'd understand what was really wrong with me. I'm sorry."

"You tosser," said Jess.

"That's awful," said Maureen.

"You arsehole," said Jess.

Martin smiled. Telling people you have an incurable disease when you don't is probably right up there with seducing a fifteen-year-old, so he was enjoying my embarrassment. Plus, he was maybe even entitled to a little moral superiority, because he'd done the decent thing when he got humiliated: He'd walked to the top of Toppers' House and dangled his feet over the edge. OK, he didn't go over, but, you know, he'd shown he was taking things seriously. Me, I'd thought about offing myself first and then disgraced myself afterward. I'd become an even bigger asshole since New Year's Eve, which was kind of depressing.

"So why did you say it?" Jess asked.

"Yes," said Martin. "What were you attempting to simplify?"

"It just . . . I don't know. Everything seemed so straightforward with you guys. Martin and the, you know. And Maureen and—" I nodded over to Matty.

"Wasn't straightforward with me," said Jess. "I was crapping on about Chas and explanations."

"Yeah, but, no offense, but you were nutso. Didn't really matter what you said."

"So what *was* wrong with you?" Maureen asked.

"I don't know. Depression, I suppose you'd call it."

"Oh, we understand depression," said Martin. "We're all depressed."

"Yeah, I know. But mine seemed too . . . too fucking vague. Sorry, Maureen."

How do people, like, not curse? How is it possible? There are all these gaps in speech where you just have to put a "fuck." I'll tell you who the most admirable people in the world are: newscasters. If that was me, I'd be like, "And the motherfuckers flew the fucking plane right into the Twin Towers." How could you not, if you're a human being? Maybe they're not so admirable. Maybe they're robot zombies.

"Try us out," said Martin. "We're understanding people."

"OK. So the short version is, all I ever wanted to do was be in a rock 'n' roll band."

"Rock 'n' roll? Like Bill Haley and the Comets?" said Martin.

"No, man. That's not . . . Like, I don't know. The Stones. Or—"

"They're not rock 'n' roll," said Jess. "Are they? They're rock."

"OK, OK, all I wanted to do was be in a rock band. Like the Stones, or, or—"

"Crusty music," said Jess. She wasn't being rude. She was just clarifying my terms.

"Whatever. Jeez. And a few weeks before Christmas my band finally split up for good. And soon after we split, I lost my girl. She was English. That's why I was here."

There was a silence.

"That's it?" said Jess.

"That's it."

"That's pathetic. I see why you came out with all that crap about the disease now. You'd rather die than not be in a band that sounds like the Rolling Stones? I'd be the opposite. I'd rather die if I was. Do people still like them in America? No one does here."

"That's Mick Jagger, isn't it, the Rolling Stones?" Maureen asked. "They were quite good, weren't they? They did well for themselves."

"Mick Jagger's not sitting here eating stale Custard Creams like JJ, is he?"

"They were new right before Christmas," said Maureen. "Maybe I didn't put the lid back on the biscuit tin properly."

I was starting to think we were losing focus on my issues.

"The Stones thing . . . That's kind of not important. That was just, like, an illustration. I just meant . . . songs, guitars, energy."

"He's about eighty," said Jess. "He hasn't got any energy."

"I saw them in '90," said Martin. "The night England lost to Germany in the World Cup on penalties. A chap from Guinness took a whole crowd of us, and everyone spent most of the evening listening to the radio. Anyway, he had a lot of energy then."

"He was only seventy then," said Jess.

"Will you shut the fuck up? Sorry, Maureen." (From now on, just presume that every time I speak I say "fuck," "fucking," or "motherfucker," and "Sorry, Maureen," OK?) "I'm trying to tell you about my whole life."

"No one's stopping you," said Jess. "But you've got to make

it more interesting. That's why we drift off and talk about biscuits."

"OK, all right. Look, there's nothing else for me. I'm qualified for nothing. I didn't graduate from high school. I just had the band, and now it's gone, and I didn't make a cent out of it, and I'm looking at a life of flipping burgers."

Jess snorted.

"Now what?"

"Just sounds funny, hearing a Yank say 'flipping' instead of . . . you know what."

"I don't think he meant 'flipping' like 'flipping heck,'" said Martin. "I think he meant 'flipping' as in 'turning them over.' That's what they call it."

"Oh," said Jess.

"And I'm worried it will kill me."

"Hard work never killed anyone," said Maureen.

"I don't mind hard work, you know? But when we were touring and recording . . . that was me, that was who I was, and, and I just feel empty and frustrated and, and . . . See, when you know you're good, you think that will be enough, that'll get you there, and when it doesn't . . . What are you supposed to do with it all? Where do you put it, huh? There's nowhere for it to go, and, and it was . . . Man, it used to eat me up even when things were going OK, because even when things were going OK, I wasn't onstage or recording, like, every minute of the day, and sometimes it felt like I needed to be, otherwise I'd explode, you know? So now, now there's nowhere for it to go. We used to have this song . . ." I have no idea why I started up on this. "We used to have this song, this little, like, Motown-y thing called 'I Got Your Back,' which me and Eddie wrote together, *really* together, which we didn't usually do, and it was like, you know, a tribute to our friendship and how far back we went and blah-blah. Anyhow, it was on our first album and it was like two minutes and thirty seconds long and no one really noticed it. I mean, people who actually bought the album didn't even notice it. But we started playing it live, and it kind of got longer, and Eddie worked out this sweet solo. It wasn't like a rock guitar solo; it was more like something maybe, I don't know, Curtis Mayfield or Ernie Isley might have played. And sometimes, when we played around Chicago and we'd jam with friends onstage, we'd have maybe a sax solo or a piano solo or maybe even, like, a pedal steel or something, and after, like, a year or two it got to be this, like, ten-, twelve-minute *showstopper*. And we'd open with it or close with it or stick it in the middle somewhere if we were playing a long set, and to me it became the sound of pure fucking joy, sorry, Maureen, you know? Pure joy. It felt like surfing, or, or whatever, a natural high. You could ride those chords like waves. I had that feeling maybe a hundred times a year, and not many people get it even once in their lives. And that's what I had to give up, man, the ability to create that routinely, whenever I felt like it, as part of my working day, and . . . You know, now that I think about it, I can see why I made up that bullshit, sorry, Maureen, about dying of some fucking disease, sorry again. Because that's what it feels like. I'm dying of some disease that dries up all the blood in your veins and all your sap and, and everything that makes you feel alive, and—"

"Yeah, and?" said Martin. "You seem to have omitted the part about why you want to kill yourself."

"That's it," I said. "This disease that dries up all the blood in your veins."

"That's just what happens to everyone," said Martin. "It's called 'getting older.' I felt like that even before I'd been to prison. Even before I slept with that girl. It's probably why I slept with her, come to think of it."

"No, I get it," said Jess.

"Yeah?"

"Course I do. You're fucked." She waved an apologetic hand in Maureen's direction, like a tennis player acknowledging a lucky net cord. "You thought you were going to be someone, but now it's obvious you're nobody. You haven't got as much talent as you thought you had, and there was no Plan B, and you got no skills and no education, and now you're looking at forty or fifty years of nothing. Less than nothing, probably. That's pretty heavy. That's worse than having the brain thing, because what you got now will take a lot longer to kill you. You've got the choice of a slow, painful death, or a quick, merciful one."

She shrugged.

She was right. She got it.

MAUREEN

I would have got away with it if Jess hadn't gone to the toilet. But you can't stop people going to the toilet, can you? I was green. It never occurred to me that she'd be nosing around where she had no business.

She was gone for a while, and she came back grinning all over her stupid face, holding a couple of the posters.

In one hand she had the poster of the girl, and in the other the poster of the black fella, the footballer.

"So whose are these, then?" she said.

I stood up and shouted at her, "Put those back! They're not yours!"

"I'd never have thought it of you," she said. "So let's work this out. You're a dyke who has a bit of a thing for black guys with big thighs. Kinky. Hidden depths."

It was typical of Jess, I thought. She only has a filthy imagination, which is to say, no imagination at all.

"Do you even know who these people are?" she said.

They're Matty's, the posters, not mine. He doesn't know they're his, of course, but they are; I chose them for him. I knew that the girl was called Buffy, because that's what it said on the poster, but I didn't really know who Buffy was; I just thought it would be nice for Matty to have an attractive young woman around the place, because he's that age now. And I knew that the black fella played for Arsenal, but I only caught his first name, Paddy. I took advice from John at the church, who goes along to Highbury every week, and he said everyone loved Paddy, so I asked him if he'd bring me back a picture for my lad next time he went to a game. He's a nice man, John, and he bought a great big picture of Paddy celebrating a goal, and he didn't even want paying for it, but things got a little awkward afterward. For some reason he decided my lad was a little lad, ten or twelve, and he promised to take him to a game. And sometimes on Sunday mornings, when Arsenal had lost on the Saturday, he'd ask how Matty was taking it, and sometimes when they'd won a big game he'd say, I'll bet your lad's happy, and so on. And then one Friday morning when I was wheeling Matty back from the shops, we bumped into him. And I could have said nothing, but sometimes you have to admit to yourself and to everyone else, *This is Matty. This is my lad.* So I did, and John never mentioned Arsenal again after that. I don't miss that on a Sunday morning. There are lots of good reasons to lose your faith.

I chose the posters the same as I chose all the other things that Jess had probably been rummaging through, the tapes and the books and the football boots and the computer games and the videos. The diaries and the trendy address books. (Address books! Dear God! Of all the things that spell it out. I can put a tape on for him, and hope he is listening to it, but what am I going to fill an address book with? I haven't even got one of my own.) The jazzy pens, the camera, and the Walkman. Lots of watches. There's a whole unlived teenaged life in there.

This all began years ago, when I decided to decorate his bedroom. He was eight, and he still slept in a nursery—clowns on the curtains, bunny rabbits on the frieze round the wall, all the things I'd chosen when I was waiting for him and I didn't know what he was. And it was all peeling away, and it looked terrible, and I hadn't done anything about it because it made me think too much about what wasn't happening to him, all the ways he wasn't growing up. What was I going to replace the bunny rabbits with? He was eight, so perhaps trains and rocket ships, and maybe even footballers were the right sort of thing for him—but of course he didn't know what any of those things were, what they meant, what they did. But there again, he didn't know what the rabbits were, either, or the clowns. So what was I supposed to do? Everything was pretending, wasn't it? The only thing I could do that wasn't

A

L

O

N

G

W

A

Y

152

make-believe was paint the walls white, get a plain pair of curtains. That would be a way of telling him and me and anyone else who came in that I knew he was a vegetable, a cabbage, and I wasn't trying to hide it. But then, where does it stop? Does that mean you can never buy him a T-shirt with a word on it, or a picture, because he'll never read, and he can't make any sense of pictures? And who knows whether he even gets anything out of colors, or patterns. And it goes without saying that talking to him is ridiculous, and smiling at him, and kissing him on the head. Everything I do is pretending, so why not pretend properly?

In the end, I went for trains on the curtains, and your man from *Star Wars* on the lampshade. And soon after that I started buying comics every now and again, just to see what a lad of his age might be reading and thinking about. And we watched the Saturday morning television together, so I learned a little bit about pop singers he might like, and sometimes about the TV programs he'd be watching. I said before that one of the worst things was never moving on, and pretending to move on doesn't change anything. But it helps. Without it, what is there left? And anyway, thinking about these things helped me to see Matty, in a strange sort of way. I suppose it must be what they do when they think of a new character for *EastEnders*: They must say to themselves, Well, what does this person like? What does he listen to? Who are his friends? What football team does he support? That's what I did—I made up a son. He supports Arsenal, he likes fishing, although he doesn't have a rod yet. He likes pop music, but not the sort of pop music where people sing half-naked and use a lot of swear words. Very occasionally, people ask what he wants for his birthday or

Christmas, and I tell them, and they know better than to act surprised. Most distant family members have never met him, and never asked to. All they know about him is just that he's not all there, or there's something not right with him. They don't want to know any more, so they never say, Oh, he can fish? Or, in the case of my uncle Michael, Oh, he can swim underwater and then look at his watch while he's down there? They're just grateful to be told what to do.

Matty took over the whole flat, in the end. You know how kids do. Stuff everywhere.

"It doesn't matter whether I know who they are or not," I said. "They belong to Matty."

"Oh, he's a big fan of—"

"Just do as you're told and put them back," said Martin. "Put them back or get out. How much of a bitch do you really want to be?"

One day, I thought, I'll learn to say that for myself.

MARTIN

Matty's posters weren't mentioned again that day. We were all curious, of course, but Jess had ensured that JJ and I couldn't express this curiosity: Jess set things up so that you were either for her or against her, and in this matter, as in so many others, we were against her—which meant staying quiet on this issue. But because we resented being made to stay quiet, we became aggressive and noisy on any other issue we could bring to mind.

"You can't stand your dad, can you?" I asked her.

"No, course not. He's a tosser."

"But you live with him?"

"So?"

"How can you stand it, man?" JJ asked her.

"Can't afford to move out. Plus they've got a cleaner and cable and broadband and all that."

"Ah, to be young and idealistic and principled!" I said. "Antiglobalization, pro-cleaner, eh?"

"Yeah, I'm really going to be lectured by you two jerks. Plus, there's the other thing. The Jen thing. They worry."

Ah, yes. The Jen thing. JJ and I were momentarily chastened. Looked at in a certain light, the previous conversation could be summarized as follows: A man recently imprisoned for having sex with a minor, and another, who had fabricated a fatal disease because to do so saved him some time, trouble, and face, had ridiculed a grieving teenager for wanting to be at home with her grieving parents. I made a note to put aside some time later so that I could synopsize it differently.

"We were sorry to hear about your sister," said Maureen.

"Yeah, well, it didn't happen yesterday, did it?"

"We were sorry anyway," said JJ wearily. Conceding the moral high ground to Jess simply meant that she could piss all over everyone until she got thrown off again.

"Got used to it now."

"Have you?" I asked.

"Sort of."

"Must be a strange thing to have to get used to."

"Bit."

"Don't you think about it all the time?" JJ asked her.

D

O

W

N

155

"Can't we talk about what we're supposed to be talking about?"

"Which is what, exactly?"

"About what we're going to do. About the papers and all that."

"Do we have to do anything?"

"I think so," said JJ.

"They'll forget about us soon, you know," I said. "It's only because fuck all happens, sorry, Maureen, at the beginning of the year."

"What if we don't want them to forget about us?" said Jess.

"Why the hell would we want them to remember?" I asked her.

"We could make some dosh. And it'd be something to do."

"*What* would be something to do?"

"I dunno. I just . . . I get the feeling that we're different. That people would like us, and be interested in us."

"You're mad."

"Yeah. Exactly. That's why they'd be interested in me. I could even play it up a bit, if you like."

"I'm sure that won't be necessary," I said quickly, on behalf of the three of us and, indeed, on behalf of the entire population of Britain. "You're fine as you are."

Jess smiled sweetly, surprised by the unsought compliment. "Thanks, Martin. So are you. And you—they'd want to know how you fucked up your life with the girl. And you, JJ, they'd want to know about pizzas and all that. And Maureen could tell everyone about how shit it is living with Matty. See, we'd be like superheroes, the X-Men or whatever. We've all got some secret superpower."

"Yeah," said JJ. "Right on. I have the superpower of delivering pizzas. And Maureen has the superpower of a disabled son."

"Well, all right, 'superpower' is the wrong word. But, you know. Some *thing*."

"Ah, yes. 'Thing.' *Le mot juste*, as ever."

Jess scowled, but was too besotted by her theme to hit me with the insult my knowledge of a foreign phrase demanded and deserved. "And we could say that we still haven't decided whether we're going to actually top ourselves—they'd like that."

"And if we, like, actually sold the TV rights to Valentine's Night maybe they could turn it into a *Big Brother* kinda thing. You could root for the person you wanted to go over," said JJ.

Jess looked dubious. "I don't know about that," she said. "But you know about papers, Martin. We could make some money, couldn't we?"

"Has it occurred to you that I've had enough trouble with the papers?"

"Oh, it's always about you, isn't it?" said Jess. "What about if there's a few quid in it for us?"

"But what's the story?" said JJ. "There's no story. We went up, we came down, that's it. People must do that all the time."

"I've been thinking about this. How about if we saw something?" said Jess.

"Like what? What are we supposed to have seen?"

"OK. How about if we saw an angel?"

"An angel," said JJ flatly.

"Yeah."

"I didn't see an angel," said Maureen. "When did you see an angel?"

"No one saw an angel," I explained. "Jess is proposing that we invent a spiritual experience for financial gain."

"That's terrible," said Maureen, if only because it was so clearly expected of her.

"It's not really *inventing*, is it?" said Jess.

"No? In what sense did we actually see an angel?"

"What do you call it in poems?"

"I'm sorry?"

"You know, in poems. And in English literature. Sometimes you say something is like something and sometimes you say something is something. You know, my love is like a fuckbloody rose or whatever."

"Similes and metaphors."

"Yeah. Exactly. Shakespeare invented them, didn't he? That's why he was a genius."

"No."

"Who was it, then?"

"Never mind."

"So why was Shakespeare a genius? What did he do?"

"Another time."

"OK. Anyway. So which is the one where you say something *is* something, like 'You are a prick,' even if you're not actually a prick. As in a penis. Obviously."

Maureen looked close to tears.

"Oh, for God's sake, Jess," I said.

"Sorry. Sorry. I didn't know if we had the same swearing rules if it was only for discussion about grammar and that."

"We do."

"Right. Sorry, Maureen. OK, 'You are a pig,' when you're not a pig."

"Metaphor."

"Exactly. We didn't literally see an angel. But we sort of did metaphorically."

"We sort of metaphorically saw an angel," repeated JJ. He had the flat disbelief thing down pat now.

"Yeah. Yeah, I mean, something turned us back. Something saved our lives. Why not an angel?"

"Because there wasn't one."

"OK, we didn't see one. But you could say that anything was an angel. Any girl, anyway. Me, or even Maureen."

"Any girl could be an angel." JJ again.

"Yeah. Because of angels. Girls. "

"Have you ever heard of the angel Gabriel, for example?"

"No."

"Well, he—*he*—was an angel."

"Yeah?"

For some reason I suddenly lost patience.

"What is this nonsense? Can you *hear* yourself, Jess?"

"What have I said now?"

"We didn't see an angel, literally or metaphorically. And, incidentally, seeing something metaphorically, whatever that means, is not the same as seeing something. With your eyes. Which, as I understand it, is what you're proposing we say. That's not embellishing. That's talking bullshit, sorry, Maureen. To be honest, I'd keep this to yourself. I wouldn't tell anyone about the angel. Not even the national press."

"But say if we get on telly and get a chance to, you know, spread our message?"

We all stared at her.

"What the hell is our message?"

"Well. That's sort of up to us, isn't it?"

How was one supposed to argue with a mind like this? The

three of us never managed to find a way, so we contented ourselves with ridicule and sarcasm, and the afternoon ended with an unspoken agreement that as three-quarters of us hadn't really enjoyed our brief moment of media exposure, we would allow the current interest in our mental health to dwindle away to nothing. And then, a couple of hours after I got home, there was a phone call from Theo, my agent, asking me why I hadn't told him that I'd seen an angel.

JESS

They weren't happy. Martin was the worst: He went up the fucking wall. He called me at home, and went off on one for about ten minutes. But I knew he was going to be all right about it, because Dad answered the phone, and Martin never said anything to him. If he'd said anything to Dad, then the story would have come apart. It needed the four of us to stick to our guns, and as long as we did that, we could say we'd seen whatever we wanted to have seen. The thing is, it was too good an idea to waste, wasn't it? And they knew that, which is why I thought they'd come round to it in the end—which they did, sort of. And for me, it was our first big test as a group. They all had a straightforward choice to make: Were they on my side or not? And to be honest, if they'd decided that they weren't, I doubt whether I'd have had anything more to do with them. It would have said a lot about them as people, none of it good.

I admit I was a bit sneaky. First of all, I asked JJ the name of the woman who'd come round to see him that morning, and he told me her name and the paper she worked for, which was a bonus. He thought I was just making conversation, but I thought it might come in handy at some stage. And then when I got home, I called the paper. I said I'd only speak to her, and when I told them my name they gave me her mobile number.

She was called Linda, and she was really friendly. I thought she might think it was all a bit weird, but she was very interested and encouraging, really. If she had a fault as a journalist, I'd say it was that she was too encouraging, if anything. Too believing and trusting. You'd expect a good journalist to be all, you know, How do I know you're telling the truth? but I could have told her anything and she'd have written it down. She was slightly unprofessional, between you and me.

So she was all, What did this angel look like, Jess? She said "Jess" a lot, to show that we were friends.

I'd thought about this. The stupid thing to say would have been that he—I'd decided he was a he, because of Gabriel—looked like a church angel, with wings and all that. That would give off the wrong signals, I thought.

Not what you'd expect, I said. And Linda went, What, no wings or halo, Jess? And she laughed—like, What kind of berk would say they'd seen an angel with wings and a halo? So I knew I'd made the right decision. I laughed as well, and I went, No, he looked all modern, and she was like, Really?

(I always do this, when I'm talking about what someone said. I'm always, like, So I was like, and She went, and all like that. But when a conversation goes on a bit, it's a drag, isn't it? Like, went, like, went. So I'm going to do it like a play from

D
O
W
N

161

now on, OK? I'm not so good on speech marks or whatever, but I can remember plays from reading them at school.)

> ME: Yeah. He was dressed modern. He looked like he could have been in a band or something.
>
> LINDA: A band? Which band?
>
> ME: I don't know. Radiohead or someone like that.
>
> LINDA: Why Radiohead?

You couldn't say anything without her asking a question. I said Radiohead because they don't look like anything much. They're just blokes, aren't they?

> ME: I don't know. Or Blur. Or . . . Who's that guy? In that film? He's not the one who's not married to Jennifer Lopez, he's the other one, and they won an Oscar, because he was good at maths even though he was only a cleaner . . . The blond one. Matt.
>
> LINDA: The angel looked like Matt Damon?
>
> ME: Yeah, I suppose. A bit.
>
> LINDA: So. A handsome angel who looked like Matt Damon.
>
> ME: He's not all that, Matt Damon. But, yeah.
>
> LINDA: And when did he appear, this angel?
>
> ME: When?
>
> LINDA: Yes, when. I mean, how close to . . . to jumping were you?
>
> ME: Oh, really close, man. He came in at the last minute.
>
> LINDA: Wow. So you were standing on the ledge? All of you?
>
> ME: Yeah. We'd decided we were going to go over

together. For company, sort of thing. So we were
standing there saying our goodbyes to each other and
that. And we were going to do One, Two, Three, Jump
and we heard this voice behind us.

LINDA: You must have been frightened out of your wits.

ME: Yeah.

LINDA: It was a wonder you didn't fall off.

ME: Yeah.

LINDA: So you all turned around . . .

ME: Yeah. We all turned around, and he said—

LINDA: Sorry. What was he wearing?

ME: Just a sort of . . . like a baggy suit, sort of thing. A
baggy white suit. Quite fashionable, really. Looked like
it had set him back a few quid.

LINDA: A designer suit?

ME: Yeah.

LINDA: Tie?

ME: No. No tie.

LINDA: An informal angel.

ME: Yeah. Smart-casual anyway.

LINDA: And did you know immediately he wasn't a
human man?

ME: Oh, yeah.

LINDA: How?

ME: He was all . . . fuzzy. Like he wasn't tuned in
properly. And you could see right through him. You
couldn't see his liver or anything like that. You could
just see like the buildings on the other side of him.
Oh, yeah—plus, he was hovering above the roof.

LINDA: How high?

ME: High, man. When I first saw him, I was like, that guy

is five meters tall. But when I looked down at his feet, they were a meter above the ground.

LINDA: So he was about twelve feet tall?

ME: Two meters above the ground, then.

LINDA: So he was nine feet tall.

ME: Three meters. Whatever.

LINDA: So his feet were above your heads.

ME: (*Becoming fucked off with her going on about meters, but trying not to show it*) To begin with. But then he sort of worked out that he'd overdone it, and he, you know. Came down a bit. I got the impression that he hadn't done any hovering for a while. He was a bit rusty.

I was just making this stuff up as I went along. I mean, you know already I was making it up. But seeing as how I'd called her without thinking any of it through, I thought I was doing really well. She seemed to like it anyway.

LINDA: Amazing.

ME: Yeah. It really was.

LINDA: So what did he say?

ME: He said, you know. Don't jump. But he said it very peacefully. Calmly. He had this, like, inner wisdom. You could tell he was a messenger from God.

LINDA: Did he say that?

ME: Not in so many words. But you could work it out.

LINDA: Because of the inner wisdom.

ME: Yeah. He had that sort of air about him, like he'd met God personally. It was wicked.

LINDA: That's all he said?

ME: He was like, Your time hasn't come yet. Go back

down and send people this message of comfort and joy. And tell them that war is stupid. Which is something I personally believe. (That last bit, the Which I personally believe bit, wasn't part of the play. I'm just giving you extra information, so you can get a better picture of the kind of person I am.)

LINDA: And do you intend to spread that message?

ME: Yeah. Course. That's one of the reasons we want to do this interview. And if any of your readers are, like, world leaders or generals or terrorists or whatever, then they should know that God is not a happy bunny at the moment. He's well pissed off with that side of things.

LINDA: I'm sure our readers will find that very thought-provoking. And you all saw it?

ME: Oh, yeah. You couldn't miss him.

LINDA: Martin Sharp saw it?

ME: Oh, yeah. Course. He saw it . . . he saw it more than any of us.

I didn't quite know what that meant, but I could tell it was important to her that Martin was involved.

LINDA: So now what?

ME: Well. We've got to work out what we're going to do.

LINDA: Of course. Will you be talking to any other newspapers?

ME: Oh, yeah. Definitely.

I was pleased with that. I got her up to five grand in the end. I had to promise that she'd have a chance to speak to everybody, though.

J J

It didn't seem like it was going to be too difficult, at first. OK, none of us was thrilled that Jess had got us into this angel thing, but it didn't seem worth falling out over. We'd grit our teeth, say we'd seen an angel, take the money, and try and forget it ever happened.

But then the next day you're sitting in front of a journalist, and you're all agreeing with a straight face that this fucking angel looked like Matt Damon, and loyalty seemed like the dumbest of all the virtues. It wasn't like you could just go through the motions, either, when you're supposed to have seen an angel. You can't just say, "Yeah, blah, angel, whatever." Seeing an angel is clearly a big deal, so you've got to act like it's a big deal, with excitement and openmouthed awe, and it's hard to do openmouthed awe through gritted teeth. Maureen was maybe the one person who could have been convincing, because she believed in that stuff, kind of. But because she believed in it, she was the one who had the most trouble with the lies. "Maureen," said Jess patiently and slowly, as if Maureen were simply being dumb, rather than fearing for her immortal soul, "it's for *five thousand pounds*."

The paper arranged for someone from the care home to sit for Matty, and we met Linda in the café where we'd had breakfast on New Year's morning. We had our photos taken—mostly group shots, but then they took one or two more outside, with us pointing at the sky, our jaws unhinged with wonder. They didn't end up using those, probably because one or two of us overdid it a little, and one of us wouldn't do it at all. And then, after the shoot, Linda asked us questions.

It was Martin she was after—he was the prize. If she could get Martin Sharp to say that an angel had kept him from killing himself—i.e., if she could get Martin Sharp to say "I AM A WACKO—OFFICIAL"—she had a front-page story. Martin knew it, too, so his performance was heroic, or as close to heroism as you can come if you're a sleazy talk-show host who is never likely to do anything involving actual heroism. Martin telling Linda that he'd seen an angel reminded me of that Sidney Carton guy in *A Tale of Two Cities* going to the guillotine so that his buddy could live: Martin wore the expression of a man about to have his head sliced off for the greater good. That Sidney guy, though, he'd discovered his inner nobility, so he probably looked noble, but Martin just looked pissed off.

Jess did all the talking to begin with, and then Linda got tired of her, and started to ask Martin questions directly.

"So when this figure began hovering . . . Hovering? Is that right?"

"Hovering," confirmed Jess. "Like I said, he hovered too

high at first, because of being out of practice, but then he found the right level."

Martin winced, like the angel's refusal to put his feet on the ground somehow made things more embarrassing for him.

"So when the angel was hovering in front of you, Martin, what did you think?"

"Think?" Martin repeated.

"We didn't think much, did we?" said Jess. "We were too stunned."

"That's right," said Martin.

"But you must have thought something," Linda said. "Even if it was only, Bloody hell, I wonder if I could get him on *Rise and Shine with Penny and Martin*." She chuckled encouragingly.

"Well," said Martin, "I haven't been presenting the show for a while now, remember. So it would have been a waste of time asking him."

"You've got your cable show, though."

"Yes."

"So maybe he would have gone on that." She chuckled encouragingly again.

"We tend to book mainly showbiz stuff. Stand-up comedians, soap stars, the odd sportsman."

"So you're saying you wouldn't have had him on." Once she'd started this line of questioning, Linda seemed kind of reluctant to let it drop.

"I don't know."

"You don't know?" She snorted. "I mean, it's not *David Letterman*, your show, is it? It's not like people are swarming all over you to get on it."

"We do all right."

I couldn't help feeling that she was missing the point of the story. An angel—possibly like an emissary from the Lord Himself, who knows?—had visited a tower block in Archway to stop us all from killing ourselves, and she wanted to know why he hadn't been booked on a talk show. I don't know, man. You'd have thought that would be one of the questions nearer the end of the interview.

"He'd have been the first person on that we'd ever heard of, anyway."

"You'd heard of him before, had you?" said Martin. "This particular angel? The one who looked like Matt Damon?"

"I've heard of *angels*," she said.

"Well, I'm sure you've heard of *actresses*," said Martin. "We've had them on, too."

"Where are we going with this?" I said. "You really wanna write a piece about why the angel Matt wasn't a guest on Martin's show?"

"Is that what you call him?" she said. " 'The angel Matt'?"

"Usually we just call him 'The Angel,' " said Jess. "But—"

"Would you mind if Martin answered a couple of questions?"

"You've asked him loads already," said Jess. "Maureen hasn't said anything. JJ hasn't said very much."

"Martin's the one that most people will have heard of," said Linda. "Martin? Is that what you call him?"

"Just 'The Angel,' " said Martin. He looked happier than this on the night he tried to kill himself.

"Can I just check something?" said Linda. "You did see him, Martin, didn't you?"

Martin shifted in his seat. You could tell he was scouting around the inside of his head, just to make sure that there were no escape routes he'd overlooked.

"Oh, yes," said Martin. "I saw him, all right. He was . . . He was awesome."

And with that, he finally walked into the cage that Linda had opened for him. The public at large were now free to poke sticks at him and call him names, and he just had to sit there and take it, like an exhibit in a freak show.

But then, we were all freaks now. When friends and family and ex-lovers opened their newspapers the next morning, they could come to one of only two possible conclusions: (1) We'd all looped the loop, or (2) We were scam artists. OK, strictly speaking, there was a third conclusion—we were telling the truth. We saw an angel that looked like Matt Damon, who for reasons best known to himself told us to get down off the roof. But I gotta say, I don't know anyone who'd believe that. Maybe my great-aunt Ida, who lives in Alabama and handles snakes every Sunday morning in her church, but then, she's nuts, too.

And I don't know, man, but to me it seemed a long way back from there. If you were gonna draw a map, you'd say that mortgages and relationships and jobs and all that stuff, all the things that constitute a regular life, were in, like, New Orleans, and by coming out with all this horseshit we'd just put ourselves somewhere north of Alaska. Who's going to give a job to a guy who sees angels? And who's going to give a job to a guy who says he sees angels because he might make a few bucks for himself? No, we were finished as serious people. We had sold our seriosity for twelve hundred and fifty of your English pounds, and as far as I could tell that money was going to have to last us for the rest of our lives, unless we saw God, or Elvis, or Princess Di. And next time we'd have to see them for real, and take photos.

Just over two years ago, R.E.M.'s manager came to see Big

Yellow and asked whether we were interested in his company representing us, and we said we were happy with what we had. R.E.M.! Twenty-six months ago! We were sitting around in this fancy office, and this guy, he was trying to persuade *us*, you know? And now I was sitting around with people like Maureen and Jess, taking part in a pathetic attempt to squeeze a few bucks out of someone who was desperate to give it to us, so long as we were prepared to totally embarrass ourselves. One thing the last couple of years has taught me is that there's nothing you can't fuck up if you try hard enough.

My only consolation was that I didn't have any friends and family here; no one knew who I was, except for a few fans of the band, maybe, and I like to think that they weren't the type to read Linda's paper. And some of the guys at the pizza place might see a copy lying around somewhere, but they'd have smelled the cash, and the desperation, and they could have cared less about the humiliation.

So that just left Lizzie, and if she saw a picture of me looking insane, then so be it. You know why she dumped me? She dumped me because I wasn't going to be a rock 'n' roll star after all. Can you fucking believe that? No, you can't, because it's beyond belief, and therefore unbelievable. "Shittiness, thy name is Woman." That was my thinking at that point in time; you know, that it wouldn't hurt her to see how she'd messed me up. In fact, if I could be temporarily invisible, then one of the first things I'd do, after robbing a bank and going into the women's showers at the gym and all the usual stuff, is put the paper down in front of her and watch her read it.

See, I didn't know anything about anything then. I thought I knew things, but I didn't.

MAUREEN

I didn't think I'd ever be able to go back to the church again after the interview with Linda. I'd been thinking about it a bit, the day before; I missed it terribly, and I wondered whether God would really mind if I just sat at the back and didn't go to confession—sneaked out somehow before communion. But once I'd told Linda that I'd seen an angel, I knew that I'd have to keep away, that I wouldn't be able to go back before I died. I didn't know exactly what sin I'd committed, but I was sure that sins involving making up angels were mortal.

I still thought I was going to kill myself when the six weeks were up; what would have changed my mind? I was busier than I'd ever been, what with the press interviews and the meetings, and I suppose that took my mind off things. But all the running around just felt like last-minute activity, as if I had some things to get done before I went on holiday. That was who I was then: a person who was going to kill herself soon, the moment she could get round to it.

I was going to say that I saw the first little glimmer of light that day, the day of the interview with Linda, but it wasn't really like that. It was more as if I'd already chosen what I was going to watch on TV, and I was beginning to look forward to it, and then noticed that there was something else on that might be more interesting. I don't know about you, but choice isn't always what I want. You can end up flicking between one channel and another, and not watching either program properly. I don't know how people with the cable television cope.

What happened was that after the interview, I found myself talking to JJ. He was going back to his flat, and I was heading toward the bus stop, and we ended up walking along together. I'm not sure he wanted to, really, because we've hardly spoken since I slapped that man on New Year's Eve, but it was one of those awkward situations where I was walking five paces behind him, so he stopped for me.

"That was kind of hard, wasn't it?" he said, and I was surprised, because I thought I was the only one who'd found it difficult.

"I hate lies," I said.

He looked at me and laughed, and then I remembered about his lie.

"No offense," I said. "I lied, too. I lied about the angel. And I lied to Matty as well. About going to a party on New Year's Eve. And to the people in the respite home."

"God'll forgive you for those, I think." We walked along a little bit more, and then he said, for no reason that I could tell, "What would it take to change your mind?"

"About what?"

"About . . . you know. Wanting To End It All."

I didn't know what to say.

"If you could make a deal with God, kind of thing. He's sitting there, the Big Guy, across the table from you. And he's saying, OK, Maureen, we like you, but we really want you to stay put, on earth. What can we do to persuade you? What can we offer you?"

"God's asking me personally?"

"Yeah."

"If He was asking me personally, He wouldn't have to offer me anything."

"Really?"

"If God in His infinite wisdom wanted me to stay on earth, then how could I ask for anything?"

JJ laughed. "OK, then. Not God."

"Who, then?"

"A sort of . . . I don't know. A sort of cosmic, you know, president. Or prime minister. Tony Blair. Someone who can get things done. You don't have to do what Tony Blair says without asking for something in return."

"Can he cure Matty?"

"Nope. He can only *arrange* things."

"I'd like a holiday."

"God. You're a cheap date. You'd choose to live out the rest of your natural life for a week in Florida?"

"I'd like to go abroad. I've never been."

"You've never been abroad?"

He said it as though I should be ashamed, and for a moment I was.

"When was the last time you had a vacation?"

"Just before Matty was born."

"And he's how old?"

"He's nineteen."

"Okay. Well, as your manager, I'm going to be asking the Big Guy for one vacation a year. Maybe two."

"You can't do that!" I really felt scandalized. I can see now I was taking it all too seriously, but it felt real to me, and it seemed like a holiday a year was too much.

"Trust me," said JJ. "I know the market. Cosmic Tony won't blink an eye. Come on, what else?"

"Oh, I couldn't ask for anything else."

"Say he does give you two weeks' vacation a year. Fifty weeks is a long time to wait for it, you know? And you're not going to get another appointment with Cosmic Tony. You got one shot. Everything you want, you've got to ask for in one go."

"A job."

"You want a job?"

"Yes. Of course."

"What kind of job?"

"Anything. Working in a shop, maybe. Anything to get me out of the house."

I used to work, before Matty was born. I had a job in an office stationer's in Tufnell Park. I liked it; I liked all the different pens, and sizes of paper and envelopes. I liked my boss. I haven't worked since.

"OK. Come on, come on."

"Maybe a bit of a social life. The church has quizzes sometimes. Like pub quizzes, but not in the pub. I'd like to have a go at one of those."

"Yep, we can allow you a quiz."

I tried to smile, because I knew JJ was joking a bit, but I was finding the conversation hard. I couldn't really think of anything very much, and that annoyed me. And it made me feel afraid, in a strange sort of a way. It was like finding a door that you'd never seen before in your own house. Would you want to know what was behind it? Some people would,

I'm sure, but I wouldn't. I didn't want to carry on talking about me.

"What about you?" I said to JJ. "What would you say to Cosmic Tony?"

"Ha. I'm not sure, man." He calls everyone "man," even if you're not a man. You get used to it. "Maybe, I don't know. Live the last fifteen years all over again or something. Finish high school. Forget about music. Become the kind of person who's happy to settle for what he is, rather than what he wants to be, you know?"

"But Cosmic Tony can't arrange that."

"No. Exactly."

"So you're worse off than me, really. Cosmic Tony can do things for me, but not for you."

"No, no, shit, I'm sorry, Maureen. I didn't mean to imply that. You have a . . . You have a really hard life, and none of it's your fault, and everything that's happened to me is just 'cause of my own stupidity, and . . . There's no comparison. Really. I'm sorry I ever mentioned it."

But I wasn't sorry. I liked thinking about Cosmic Tony much more than I liked thinking about God.

MARTIN

The headline in Linda's paper—page one, accompanied by the picture of me flat on my face outside a nightclub—read FOR HARPS—SEE SHARP. The story did not, as Linda had promised it would, emphasize the beauty and mystery of our experience on the roof; rather, it chose to concentrate on another angle, namely, the sudden, gratifying, and amusing lunacy of a former television personality. The journalist in me suspects that she got the story about right.

"What does that mean?" Jess asked me on the phone that morning.

"It's an old lager ad," I said. "HARP — STAYS SHARP."

"What has lager got to do with anything?"

"Nothing. But the name of the lager was Harp. And my name's Sharp, you see."

"OK. Then what have harps got to do with anything?"

"Angels are supposed to play them."

"Are they? Should we have said he was playing a harp? To make it more convincing?"

I told her that, in my opinion, the addition of a harp to the portrait of the angel Matt Damon that we had painted was unlikely to have helped convince people of its authenticity.

"And anyway, how come it's all about you? We hardly get a fucking mention."

I had many other phone calls that morning—from Theo, who said that there was a lot of interest in the story, and who thought I'd finally given him something he could work with, as long as I was comfortable talking to the public about what was obviously a private spiritual moment; from Penny, who wanted us to meet and talk; and from my daughters.

I hadn't been allowed to speak to them for weeks, but Cindy's maternal instinct had obviously told her that the day Daddy was in the papers talking about seeing messengers from God was a good day to reinstate contact.

"Did you see an angel, Daddy?"

"No."

"Mummy said you did."

"Well, I didn't."

"Why did Mummy say you did?"

"You'd better ask her."

"Mummy, why did you say Daddy saw an angel?"

I waited patiently while a brief conversation took place away from the receiver.

"She says she didn't say it. She says the newspaper says it."

"I told a fib, sweetie. To make some money."

"Oh."

"So I can buy you a nice birthday present."

"Oh. Why do you get money for saying you saw an angel?"

"I'll tell you another time."

"Oh."

And then Cindy and I spoke, but not for very long. During our brief conversation I managed to refer to two different types of domesticated female animals.

I also received a phone call from my boss at FeetUp!TV. He was calling to tell me that I was fired.

"You're joking."

"I wish I was, Sharpy. But you've left me with no alternative."

"By doing what, exactly?"

"Have you seen the paper this morning?"

"That's a problem for you?"

"You come across as a bit of a nutter, to be honest."

"What about the publicity for the channel?"

"All negative, in my book."

"You think there's such a thing as negative publicity for FeetUp!TV?"

"How do you mean?"

"What with no one ever having heard of us. You."

There was a long, long silence, during which you could hear the rusting cogs of poor Declan's mind turning over.

"Ah. I see. Very cunning. That hadn't occurred to me."

"I'm not going to beg, Dec. But it would seem a little perverse to me. You hire me when no one else in the world would give me the time of day. And then you fire me when I'm hot. How many of your presenters are all over the papers today?"

"No, no, fair point, fair point. I can see where you're coming from. What you're saying, if I read you correctly, is that there's no such thing as bad publicity for a . . . a *fledgling* cable channel."

"Obviously I couldn't have put it as elegantly as that. But yes, that's the long and the short of it."

"OK. You've turned me round, Sharpy. Who've we got on this afternoon?"

"This afternoon?"

"Yeah. It's Thursday."

"Ah."

"Had you forgotten?"

"I sort of had, really, yeah."

"So we've got no one?"

"I reckon I could get JJ, Maureen, and Jess to come on."

"Who are they?"

"The other three."

"The other three who?"

"Have you read the story?"

"I only read the one about you seeing the angel."

"They were up there with me."

"Up where?"

"The whole angel thing, Declan, came about because I was going to kill myself. And then I bumped into three other people on the top of a tower block who were thinking of doing the same thing. And then . . . well, to cut a long story short, the angel told us to come down again."

"Fuck me."

"Exactly."

"And you reckon you can get the other three?"

"Almost sure of it."

"Jesus Christ. How much will they cost, d'you reckon?"

"Three hundred quid for the three of them, maybe? Plus expenses. One of them's a . . . well, she's a single parent, and her kid will need looking after."

"Go on, then. Fuck it. Fuck the expense."

"Top man, Dec."

"I think it's a good idea. I'm pleased with that. Old Declan's still got it, eh?"

"Too right. You're a newshound. You're the Newshound of the Baskervilles."

"What you've got to tell yourself," I told them, "is that no one will be watching."

"That's one of your old pro tricks, right?" said JJ knowingly.

"No," I said. "Believe me. Literally no one will be watching. I have never met anyone who has ever seen my show."

The world headquarters of FeetUp!TV—known, inevitably, to its staff as TitsUp!TV—is in a sort of shed in Hoxton. The shed contains a small reception area, two dressing

rooms, and a studio, where all four of our homegrown programs are made. Every morning, a woman called Candy-Ann
sells cosmetics; I split Thursday afternoons with a man called
DJ GoodNews, who speaks to the dead, usually on behalf of
the receptionist, the window cleaner, the minicab driver
booked to take him home, or anyone else who happens to be
passing through: "Does the letter 'A' mean anything to you,
Asif?" and so on. The other afternoons are taken up by tapes
of old dog races from the U.S.—once upon a time the intention was to offer viewers the chance to bet, but nothing ever
came of it, and in my opinion, if you can't bet, then dog racing, especially old dog racing, loses some of its appeal. During
the evening, two women sit talking to each other, in and usually about their underwear, while viewers text them lewd messages, which they ignore. And that's more or less it. Declan
runs the station on behalf of a mysterious Asian businessman,
and those of us who work for FeetUp!TV can only presume
that somehow, in ways too obtuse and sophisticated for us to
decipher, we are involved in the trafficking of class A drugs
and child pornography. One theory is that the dogs in the
races are sending out encoded messages to the traffickers: If,
say, the dog in the outside lane wins, then that is a message to
the Thai contact that he should send a couple of kilos of
heroin and four thirteen-year-olds first thing in the morning.
Something like that anyway.

My guests on *Sharp Words* tend to be old friends who want
to do something to help, or former celebrities in a boat not dis-
similar to my own—holed under the waterline and sinking fast.
Some weeks I get has-beens, and everyone gets wildly overex-
cited, but most weeks it's had-beens. Candy-Ann, DJ Good-

News, and the two semiclothed ladies have appeared on my show not just once but several times, in order to give viewers a chance to get to know them a little better. (*Sharp Words* is two hours long, and though the advertising department—namely, Karen on reception—does its best, we are rarely interrupted by messages from our sponsors. The theoretical viewer is highly unlikely to feel as though we have barely scratched the conversational surface.) Attracting people of the caliber of Maureen and Jess, then, constituted something of a coup: Only rarely have my guests appeared on the show during the same decade that they have appeared in the newspapers.

I took pride in my interviewing. I mean, I still do, but at a time when I seemed to be able to do nothing else properly, I hung on to my competence in a studio as I would to a tree root on the side of a cliff. I have, in my time, interviewed drunken, maudlin actors at eight in the morning, and drunken, aggressive footballers at eight in the evening. I have forced lying politicians to tell something like the truth, and I have had to cope with mothers whose grief has made them uncomfortably verbose, and not once have I let things become sloppy. My studio sofa was my classroom, and I didn't tolerate any waywardness. Even in those desperate FeetUp!TV months spent talking to nobodies and never-weres, people with nothing to say and no ability to say it, it was comforting to think that there was some area of my life in which I was competent. So when Jess and JJ decided that my program was a joke and acted accordingly, I suffered something of a sense-of-humor failure. I wish, of course, that I hadn't; I wish that I could have found it in me to be a little less pompous, a little more relaxed. True, I was encouraging them to talk about an unforgettable experience that they hadn't had, and which I knew they hadn't had. And granted, that imaginary unforgettable experience was preposterous. And yet, despite those impediments, I had somehow expected a higher level of professionalism.

I don't wish to overstate my case; it's not bloody rocket science, doing a TV interview. You chat to your guests beforehand, agree on a rough conversational course, remind them of their hilarious anecdotes and, in this case, of the known facts about the fictions we were about to discuss, as provided by Jess in her original interview—namely, that the angel looked like Matt Damon, he floated above the roof, and he was wearing a baggy white suit. Don't fuck about with those bits, I told them, or we'll get into a mess. So what happens? Almost immediately? I ask JJ what the angel was wearing, and he tells me that the angel was wearing a promotional T-shirt for the Sandra Bullock film *While You Were Sleeping*—a film which, as luck would have it, Jess had seen on TV, and was thus able to synopsize at considerable length.

"If we can just stick to the subject," I said. "Lots of people have seen *While You Were Sleeping*. Very few people have seen an angel."

"Fuck off. No one's watching. You said."

"That was just one of my old pro's tricks."

"We'll be in trouble now, then. Because I just said 'Fuck off.' You'll get loads of complaints for that."

"I think that our viewers are sophisticated enough to know that extreme experiences sometimes produce extreme language."

"Good. Fuckofffuckofffuckoff." She made her apologetic wave at Maureen, and then into the camera, at the outraged people of Britain. "Anyway, watching rubbish Sandra Bullock films isn't a very extreme experience."

"We were talking about the angel, not Sandra Bullock."

"What angel?"

And so on, and on, until Declan walked in with the cosmetics lady and ushered us off the air, into the street, and, in my case, out of a job.

JESS

Someone should write a song or something called, "They Fuck You Up, Your Mum and Dad." Something like, "They fuck you up, your mum and dad. / They make you feel fucking bad." Because they do. Especially your dad. That's why he gets the rhyme. He wouldn't like me saying this, but if it wasn't for me and Jen, no one would ever have heard of him. He's not like the boss of education—that's the secretary of state. There are loads of ministers, and he's only one of them, so he's what they call a junior minister, which is a laugh and a half because he's not very junior at all. So he's sort of a loser politician, really. You wouldn't mind if he was a loser because he shot his mouth off and said what he thought about Iraq or whatever, but he doesn't; he says what he's told to say, and it still doesn't do him much good.

Most people have a rope that ties them to someone, and that rope can be short or it can be long. (Be long. Belong. Get it?) You don't know how long, though. It's not your choice. Maureen's rope ties her to Matty and it's about six inches long and it's killing her. Martin's rope ties him to his daughters and, like a stupid dog, he thinks it isn't there. He goes running off somewhere—into a nightclub after a girl, up a building, whatever—and then suddenly it brings him up short and chokes him and he acts surprised, and then he does the same thing again the next day. I think JJ is tied to this bloke Eddie he keeps talking about, the one he used to be in the band with.

And I'm learning that I'm tied to Jen, and not to my mum and dad—not to home, which is where the rope should be. Jen thought she was tied to them, too, I'm sure of it. She felt safe, just because she was a kid with parents, so she kept walking and walking and walking until she walked off a cliff or into the desert or off to Texas with her mechanic. She thought she'd get jerked back by the rope, but there wasn't one. She learned that the hard way. So I'm tied to Jen now, but Jen isn't solid, like a house. She's floating, blowing around, no one knows where she is; she's sort of fucking useless, really, isn't she?

Anyway, I don't owe Mum and Dad anything. Mum understands that. She gave up expecting anything ages ago. She's still a mess because of Jen, and she hates Dad, and she's given up on me, so everything's all aboveboard there. But Dad really thinks that he's entitled to something, which is a joke. For example: He kept showing me these articles that people were writing about him, saying he should resign because his daughter was in such a fucking state, as if it was any of my business. And I was like, So? Resign. Or don't. Whatever. He needed to talk to a career adviser, not a daughter.

It wasn't as if we were in the papers for long anyway. We made one more chunk of money, from a new Channel 5 chat show. We were going to really try and do it straight that time, but the woman who interviewed us really got on my tits, so I told her we'd made it all up to earn a few bob, and she told us off, and all these stupid brain-dead old bags in the audience booed us. And that was it, no one wanted to speak to us anymore. We were left to entertain ourselves. It wasn't too hard. I had loads of ideas.

For example: It was my idea that we met for a coffee regularly—either at Maureen's, or somewhere in Islington, if we could find someone to sit with Matty. We didn't mind spending bits of the money on babysitters or whatever you want to call them; we pretended we were up for it because we wanted Maureen to have a break, but really it was because we didn't want to go round hers all the time. No offense, but Matty put, like, a real downer on everything.

Martin didn't like my idea, of course. First he wanted to know what "regularly" meant, because he didn't want to commit himself. And I was like, Yeah, well, what with no kids and no wife and no girlfriend and no job, it must be hard to find the time, and he said it wasn't a question of time actually it was a question of choice, so I had to remind him that he had agreed to be part of a gang. And he was like, So what, so I went, Well, what's the point of agreeing? And he said, No point. Which he thought was funny, because it was more or less what I'd said on the roof on New Year's Eve. And I was like, Well, you're a lot older than me, and my young mind isn't fully formed yet, and he went, You can say that again.

And then we couldn't agree on where we'd meet. I wanted to go to Starbucks, because I like Frappuccinos and all that, but JJ said he wasn't into global franchises, and Martin had read in some posey magazine about a snooty little coffee bar between Essex Road and Upper Street where they grow their own beans while you wait or something. So to keep him happy, we met up there.

Anyway, this place had just changed its name and its vibe. The snootiness hadn't worked out, so it wasn't snooty anymore. It used to be called Tres Marias, which is the name of a dam in Brazil, but the guy who ran it thought the name confused people, because what did one Mary have to do with coffee, let alone three? And he didn't even have one Mary. So now it was called Captain Coffee, and everyone knew what it sold, but it didn't seem to make much difference. It was still empty.

We walked in, and the guy who ran it was wearing this old army uniform, and he saluted us, and said, Captain Coffee at your service. I thought he was funny, but Martin was like, Jesus Christ, and he tried to leave, but Captain Coffee wouldn't let us, he was that desperate. He told us we could have our coffee for free on our first visit, and a cake, if we wanted. So we didn't walk out, but the next problem was that the place was tiny. There were, like, three tables, and each table was six inches away from the counter, which meant that Captain Coffee was leaning on the counter listening to everything we said. And because of who we were and what had happened to us, we wanted to talk about personal things, so it was embarrassing, him standing there.

Martin was like, Let's drink up and go, and he stood up. But Captain Coffee went, What's the matter now? So I said, The thing is, we need to have a private conversation, and he said he understood completely, and he'd go outside until we'd finished. And I said, But really, everything we say is private, for reasons I can't go into. And he said it didn't matter, he'd still wait outside unless anyone else came. And that's what he did, and that's why we ended up going to Starbucks for our coffee meetings. It was hard to concentrate on how miserable we were, with this berk in an army uniform leaning against the window outside checking that we weren't stealing his biscuits or biscotties as he called them. People go on about places like Starbucks being unpersonal and all that, but what if that's what you want? I'd be lost if JJ and people like that got their way, and there was nothing unpersonal in the world. I like to know that there are big places without windows where no one gives a shit. You need confidence to go into small places with regular customers—small bookshops and small music shops and small restaurants and cafés. I'm happiest in the Virgin Megastore and Borders and Starbucks and PizzaExpress, where no one gives a shit, and no one knows who you are. My mum and dad are always going on about how soulless those places are, and I'm like, Der. That's the point.

The book group thing was JJ's idea. He said people do it a lot in America, read books and talk about them; Martin reckoned it was becoming fashionable here, too, but I'd never heard of it, so it can't be that fashionable, or I'd have read about it in *Dazed and Confused*. The point of it was to talk about Something Else, sort of thing, and not get into rows about who was a berk and who was a prat, which was how the afternoons in Starbucks usually ended up. And what we decided was, we were going to read books by people who'd killed themselves. They were, like, our people, and so we thought we ought to find out what was going on in their heads. Martin said he thought we might learn more from people who hadn't killed themselves—we should be reading up on what was so great about staying alive, not what was so great about topping yourself. But it turned out there were like a billion writers who hadn't killed themselves, and three or four who had, so we took the easy option, and went for the smaller pile. We voted on using funds from our media appearances to buy ourselves the books.

Anyway, it turned out not to be the easy option at all. Fucking hell! You should try and read the stuff by people who've killed themselves! We started with Virginia Woolf, and I only read like two pages of this book about a lighthouse, but I read enough to know why she killed herself: She killed herself because she couldn't make herself understood. You only have to read one sentence to see that. I sort of identify with her a bit, because I suffer from that sometimes, but her mistake was to go public with it. I mean, it was lucky in a way, because she left a sort of souvenir behind so that people like us could learn from her difficulties and that, but it was bad luck for her. And she had some bad luck, too, if you think about it, because in the olden days anyone could get a book published because there wasn't so much competition. So you could march into a publisher's office and go, you know, I want this published, and they'd go, Oh, OK, then. Whereas now they'd go, No, dear, go away, no one will understand you. Try Pilates or salsa dancing instead.

JJ was the only one who thought it was brilliant, so I had a go at him, and he had a go back because I didn't like it. He was all, Is it because your daddy reads books? Is that why you come on like such a dork? Which was an easy one to answer, because Daddy doesn't read books, bad luck, and I told him so. And then I said, Is it because you didn't go to school? Is that why you think all books are great even when they're shit? Because some people are like that, aren't they? You're not allowed to say anything about books because they're books, and books are, you know, God. Anyway, he didn't like that much, which means I got him right where it hurts. He said that he could see that what was going to happen to our reading group was that I would wreck it, and how had he been so stupid as to expect anything else? And I was like, I'm not going to wreck anything. If a book's shit, I'll say so. And he went, Yeah, but you're gonna say they're all shit, aren't you, because you're so fucking contrary, sorry, Maureen. And I said, Yeah, and you're gonna say they're all great, because you're such a creep. And he said, They are all great, and he went through all these people we were supposed to be talking about in the group— Sylvia Plath, Primo Levi, Hemingway. So I said, Well, what's the point of doing the reading group if you know in advance they're all great? What's fun about that? And he said, It's not *Pop Idol*, man. You don't vote for the best one. They're all good, and we accept that, and we talk about their ideas. And I was like, Well, if she's anything to go by, I don't accept they're all great. In fact, I now accept the opposite. And JJ got really worked up about that, and there was some unpleasantness then, and Martin stepped in and we decided not to do any more books for a while—in other words, ever. That was when we decided to have a go at musical suicide instead. Maureen had never heard of Kurt Cobain, can you believe it?

I do think. I know no one believes it, but I do. It's just that my way of thinking is different from everyone else's. Before I think, I have to get angry and maybe a bit violent, which I can see is sort of annoying for everyone else, but tough shit. Anyway, that night, in bed, I thought about JJ, and what he'd said about how I hated books because Daddy read them. And it's true what I said, that he doesn't, not really, although because of his job he has to pretend that he does.

Jen was a reader, though. She loved her books, but they scared me. They scared me when she was around, and they scare me even more now. What was in them? What did they say to her, when she was unhappy and listening only to them and to no one else—not her friends, not her sister, no one? I got out of bed and went into her room, which has been left exactly as it was on the day she left. (People are always doing that in films, and you think, Yeah, right, like you don't want a guest bedroom, or somewhere to put all your crap. But you try going in there and fucking everything up.) And there they all are: *The Secret History*, *Catch-22*, *To Kill a Mockingbird*, *The Catcher in the Rye*, *No Logo*, *The Bell Jar* (which is a coincidence or maybe not because that was one of the books JJ wanted us to read), *Crime and Punishment*, *1984*, *Good Places to Go When You Want to Disappear* . . . That was just a joke, that last one.

I don't think I was ever going to be a big reader, because she was the brainy one, not me, but I'm sure I would have been better at it if she hadn't put me off by disappearing. It wasn't the first time I'd been in her room, and it wouldn't be the last, I knew, and the books all sit there and look at me, and what I hate most is knowing that one of them might help me to understand. I don't mean that I'll find some sentence she's underlined that will give me a clue about where she is, although I looked a while ago. I flicked through, just in case she'd put, like, an exclamation mark by the word "Wales," or a ring around "Texas." I just mean that if I read everything she loved, and everything that took her attention in those last few months, then I'd get some picture of where her head was at. I don't even know whether these books are serious or sad or scary. And you'd think I'd want to find out, wouldn't you, considering as how much I loved her and everything. But I don't. I can't. I can't because I'm too lazy, too stupid, and I can't even make the effort because something stops me. They just sit there looking at me, day after day, and one day I know I'll put them all in a big pile and burn them.

So, no, I'm not a big reader.

J J

Our cultural program was all on my shoulders, because none of the others knew anything about anything. Maureen got books out of the library every couple weeks, but she didn't read stuff we could talk about, if you know what I'm saying, unless we wanted to talk about whether the nurse should marry the bad rich guy or the good poor guy. And Martin wasn't a big fan of literature. He said he read a lot of books in prison, but mostly biographies of people who had overcome great adversities, like Nelson Mandela and those guys. My guess is Nelson Mandela wouldn't have thought of Martin Sharp as a soul brother. When you looked at their lives closely, you'd see that they'd wound up in jail for different reasons. And, believe me, you don't want to know what Jess thought of books. You'd find it offensive.

She was right about me, though, kind of. How could she not be? I've spent my entire life with people who don't read—my folks, my sister, most of the band, especially the rhythm section—and it makes you really defensive, after a while. How many times can you be called a fag before you snap? Not that I mind being called a fag, blah-blah-blah, and some of my best friends, blah-blah, but to me, being a fag is about whether you like guys, not whether you like Don DeLillo—who is a guy, admittedly, but it's his books I like, not his ass. Why does reading freak people out so much? Sure, I could be pretty antisocial when we were on the road, but if I was playing a Game Boy hour after hour, no one would be on my case. In my social circle, blowing up fucking space monsters is socially acceptable in a way that *American Pastoral* isn't.

Eddie was the worst. It was like we were married, and picking up a book was my way of telling him that I had a headache every night. And like a marriage, the longer we were together, the worse it got; but now that I think about it, the longer we were together, the worse everything got. We knew we weren't going to make it, as a band and maybe even as friends, and so we were both panicking. And me reading just made Eddie panic more, because I think he had some bull-shit idea that reading was going to help me find some sort of new career. Yeah, like that's what happens in life. "Hey, you like Updike? You must be a cool guy. Here's a $100,000 job in our advertising agency." We spent all those years talking about the stuff we had in common, and the last few months notic-ing all the ways we were different, and it broke both of our hearts.

And all that is a long-ass way of explaining why I freaked out at Jess. I'd left one band full of aggressive illiterates, and I sure as hell wasn't going to join another one. When you're unhappy, I guess everything in the world—reading, eating, sleeping—has something buried somewhere inside it that just makes you unhappier.

And for some reason, I thought music was going to be easier, which, considering I'm a musician, wasn't real smart. I only have a lot invested in books, but I got my whole life invested in music. I thought I couldn't go wrong with Nick Drake, especially in a room full of people who've got the blues. If you haven't heard him . . . man, it's like he boiled down all the melancholy in the world, all the bruises and all the fucked-up dreams you've let go, and poured the essence into a little tiny bottle and corked it up. And when he starts to play and sing, he takes the cork out, and you can smell it. You're pinned into your seat, as if it's a wall of noise, but it's not—it's still, and quiet, and you don't want to breathe in case you frighten it away. And we were listening to him over at Maureen's, because we couldn't play our own music at Starbucks, and at Maureen's you've got the sound of Matty breathing, which was like this whole extra freaky instrument. So I was sitting there thinking, Man, this is going to change these people's lives *forever*.

At the end of the first song, Jess started putting her fingers down her throat and making faces.

"But he's such a *drip*," she said. "He's like, I dunno, a *poet* or something." This was meant to be an insult: I was spending my days with someone who thought that poets were creatures you might find living in your lower intestine.

"I don't mind it," said Martin. "I wouldn't walk out if he was playing in a wine bar."

"I would," said Jess.

I wondered whether it would be possible to punch both of them out simultaneously, but rejected the idea on the grounds that it would all be over too quickly, and there wouldn't be enough pain involved. I'd want to keep on pummeling them after they were down, which would mean doing them one at a time. It's music rage, which is like road rage, only more righteous. When you get road rage, a tiny part of you knows you're being a jerk, but when you get music rage, you're carrying out the will of God, and God wants these people dead.

And then this weird thing happened, if you can call a deep response to *Five Leaves Left* weird.

"Have you not got ears?" Maureen said suddenly. "Can't you hear how unhappy he is, and how beautiful his songs are?"

We looked at her, and then Jess looked at me.

"Ha-ha," said Jess. "You like something Maureen likes." She sang this last part, like a little kid, nah, nah, nah, nah, nah, nah.

"Don't pretend to be more foolish than you are, Jess," said Maureen. "Because you're foolish enough as it is." She was steamed. She had the music rage, too. "Just listen to him for a moment, and stop blathering."

And Jess could see that she meant it, and she shut up, and we listened to the whole rest of the album in silence, and if you looked at Maureen closely you could see her eyes were glistening a little.

"When did he die?"

"Nineteen seventy-four. He was twenty-six."

"Twenty-six." She was quiet for a moment, thoughtful, and I was really hoping that she was feeling sorry for him and his family. The alternative was that she was envying him for having spared himself all those unnecessary extra years. You want people to respond, but sometimes they can overdo it, you know?

"People don't want to hear it, do they?" she said.

No one said anything, because we weren't sure where she was at.

"This is how I feel, every day, and people don't want to know that. They want to know that I'm feeling what Tom Jones makes you feel. Or that Australian girl who used to be in *Neighbours*. But I feel like this, and they won't play what I feel on the radio, because people that are sad don't fit in."

We'd never heard Maureen talk like this, didn't even know she could, and even Jess didn't want to stop her.

"It's funny, because people think it's Matty that stops me fitting in. But Matty's not so bad. Hard work, but . . . it's the way Matty makes me feel that stops me fitting in. You get the weight of everything wrong. You have to guess all the time whether things are heavy or light, especially the things inside you, and you get it wrong, and it puts people off. I'm tired of it."

And so, suddenly Maureen was like my girl, because she got it, and because she felt the music rage, too, and I wanted to say the right thing to her.

"You need a vacation."

I said it because I wanted to be sympathetic, but then I remembered Cosmic Tony, and I realized that now Cosmic Tony had the money.

"Hey. What about that? Why not?" I said. "Let's all take Maureen on vacation somewhere."

Martin burst out laughing.

"Yeah, right," said Jess. "What are we? Volunteers for like an old folks' home or something?"

"Maureen's not old," I said. "How old are you, Maureen?"

"I'm fifty-one," she said.

"OK, not an old folks' home. A boring folks' home."

"And what makes you the most fascinating person on the planet?" Martin said.

"I don't look like that, for a start. Anyway, I thought you were on my side."

And almost unnoticed, amid all the laughter and the general scorn, Maureen had started to cry.

"I'm sorry, Maureen," said Martin. "I wasn't being ungallant. I just couldn't imagine the four of us sitting around a swimming pool on our sun loungers."

"No, no," said Maureen. "I took no offense. Not much, anyway. And I know nobody wants to go on holiday with me, and that's fine. I just got a bit weepy because JJ suggested it. It's been a long . . . Nobody's . . . I haven't . . . It was just nice of him, that's all."

"Oh, fucking hell," said Martin quietly. Now, "Oh, fucking hell" can mean a lot of different things, as you know, but there was no ambiguity here; we all understood. What Martin meant by "Oh, fucking hell" in this context, if I can explain an obscenity with an obscenity, is that he was fucked. Because what kind of asshole was going to say to Maureen, you know, "Yeah, well, it's the thought that counts. Hope that's enough for you."

And, like, five days later we were on a plane to Tenerife.

MAUREEN

It was their decision, not mine. I didn't feel that I had the right to decide, not really, even though a quarter of the money did belong to me. I was the one who'd suggested the holiday in the first place, to JJ, when we were talking about Cosmic Tony, so I didn't think it was right that I should join in when they took a vote on it. I think what I did is, I abstained.

It wasn't as if there was a big argument, though. Everyone was all for it. The only debate was about whether to go now or in the summer, because of the weather, but there was a general feeling that, what with one thing and another, it was better to go now, before Valentine's Day. For a moment they thought we could afford the Caribbean—Barbados or somewhere—until Martin pointed out that the money we had would have to cover Matty's time in the care center as well.

"Let's go without Maureen, then," said Jess, and I was hurt, for a moment, until it turned out she was joking.

I can't remember the last time I wept because I was happy. I'm not saying that because I want people to feel sorry for me;

it's just that it was a strange feeling. When JJ said he had an idea, and then explained what it was, I didn't even allow myself to think for a moment that it would ever come to anything.

It was funny, but up to that point, we hadn't really ever been nice to each other. You'd think that would have been a part of the story, considering how we'd met. You'd think this would be the story of four people who met because they were unhappy, and wanted to help each other. But it hadn't been up until then, not at all, nothing like, unless you count me and Martin sitting on Jess's head. And even that was being cruel to be kind, rather than kind plain and simple. Up until then it had been the story of four people who met because they were unhappy and then swore at each other. Three of them swore anyway.

I was making little sobbing noises that embarrassed everyone, myself included.

"F——ing hell," said Jess. "It's only a week in the poxy Canary Isles. I've been there. It's just beaches and clubs and that."

I wanted to tell Jess that I hadn't even seen an English beach since Matty left school; they used to take them to Brighton every year, and I went with them once or twice. I didn't say anything, though. I may not know the weight of many things, but I could feel the weight of that one, so I kept it to myself. You know that things aren't going well for you when you can't even tell people the simplest fact about your life, just because they'll presume you're asking them to feel sorry for you. I suppose it's why you feel so far away from everyone, in the end; anything you can think of to tell them just ends up making them feel terrible.

. . .

I want to describe every moment of the journey, because it seemed so exciting, but that would probably be a mistake, too. If you're like everybody else, then you'll already know what an airport looks like, what it sounds and smells like, and if I tell you about it, then it would be just another way of saying that I haven't seen the sea for ten years. I'd got a one-year passport from the post office, and even that caused too much excitement, because I saw one or two people from the church in the queue, and they know I'm not a big traveler. One of the people I saw was Bridgid, the woman who didn't invite me to the New Year's Eve party I didn't go to; one day, I thought, I'll tell her how she helped me to take my first trip abroad. I'd really have to know how much things weighed before I tried that, though.

You probably know that you sit in a row of three. They let me sit in the window seat, because they'd all been on planes before. Martin sat in the middle and JJ sat next to him on the aisle for the first few minutes. After a little while, Jess had to swap places with JJ, because she had an argument with the woman sitting next to her about the wee bag of nuts they give you, and there was some shouting and carrying on. Another thing you probably know is that there's a terrible noise when you take off, and sometimes the plane shakes in the air. Well, of course I didn't know any of those things, and my stomach turned to water, and Martin had to hold my hand and talk to me.

And you probably also know that when you look out of an aeroplane window and see the world shrink like that, you can't help but think about the whole of your life, from the begin-

A LONG WAY

ning until where you are now, and everyone you've ever known. And you'll know that thinking about those things makes you feel grateful to God for providing them, and angry with Him for not helping you to understand them better, and so you end up in a terrible muddle and needing to talk to a priest. I decided I wouldn't sit in the window seat on the way back. I don't know how these jet-set people who have to fly once or twice a year cope, I really don't.

Not having Matty with me was like missing a leg. It felt that strange. But I also enjoyed the lightness of it, so it probably wasn't at all like missing a leg, because I don't suppose people who've had a leg taken off do enjoy the lightness of it very much. And I was going to say that it was much easier to move around without Matty, but it's much harder to move around with only one leg, isn't it? So maybe it would be more truthful to say that being on the plane without Matty was like being without a third leg, because a third leg would feel heavy, I expect, and it would get in the way, and you would be relieved if it was taken off. I missed him most when the plane was doing its shaking; I thought I was going to die, and I hadn't said goodbye to him. I panicked then.

We didn't fall out on the first night. Everyone was happy then, even Jess. The hotel was nice, and clean, and we all had our own toilets and bathrooms, which I hadn't been expecting. And when I opened the shutters, the light poured into the room like a torrent of water through a burst dam, and it nearly knocked me over. My knees buckled for a moment, and I had to lean against the wall. The sea was there, too, but it wasn't fierce and strong, like the light; it just sat quiet and blue, and made tiny little murmuring noises. Some people can see this whenever they want to, I thought, but then I had to stop thinking that because it would have got in the way of the things I wanted to think about. It was a time to be feeling grateful, not to be coveting my neighbor's wife, or his sea views.

We ate in a seafront restaurant not far from the hotel. I had a nice piece of fish, and the men ate squid and lobster, and Jess had a hamburger, and I drank two or three glasses of wine. I won't tell you when I'd last eaten out in a restaurant, or had wine with a meal, because I'm learning not to do that. I didn't even try to tell the others, because I could feel the weight for myself, and knew it was more than they would want to carry. Anyway, they knew by this time that it was donkey's years since I'd done anything at all, apart from the things I do every day of my life. They took it for granted.

I would like to say this, though, and I don't care how it sounds: It was the nicest meal I've ever had in my life, and perhaps the nicest evening I've ever had in my life. Is that so terrible, to be so positive about something?

MARTIN

The first evening wasn't too bad, I suppose. I was recognized once or twice, and ended up wearing JJ's baseball cap pulled down over my eyes, which depressed me. I am not a baseball cap sort of a chap, and I abhor people who wear any sort of headgear during dinner. We ate so-so seafood in a tourist trap on the seafront, and the only reason I didn't complain about just about everything was because of the look on Maureen's face: She was transported by her microwaved plaice and her warm white wine, and it seemed churlish to spoil it.

Maureen had never been anywhere, and I'd had a holiday just a few months before. Penny and I went away for a few days after I'd come out of prison, to Majorca. We stayed in a private villa outside Deya, and I thought it was going to be the best few days of my life, because the worst three months were over. But of course it wasn't like that at all; to describe prison as the worst three months of one's life is like describing a horrible car crash as the worst ten seconds. It sounds logical and neat; it sounds truthful. But it's not, because the worst time is afterward, when you wake up in hospital and learn that your wife is dead, or you've had your legs amputated, and that therefore the worst has just begun. I appreciate that this is a gloomy way of talking about a mini-break on a perfectly pleasant Mediterranean island, but it was on Majorca that I realized that the worst was nowhere near over, and might never be over. Prison was humiliating and terrifying, mind-numbing, savagely destructive of the soul in a way that the expression "soul-destroying" can no longer convey. Do you know what "quizzies" are? Neither did I, until my first night. Quizzies are when drugged-up psychos hurl questions at each other across the blocks, all of them centered around what the participants would like to see done to unpopular and/or celebrated newcomers. I was the subject of a quizzie on my first night; I won't bother to list even the more imaginative suggestions, but suffice to say that I didn't sleep very well that night, and that for the first time in my life I had intensely violent fantasies of revenge. I focused everything on the day of my release, and though that day brought with it an overwhelming relief, it didn't last very long.

Criminals serve their time, but with all due respect to my friends in B Wing, I was not a criminal, not really; I was a television presenter who had made a mistake, and paradoxically, this meant that I would never serve my time. It was a class issue, and I'm sorry, but there's no point in pretending it wasn't. You see, the other inmates would eventually return to their lives of thieving and drug dealing and possibly even roofing or whatever the hell it was they did before their careers were interrupted; prison would prove to be no impediment, either socially or professionally. Indeed, they may even find their prospects and social standing enhanced.

But you don't return to the middle class when you've been banged up. It's over, and you're out. You don't go and see the head of daytime TV and tell her you're ready to reclaim your seat behind the *Rise and Shine* desk; you don't knock on your friends' doors and tell them that you're once again available for dinner parties. You needn't even bother telling your ex-wife you want to see your kids again. I doubt whether Mrs. Big Joe would have attempted to deny him access to his children, and I doubt whether many of his mates in the pub would have stood in the corner muttering their disapproval. I'll bet they bought him a drink and got him laid, in fact. I have thought long and hard about this, and have turned into something of a radical on the subject of penal reform: I have come to the conclusion that no one who earns more than, say, £75,000 a year should ever be sent to jail, because the punishment will always be more severe than the crime. You should just have to see a therapist, or give some money to charity, or something.

That holiday with Penny was the first time I fully apprehended the trouble I was in, and the trouble I would always be in. The villa at the end of the road was owned by people we both knew, a couple who ran their own production company and had, in happier times, offered us both work. We ran into them one night in a local bar, and they pretended they didn't know us. Later, the woman took Penny aside in the supermarket and explained that they were worried about their teenaged daughter, a particularly unprepossessing fourteen-year-old who, to be perfectly frank, is unlikely to lose her virginity for a good many years to come, and certainly not to me. It was all nonsense, of course, and she was no more worried about my proximity to her daughter than she was about my proximity to her purse. It was her way of telling me, as so many others have done since, that I've been cast out of the Garden of Islington, doomed to roam the offices of crap cable companies forevermore.

So the dinner that first night in Tenerife just made me gloomy. These weren't my people. They were just people who would talk to me because I was in their boat, but it was a bad boat to be in—an unseaworthy, shabby little boat, and I could suddenly see that it was going to break up and sink. It was a boat made for pootling around the lake in Regent's Park, and we were attempting to sail to fucking Tenerife in it. You'd have to be an idiot to think it was going to stay afloat for much longer.

JESS

I don't think everything the next day was my fault. I take some
of the blame, but when things go wrong, you just make them
worse if you overreact, don't you? And I think some people
overreacted. Because my dad is New Labour and all that, he's
always going on about tolerance for people of different cul-
tures, and I think what happened was that some people, in
other words Martin, were not tolerant of my culture, which is
more of a drinking and drug-taking and shagging sort of a culture than his culture. I like to think that I'm respectful of his.
I don't tell him that he should get pissed up and fucked up on
drugs and pick up more girls. So he should be respectful of
mine. He wouldn't tell me to eat pork if I was Jewish, so why
should he tell me not to do the other stuff?

There were only seven years between the first and last
Beatles albums. That's nothing, seven years, when you think
of how their hairstyles changed and their music changed.
Some bands now go seven years without hardly bothering to
do anything. Anyway, at the end of their seven years, they'd

probably got sick of the sight of each other, and you can see that they wanted different things. John wanted to be in a bag or whatever, and Paul wanted to be on his farm or whatever, and it's hard to see how you can keep a relationship going when you're so different, and one of you is in a bag. OK, we hadn't even been going for seven weeks, but we were different in the first place, whereas John and Paul liked the same music and went to the same schools and so on. We didn't have any of that to go on. We weren't even all from the same country. So in a way, it's no wonder that our seven years got condensed into about three weeks.

What happened was, we had breakfast together, and we agreed that we'd go our separate ways until the evening, when we were all going to meet up in the hotel bar, have a cocktail, and find somewhere to eat. And then JJ and I went for a swim in the hotel pool while Maureen sat and watched us, and then I decided to go out on my own.

We were staying on the north of the island, in this place called Puerto de la Cruz, which was OK. When I came before we were in the south, which is really mental, but probably too mental for Maureen, and as it was supposed to be her holiday, I didn't mind too much. I did want to buy some blow, though, and it was harder to find up here than it would have been down there, and that's how come I ended up getting myself into the trouble that Martin was, in my opinion, disrespectful of.

I went into a couple of bars looking for the kinds of people who might sell spliff, and in the second bar I saw a girl who looked exactly like Jen. I'm not exaggerating; when she looked at me and didn't recognize me, I thought she was messing about, until I noticed that her eyes weren't quite big enough, and her hair was bleached; Jen would never have bleached her hair, however much she wanted to disguise herself. Anyway, this girl didn't like me staring at her, so I had to have a few words, and she was English and unfortunately understood those words, so she gave me a mouthful back, and I sort of took it on from there. And after we'd been at it for a while, we were both asked to leave. I'll be truthful and say that I'd already had a couple of Bacardi Breezers, even though it was still quite early, and I think they made me aggressive, although she didn't take up my offer of a fight. And then the usual stuff happened: NotJen's brother, this bar, this guy, money, dope, and a couple of Es, wasn't going to do any of it until later, ended up doing most of it straightaway, some people from a place called Nantwich, this guy, freaked, left to freak on my own. Puke, sleep on the beach, woken up, freaked, driven back to the hotel in a police car. I don't think I'd ever met anyone from Nantwich before, and this all happened during the day, but other than that it was a pretty typical night out. I told the police that Maureen and Martin were my parents, and Martin wasn't happy. I don't think there was any need for him to check out of our hotel, though. It would have all blown over.

I felt terrible the next morning, mostly because I'd gone to bed without anything to eat, although I'm sure the Es and the Breezers and the blow didn't help. I felt low, too. I had that terrible feeling you get when you realize that you're stuck with who you are, and there's nothing you can do about it. I mean, you can make characters up, like I did when I became like a Jane Austen-y person on New Year's Eve, and that gives you some time off. But it's impossible to keep it going for long, and then you're back to being sick outside some dodgy club and offering to fight people. My dad wonders why I choose to be like this, but the truth is, you have no choice, and that's what makes you feel like killing yourself. When I try to think of a life that doesn't involve being sick outside a dodgy club, I can't manage it; I picture nothing at all. This is I; this is my voice, this is my body, this is my life. Jess Crichton, this is your life, and here are some people from Nantwich to talk about you.

I once asked Dad what he'd do if he wasn't working in politics, and he said he'd be working in politics, and what he meant, I think, is that wherever he was in the world, whatever job he was doing, he'd still find a way back, in the way that cats are supposed to be able to find a way back when they move house. He'd be on the local council, or he'd give out pamphlets, or something. Anything that was a part of that world, he'd do. He was a little sad when he said it; he told me it was, in the end, a failure of imagination.

And that's me: I suffer from a failure of imagination. I could do what I wanted, every day of my life, and what I want to do, apparently, is to get walloped out of my head and pick fights. Telling me I can do anything I want is like pulling the plug out of the bath and then telling the water it can go anywhere it wants. Try it, and see what happens.

JJ

I had a good day, that first day. In the morning I read *The Sportswriter* by the pool, and that's one fucking cool book. And then I ordered a sandwich, and then . . . Well, the truth of the matter is, I thought it was about time to jump-start my libido, which had been on life support and demonstrating no outward signs of life for maybe four or five months. You ever read that book some dude wrote with, like, his eyelid? He had to flicker it every time whoever was helping him got to the right letter of the alphabet. True story. Anyway, my fucking libido couldn't even have written that book. But sitting by the pool in my shorts, with the sun warming parts of me that had been frozen for a long time, in all the ways there are to be frozen, there were dim but unmistakable signs of life.

It wasn't like I went out with the express purpose of doing anything about it. I just thought I'd go for a walk and look around, maybe get back in touch with that side of life. I went back to the room to get dressed first, though. I'm not a bare-chested kind of guy. I'm like a hundred and thirty pounds, skinny as fuck, white as a ghost, and you can't walk around next to guys with tans and six-packs when you look like that. Even if you found a chick who dug the skinny ghost look, she wouldn't remember she dug it in this context, right? If you were into Dolly Parton and they played a blast of her album during a hip-hop show, she just wouldn't sound good. In fact, you wouldn't even be able to fucking *hear* her. So putting on my faded black jeans and my old Drive-By Truckers T-shirt was my way of being heard by the right people.

And get this: Not only did I get heard, if I may use a euphemism, but I got heard by someone who'd seen the band and liked us. I mean, what are the chances? OK, she couldn't remember us real clearly, and I kind of had to tell her she'd liked us, but, you know. Still. What happened was, I found this cool saltwater pool in the town, designed by some local artist, and I stopped for a beer right across from there. And this English chick was sitting by herself, and she was reading this book called *Bel Canto*, so I told her I'd read it, too, and we started to talk about it, and I scooted over to her table. And then we started talking about music, because *Bel Canto* is kind of about music—opera anyway, which some people think is music—and she said she was more into rock 'n' roll than opera, so I was, like, Which bands? And she listed a whole bunch, and one of them, this band called the Clockers, we'd done a tour with a few years back. And she'd seen them on that tour, in Manchester, where she lives, and she thought she might have gotten there early enough to see the opener, and I said, Well, that was us. And she said, Oh, right, I remember, you were cool. I know, I know, but I was at a period in my life where I took what I could get.

We ended up spending the afternoon together, and then I blew off the family dinner and we spent the evening together, and then, finally, we spent the night together at my hotel, because she had a roommate at hers. And that was the first time I'd gotten any since the last night with Lizzie, which was more like necrophilia anyway.

Kathy and I had breakfast together in the dining room the next morning, and not only because the hotel didn't have enough stars for room service: I was kind of looking forward to bumping into the others. For some reason I thought I'd get some props—OK, maybe not from Maureen, but from Martin, certainly, because he's got an eye for a pretty girl. I even somehow got it into my head that Jess would be kind of impressed. I could see the three of them on the other side of the room, and two of them whispering dirty jokes, and I'd feel cool again.

. . .

Maureen was first down. I waved to her as she came in, to be friendly, but the wave was somehow misinterpreted as an invitation, and she came and sat down at our table. She looked at Kathy suspiciously.

"Is someone not coming down for breakfast?" She wasn't being rude. She was just confused.

"No, see—" But then I didn't know what to say.

"I'm Kathy," said Kathy, who was also confused. "I'm a friend of JJ's."

"The trouble is, there isn't really room for five on the table," said Maureen.

"If everyone else shows, Kathy and I will move," I said.

"Who's 'everyone else'?" Kathy asked, I guess reasonably.

"Martin and Jess," said Maureen. "But Jess got brought home in a police car last night. So she might be having a lie-in."

"Oh," I said. I mean, I wanted to know why Jess had been brought home in a police car and everything. But I didn't want to know right then.

"What had she done?" asked Kathy.

"What hadn't she done?" said Maureen. The waitress came over and poured us some coffee, and Maureen went to the buffet table for her croissants.

Kathy looked at me. She had some questions, I could tell.

"Maureen is . . ." But then I couldn't think of a way to finish the sentence. I didn't have to find a way, either, because then Jess walked in and sat down.

"Fuck me," she said. That was by way of an introduction. "I feel so shit. Normally I'd think a good puke might make me feel better. But I puked my whole insides up last night. There's nothing left."

"I'm Kathy," said Kathy.

"Hello," said Jess. "I'm in such a state I didn't even realize I don't know you."

"I'm a friend of JJ's," said Kathy, and Jess's eyes lit up ominously.

"What sort of friend?"

"We just met yesterday."

"And you're having breakfast together?"

"Shut up, Jess."

"What have I said?"

"It's what you're going to say."

"What am I going to say?"

"I have no idea."

"Have you met our mum and dad yet, Kathy?"

Kathy's eyes flickered nervously over to Maureen.

"You're braver than me, JJ," said Jess. "I wouldn't bring a one-night stand down to the family breakfast table. That's fucking modern, man."

"That's your mother?" said Kathy. She was trying to be real casual, but I could tell she was freaking a little.

"Of course it's not my mother. We're not even the same nationality. Jess is being—"

"Did he tell you he was a musician?" said Jess. "I'll bet he did. He always does. That's the only way he can ever get a girlfriend. We keep telling him not to try that one, because people always find out in the end. And then they're disappointed. I'll bet he said he was a singer, right?"

Kathy nodded, and looked at me.

"That's a laugh. Sing for her, JJ. You should hear him. Fucking hell."

"Kathy saw my band," I said. But as soon as I'd said it, I remembered that I'd told Kathy she'd seen the band, which isn't quite the same thing; Kathy turned to look at me, and I could tell she was remembering the same thing. Oh, man.

Maureen and her croissants sat down at the table.

"What are we going to do if Martin comes down? There's no room."

"Oh, no," said Jess. "Aaaaagh. Help. We'll just panic, I s'pose."

"Maybe I should make a move," said Kathy. She stood up and gulped some coffee down. "Anna will be wondering what's happened to me."

"We could move to another table," I said, but I knew it was over, destroyed by a malevolent force beyond my control.

"See you later," said Jess cheerily.

And that was the last time I saw Kathy. If I were her, I'd still be reconstructing the dialogue in my head, writing it down and getting friends to act it out, looking for any kind of clue that would help me make sense of that breakfast.

You never know with Jess whether she's being sharp or lucky. When you shoot your mouth off as fast and as frequently as she does, you're bound to hit something sometime. But for whatever reason, she was right: Kathy wouldn't have happened without music. She was supposed to be a little pick-me-up, my first since the band broke up—my first ever as a nonpracticing musician, because I was already in a band when I lost my virginity, and I've been in a band ever since. So after she left, I started to worry about how this was ever going to work and, like, whether I'd be in some fucking old folks' home in forty years telling some little old lady with no teeth that R.E.M.'s manager had wanted to represent my band. When was I ever going to be a person—someone with maybe a job, and a personality that people could respond to? It's no fucking use, giving something up if there's nothing to take its place. Say I'd just kept talking about the books we were both reading, and we'd never mentioned music . . . Would we still have gone to bed? I couldn't see it. It seemed to me that without my old life, I had no life at all. My morale-booster ended up making me feel totally fucking crushed and desperate.

MAUREEN

We didn't really think anything of Martin missing his breakfast, even though breakfast was included. I was getting used to the idea that once or twice a day, something would happen that I wouldn't understand. I didn't understand what Jess had been up to the night before, and I didn't understand why there was a strange woman—a girl, really—sitting at our breakfast table. And now I didn't understand where Martin had gone. But not understanding didn't seem to matter very much. Sometimes, when you watch a cops-and-robbers film on the television, you don't understand the beginning, but you know you're not meant to. You watch anyway, though, because in the end someone will explain some of the things to you if you pay close attention. I was trying to think of life with Jess and

JJ and Martin as a cops-and-robbers film; if I didn't get every-thing, I told myself not to panic. I'd wait until someone gave me a clue. And anyway, I was beginning to see that it didn't really matter even if you understood almost nothing. I hadn't really understood why we had to say we'd seen an angel, or how that got us onto the television. But that was all forgotten about now, apparently, so why make a fuss? I must admit, I was worried about where everyone was going to sit at break-fast, but that wasn't because I was confused. I just didn't want Martin to think us rude.

After breakfast I tried to telephone the care home, but I couldn't manage on my own. In the end I had to ask JJ to do it for me, and he explained that there were lots of extra numbers to dial, and some you had to leave out, and I don't know what else. I wasn't being cheeky, using the telephone, because the others told me I could call once a day whatever the expense; otherwise, they said, I wouldn't relax properly.

And the telephone call . . . Well, it changed everything. Just those two or three minutes. More happened to me in my head during the telephone call than during all that time up on the roof. And it wasn't as if there was any bad news, or any news at all. Matty was fine. How could he not be? He needed care, and he was getting care, and there wasn't much else they could tell me, was there? I tried to make the conversa-tion last longer, and, fair play to him, the nurse tried to help me make it last longer, God love him. But neither of us could think of anything to say. Matty doesn't do anything in the course of a day, and he hadn't done anything on that particu-lar day. He'd been out in his wheelchair, and we talked about that, but mostly we were talking about the weather, and the garden.

And I thanked him and put the phone down and thought for a moment, and tried not to feel sorry for myself. Love and concern and the rest of it, the things that only a mother can provide . . . For the first time in his life I could finally see that those things were no use to him anyway. The point of me was exactly the same as the point of the people in the care home. I was probably still better at it than they were, because of the practice I'd had. But I could have taught them all they'd need to know in a couple of weeks.

What that meant was that when I died, Matty would be fine. And what that meant was, the thing I'd been most afraid of, ever since he was born, wasn't frightening in the least. And I didn't know whether I wanted to kill myself more or less, knowing that. I didn't know whether my whole life had been a waste of time or not.

I went downstairs, and I saw Jess in the lobby.

"Martin's checked out of the hotel," she said.

And I smiled at her politely, but I didn't stop, and I kept walking. I didn't care that Martin had checked out of the hotel. If I hadn't made the telephone call I would have cared, because he was in charge of our money. But if he'd gone off with the money, it wouldn't matter much, would it? I'd stay there, or not, and I'd eat, or not, and I'd drink, or not, and go home, or not, and what I did or didn't do wouldn't matter to anyone at all. And I walked for most of the day. Do people get sad on holiday sometimes? I can imagine they do, having all that time to think.

For the rest of the week, I tried to keep out of everybody's way. Martin was gone anyway, and JJ didn't seem to mind. Jess didn't like it much, and once or twice she tried to make me eat with her, or sit on the beach with her. But I just smiled and said, No, thank you. I didn't say, But you're always so rude to me! Why do you want to talk to me now?

I borrowed a book from the little bookcase in reception, a silly one with a bright pink cover called *Paws for Beth*, about a single girl whose cat turns into a handsome young fella. And the young fella wants to marry her, but she's not sure because he's a cat, so she takes a while to decide. And sometimes I read that, and sometimes I slept. I've always been fine on my own.

And the day before we flew home I went to Mass, for the first time for a month or so. There was a lovely old church in the town—much nicer than ours at home, which is modern and square. (I've often wondered whether God would even have found ours, but I suppose He must have done by now.) It was easier than I thought it would be to walk in and sit down, but that's mostly because I didn't know anybody there. But after that everything seemed a little harder, because the people seemed so foreign, and I didn't know where we were very often because of the language.

I got used to it, though. It was like walking into a dark room—and it was dark in there, much darker than ours. After a little while, I started to be able to see things, and what I could see were people from home. Not the actual people, of course, but the Tenerife versions. There was a woman like Bridgid, who knew everyone and kept looking down the pews and smiling and nodding. And there was a fella who was a little unsteady on his feet, even at that time of day, and that was Pat.

And then I saw me. She was my age, on her own, and she had a grown-up son in a wheelchair who didn't know what day it was, and for a little while I stared at them, and the woman

A

L

O

N

G

W

A

Y

caught me staring and she obviously thought I was being rude. But it seemed so strange, such a coincidence, until I thought about it. And what I thought was, you could probably go into any church anywhere in the world and see a middle-aged woman, no husband in sight, pushing a young lad in a wheelchair. It was one of the reasons churches were invented, probably.

MARTIN

I have never been a particularly introspective man, and I say this unapologetically. One could argue that most of the trouble in the world is caused by introspection. I'm not thinking of things like war, famine, disease, or violent crime—not that sort of trouble. I'm thinking more of things like annoying newspaper columns, tearful chat-show guests, and so on. I can now see, however, that it's hard to prevent introspection when one has nothing to do but sit around and think about oneself. You could try thinking about other people, I suppose, but the other people I tried to think about tended to be people I knew, and thinking about people I knew just brought me right back to where I didn't want to be.

So in some ways it was a mistake, checking out of the hotel and going off on my own, because even though Jess irritated the hell out of me, and Maureen depressed me, they occupied a part of me that should never be left untenanted and unfurnished. It wasn't just that, either: They also made me feel relatively accomplished. I'd done things, and because I'd done things, there was a possibility that I might do other things. They'd done nothing at all, and it was not difficult to imagine that they would continue to do nothing at all, and they made me look and feel like a world leader who runs a multinational company in the evenings and a scout troop at weekends.

I moved into a room that was more or less identical to the one I'd been staying in, except I treated myself to a sea view and a balcony. And I sat on the balcony for two solid days, staring at the sea view and being introspective. I can't say that I was particularly inventive in my introspection; the conclusions I drew on the first day were that I'd made a pig's ear of just about everything, and that I'd be better off dead, and if I died no one would miss me or feel bad about my death. And then I got drunk.

The second day was only very slightly more constructive. Having reached the conclusion the previous evening that no one would miss me if I died, I realized belatedly that most of my woes were someone else's fault: I was estranged from my children because of Cindy, and Cindy was also responsible for the end of my marriage. I made one mistake! OK, nine mistakes. Nine mistakes out of, say, a hundred opportunities! I got 91 percent and I still failed the test! I was imprisoned (a) due to entrapment, and (b) because society's attitudes to teenage sexuality are outmoded. I lost my job because of the hypocrisy and disloyalty of my bosses. So at the end of the second day, I wanted to kill other people, rather than kill myself, and that's got to be healthier, surely?

Jess found me on the third day. I was sitting in a café reading a two-day-old *Daily Express* and drinking *café con leche*, and she sat down opposite me.

"Anything about us in there?" she said.

"I expect so," I said. "But I've only read the sport and the horoscopes so far. Haven't looked at the front page yet."

"Fun-nee. Can I sit with you?"

"No."

She sat down anyway.

"What's all this about, then?"

"All what?"

"This . . . big sulk."

"You think I'm sulking?"

"What would you call it, then?"

"I'm sick to death of you."

"What have we done?"

"Not you, plural. You, singular. *Toi*, not *vous*."

"Because of the other night?"

"Yes, because of the other night."

"You just didn't like me saying you were my dad, did you? You're old enough to be."

"I'm aware of that."

"Yeah. So get over it. Take a chill pill."

"I'm over it. I've taken one."

"Looks like it."

"Jess, I'm not sulking. You think I moved out of a hotel because you said I was your father?"

"I would."

"Because you hate him? Or because you'd be ashamed of your daughter?"

"Both."

This is what happens with Jess. When she thinks you're withdrawing, she pretends to be thoughtful (and by "thoughtful," I mean "self-loathing," which to me is the only possible outcome of any prolonged thought on her part). I decided I wasn't going to be taken in.

"I'm not going to be taken in. Get lost."

"What have I done now? Fucking hell."

"You're pretending to be a remorseful human being."

"What does 'remorseful' mean?"

"It means you're sorry."

"For what?"

"Go away."

"For what?"

"Jess, I want a holiday. Most of all, I want a holiday from you."

"So you want me to get pissed up and take drugs."

"Yes. I want that very much."

"Yeah, right. And if I do I'll get a bollocking."

"Nope. No bollocking. Just go away."

"I'm bored."

"So go and find JJ or Maureen."

"They're boring."

"And I'm not?"

"Which celebrities have you met? Have you met Eminem?"

"No."

"You have, but you won't tell me."

"Oh, for Christ's sake."

I left some money on the table, got up, and walked out. Jess followed me down the street.

"What about a game of pool?"

"No."

"Sex?"

"No."

"You don't fancy me?"

"No."

"Some men do."

"Have sex with them, then. Jess, I'm sorry to say it, but I think our relationship is over."

"Not if I just follow you around all day it isn't."

"And you think that would work in the long term?"

"I don't care about the long term. What about what my dad said about looking out for me? And I'd have thought you'd want to. I could replace the daughters you've lost. And that way you could find inner peace, see? There are loads of films like that."

She offered this last observation matter-of-factly, as if it were somehow indicative of the truth of the scenario she'd imagined, rather than the opposite.

"What about the sex you were offering? How would that fit in with you replacing the daughters I've lost?"

"This would be a different, you know, thing. Route. A different way to go."

We passed a ghastly-looking bar called New York City.

"That's where I got thrown out for fighting," said Jess proudly. "They'll kill me if I try to go in again."

As if to illustrate the point, a grizzled-looking owner was standing in the doorway with a murderous look on his face.

"I need a pee. Don't go anywhere."

I walked into New York City, found a lavatory somewhere in the Lower East Side, put the TV pages of the *Express* over the seat, sat down, and bolted the door. For the next hour or two I could hear her yelling at me through the wall, but eventually the yelling stopped; I presumed she'd gone, but I stayed in there anyway, just in case. It was eleven in the morning when I bolted the door, and three in the afternoon when I came out. I didn't resent the time. It was that sort of holiday.

J J

The last band I was in broke up after a show at the Hope and Anchor in Islington, just a few blocks from where my apartment is now. We knew we were breaking up before we went onstage, but we hadn't talked about it. We'd played in Manchester the night before, to a very small crowd, and on the way down to London we'd all been a little snappy, but mostly just morose and quiet. It felt exactly the same as when you break up with a woman you love—the sick feeling in the stomach, the knowledge that nothing you can say will make any fucking difference. Or, if it does, it won't make any difference for any longer than, like, five minutes. It's weirder with a band, because you kind of know that you won't lose touch with the people the way you lose touch with a girlfriend. I could have sat in a bar with all three of them the next night without arguing, but the band would still have ceased to exist. It was more than the four of us; it was a house, and we were the people in it, and we'd sold it, so it wasn't ours anymore. I'm talking metaphorically here, obviously, because no one would have given us a fucking dime for it.

Anyway, after the show at the Hope and Anchor—and the show had an unhappy intensity to it, like a desperate breakup fuck—we walked into this shitty little dressing room, and sat down in a line, and then Eddie said, "That feels like it." And he did this thing that was so unlike him, so not just-like-Eddie: He reached out to either side of him and took my hand and Jesse's hand, and squeezed. And Jesse took Billy's hand, just so that we'd all be joined for one last time, and Billy said, "Fuck you, queer boy," and stood up real quick, which kind of tells you all you need to know about drummers.

I had only known my holiday companions for a few weeks, but there was the same kind of sick feeling on the way from the hotel to the airport. There was a breakup coming, you could smell it, and no one was saying anything. And it was for the same reason, which was that we'd taken things as far as we could, and there was nowhere for us to go. That's why everyone breaks up, I guess: bands, friends, marriages, whatever. Parties, weddings, anything.

It's funny, but when the band split, one of the reasons I felt sick was because I was worried about the other guys. What the fuck were they going to do, you know? None of us were overqualified. Billy wasn't real big on reading and writing, if you hear what I'm saying, and Eddie was too, like, pugilistic to hold down a job for long, and Jesse liked his spliff . . . The one person I had no real concerns about was me. I was going to be OK. I was smart, and stable, and I had a girlfriend; even though I knew I'd miss making music every fucking day of my life, I could still be something and someone without it. So what happens? A few weeks later, Billy and Jesse get a gig with a band back home whose rhythm section had walked out on

D
O
W
N

225

them, Eddie goes to work for his dad, and I'm delivering pizzas and nearly jumping off a fucking roof.

So this time around, I was determined not to fret about my fellow band members. They'd be OK, I told myself. It didn't look that way, maybe, but they'd survived so far, just about, and it wasn't my problem anyway.

In the taxi to the airport we talked some about what we'd done, and what we'd read, and the first thing we were going to do when we got home, and shit like that, and on the plane we all dozed, because it was an early flight. And then we got the tube from Heathrow to King's Cross, and took a bus from there. It was on the bus that we started to recognize that maybe we wouldn't be hanging out so much.

"Why not?" said Jess.

"Because we have nothing in common," said Martin. "The holiday proved that."

"I thought it went OK."

Martin snorted. "We didn't speak to each other."

"You were hiding in a toilet most of the time," said Jess.

"And why was that, do you think? Because we're soul mates? Or because ours is not one of my most fulfilling relationships?"

"Yeah, and what is your most fulfilling relationship?"

"What's yours?"

Jess thought for a moment, and then shrugged.

"With you lot," she said.

There was a silence that was long enough for us to see the truth of Jess's observation as it applied to her. And luckily for us, Martin spoke up just as we were starting to see how it might possibly apply to us, too.

"Yes. Well. It shouldn't be, should it?"

"Are you giving me the push?"

"If you want to put it like that. Jess, we got through the holiday. And now it's time to go our separate ways."

"What about Valentine's Day?"

"We can meet on Valentine's Day, if you want. We said we'd do that."

"Up on the roof?"

"Do you still think you might throw yourself off?"

"I dunno. It changes day by day."

"I'd like to meet up," said Maureen.

"I suppose Valentine's must be a pretty important day for you, Maureen," said Jess. She said it as if she were making conversation, but Maureen recognized the disguised nastiness, and didn't bother to respond. Just about everything Jess said could be bounced right back at her, but none of us had the energy anymore. We looked out the window at the traffic in the rain, and at Angel I said goodbye and got off. As I watched the bus drive away, I could see Maureen offer the others, even Jess, her packet of Polo mints, and the gesture seemed kind of heartbreaking.

For the next week I did nothing, pretty much. I read a lot, and wandered around Islington to see if there was any sign of a bad job for me. One night I blew ten pounds on a ticket for a band called Fat Chance, who were playing in the Union Chapel. They started up around the same time as us, and now they had a decent deal, and there was a buzz about them, but they were lame, in my opinion. They stood there and played their songs, and people clapped, and there was an encore, and then we left, and I wouldn't say any of us was the richer for the experience.

I was recognized on the way out, by a guy who must have been in his forties.

"All right, JJ?" he said.

"Do I know you?"

"I saw you at the Hope and Anchor last year. I heard the band had split. You living here?"

"Yeah, for now."

"What you doing? You gone solo?"

"Yeah, that's right."

"Cool."

We met at eight in the evening on Valentine's Day, and everyone was on time. Jess wanted to meet later, like at midnight or something, for full tragic effect, but no one else thought it was such a good idea, and Maureen didn't want to travel home so late. I ran into her on the stairs on the way up, and told her I was glad to hear she was thinking about traveling home afterward.

"Where else would I go?"

"No, I just meant . . . Last time you weren't gonna go home, you know? Not, like, on the bus anyway."

"On the bus?"

"Last time, you were going to get off the roof the quick way." I walked my fingers through the air and then plunged them downward, as if they were jumping off the roof. "But tonight, it sounds as though you'll be taking the long way down."

"Oh. Yes. Well. I've come on a bit," she said. "In my head, I mean."

"That's great."

"I'm still feeling the benefit of the holiday, I think."

"Right on."

And then she didn't want to talk anymore, because it was a long way up, and she was short of breath.

Martin and Jess arrived a couple of minutes later, and we said hello, and then we all stood there.

"What was the point of this, actually?" said Martin.

"We were going to meet up and see how we were all feeling and all that," said Jess.

"Ah."

We shuffled our feet.

"And how are we all feeling?"

"Maureen's doing good," I said. "Aren't you, Maureen?"

"I am. I was saying to JJ, I think I'm still feeling the benefit of the holiday."

"Which holiday? The holiday we just had?" He looked at her and then shook his head, with a mixture of amazement and admiration.

"How about you, Mart?" I said. "How you doing?" But I could kind of tell what the answer to that question was going to be.

"Oh, you know. *Comme ci, comme ça.*"

"Tosser," said Jess.

We shuffled our feet some more.

"I read something I thought might interest you all," Martin said.

"Yeah?"

"I was wondering . . . Maybe it would be good to talk about it somewhere other than here. In a pub, say."

"Sounds good to me," I said. "I mean, maybe we should celebrate anyway, you know?"

"Celebrate," said Martin, like I was nuts.

"Yeah. I mean, we're alive, and, and—"

The list kind of ran out after that. But being alive seemed worth the price of a round of drinks. Being alive seemed worth celebrating. Unless, of course, it wasn't what you wanted, in which case . . . Oh, fuck it. I wanted a drink anyway. If we couldn't think of anything else, then me wanting a drink was worth celebrating. An ordinary human desire had emerged through the fog of depression and indecision.

"Maureen?"

"Yes, I don't mind."

"It doesn't look to me like anyone's going to jump," I said. "Not tonight. Is that right? Jess?"

She wasn't listening.

"Fuck me," she said. "Jesus Christ."

She was staring at the corner of the roof, the spot where Martin had snipped the wire on New Year's Eve. There was a guy sitting there, exactly where Martin had sat, and he was watching us. He was maybe a few years older than me, and he looked real frightened.

"Hey, man," I said quietly. "Hey. Just stay there."

I started to walk slowly over to him.

"Please don't come any closer," he said. He was panicky, near tears, dragging furiously on a smoke.

"We've all been there," I said. "Come on back over and you can join our gang. This is our reunion." I tried another couple of steps. He didn't say anything.

"Yeah," said Jess. "Look at us. We're OK. You think you're never going to get through the evening, but you do."

"I don't want to," said the guy.

"Tell us what the problem is," I said. I walked a little closer. "I mean, we're all fucking experts in the field. Maureen here—"

But I never got any further. He flipped the cigarette over the edge, and then with a little moan he pushed himself off. And there was silence, and then there was the noise of his body hitting the concrete all those floors below. And those two noises, the moan and the thud, I've heard every single day since, and I still don't know which is scarier.

PART THREE

MARTIN

The guy who jumped had two profound and apparently con-
tradictory effects on us all. Firstly, he made us realize that we
weren't capable of killing ourselves. And secondly, this information made us suicidal again.

That isn't a paradox, if you know anything about the perversity of human nature. A long time ago, I worked with an
alcoholic—someone who must remain nameless because you
will almost certainly have heard of him. And he told me that
the first time he failed on an attempt to quit the booze was
the most terrifying day of his life. He'd always thought that
he could stop drinking if he ever got round to it, so he had a
choice stashed away in a sock drawer somewhere at the back
of his head. But when he found out that he had to drink,
that the choice had never really been there . . . Well, he
wanted to do away with himself, if I may temporarily confuse
our issues.

I didn't properly understand what he meant until I saw
that guy jump off the roof. Up until then, jumping had always

been an option, a way out, money in the bank for a rainy day. And then suddenly the money was gone—or rather, it had never been ours in the first place. It belonged to the guy who jumped, and people like him, because dangling your legs over the precipice is nothing unless you're prepared to go that extra two inches, and none of us had been. We could tell each other and ourselves something different—Oh, I would have done it if she hadn't been there, or he hadn't been there, or if someone hadn't sat on my head—but the fact of the matter was that we were all still around, and we'd all had ample opportunity not to be. Why had we come down that night? We'd come down because we thought we should go and look for some twit called Chas, who turned out not to be terribly germane to our story. I'm not sure we could have persuaded old matey, the jumper, to go and look for Chas. He had other things on his mind. I wonder how he would have scored on Aaron T. Beck's Suicide Intent Scale. Pretty high, I should think, unless Aaron T. Beck has been barking up the wrong tree. No one could say the intent wasn't there.

We got off that roof sharpish once he'd gone over. We decided it was best not to hang around and explain our role, or lack of it, in the poor chap's demise. We had a little Toppers' previous, after all, and by owning up, we'd only be confusing the issue. If people knew we'd been up there, then the clarity of the story—unhappy man jumps off building—would be diminished, and people would understand less of it, rather than more. We wouldn't want that.

So we charged down the stairs as fast as damaged lungs and varicosed legs would let us, and went our separate ways. We were too nervous to go for a drink in the immediate vicinity, and too nervous to travel in a taxi together, so we scattered the moment we reached the pavement. (What, I wondered on the way home, was the nearest pub to Toppers' House like of an evening? Was it full of unhappy people on their way up, or half-confused, half-relieved people who'd just come down? Or an awkward mix of the two? Does the landlord recognize the uniqueness of his clientele? Does he exploit their mood for financial gain—by offering a Miserable Hour, for example? Does he ever try to get the Uppers—in this context, the very unhappy people—to mix with the Downers? Or the Uppers to mix with each other? Has there ever been a relationship born there? Could the pub even have been responsible for a wedding, and thus maybe a child?)

We met again the following afternoon, in Starbucks, and everyone had the blues. A few days previously, in the immediate aftermath of the holiday, it had been perfectly clear that we no longer had much use for each other; now it was hard to imagine who else would be suitable company. I looked around the café at the other customers: young mothers with prams, young men and women in suits with mobile phones and pieces of paper, foreign students . . . I tried to imagine talking to any of them, but it was impossible. They wouldn't want to hear about people jumping off tower blocks. No one would, apart from the people I was sitting with.

"I was up all fucking night thinking about that guy," said JJ. "Man. What was going on there?"

"He was probably just, you know. A drama queen. A male drama queen. A drama king," said Jess. "He looked the sort."

"That's very shrewd, Jess," I said. "In the brief glimpse we got of him before he plunged to his death, he didn't strike me as someone with serious problems. Nothing on your scale, anyway."

"It'll be in the local paper," said Maureen. "They usually are. I used to read the reports. Especially when it was coming up to New Year's Eve. I used to compare myself with them."

"And? How did you get on?"

"Oh," said Maureen. "I did OK. Some of them I couldn't understand."

"What sort of things?"

"Money."

"I owe loads of people money," said Jess proudly.

"Perhaps you should think of killing yourself," I said.

"It's not much," said Jess. "Only twenty quid here and twenty quid there."

"Even so. A debt's a debt. And if you can't pay . . . maybe you should take the honorable way out."

"Hey. Guys," JJ said. "Let's keep some focus, huh?"

"On what? Isn't that the problem? Nothing to focus on?"

"Let's focus on that guy."

"We don't know anything about him."

"No, but, I don't know. He seems kind of important to me. That was what we were gonna do."

"Were we?"

"I was," said Jess.

"But you didn't."

"You sat on my head."

"But you haven't done anything about it since."

"Well. We went to that party. And we went on holiday. And, you know. There's been one thing after another."

"Terrible, isn't it, how that happens? You'll have to block out some time in your diary. Otherwise life will keep getting in the way."

"Shut up."

"Guys, guys . . ."

I had, once again, allowed myself to be drawn into an undignified spat with Jess. I decided to act in a more statesmanlike manner.

"Like JJ, I have spent a long night cogitating," I said.

"Tosser."

"And my conclusion is that we are not serious people. We were never serious. We got closer than some, but nowhere near as close as others. And that puts us in something of a bind."

"I agree. We're fucked," said JJ. "Sorry, Maureen."

"I'm missing something," said Jess.

"This is it," I said. "This is us."

"What is?"

"This." I gestured vaguely at our surroundings, the company we were keeping, the rain outside, all of which seemed to speak eloquently of our current condition. "This is it. There's no way out. Not even the way out is the way out. Not for us."

"Fuck that," said Jess. "And I'm not sorry, Maureen."

"The other night, I was going to tell you about something I'd read in a magazine. About suicide. Do you remember? Anyway, this guy reckoned that the crisis period lasts ninety days."

"What guy?" JJ asked.

"This suicidologist guy."

"That's a job?"

"Everything's a job."

"So what?" said Jess.

"So we've had forty-six of the ninety days."

"And what happens after the ninety days?"

"Nothing *happens*," I said. "Just . . . things are different. Things change. The exact arrangement of stuff that made you think your life was unbearable . . . It's got shifted around somehow. It's like a sort of real-life version of astrology."

"Nothing's going to change for you," said Jess. "You're still going to be the geezer off the telly who slept with the fifteen-year-old and went to prison. No one will ever forget that."

"Yes. Well. I'm sure the ninety-days thing won't apply in my case," I said. "If that makes you happier."

"Won't help Maureen, either," said Jess. "Or JJ. I might change, though. I do, quite a lot."

"My point, anyway, is that we extend our deadline again. Because, well, I don't know about you lot. But I realized this morning that I'm not, you know. Ready to go solo just yet. It's funny, because I don't actually like any of you very much. But you seem to be, I don't know . . . What I need. You know how sometimes you know you should be eating more cabbage? Or drinking more water? It's like that."

There was a general shuffling of feet, which I interpreted as a declaration of reluctant solidarity.

"Thanks, man," said JJ. "Very touching. When's the ninety days up?"

"March 31."

"That's a bit of a coincidence, isn't it?" said Jess. "Exactly three months."

"What's your point?"

"Well. It's not scientific, is it?"

"What, and eighty-eight days would be?"

"More scientific, yeah."

"No, I get it," said JJ. "Three months sounds about right. Three months is like a season."

"Very much like," I agreed. "Given there are four seasons, and twelve months in a year."

"So we're seeing the winter through together. That's cool. Winter is when you get the blues," JJ said.

"So it would appear," I said.

"But we gotta *do* something," said JJ. "We can't just sit around waiting for three months to be up."

"Typical American," said Jess. "What do you want to do? Bomb some poor little country somewhere?"

"Sure. It would take my mind off things, some bombing."

"What should we do?" I asked him.

"I don't know, man. I just know that if we spend six weeks pissing and moaning, then we're not helping ourselves."

"Jess is right," I said. "Typical bloody American. 'Helping ourselves.' Self-help. You can do anything if you put your mind to it, right? You could be president."

"What is it with you assholes? I'm not talking about becoming president. I'm talking about, like, finding a job waiting tables."

"Great," said Jess. "Let's all not kill ourselves because someone gave us a fifty-pence tip."

"No fucking chance of that in this fucking country," said JJ. "Sorry, Maureen."

"You could always just go back where you came from," said Jess. "That would change something. Also, your buildings are higher, aren't they?"

"So," I said. "Forty-four days to go."

There was something else in the article I read: an interview with a man who'd survived after jumping off the Golden Gate Bridge in San Francisco. He said that two seconds after jumping, he realized that there was nothing in his life he couldn't deal with, no problem he couldn't solve—apart from the problem he'd just given himself by jumping off the bridge. I don't know why I didn't tell the others about that; you'd think it might be relevant information. I wanted to keep it to myself for the time being, though. It seemed like something that might be more appropriate later, when the story was over. If it ever was.

MAUREEN

It was in the local paper, the following week. I cut the story out and kept it, and I read it every so often, just to try to understand the poor man better. I couldn't keep him out of my head. He was called David Fawley, and he'd jumped because of problems with his wife and children. She'd met someone else, and moved away to be with him, and taken the kiddies with her. He only lived two streets away, which seemed very strange to me, a coincidence, until I realized that people in my local paper always lived locally, unless someone had visited to open a school or something. Glenda Jackson came to Matty's school once, for example.

Martin was right. When I saw David Fawley jump, it made

A

L

O

N

G

W

A

Y

me see that I hadn't been ready on New Year's Eve. I'd been ready to make the preparations, because it gave me something to do—New Year's Eve was something to look forward to, in a strange sort of way. And when I'd met some people to talk to, then I was happy to talk, instead of jump. They'd have let me jump, I think, once I'd told them why I was up there. They wouldn't have got in my way, or sat on my head. But even so, I'd gone down the stairs and on to the party. This poor David hadn't wanted to talk to us, that was the thing I'd noticed. He'd come to jump, not to natter. I thought I'd gone to jump, but I ended up nattering anyway.

If you thought about it, this David fella and me, we were opposites. He'd killed himself because his children were gone, and I'd thought about it because my son was still around. There must be a lot of that goes on. There must be people who kill themselves because their marriage is over, and others who kill themselves because they can't see a way out of the one they're in. I wondered whether you could do that with everyone, whether every unhappy situation had an unhappy opposite situation. I couldn't see it with the people who had debts, though. No one ever killed himself because he had too much money. Those sheikhs with the oil don't seem to commit suicide very often. Or if they do, no one ever talks about it. Anyway, perhaps there was something in this opposites idea. I had someone, and David had no one, and he'd jumped and I hadn't. When it comes to committing suicide, nobody beats somebody, if you see what I mean. There's no rope holding you back.

I prayed for David's soul, even though I knew it wouldn't do him any good, because he had committed the sin of despair, and my prayers would fall on deaf ears. And then after Matty had gone to sleep, I left him alone for five minutes and walked down the road to see where David had lived. I don't know why I did that, or what I hoped to see, but there was nothing there, of course. It was one of these streets full of big houses that have been turned into flats, so that's what I found out, that he lived in a flat. And then it was time to turn around and go home.

That evening, I watched a program on the television about a Scottish detective who doesn't get on with his ex-wife very well, so I thought about David some more, because I don't suppose he got on very well with his ex-wife either. And I'm not sure this was the point of the program, but there wasn't much room in it for lots of arguments between the Scottish detective and his ex-wife, because most of the time he had to find out who'd killed this woman and left her body outside her ex-husband's house to make it look as though he'd killed her. (This was a different ex-husband.) So in an hour-long program, there were probably only ten minutes of him arguing with his ex-wife and his children, and fifty minutes of him trying to find who'd put the woman's body in the dustbin. Forty minutes, I suppose, if you took out the advertisements. I noticed because I was a bit more interested in the arguments than I was in the body, and the arguments didn't seem to come around very often.

And that seemed about right to me, ten minutes an hour. It was probably about right for the program, because he was a detective, and it was more important for him and for the viewers that he spent the biggest chunk of his time on solving the murders. But I think even if you're not in a

TV program, then ten minutes an hour is about right for your problems. This David Fawley was unemployed, so there was a fair old chance that he spent sixty minutes an hour thinking about his ex-wife and his children, and when you do that, you're bound to end up on the roof of Toppers' House.

I should know. I don't have arguments, but there have been lots of times in my life when I couldn't stop Matty becoming sixty minutes an hour. There was nothing else to think about. I'd had more on my mind recently, because of the others, and the things that have happened in their lives. But most of the time, on most days, it was just me and my son, and that meant trouble.

Anyway, that evening there was a whole jumble of thoughts. I lay in bed half-asleep, thinking about David, and the Scottish detective, and coming down off the roof to find Chas, and eventually I got these thoughts unknotted, and when I woke up in the morning I decided it would be a good idea to find out where Martin's wife and children lived, and then go and talk to them all and see if there was any chance of getting the family back together. Because if that worked, then Martin wouldn't get so eaten up about some things, and he'd have somebody rather than nobody, and I'd have something to do for forty or fifty minutes an hour, and it would help everybody.

But I was a hopeless detective. I knew Martin's wife's name was Cindy, so I looked Cindy Sharp up in the phone book, and she wasn't there, and I ran out of ideas after that. So I asked Jess, because I didn't think JJ would approve of my plan, and she found all the information we needed in about five minutes, on a computer. But then she wanted to come with me to see Cindy, and I said she could. I know, I know. But you try telling her she can't have something she wants.

JESS

I got on Dad's computer and put "Cindy Sharp" into Google, and I found an interview she'd given to some women's magazine when Martin had gone to prison. "Cindy Sharp Talks for the First Time About Her Heartbreak," and all that. You could even click on a picture of her and her two girls. Cindy looked like Penny, except older and a bit fatter, because of having had kids. And what's the betting that Penny looked like the fifteen-year-old, except that the fifteen-year-old was even slimmer than Penny, and had bigger tits or whatever? They're tossers, aren't they, men like Martin? They think women are like fucking laptops or whatever; like, My old one's knackered and anyway, you can get ones that are slimmer and do more stuff now.

So I read the interview, and it said she lived in this village called Torley Heath, about forty miles outside London. And if she was trying to stop people like us from knocking on the door to tell her to get back with her husband, then she made a big mistake, because the interviewer described exactly where her house is in the village—opposite an old-fashioned corner shop, next door but one to the village school. She told us all this because she wanted us to know how idealistic or whatever Cindy's life is. Apart from her ex-husband being in prison for sleeping with a fifteen-year-old.

We decided not to tell JJ. We were pretty sure he'd stop us for some bullshit reason or another. He'd say, It's none of your business, or, You'll fuck up the last chance he's got. But we thought we had a strong argument, Maureen and I. Our argument was this: Maybe Cindy did hate Martin because he was a real playa who went anywhere with anyone. But now he was suicidal, and he probably wouldn't go anywhere with anyone, or at least not for a while. So basically, if she wouldn't take him back, she had to hate him enough to want him to die. And that's a lot of hate. True, he hadn't ever said he wanted to get back with her, but he needed to be in a secure domestic environment, in a place like Torley Heath. It was better to do nothing in a place where there was nothing to do than in London, where there was trouble—teenaged girls and nightclubs and tower blocks. That's what we felt.

So we had a day out. Maureen made horrible, like, old-fashioned sandwiches with egg and stuff in them, which I couldn't eat. And we got the tube to Paddington, then the train to Newbury, and then a bus to Torley Heath. I'd been worried that Maureen and I wouldn't have much to say to each other, and we'd get really bored, and I'd end up doing something stupid, because of the boredom. But it really wasn't like that, mostly because of me, and the effort I put in. I decided that I was going to be like an interviewer-type person, and I'd spend the journey finding out about Maureen's life, no matter how boring or depressing it was. The only trouble was that it was actually too boring and depressing to listen to, so I sort of switched off when she was talking, and thought up the next question. A couple of times she looked at me funny, so I'm guessing that quite often she had just told me something and then I asked her about it again. Like once, I tuned back in to hear her go, Something, something, something met Frank. So I went, When did you meet Frank, but I think what she'd just said was, That was when I met Frank. So I'd have to work on that, if I was ever to be an interviewer. But let's face it, I wouldn't be interviewing people who did nothing and had a disabled son, would I? So it would be easier to concentrate, because they'd be talking about their new films and other stuff you'd actually want to know about.

Anyway, the point was that we went through a whole journey to the middle of fucking nowhere without me asking her whether she had sex doggy style or anything like that. And what I realized then was that I'd come a long way since New Year's Eve. I'd grown as a person. And that made me think that our story was sort of coming to an end, and it was going to be a happy ending. Because I'd grown as a person, and also we were in this period where we were sorting out each other's problems. We weren't just sitting around moping. That's when stories end, isn't it? When people show they've learned things, and problems get solved. I've seen loads of films like that. We'd sort out Martin today, and then turn our minds to JJ, and then me, and then Maureen. And we'd meet on the roof after ninety days, and smile, and hug, and know that we had moved on.

The bus stop was right outside the village shop that the article in the magazine had gone on about. So we got off the bus and stood outside the shop and looked across the road to see what

A
L
O
N
G
W
A
Y

we could see. What we saw was this little cottagey sort of place with a low wall, and you could look into the garden, and in the garden there were two little girls all wrapped up in hats and scarves and they were playing with a dog. So I went to Maureen, Do you know the names of Martin's kids. And she was like, Yes, they're called Polly and Maisie—which seemed about right, I thought. I could imagine Martin and Cindy having kids called Polly and Maisie, which are sort of old-fashioned posh names, so everyone could pretend that Mr. Darcy or whatever lived next door. So I shouted, Oo-o, Polly! Maisie! And they looked at us and came toward us, and that was my detective work over.

We knocked on the door and Cindy answered, and she looked at me as if she half-recognized me, and I was like, I'm Jess. I'm one of the Toppers' House Four, and I was, you know, linked to your husband or whatever in the newspapers. Which was a lie, by the way. (That was me telling her it was a lie, not me telling you. I really wish I knew where speech marks or whatever went. I can see the point of them now.)

And she said, Ex-husband, which was sort of an unfriendly and unhelpful start.

And I went, Well, that's the thing, isn't it?

And she went, Is it?

And I went, Yes, it is. Because he doesn't have to be your ex-husband.

And she went, Oh, yes he does.

And we hadn't even gone through the front door.

At that point Maureen goes, Do you think we could come in and talk to you? I'm Maureen. I'm also a friend of Martin's. We've come down from London on the train.

And the bus, I said. I just wanted her to know we'd made an effort.

And Cindy said, I'm sorry, come in. Not, I'm sorry, fuck off home, which is what I thought she was going to say. She was apologizing for her bad manners in making us stand out on the doorstep. So I was like, Oh, this is going to be easy. In ten minutes I'll have bullied her into taking him back.

So we walk into the cottage, and it's cozy in there, but not all like out of a magazine, which I thought it would be. The furniture didn't really match, and it was old, and it smelled of the dog a bit. She showed us through to the sitting room and there was this geezer in there sitting by the fire. He was nice-looking, younger than her, and I thought, Oh-oh, he's got his feet under the table. Because he was listening to a Walkman with his shoes off, and you don't listen to a Walkman with your shoes off in someone's house if you're just visiting, do you?

Cindy went up to him and tapped him on the shoulder and said, We've got visitors, and he was like, Oh, I'm sorry. I was listening to Stephen Fry reading *Harry Potter*. The children love it, so I thought I should give it a whirl. Have you heard it? So I was like, Yeah, do I look nine years old to you? And he didn't know what to say to that. He took the headphones off and pressed a button on the machine.

And Cindy said, It's Paul's dog that the girls are playing with. And I was like, Yeah, so? But I didn't say that.

Cindy told him that we were friends of Martin's, and he asked whether she wanted him to leave, and she said, No, of course not, whatever they've come to say I want you to hear. So I said, Well, we've come to tell Cindy she should get back with Martin, so you might not want to hear that. And he didn't know what to say to that either.

Maureen looked at me, and then she goes, We're worried about him. And Cindy said, Yes, well, I can't say I'm surprised. And Maureen tells her about the bloke who topped himself, and how it was because of how his wife and kids had left him, and Cindy said, You know Martin left us? We didn't leave him? And I was like, Yeah, that's why we've come. Because if you'd left him, this whole trip would have been a waste of time. But, you know. We've come down here to tell you he's changed his mind, sort of thing. And Maureen said, I think he knows that was a mistake. And Cindy goes, I had no doubt he'd realize it in the long term, and I also had no doubt that by the time he did it would be too late. And I went, It's never too late to learn. And she went, It is for him. And I said I thought she owed him another chance, and she sort of smiled and said she disagreed and I said I disagreed with her disagreeing and she said we must agree to disagree. And I was like, So you want him to die, then?

And she went a bit quiet, and I thought I'd got her. But then she goes, I thought about killing myself, too, when things were really bad, a while ago. But I didn't have the option, be-cause of the girls. And it's indicative of the way things are that he does have the option. He's not part of a family. He hated being part of a family. And that's when I decided it was his business. If he had the freedom to fuck around, then he had the freedom to kill himself, too. Don't you think?

And I went, Well, I can see why you say that. Which was a mistake, because it didn't help my argument.

Cindy said, Did he tell you I wouldn't let him see the girls?

And Maureen said, Yes, he did mention that. And Cindy went, Well, that's not true. I just won't let him see them here. He could take them for weekends in London, but he won't. Or he says he will, but then he makes excuses. He doesn't want to be that sort of dad, you see. It's too much effort. He wants to come home from work, read them a story some nights but not every night, and go to see them in the Christmas play. He doesn't want all the other stuff. And then she was like, I don't know why I'm telling you this.

And I went, He's a bit of a tosser, really, isn't he? And she laughed. He's made a lot of mistakes, she said. And he continues to make them.

And that Paul bloke goes, If he were a computer, you'd have to say that there's a programming fault, so I was like, What's it got to do with you? And Cindy said, Listen, I've been very patient with you up until now. Two strangers knock on my door and tell me to get back together with my ex-husband, a man who nearly destroyed me, and I invite them in and actually listen to them. But Paul is my partner, and part of my family, and a wonderful stepfather to the girls. And that's what it's got to do with him.

And then Paul stood up and said, I think I'll take *Harry Potter* upstairs, and he nearly tripped over my feet, and Cindy dived over and was like, Careful, darling, and then I worked out he was blind. Blind! Fucking hell! That's why he had a dog. That's why she was trying to *tell* me he had a dog (because I was giving it all that stuff like, Do I look nine years old? Oh, God, oh, God). So we'd gone all the way down there to tell Cindy she had to leave a blind man and get back together with a man who shagged fifteen-year-olds and treated her like shit. It shouldn't really have made any difference, though, should it? They're always going on about how they want to be treated the same as everyone else. So I'll leave the blind thing out of it. I'll just say that we went all the way down there to tell Cindy she had to leave an OK bloke who was good to her and her kids, and get back with an arsehole. And that still didn't sound great.

I'll tell you what really got me, though. The only proof that Martin had ever had anything to do with Cindy was us turning up in her house. Us and his kids, anyway, but they would only be proof if you took them for a DNA test and that. Anyway, what I mean is, as far as Cindy was concerned, he might as well have never existed. They'd all moved on. Cindy had a whole new life now. On the way down, I'd been thinking about how I'd moved on, but all I'd done was gone one train ride and one bus journey without asking Maureen about sexual positions. After I'd seen Cindy, that didn't seem like such a long journey. Cindy had got rid of Martin, moved, and met someone else. Her past was in the past, but our past, I don't know . . . Our past was still all over the place. We could see it every day when we woke up. It was like Cindy lived in a modern place like Tokyo and we lived in an old place like Rome or somewhere. Except it couldn't be exactly like that, because Rome is probably a cool place to live, what with the clothes and the ice cream and the lush boys and that—just as cool as Tokyo. And where we lived wasn't cool. So maybe it was more like she lived in a modern penthouse, and we lived in some old shithole that should have been pulled down years ago. We lived in a place where there were holes in the walls, and any-one could stick their head through them if they wanted to, and make faces at us. And Maureen and I had been trying to persuade Cindy to move out of her cool penthouse and move into our dump with us. It wasn't much of an offer, I could see that now.

As we were leaving, Cindy was like, I'd have more respect for him if he asked me himself. And I went, Ask you what? And she said, If I can help him, I will. But I don't know what he wants help with.

And when she said that, I could see we'd done the after-noon all wrong, and there was a much better way.

J J

The only trouble was, the American self-help guy didn't have the first fucking idea of how to help himself. And to be hon-est with you, the more I thought about the ninety-day theory, the less I could see how it applied to me. As far as I could tell, I was fucked for a lot longer than ninety days. I was giving up being a musician forever, man, and giving up music wasn't go-ing to be like giving up cigarettes. It was going to get worse and worse, harder and harder, every day I went without. My first day working at Burger King wouldn't be so bad, because I'd tell myself, you know . . . Actually, I don't know what the fuck I'd tell myself, but I'd think of something. But by the fifth day I'd be miserable, and by the thirtieth *year* . . . Man. Don't try talking to me on my thirtieth anniversary of burger-flipping. I'll be real grouchy that day. And I'll be sixty-one years old.

And then, when this stuff had gone around and around in my head for a while, I'd kind of stand up, mentally speaking, and say, OK, fuck it, I'm going to kill myself. And then I'd remember the guy we saw do exactly that, and I'd sit down again feeling truly terrible, worse than when I'd stood up in the first place. Self-help was a crock of shit. I couldn't help myself to a free drink.

The next time we met up, Jess told us all that she and Maureen had gone to see Cindy out in the countryside.

"My ex-wife was called Cindy," said Martin. He was sipping a latte and reading the *Telegraph*, and not really listening to anything Jess had to say.

"Yeah, that's a coincidence," said Jess.

Martin continued to sip his coffee.

"Der," said Jess.

Martin put the *Telegraph* down and looked at her.

"What?"

"It was your Cindy, you doughnut."

Martin looked at her.

"You've never met my Cindy. Ex—my Cindy. My ex."

"That's what we're saying to you. Maureen and I went down wherever it was to talk to her."

"Torley Heath," said Maureen.

"That's where she lives!" said Martin, scandalized.

Jess sighed.

"You went to see Cindy?"

Jess picked up his *Telegraph* and started leafing through it, kind of a spoof on his previous lack of interest. Martin snatched the paper away from her.

"What the hell did you do that for?"

"We thought it might help."

"How?"

"We went down to ask her whether she'd take you back. But she wouldn't. She's shacked up with this blind geezer. She's well sorted. Isn't she, Maureen?"

Maureen had the good sense to stare at her own shoes.

Martin stared at Jess.

"Are you insane?" he said. "On whose authority did you do that?"

"On whose authority? On my authority. Free country."

"And what would you have done if she'd burst into tears and said, you know, 'I'd love him to come back'?"

"I would have helped you pack. And you'd have fucking well done what we'd told you."

"But—" He made some spluttering noises, and then stopped. "Jesus Christ."

"Anyway, there's no chance of that. She thinks you're a right bastard."

"If you'd ever listened to anything I'd ever said about my ex-wife, you could have saved yourself a trip. You thought she'd take me back? You thought I'd go back?"

Jess shrugged. "It was worth a try."

"You," said Martin. "Maureen. There's nothing on the floor. Look at me. You went with her?"

"It was her idea," said Jess.

"So you're an even bigger fool than she is."

"We all need help," said Maureen. "We don't all know

what we want. You've all helped me. I wanted to help you. And I thought that was the best way."

"How would it work now when it didn't work before?"

Maureen didn't say anything, so I did.

"So which of us wouldn't try to make something work now that didn't work before? Now that we've seen what the alternative is. A big fat fucking nothing."

"So what would you want back, JJ?" Jess asked.

"Everything, man. The band. Lizzie."

"That's stupid. The band was rubbish. Well," she said quickly when she saw my face. "Not rubbish. But not—you know."

I nodded. I knew.

"And Lizzie packed you in."

I knew that, too. What I didn't say, because it sounded too fucking lame, was that if it were possible to rewind, I'd rewind back to the last few weeks of the band, and the last few weeks of Lizzie, even though everything was fucked up. I was still playing music, I was still seeing her—there wasn't anything to complain about, right? OK, everything was dying. But it wasn't dead.

I don't know why, but it was kind of liberating, saying what you really wanted, even if you couldn't have it. When I'd invented that Cosmic Tony guy for Maureen, I'd put limits on his superpowers because I thought we might see what kind of practical assistance Maureen needed. And as it turned out, she needed a vacation, and we could help, so Cosmic Tony turned out to be a guy worth knowing. But if there's no superpower limit, then you get to find out all kinds of other shit, like, I don't know, the thing that's wrong with you in the first place. We all spend so much time not saying what we want,

D
O
W
N

257

because we know we can't have it. And because it sounds ungracious, or ungrateful, or disloyal, or childish, or banal. Or because we're so desperate to pretend that things are OK, really, that confessing to ourselves they're not looks like a bad move. Go on, say what you want. Maybe not out loud, if it's going to get you into trouble: "I wish I'd never married him." "I wish she was still alive." "I wish I'd never had kids with her." "I wish I had a whole shitload of money." "I wish all the Albanians would go back to fucking Albania." Whatever it is, say it to yourself. The truth will set you free. Either that or it'll get you a punch in the nose. Surviving in whatever life you're living means lying, and lying corrodes the soul, so take a break from the lies just for one minute.

"I want my band back," I said. "And my girl. I want my band back and my girl back."

Jess looked at me. "You just said that."

"I haven't said it often enough. I want my band back and my girl back. *I want my band back and my girl back.* What do you want, Martin?"

He stood up. "I want another cappuccino," he said. "Anyone else?"

"Don't be such a pussy. What do you want?"

"And what good will it do me if I tell you?"

"I don't know. Say it, and we'll see what we see."

He shrugged and sat down.

"You got three wishes," I said.

"OK. I wish I'd been able to make my marriage work."

"Yeah, well, that was never going to happen," said Jess. "Because you couldn't keep your prick in your trousers. Sorry, Maureen."

Martin ignored her.

"And of course I wish I'd never slept with that girl."

"Yeah, well . . ." said Jess.

"Shut up," I said.

"I don't know," said Martin. "Maybe I just wish that I wasn't such an arsehole."

"There, now. That wasn't so hard, was it?"

I was joking, kind of, but no one laughed.

"Why don't you just wish that you'd slept with the girl and got away with it?" said Jess. "That's what I'd wish, if I were you. I think you're still lying. You're wishing for stuff that makes you look good."

"That wish wouldn't really solve the problem, though, would it? I'd still be an arsehole. I'd still get caught for something else."

"Well, why not just wish that you never got caught for anything ever? Why not wish that you . . . What's that one with the cake?"

"What are you talking about?"

"Something about eating a cake?"

"Having it and eating it?"

Jess looked kind of doubtful. "Are you sure that's it? How can you eat a cake without having it in the first place?"

"The idea," said Martin, "is that you get it both ways. You eat the cake, but it somehow remains untouched. So 'have' here means 'keep.'"

"That's mental."

"Indeed."

"How could you do that?"

"You can't. Hence the expression."

"And what's the point of the fucking cake? If you're not going to eat it?"

"We're kind of getting off the subject here," I said. "The point is to wish for something that would make us happier. And I can see why Martin wants to be, you know, a different person."

"I wish Jen would come back," said Jess.

"Yeah, well. I can see that. What else?"

"Nothing. That's it."

Martin snorted. "You don't wish you were less of an arsehole?"

"If Jen came back, I wouldn't be."

"Or less mad?"

"I'm not mad. Just, you know. Confused."

There was a thoughtful silence. You could tell that not everyone around the table was convinced.

"So you're just gonna waste two wishes?" I said.

"No. I can use them up. Ummm . . . An everlasting supply of blow, maybe? And, I dunno . . . Oooh, I wouldn't mind being able to play the piano, I suppose."

Martin sighed. "Jesus Christ. That's the only problem you've got? You can't play the piano?"

"If I was less confused, I'd have the time to play the piano."

We left it there.

"How 'bout you, Maureen?"

"I told you before. When you said Cosmic Tony could only arrange things."

"Tell everyone else."

"I wish they could find a way to help Matty."

"You can do better than that, can't you?" said Jess.

We winced.

"How?"

"No, well, see, I was wondering what you'd say. 'Cause you could have wished that he'd been born normal. And then you could have saved yourself all those years of clearing up shit."

Maureen was quiet for a minute.

"Who would I be then?"

"Eh?"

"I don't know who I'd be."

"You'd still be Maureen, you stupid old trout."

"That's not what she means," I said. "She means, like, we are what's happened to us. So if you take away what's happened to us, then, you know . . ."

"No, I don't fucking know," said Jess.

"If Jen hadn't happened to you, and, and all the other things . . ."

"Like Chas and that?"

"Exactly. Events of that magnitude. Well, who would you be?"

"I'd be someone different."

"Exactly."

"That'd be fucking excellent."

We stopped playing the wishing game then.

MARTIN

It was intended to be this enormous gesture, I think, a way of wrapping the whole thing up, as if the whole thing could or would ever be wrapped up. That's the thing with the young these days, isn't it? They watch too many happy endings.

Everything has to be wrapped up, with a smile and a tear and a wave. Everyone has learned, found love, seen the error of their ways, discovered the joys of monogamy, or fatherhood, or filial duty, or life itself. In my day, people got shot at the end of films, after learning only that life is hollow, dismal, brutish, and short.

It was about two or three weeks after the "I wish" conversation in Starbucks. Somehow Jess had managed to keep her trap shut—an impressive achievement for someone whose usual conversation technique is to describe everything as, or even before, it happens, using as many words as possible, like a radio sports commentator. Looking back on it, it is true that she had occasionally given the game away—or would have done, if any of us had known there was a game.

One afternoon, when Maureen said that she had to get back to see Matty, Jess stifled a giggle and observed enigmatically that she'd see him soon enough.

Maureen looked at her.

"I'll be seeing him in twenty minutes if I'm lucky with the bus," she said.

"Yeah, but after that," said Jess.

"Soon enough but after that?" I said.

"Yeah."

"I see him most minutes of every day," said Maureen.

And we forgot all about it, just as we forgot all about so much that Jess said.

Perhaps a week later, she started to show a hitherto concealed interest in Lizzie, JJ's ex-girlfriend.

"Where does Lizzie live?" she asked JJ.

"King's Cross. And before you say anything, no, she isn't a hooker."

"What is she, a hooker? Ha-ha. Just messing around."

"Yeah. Totally excellent joke."

"So where is there to live in King's Cross, then? If you're not a hooker."

JJ rolled his eyes. "I'm not telling you where she lives, Jess. You think I'm some kinda sucker?"

"I don't want to talk to her. Stupid old slapper."

"Why is she a slapper, precisely?" I asked her. "As far as we are aware, she has slept with only one man in her entire life."

"What's that word again? The prick one? Sorry, Maureen."

"'Metaphorically,'" I said. When someone uses the phrase "the prick one," and you know immediately that this is a synonym for the word "metaphorically," you are entitled to wonder whether you know the speaker too well. You are even entitled to wonder whether you should know her at all.

"Exactly. She's a metaphorical slapper. She dumped JJ and probably went out with someone else."

"Yeah, I dunno," said JJ. "I'm not sure that dumping me condemns a person to eternal celibacy."

And thus we moved on, to a discussion about the appropriate punishment for our exes, whether death was too good for them, and so on, and the Lizzie moment passed, like so many moments in those days, without us noticing. But it was in there, if we'd wanted to rootle around in the rubbish-strewn teenaged bedroom of Jess's mind.

On the big day itself, I had lunch with Theo, my agent— although of course while I was having lunch with Theo, I had no idea that it was going to be a big day. Having lunch with Theo was momentous enough. I hadn't spoken to him face-to-face since I'd come out of prison.

He wanted to talk to me because he'd had, he said, a "substantial" offer from a reputable publisher for an autobiography.

"How much?"

"They're not talking money yet."

"May I ask, then, in what way it could be described as 'substantial'?"

"Well. You know. It has substance."

"What does that mean?"

"It's real, not imaginary."

"And what does 'real' mean, in real terms? Really?"

"You're becoming very difficult, Martin. If you don't mind me saying so. You're not my easiest client at the best of times, what with one thing and another. And I've actually been working quite hard on this project."

I was momentarily distracted by the realization that there was straw underneath my feet. We were eating in a restaurant called Farm, and everything we were eating came from a farm. Brilliant, eh? Meat! Potatoes! Green salad! What a concept! I suppose they needed the straw, without which their theme would have begun to look a little short on inspiration. I would like to report that the waitresses were all jolly and large and red-cheeked and wearing aprons, but of course they were surly, thin, pale, and dressed in black.

"But what did you have to do, Theo? If, as you say, someone phoned up and offered for my autobiography, in some kind of indescribably substantial way?"

"Well, I phoned them up and suggested they might want it."

"Right. And they seemed interested?"

"They phoned back."

"With a substantial offer."

Theo smiled condescendingly.

"You don't really know much about the publishing world, do you?"

"Not really. Only what you've told me over this lunch. Which is that people have been phoning up with substantial offers. That's why we're here, apparently."

"We mustn't run before we can walk."

Theo was beginning to annoy me.

"OK. Agreed. Just tell me the walking part."

"No, you see . . . even the walking part is running. It's more, you know, *tactical* than that."

"Asking you to tell me about walking is running?"

"Softly, softly, catchee monkey."

"Jesus Christ, Theo."

"And that sort of reaction isn't softly, softly, if I may say so. That's noisy, noisy. Tetchy, tetchy, even."

I never heard any more about the offer, and I have never been able to work out the point of the lunch.

Jess had called an extraordinary meeting for four o'clock, in the vast and invariably empty basement of the Starbucks in Upper Street, one of those rooms with a lot of sofas and tables that would feel exactly like your living room, if your living room had no windows, and you only ever drank out of paper cups that you never threw away.

"Why in the basement?" I asked her when she phoned me.

"Because I've got private things to talk about."

"What sort of private things?"

"Sexual things."

"Oh, God. The others are going to be there, aren't they?"

"You think I've got private sexual things I only want to tell you?"

"I was hoping not."

"Yeah, like I have fantasies about you all the time."

"I'll see you later, OK?"

I got a number 19 bus from the West End to Upper Street, because the money had finally run out. We'd got through the bits and pieces of money we'd picked up from chat-show appearances and junior ministers, and I had no job. So even though Jess once explained that cabs are the cheapest form of transport, because they will take you wherever you want to go for free, and it's not until you get there that money is needed, I decided that inflicting my poverty on a cabbie was not such a good idea. In any case, the cabbie and I would almost certainly spend the journey talking about the unfairness of my incarceration, perfectly normal thing to want to do, her fault for going out looking like that, and so on. I have preferred minicab drivers for some time now, because they are as ignorant of London's inhabitants as they are of its geography. I got recognized twice on the bus, once by someone who wanted to read me a relevant and apparently redemptive passage in the Bible.

As I approached Starbucks, a youngish couple walked in just ahead of me, and immediately went downstairs. Initially I was pleased, of course, because it meant that Jess's sexual revelations would have to be conducted sotto voce, if at all; but then as I was queuing for my chai tea latte, I realized that this meant no such thing, given Jess's immunity to embarrassment; and my stomach started to do what it has done ever since I turned forty. It doesn't *churn*, that's for sure. Old stomachs don't *churn*. It's more as if one side of the stomach wall is a tongue, and the other side a battery. And at moments of tension the two sides touch, with disastrous consequences.

The first person I saw at the bottom of the stairs was Matty, in his wheelchair. He was flanked by two burly male nurses, who I presumed must have carried him down, one of whom was talking to Maureen. And as I was trying to work out what had brought Matty to Starbucks, two small blonde girls came belting toward me shouting, "Daddy! Daddy!" and even then I did not instantaneously realize that they were my daughters. I picked them up, held them, tried not to weep, and looked around the room. Penny was there, smiling at me, and Cindy was at a table in the far corner, not smiling at me. JJ had his arms around the couple who'd walked in ahead of me, and Jess was standing with her father and a woman whom I presumed to be her mother—she was unmistakably the wife of a Labour junior minister. She was tall, expensively dressed, and disfigured by a hideous smile that clearly bore no relation to anything she might be feeling, a real election night of a smile. Round her wrist there was one of those bits of red string that Madonna wears, so despite all appearances to the contrary, she was obviously a deeply spiritual woman. Given Jess's flair for the melodramatic, I wouldn't have been alto-gether surprised to see her sister, but I checked carefully, and she wasn't there. Jess was wearing a skirt and a jacket, and for once, you had to get up quite close to become scared by her eye makeup.

I put the girls down and led them over to their mother. I waved to Penny on the way, though, just so that she wouldn't feel left out.

"Hello." I leaned down to kiss Cindy on the cheek, and she moved smartly out of the way.

"What brings you here, then?" I said.

"The mad girl there seemed to think it might help in some way."

"Oh. Did she explain how?"

Cindy snorted. I got the feeling that she was going to snort whatever I said, that snorting was going to be her preferred method of communication, so I knelt down to talk to the children.

Jess clapped her hands together and stepped into the center of the room.

"I read about this on the Internet," she said. "It's called an intervention. They do it all the time in America."

"All the time," JJ shouted. "It's all we do."

"See, if someone is fucked . . . messed up on drugs or drink or whatever, then the, like, friends and family and whatever all gather together and confront him and go, you know, Fucking pack it in. Sorry, Maureen. Sorry, Mum and Dad. Sorry, little girls. This one's sort of different. In America, they have a skilled . . . Oh, shit, I've forgotten the name. On the Web site I was on he was called Steve."

She fumbled in the pocket of her jacket and pulled out a piece of paper.

"A facilitator. You're supposed to have a skilled facilitator, and we haven't got one. I didn't know who to ask, really. I don't know anyone with skills. Also, this intervention is sort of the other way round. Because we're asking you to intervene. It's us coming to you, rather than you coming to us. We're saying to you, We need your help."

The two nurses who'd come with Matty started to look a little uncomfortable at this point, and Jess noticed.

"Not you guys," she said. "You don't have to do anything. To tell you the truth, you're only really here to bump up Maureen's numbers, 'cause, well, I mean, she hasn't really got anybody, has she? And I thought you two and Matty would be better than nobody, see? It would have been a bit grim for you, Maureen, seeing all these reunions and standing there on your own."

You had to hand it to Jess. Once she got a theme between her teeth, she was unwilling to let it go. Maureen attempted a grateful smile.

"Anyway. Just so's you know who's who. In the JJ corner we have his ex, Lizzie, and his mate Ed, who used to be in his crappy band with him. Ed's flown over from America special. I've got my mum and dad, and it's not often you'll catch them in the same room together, ha-ha. Martin's got his ex-wife, his daughters, and his ex-girlfriend. Or maybe not ex-, who knows? By the end of this he might have his wife back *and* his girlfriend back."

Everyone laughed, looked at Cindy, and then stopped laughing when they realized that laughing would have consequences.

"And Maureen's got her son, Matty, there, and the two guys from the care home. So here's my idea: We spend some time talking to our people, have a little catch-up. And then we swap round, and go and talk to some other person's people. So it's a cross between the American thing and a school parents' evening, 'cause the friends and family sort of sit in a corner, waiting for people to visit them."

"Why?" I said. "What for?"

"I don't know. Whatever. Just for a laugh. And we'll learn things, won't we? About each other? And about ourselves?"

There she went again, with her happy endings. It was true that I had learned things about the others, but I had learned absolutely nothing that wasn't factual. So I could tell Ed the name of the band that he used to play in, and I could tell the Crichtons the name of their missing daughter; it seemed to me unlikely that they would find this in any way useful or even comforting, however.

And anyway, what does or can one ever learn, apart from times tables, and the name of the Spanish prime minister? I hope that I've learned not to sleep with fifteen-year-olds, but I learned that a long time ago—decades before I actually slept with a fifteen-year-old. The problem there was simply that she told me she was sixteen. So, have I learned not to sleep with sixteen-year-olds, or attractive young women? No. And yet just about everyone I've ever interviewed has told me that by doing something or other—recovering from cancer, climbing a mountain, playing the part of a serial killer in a movie—they have learned something about themselves. And I always nod and smile thoughtfully, when really I want to pin them down: What *did* you learn from the cancer, actually? That you don't like being sick? That you don't want to die? That wigs make your scalp itch? Come on, be specific. I suspect it's something they tell themselves in order to turn the experience into something that might appear valuable, rather than a complete and utter waste of time.

In the last few months, I have been to prison, lost every last molecule of self-respect, become estranged from my children, and thought very seriously about killing myself. I mean, that little lot has got to be the psychological equivalent of cancer, right? And it's certainly a bigger deal than acting in a bloody film. So how come I've learned absolutely bugger all? What was I supposed to learn? True, I have discovered that I was quite attached to my self-esteem, and regret its passing. Also, I've found out that prison and poverty aren't really *me*. But, you know, I could have had a wild stab in the dark about both of those things beforehand. Call me literal-minded, but I suspect people might learn more about themselves if they didn't get cancer. They'd have more time, and a lot more energy.

"So," Jess went on. "Who's going to go where?"

At that moment, several French teenage punks appeared in our midst, carrying coffee mugs. They headed for an empty table next to Matty's wheelchair.

"Oi," said Jess. "Where do you think you're going? Upstairs, all of you."

They stared at her.

"Come on, we haven't got all day. Hup, hup, hup. *Schnell. Plus vitement.*" She shooed them toward the stairs, and away they went, uncomplainingly; Jess was just another incomprehensible and aggressive native of an incomprehensible and aggressive country. I sat down at my ex-wife's table, and waved toward Penny again. It was a sort of all-purpose crowded-party gesture, some kind of cross between "I'm just getting a drink" and "I'll give you a ring," with maybe a little bit of "Can we have the bill, please?" thrown in. Penny nodded, as if she understood. And then, equally inappropriately, I rubbed my hands together, as if I were relishing the prospect of all the delicious and nutritious self-knowledge I was about to tuck into.

MAUREEN

I didn't think there was going to be very much for me to say. I mean, there wasn't really anything I could say to Matty. But I didn't think I'd find anything to say to the two lads from the respite home, either. I asked them if they wanted a cup of tea, but they didn't; and then I asked whether it had been hard getting Matty down the stairs, and they said it wasn't, with the two of them there. And I said I couldn't have got him down there if there were ten of me, and they laughed, and then we stood there looking at each other.

And then the short one, the one who came from Australia and was shaped like the toy robot that Matty used to have, with a square head and a square body, asked what the little gathering was all about. It hadn't occurred to me that they wouldn't know.

"I've been trying to work it out, but I'm clueless."

"Yes," I said. "Well. It must be very confusing."

"So come on, then. Put us out of our misery. Steve here reckons you've all got money troubles."

"Some of us have. I haven't."

I've never had to worry about money, really. I get my carer's allowance, and I live in my mother's house, and she left me a little bit anyway. And if you never go anywhere or do anything, life is cheap.

"But you've got troubles," said the square one.

"Yes, we've got troubles," I said. "But they're all different troubles."

"Yeah, well, I know he's got troubles," said the other one, Stephen. "The guy off of the TV."

"Yes, he's got troubles," I said.

"So how do you know him? I can't imagine you go to the same nightclubs."

And I ended up telling them everything. I didn't mean to. It just sort of came out. And once I'd started, it didn't seem to matter much what I'd told them. And then, when I got to the end of the story, I realized I shouldn't have said anything, even though they were nice about it, and said how sorry they were, and that kind of thing.

"You won't tell them back at the center, will you?" I said.

"Why would we tell them?"

"Because if they found out that I'd been planning to leave Matty with them forever, they might refuse to take him again. They might think that whenever I called for you to take him, I was thinking of jumping off a roof somewhere."

So we made a deal. They gave me the name of another center in the area, a private one that they said was nicer than theirs, and I promised that if I was going to do away with myself, I'd call that one.

"It's not that we don't want to know," said the square one,

Sean. "And it's not that we don't want our center to be stuck with Matty. It's just that we don't want to feel that every time you call us up, you're in trouble."

I don't know why, but this made me feel happy. Two men I didn't really know had told me not to call them if I was feeling suicidal, and I felt like hugging them. I didn't want people feeling sorry for me, you see. I wanted them to help, even if helping meant saying that they wouldn't help, if that doesn't sound too Irish. And the funny thing was that this was what Jess was after when she arranged the get-together. And she didn't expect me to get anywhere, and she'd only asked the two young fellas along because Matty couldn't have got here without them, and in five minutes they'd made me feel better about something.

Stephen and Sean and I watched the others for a few moments, to see how they were getting on. JJ was doing the best, because he and his friends hadn't really started fighting yet. Martin and his ex-wife were watching in silence as their daughters drew a picture, and Jess and her parents were shouting. Which might have been a good sign, if they were shouting about the right things, but every now and again you could hear Jess yelling the loudest about something or other, and it never seemed to be anything that would help. For example, "I never touched any stupid bloody earrings!" Everyone in the room heard that, and Martin and JJ and I looked at each other. None of us knew the situation with these earrings, so we didn't want to judge, but it was hard to imagine that earrings were the root of Jess's problems.

I felt sorry for Penny, who was still sitting on her own, so I went over and asked her if she wanted to come to my corner.

"I'm sure you've got plenty to talk about over there," she said.

"No," I said. "We're done, really."

"Well, you've got the best-looking chap in the place," she said. She was talking about Stephen, the tall nurse, and when I looked at him from the other side of the room, I could see what she meant. He was blond, with long, thick hair, and bright blue eyes, and he had a smile that warmed the room. It was sad that I hadn't noticed, but I don't really think about things like that anymore.

"So come on over and talk to him. He'd be pleased to meet you," I said. I didn't know for sure that he would be, but if you've got nothing to do but stand beside a boy in a wheel-chair, then I'd have thought you'd be happy enough to meet a pretty woman who appears on the television. And I can't take much credit for it, because I didn't really do anything, apart from say what I said; but it was funny that so much happened because Penny walked across a coffee bar to talk to Stephen.

JESS

Everyone seemed to be having an OK time except for me. I had a shit time. And that wasn't fair, because I'd spent ages organizing that intervention parents' evening thing. I'd gone on the Internet and got hold of the e-mail address of the bloke who used to manage JJ's band. And he gave me Ed's phone number, and I stayed up until, like, three in the morning so I could ring him when he got home from work. And when I told him how messed up JJ was, he said he'd come over, and then he phoned Lizzie and told her, and she was up for it, too. And there was all sorts with Cindy and her kids, and it was like a fucking full-time job for a week, and what did I get out of it? Fuck all. Why did I think that talking to my fucking father and my fucking mother would be any fucking use at all? I talk to them every fucking day, and nothing ever changes. So what did I think would make a difference? Having Matty and Penny and all them around? Being in Starbucks? I suppose I'd hoped that they might listen, especially when I'd announced that we'd all got together because we needed their help; but when Mum brought up that thing about the earrings, I knew I might as well have dragged someone in off of the street and asked them to adopt me or whatever.

We're never going to forget about the earrings. We'll be talking about them on her deathbed. They're almost like her way of swearing. When I'm angry with her, I say "fuck" a lot, and when she's angry with me she says "earrings" a lot. They weren't her earrings anyway; they were Jen's, and like I told her, I never touched them. She has this thing that all through those horrible first few weeks, when all we did was sit by the phone and wait for the police to tell us they'd found her body, the earrings were on Jen's bedside table. Mum reckons she went and sat on the bed every night, and that she has, like, this photographic memory of the things she saw every night, and she can still see the earrings now, next to an empty coffee cup and some paperback or other. And then, when we started to sort of drift back to work and school and a normal life, or as close to a normal life as we've ever had since, the earrings disappeared. So of course I must have taken them, because I'm always thieving. And I am, I admit it. But what I thieve mostly is money, off of them. Those earrings were Jen's, not theirs, and anyway she bought them at Camden Market for, like, five quid.

I don't know this for sure, and I'm not being all self-pitiful or whatever. But parents must have favorite kids, right? How could they not? How could, like, Mr. and Mrs. Minogue not prefer Kylie to the other one? Jen never thieved off of them; she read books all the time, did well at school, talked to Dad about shuffling and all those political things, never puked on the floor in front of the treasury minister or whatever. Take the puking, just for instance. It was a bad falafel, right? I'd bunked off of school, and we'd had maybe two spliffs and a couple of Breezers, so it wasn't what you'd call a mental afternoon. I really hadn't been giving it large. And then I ate this falafel just before I went home. Well, I could feel the falafel coming up again as I was turning the key in the front door, so I knew that was what had made me sick. And I had no chance of getting to the toilet, right? And Dad was in the kitchen with the treasury bloke, and I tried to make the sink, and I didn't. Falafel and Breezers everywhere. Would I have thrown up without the falafel? No. Did he believe it was anything to do with the falafel? No. Would they have believed Jen? Yes, just because she didn't drink or smoke blow. I don't know. This is what happens—falafels and earrings. Everyone knows how to talk, and no one knows what to say.

After we'd gone over the earring thing again, my mum goes, What do you want? So I was like, Don't you listen to anything, and she went, Which bit was I supposed to be listening to? And I was like, In my speech or whatever I said we needed your help, and she goes, Well, what does that mean? What are we supposed to do that we don't do?

And I didn't know. They feed me and clothe me and give me booze money and educate me and all that. When I talk they listen. I just thought that if I told them they had to help me, they'd help me. I never realized there was nothing I could say, and nothing they could say, and nothing they could do.

So that moment, when Mum asked me how they could help, it was sort of like the moment the guy jumped off the roof. I mean, it wasn't as horrible or as scary and no one died and we were indoors, et cetera. But you know how you keep things tucked up in the back of your head in a sort of rainy-day box? For example, you think, One day, if I can't handle it anymore, then I'll top myself. One day, if I'm really fucking up badly, then I'll just give up and ask Mum and Dad to bail me out. Anyway, the mental rainy-day box was empty now, and the joke was that there had never been anything in it all the time.

So, I did what I normally do in these situations. I told my mum to fuck off and I told my dad to fuck off and then I left, even though I was supposed to be talking to someone else's friends and family afterward. And then when I got up to the top of the stairs, I felt stupid, but it was too late to go back down again, so I just walked straight out the door and down Upper Street and into the Angel underground and I got on the first train that came. No one chased after me.

JJ

The minute I saw Ed and Lizzie down in that basement, I felt this uncontrollable little flicker of hope. Like, this is it! They've come to rescue me! The rest of the band are setting up for a gig tonight, and then afterward Lizzie and I are going back to this cute apartment that she's rented for the two of us! That's what she's been doing all this time! Apartment hunting and decorating! And . . . who's that old guy talking to Jess? Could he be a record company executive? Has Ed fixed us up with a new deal? No, he hasn't. The old guy is Jess's dad, and later I found out that Lizzie had a new boyfriend, someone with a house in Hampstead and his own graphic design company.

I snapped out of it pretty quick. There was no excitement in their faces, or in their voices, so I knew that they didn't have any news for me, any grand announcement about my future. I could see love there, and concern, and it made me feel a little teary, to tell you the truth; I hugged them for a long time so that they couldn't see me being a wuss. But they'd come to a Starbucks basement because they'd been told to come to a Starbucks basement, and neither of them had any idea why.

"What's up, man?" said Ed. "I heard you weren't doing so good."

"Yeah, well," I said. "Something will turn up." I wanted to say something about that Micawber dude in Dickens, but I didn't want Eddie to get on my case even before we'd talked.

"Nothing's gonna turn up here," he said. "You gotta come home."

I didn't want to have to go into the whole ninety-day thing, so I changed the subject.

"Look at you," I said. He was wearing, like, a suede jacket, which looked like it had cost a lot of money, and a pair of white corduroys, and though his hair was still long, it looked kind of healthy and glossy. He looked like one of those ass-holes that date the girls in *Sex and the City.*

"I never really wanted to look like I used to look. I looked like that because I was broke. And we never stayed anywhere with a decent shower."

Lizzie smiled politely. It was hard, with the two of them there—like your first and your second wives coming to see you in the hospital.

"I never pegged you for a quitter," Ed said.

"Hey, be careful what you say. This is the Quitters' Club HQ."

"Yeah. But from what I hear, the rest of them had good reasons. What have you got? You got nothing, man."

"Yup. That's pretty much how it feels."

"That wasn't what I meant."

"Anyone want a coffee?" said Lizzie.

I didn't want her to go.

"I'll come with you," I said.

"We'll all go," said Ed. So we all went, and Lizzie and I

kept not talking, and Ed kept talking, and it felt like the last couple years of my life, condensed into a line for a latte.

"For people like us, rock 'n' roll is like college," said Ed after we'd ordered. "We're working-class guys. We don't get to fuck around like frat boys unless we join a band. We get a few years, then the band starts to suck, and the road starts to suck, and having no money really starts to suck. So you get a job. That's life, man."

"So, the point when everything starts to suck . . . That's like our college degree. Our graduation."

"Exactly."

"So when's it all going to start sucking for Dylan? Or Springsteen?"

"Probably when they're staying in a motel that doesn't allow them to use hot water until six p.m."

It was true that on our last tour we stayed in a motel like that in South Carolina. But I remember the show, which smoked; Ed remembers the showers, which didn't.

"Anyway, I knew Springsteen. Or at least, I saw him live on the E Street reunion tour. And, Senator JJ, you're no Springsteen."

"Thanks, pal."

"Shit, JJ. What do you want me to say? OK, you are Springsteen. You're one of the most successful performers in music business history. You were on the cover of *Time* and *Newsweek* in the same week. You fill stadiums night after fucking night. There. You feel better now? Jeez. Grow up, man."

"Oh, what, and you're all grown up because your old man took pity on you and gave you a job hooking people up with illegal cable TV?"

Ed's ears get red when he's about to start throwing

punches. This information is probably of no use to anyone in the world apart from me, because, for obvious reasons, he doesn't tend to form real deep attachments to people he's punched, so they never learn the ear thing—they don't seem to stick around long enough. I'm probably the only one who knows when to duck.

"Your ears are getting red," I said.

"Fuck you."

"You flew all this way to tell me that?"

"Fuck you."

"Stop it, the pair of you," said Lizzie. I couldn't say for sure, but I seem to remember that last time the three of us were together she said the same thing.

The guy making our coffee was watching us carefully. I knew him, to say hello to, and he was OK; he was a student, and we'd talked about music a couple times. He liked the White Stripes a lot, and I'd been trying to get him to listen to Muddy Waters and the Wolf. We were freaking him out a little.

"Listen," I said to Ed. "I come here a lot. You wanna kick my ass, then let's go outside."

"Thanks," said the White Stripes guy. "I mean, you know. You'd be welcome if there wasn't anyone else here, because you're a regular, and we like to look after our regulars. But . . ." He gestured at the line behind us.

"No, no, I understand, man," I said. "Thanks."

"Shall I leave your coffees on the counter here?"

"Sure. It won't take long. He usually calms down after he's landed a good one."

"Fuck you."

So we all went out onto the street. It was cold and dark and wet, but Ed's ears were like two little torches in the gloom.

MARTIN

I hadn't seen or spoken to Penny since the morning our brush with the angel had been in the papers. I had thought fondly of her, but I hadn't really missed her, either sexually or socially. My libido was on leave of absence (and one had to be prepared for the possibility that it might opt for early retirement and never return to its place of work); my social life consisted of JJ, Maureen, and Jess, which might suggest that it was as sickly as my sex drive, not least because they seemed to suffice for the time being. And yet when I saw Penny flirt with one of Matty's nurses, I felt uncontrollably angry.

This isn't a paradox, if you know anything about the perversity of human nature. (I believe I have used that line before, and as a consequence it is probably beginning to seem a little less authoritative and psychologically astute. Next time, I shall just own up to the perversity and the inconsistency, and leave human nature out of it.) Jealousy is likely to seize a man at any time, and in any case the blond nurse was tall, and young, and tanned, and blond. There is every chance that he would have made me uncontrollably angry if he had been standing on his own in the basement of Starbucks, or indeed anywhere in London.

I was, in retrospect, almost certainly looking for an excuse to leave the bosom of my family. As suspected, I had learned very little about myself in the previous few minutes. Neither my ex-wife's scorn nor my daughters' crayons had been as instructive as Jess might have wished.

"Thanks," I said to Penny.

"Oh, that's OK. I wasn't doing anything, and Jess seemed to think it might help."

"No," I said, immediately at something of a moral disadvantage. "Not thanks for that. Thanks for standing here flirting in front of me. Thanks for nothing, in other words."

"This is Stephen," Penny said. "He's looking after Matty, and he didn't have anyone to talk to, so I came over to say hello."

"Hi," said Stephen. I glared at him.

"I suppose you think you're pretty great," I said.

"I'm sorry?" he said.

"Martin!" said Penny.

"You heard me," I said. "Smug git."

I had the feeling that over in the corner, where the girls were coloring their picture, there was another Martin—a kinder, gentler Martin—watching in appalled fascination, and I wondered briefly whether it was possible to rejoin him.

"Go away, before you make an idiot of yourself," said Penny. It says a lot for Penny's generosity of spirit that she still saw idiocy coming toward me from off in the distance, and that I still had a chance of getting out of the way; less partial observers would have argued that idiocy had already squashed me flat. It didn't matter, though, because I wasn't moving.

"It's easy, being a male nurse, isn't it?"

"Not very," said Stephen. He had made the elementary mistake of answering my question as if it had been delivered straight, without bile. "I mean, it's rewarding, sure, but . . . long hours, poor pay, night shifts. Some of the patients are difficult." He shrugged.

"Some of the patients are difficult," I said, in a stupid, whiny voice. "Poor pay. Night shifts. Diddums."

"Sean," Stephen said to his partner. "I'm going to wait upstairs. This guy's throwing the rattle out of the pram."

"You just wait and listen to what I have to say. I did you the courtesy of listening to you banging on about what a national hero you are. Now you listen to me."

I don't think he minded staying where he was for a couple of minutes. This kind of sensationally bad behavior elicited a great deal of fascination, I could see that, and I hope I don't seem immodest when I say that my celebrity, or what remained of it, was crucial to the success of the spectacle: Usually, television personalities only behave badly in nightclubs, when surrounded by other television personalities, so my decision to cut loose, when sober, to a male nurse, in a Starbucks basement, was bold—possibly even groundbreaking. And it wasn't as if Stephen could really take it personally, just as he couldn't have taken it personally if I'd decided to crap on his shoes. The outward manifestations of an inner combustion are never very directed.

"I hate people like you," I said. "You wheel a disabled kid around for a bit and you want a medal. And how hard is it, really?"

At this point, I regret to say, I took the handles of Matty's wheelchair and pushed him up and down. And it suddenly seemed like an excellent idea to put my hand on my hip while

I was doing it, in order to suggest that pushing disabled people around in their wheelchairs was an effeminate activity.

"Look at Daddy, Mummy," one of my daughters (and I'm sorry to say that I don't know which one) yelled with delight. "He's funny, isn't he?"

"There," I said to Penny. "How's that? Do I look more attractive to you again now?"

Penny was staring at me as if I were indeed crapping on Stephen's shoes—a look that answered the question.

"Hey, everybody," I yelled, although I had already attracted all the attention I could possibly wish for. "Aren't I great? Aren't I great? You think this is hard, Blondie? I'll tell you what's hard, Sunny Jim. Hard is . . ."

But here I dried up. As it turned out, there were no examples of difficulty in my professional life readily to hand. And the difficulties I had experienced recently all stemmed from sleeping with an underage girl, which meant that they weren't much good for eliciting sympathy.

"Hard is when . . ." I just needed something with which to finish the sentence. Anything would do, even something I hadn't experienced directly. Childbirth? Tournament-level chess? But nothing came.

"Have you finished, mate?" Stephen asked.

I nodded, trying somehow to convey in the gesture that I was too angry and disgusted to continue. And then I took the only option apparently available to me, and followed Jess and JJ out the door.

MAUREEN

Jess was always walking out of everywhere, so I didn't mind her going too much. But when JJ walked out, and then Martin . . . Well, I started to feel a bit annoyed, to tell you the honest truth. It seemed rude, when everyone had gone to all that trouble to turn up. And Martin was so peculiar, pushing Matty up and down and asking everyone if he looked attractive. Why would anyone think he looked attractive? He didn't look attractive at all. He looked mad. To be fair to JJ, he'd taken his guests with him when he went—he hadn't left them behind in the coffee bar, the way Jess and Martin had done. But later on I found out that he'd taken them all outside to have a fight with them, so it was difficult to decide whether he was being rude or not. On the one hand, he was with them, but on the other hand, he was with them because he wanted to beat them up. I think that's probably still rude, but not as rude as the others.

The people left behind stood around for a little while—the nurses and Jess's parents and Martin's friends and family—

and then when we all began to realize that no one was coming back, not even JJ and his friends, no one was quite sure what to do.

"Is that it, do you think?" said Jess's father. "I mean, I don't want to . . . I don't wish to appear unsympathetic. And I know Jess took a lot of trouble organizing this. But, well, there's no one really left, is there? Would you like us to stay, Maureen? Is there anything we can usefully achieve as a unit? Because obviously, if there were . . . I mean, what do you think Jess was hoping for? Perhaps we can help her to achieve it in absentia?"

I knew what Jess was hoping for. She was hoping that her mum and dad would come and make everything better, in the way mums and dads are supposed to. I used to have that dream, a long time ago, when I was first on my own with Matty, and I think it's a dream that everyone has. Everyone whose life has gone badly wrong, anyway.

So I told Jess's father that I thought Jess just wanted people to understand better, and that I was sorry if that wasn't what had happened.

"It's those bloody earrings," he said, and so I asked about the earrings, and he told me the story.

"Were they special to her?" I said.

"To Jen? Or to Jess?"

"To Jen."

"I don't really know," he said.

"They were her favorites," said Mrs. Crichton. She had a strange face. She smiled the whole time we were speaking, but it was as though she'd only discovered smiling that afternoon—she didn't have the sort of face that looked as though it were very used to being cheerful. The lines she had were the sort you'd get from being angry about stolen earrings, and her mouth was very thin and tight.

"She came back for them," I said. I don't know why I said it, and I don't know if it was true or not. But it felt like the right thing to say. It felt true in that way.

"Who did?" she said. Her face looked different now. It was having to do things it wasn't used to doing, because she suddenly looked so desperate to hear what I had to say. I don't think she was used to listening properly. I liked making her face do something new, and that was why I went on, partly. I felt like I was in charge of a lawn mower, cutting a path into places where the grass was overgrown.

"Jen. If she loved her earrings, then she probably came back for them. You know what girls of that age are like."

"God," said Mr. Crichton. "I'd never thought of that."

"Me neither," Mrs. Crichton said. "But . . . that makes so much sense. Because, do you remember, Chris? That's when we lost a couple of other things, too. That was when that money went missing."

I didn't have the same feeling about the money. I could see that there might have been another explanation for that.

"And I said at the time that I thought there were a couple of books gone, do you remember? And we know Jess didn't take those."

And they both laughed then, as if they liked Jess, and liked it that she'd rather jump off a tower block than read a book.

I could see and feel why it would make a difference to them, this idea that Jen had come into the house for her earrings. It would mean that she had disappeared—gone to Texas or Scotland or Notting Hill Gate—rather than that she'd been killed, or she'd killed herself. It meant that they could think about where she was, imagine her life now. They could wonder about whether she'd had a baby that they'd never seen and might never see, or got a job that they'd never hear about. It meant that in their heads they could carry on being ordinary parents. It's what I was doing, when I bought Matty his posters and his tapes—I was being an ordinary mother in my head, just for a moment.

You could wreck it all for them in a second, if you chose to, rip enormous great big holes in the story, because what did it add up to, really? Jen could have come back because she wanted to die wearing her earrings. She might not have come back at all. And she was still gone, whether she came back for five minutes or not. Oh, but I know what you need to keep yourself going. That probably sounds funny, considering why we were all there in that coffee bar in the first place. But the fact is that so far I have kept myself going, even if I had to climb the stairs to the roof of Toppers' House to do it. Sometimes you just need to give things a tiny little jiggle. You just need to think that perhaps someone might have helped themselves to their own earrings, and your part of the world looks like somewhere you could live in for a while.

That was Mr. and Mrs. Crichton, though, not Jess. Jess didn't know anything about the earring theory, and Jess was the one who needed her world to look different. She was the one who'd been up on the roof with me. Mr. and Mrs. Crichton had their jobs and their friends and all the rest of it, so you could say that they didn't need any stories about earrings. You could say that stories about earrings were wasted on them.

You could say all that, but it wouldn't be true. They needed the stories—you could see it in their faces. I only know one person in the world who doesn't need stories to keep himself going, and that person is Matty. (And maybe even he does. I don't know what goes on in there. Keep talking to him, they say, so I do, and who knows whether he uses something I say?) And there are other ways of dying, without killing yourself. You can let parts of yourself die. Jess's mother had let her face die, and I watched it come to life again.

JESS

The first train that came along was southbound, and I got off at London Bridge and went for a walk. If you'd seen me leaning on the wall and looking down at the water, you'd have gone, Oh, she's thinking, but I wasn't. I mean, there were words in my head, but just because there are words in your head it doesn't mean you're thinking, just like if you've got a pocket full of pennies it doesn't mean you're rich. The words in my head were, like, "bollocks," "bastard," "bitch," "shit," "fuck," "wanker," and they were spinning round in there pretty fast, too fast even for me to make a sentence out of them. And that's not really thought, is it?

So I watched the water for a little while, and then I went to a stall by the bridge and bought some tobacco and papers and matches. Then I went back to where I'd been standing, and sat down to roll myself a few smokes, for something to do, sort of thing. I don't know why I don't smoke more, to be honest. I forget, I think. If someone like me forgets to smoke, what chance has smoking got? Look at me. You'd bet any money that I smoked like fuck, and I don't. New Year's resolution: Smoke more. It's got to be better for you than jumping off of tower blocks.

Anyway, so there I was, sitting down with my back against the wall, rolling up roll-ups, when I saw this lecturer from college. He's like an old bloke, one of those art-school people who've been knocking around since the '60s. He teaches typography and that, and I went to a couple of his classes until I got bored. I don't mind him, Colin. He doesn't have a gray ponytail and he doesn't wear a faded denim jacket. And he never wanted to be our friend, which must mean that he has his own friends. You couldn't say that about some of them.

To tell this story truthfully, I should probably say that he saw me before I saw him, because when I looked up from my rolling, he was walking over to me. And to be really properly truthful, I should also say that some of the thinking I was doing, in other words the mental swearing, probably wasn't entirely mental, if you see what I mean. It was meant to be mental, but some of it was coming out through my mouth, just because there was so much of it. It was sort of slopping out of me, as if the swearing was coming out of a tap and running into a bucket (= my head), and I hadn't bothered turning the tap off even when the bucket was full.

That's what it looked like from my point of view. From his point of view, it looked like I was sitting on the pavement rolling up fags and swearing to myself, and that's not such a good look, is it? He kind of came up to me, and then he crouched down so he was at my height, and then he started talking to me quietly. And he was like, Jess? Do you remember me?

I'd only seen him, like, two months before, so of course I

remembered him. And I went, No, and laughed, which was supposed to be a joke but which couldn't have come across as a joke, because then he goes, still in this whispery voice, I'm Colin Wearing, and I used to teach you at art college. And I go, Yeah, yeah, and he goes, No, I am, and then I see that he thought my Yeah, yeah was like Yeah, right, but it wasn't that sort of Yeah, yeah. All I was doing with the two yeahs was try-ing to tell him that I'd only been joking before, but I only made it worse. I made it look like I thought he was pretending to be Colin Wearing, which would be an utterly insane thing to do. So the whole conversation is going right off course. It's like a supermarket trolley with a wonky wheel, because all the time I'm thinking, This should be easy to push along, and everything I say just takes me in the wrong direction.

And he goes, Why are you here, sitting on the path? And I tell him that I'd had a row with my fucking mother about some earrings, and he was like, And now you can't go home? And I said that I could if I wanted to. I could just get on the Northern Line back to Angel and then jump on a bus. But I didn't want to. And he went, Well, I don't think you should sit here. Is there anywhere you can go? And then I realized that he thought I had turned into, like, a nutter, so I stood up quickly, which made him jump, and I gave him a mouthful and walked away.

But then I did think, as opposed to swear mentally. And the first thing I thought was that it would be very easy for me to be a nutter. I'm not saying it would be a piece of piss, living that life—I don't mean that. I just mean that I had a lot in common with some of the people you see sitting on pavements swearing and rolling cigarettes. Some of them seemed to hate people, and I hated just about everyone. They must have pissed off their friends and family, and I'd pretty much done that. And who knows whether Jen's a nutter now. Maybe it runs in the genes, although with my dad being a junior education minister, maybe it's one of those things that skips a generation.

And I didn't know where all this thinking was leading to, but I could see suddenly that I was in more trouble than I had thought. I know that sounds stupid, considering I'd thought about killing myself, but that was all just for a laugh, and if I'd jumped it would have been for a laugh, too. What if I had a future on this planet, though? What then? How many people could I piss off, and how many places could I run away from, before I found myself sitting by the river and swearing externally 4 real? Not many more, was the answer.

So the thing to do was to go back—to Starbucks, or home, to somewhere—anywhere that wasn't forward. If you're walking somewhere, and you come up against a brick wall, then you have to retrace your steps.

But then I sort of found a way of climbing over the wall. Or I found a little hole in the wall I could crawl through, or whatever. I met this geezer with a really nice dog, and I went and slept with him instead.

J J

So I just stood there on the sidewalk and told Ed to take a swing at me if it would make him feel any better.

"I don't want to hit you unless you hit me," he said.

There was a guy selling that homeless magazine standing watching us.

"Hit him," he said to me.

"You shut the fuck up," said Ed.

"I was only trying to get things started," said the homeless guy.

"You flew across the bloody Atlantic because JJ was in trouble," Lizzie said to Ed. "And now look at you. One conversation and you want to punch him."

"Things have to go the way they have to go," said Ed.

"Is that like 'A man's gotta do what a man's gotta do'? Because it sounds utterly meaningless to me, I'm afraid," said Lizzie. She was leaning against the window of a thrift shop, making out like she was bored, but I knew she wasn't. She was angry, too, but she didn't want to show it.

"He's on my side," said Ed. "So it doesn't matter what it sounds like to you. He understands."

"No I don't," I said. "Lizzie's right. Why would you come all this way to punch me?"

"It's a *Butch Cassidy and the Sundance Kid* thing, surely," said Lizzie. "You want to sleep with each other, but you can't, because you're both so straight."

This really tickled the homeless guy. He laughed like a hyena. "Did you ever read Pauline Kael on *Butch Cassidy*? God, she hated it," he said.

Neither Lizzie nor Ed would have had a fucking clue who Pauline Kael was, but I got two or three of her collections. I used to keep them by the toilet, because they're great for dipping into when you're on the can. Anyway, hers wasn't a name I was necessarily expecting to hear from that particular guy at that particular moment. I looked at him.

"Oh, I know who Pauline Kael is," he said. "I wasn't born homeless, you know."

"I really, really don't want to sleep with him," said Ed. "I really want to punch him. But he has to punch me first."

"You see?" said Lizzie. "Homoerotic, with a bit of sado-masochism thrown in. Just kiss him, and be done with it."

"Kiss him," the homeless guy said to Ed. "Kiss him or punch him. But let's get something going, for God's sake."

Ed's ears couldn't have gotten any redder, so I was wondering whether they might just burst into flame and then turn black. At least then I could say that I'd seen something new.

"You trying to get me killed?" I said to her.

"Why don't you just get back together?" said Lizzie. "At least you've got all that mike-sharing and those great big electric penis substitutes."

"Oh, so that's why you didn't want him to be in a band," said Ed. "You were jealous."

"Who said I didn't want him to be in a band?" Lizzie asked him.

"Yeah, you got that dead wrong, Ed," I said. "She wasn't that deep. She dumped me precisely because I wasn't in a band. She wasn't interested in being with me unless I became a rock star and made a shitload of money."

"Is that what you think I meant?" said Lizzie.

I could suddenly see my life being put back together before my eyes. It had all been a terrible misunderstanding, which was now about to be cleared up, with much laughter and many tears. Lizzie never wanted to break up with me. Ed never wanted to break up with me. I'd come out onto the sidewalk to get my ass kicked and, instead, I was going to get everything I ever wanted.

"There isn't going to be a fight, is there?" said the homeless guy sadly.

"Unless we all beat the shit out of you," said Ed.

"Just let me hear the end of this," said the homeless guy. "Don't go back inside. I never get the fucking ending of a story, stuck out here."

It was going to be a happy ending, I could feel it coming. And it was going to involve all four of us. The first show we played when we got back together, we could dedicate a song to Homeless Guy. Hey—he could maybe even be our road manager. Plus, he could make one of the toasts at the wedding. "Everyone should get back with everyone," I said, and I meant it. This was my big closing speech. "Every band that has ever come apart, every couple . . . There's too much unhappiness in the world as it is, without people splitting up every ten seconds."

Ed looked at me as if I had gone nuts.

"You're not serious," said Lizzie.

Maybe I'd misjudged the mood and the moment. The world wasn't ready for my big closing speech.

"Naaah," I said. "Well. You know. It's just . . . an idea I had. A theory I was working on. I hadn't ironed out all the kinks in it yet."

"Look at his face," said Homeless Guy. "Oh, he's serious, all right."

"How does that work with bands that grew out of other bands?" said Ed. "Like, I don't know. If Nirvana got back together. That would mean the Foo Fighters had to split up. Then they'd be unhappy."

"Not all of 'em," I pointed out.

"And what about second marriages? There are loads of happy second marriages."

"There'd have been no Clash. 'Cause Joe Strummer would have had to stay in his first band."

"And who was your first girlfriend?"

"Kathy Gorecki!" said Ed. "Ha!"

"You'd still be with her," said Lizzie.

"Yeah, well." I shrugged. "She was nice. That wouldn't have been a bad life."

"But she never gave nothin' up!" said Ed. "You never even got a hand under a bra!"

"I'm sure I'd have managed by now. We'd have been together fifteen years."

"Oh, man," said Ed, in the tone of voice that we usually used when Maureen had said something heartbreaking. "I can't punch you."

We walked down the road a little ways and went to a pub, and Ed bought me a Guinness, and Lizzie bought a pack of smokes from the machine and put it down on the table for us to share, and we just sat there, with Ed and Lizzie looking at me as if they were waiting for me to catch my breath.

"I didn't realize you felt that bad," Ed said after a while.

"The suicide thing—that wasn't a clue?"

"Yeah. I knew you wanted to kill yourself. But I didn't know you felt so bad that you wanted to patch things up with Lizzie and the band. That's this whole different level of misery, way beyond suicide."

Lizzie tried not to laugh, and the effort produced a weird snorting noise, and I took a long pull on my Guinness.

And suddenly, just for a moment, I felt good. It helped that I really love cold Guinness; it helped that I really love Ed and Lizzie. Or I used to love them, or kind of love them, or loved and hated them, or whatever. And maybe for the first time in the last few months, I acknowledged something properly, something I knew had been hiding right down in my guts, or at the back of my head—somewhere I could ignore it anyway. And what I owned up to was this: I had wanted to kill myself, not because I hated living, but because I loved it. And the truth of the matter is, I think, that a lot of people who think about killing themselves feel the same way—I think that's how Maureen and Jess and Martin feel. They love life, but it's all fucked up for them, and that's why I met them, and that's why we're all still around. We were up on the roof because we couldn't find a way back into life, and being shut out of it like that . . . It just fucking destroys you, man. So it's like an act of despair, not an act of nihilism. It's a mercy killing, not a murder. I don't know why it suddenly got to me. Maybe because I was in a pub with people I loved, drinking a Guinness, and I know I said this before, but I fucking love Guinness, like I love pretty much all alcohol— love it as it should be loved, as one of the glories of God's creation. And we'd had this stupid scene on the street, and even that was kind of cool, because sometimes it's moments like that, real complicated moments, *absorbing* moments, that make you realize that even hard times have things in them that make you feel alive. And then there's music, and girls, and drugs, and homeless people who've read Pauline Kael, and wah-wah pedals, and English potato chip flavors, and I haven't even read *Martin Chuzzlewit* yet, and . . . There's plenty out there.

And I don't know what difference it made, this sudden flash. It wasn't like I wanted to, you know, grab life in a passionate embrace and vow never to let it go until it let go of me. In a way, it makes things worse, not better. Once you stop pretending that everything's shitty and you can't wait to get out of it, which is the story I'd been telling myself for a while, then it gets more painful, not less. Telling yourself life is shit is like an anesthetic, and when you stop taking the Advil, then you really can tell how much it hurts, and where, and it's not like that kind of pain does anyone a whole lot of good.

And it was kind of appropriate that I was with my ex-lover and my ex-brother at the precise moment I realized, because it was the same kind of thing. I loved them, and would always love them. But there was no place where they could fit anymore, so I had nowhere to put all the things I felt. I didn't know what to do with them, and they didn't know what to do with me, and isn't that just like life?

"I never said anything about finishing with you because you weren't going to be a rock star," said Lizzie after a while. "You know that really, don't you?"

I shook my head. I didn't know, did I? You guys can back me up on that. Not once in this story have I ever owned up to any kind of misunderstanding, deliberate or otherwise. So far as I was concerned, she was dumping me because I was a musical loser.

"So what did you say, then? Try again. And I'll listen real hard this time."

"It's not going to make any difference now, because we've all moved on, right?"

"Kind of." I wasn't going to admit to standing still, or going backward.

"OK. What I said was, I couldn't be with you if you weren't a musician."

"It wasn't such a big deal to you at the time. You don't even like music that much."

"You're not hearing me, JJ. You're a musician. It's not just what you did. It's who you are. And I'm not saying you're going to be a successful musician. I don't even know if you're a good one. It was just that I could see you'd be no use to anyone if you stopped. And look what happened. You break the band up, and five minutes later you're standing on the top of a tower block. You're stuck with it. And without it you're dead. Or you might as well be."

"So . . . OK. Nothing to do with being unsuccessful."

"God, what do you take me for?"

But I wasn't talking about her; I was talking about me. I never looked at it that way before. I thought this whole thing had been about my failure, but that wasn't it. And at that moment I felt like crying my fucking heart out, really. I felt like crying because I knew she was right, and sometimes the truth gets you like that. I felt like crying because I was going to make music again, and I'd missed it so much. And I felt like crying because I knew that making music was never going to make me successful, so Lizzie had just condemned me to another thirty-five years of poverty, rootlessness, despair, no health plan, cold-water motels, and bad hamburgers. It's just that I'd be eating the burgers, not flipping them.

MARTIN

I walked home, turned the phone off, and spent the next forty-eight hours with the curtains drawn, drinking, sleeping, and watching as many programs about antiques as I could find.

During those forty-eight hours, I would say that I was in grave danger of turning into Marie Prevost, the Hollywood actress who was discovered sometime after her death in a state of disrepair, due to her corpse having been partially eaten by her dachshund. That I had no dachshund, or indeed any domestic pet, I can remember being a source of some consolation in those couple of days. I would certainly die alone, and my corpse would certainly be in a state of advanced decay by the time anyone found me, but I would be complete, apart from the bits that had dropped off through natural causes. So that was all right.

Here's the thing: The cause of my problems is located in my head, if my head is where my personality is located. (Cindy and others would argue that both my personality and the source of my troubles were located below, rather than above, my waist, but hear me out.) I had been given many opportunities in life, and I had thrown each of them away, one by one, through a series of catastrophically bad decisions, each one of which seemed like a good idea to me—to me and my head—at the time. And yet the only tool I had at my disposal to correct the disastrous course my life seemed to be taking was the very same head that had caused me to fuck up in the first place. What chance did I have?

A couple of weeks after Jess's *Jerry Springer* show, I read some notes I'd made during that two-day period. It wouldn't be true to say that I'd been so drunk I'd forgotten I'd ever made them, and in any case they'd been lying around the flat in plain view. But it was a fortnight before I possessed enough courage to read them, and once I'd done so, I was almost compelled to draw the curtains and reach for the Glenmorangie once again.

The object of the exercise was to analyze, with the only

head I have available to me, why I had behaved so absurdly that afternoon, and to list all possible responses to that behavior. To give my head its due—to be fair to the lad, as sports pundits would say—it was at least capable of recognizing that the behavior had been absurd. It just wasn't capable of doing very much about it. Are all heads like this, or is it just mine?

Anyway, on the backs of several unopened envelopes, mostly bills, there was depressingly conclusive evidence of the circularity of human behavior.

WHY HORRIBLE TO NURSE? I had written. And then, underneath:

(1)   Arsehole? Him? Me?

(2)   Hitting on Penny?

(3)   Good-looking and young—Pissed me off?

(4)   Annoyed by people. (This last explanation, which may have meant something brilliantly precise when I hit on it, now seemed startlingly candid in its vagueness.)

On another envelope, I had scrawled COURSES OF ACTION (and please note, by the way, the switch from numbers to letters, a switch presumably meant to indicate the scientific nature of the work):

(a)   Kill myself?

(b)   Ask Maureen not to use that nurse anymore

(c)   Don't

And "C" stopped there, either because I fell into a stupor at that point, or because "Don't" was a concise way of expressing a profound solution to all my problems. Think about it: How much better things would be for me if I didn't, wouldn't, and never had.

Neither envelope inspired much confidence in my powers of cogitation. I could see that they had both been written by the man who had recently wanted to tell a select group of people—a group that included his own young daughters—that all male nurses were effeminate and self-righteous: The word "arsehole" would surely provide a forensic psychologist with all the evidence required for that deduction. And similarly, the man who had spent some of New Year's Eve trying to work out whether to jump from the roof of a tower block was exactly the sort of man who might jot down "Kill myself?" in a "Things to Do" list. If thinking inside the box were an Olympic sport, I would have won more gold medals than Carl Lewis.

Quite clearly, I needed two heads, two heads being better than one and all that. One would have to be the old one, just because the old one knows people's names and phone numbers, and which breakfast cereal I prefer, and so on; the second one would be able to observe and interpret the behavior of the first, in the manner of a television wildlife expert. Asking the head I have now to explain its own thinking is as pointless as dialing your own telephone number on your own telephone: Either way, you get an engaged signal. Or your own answer message, if you have that kind of phone system.

It took me an embarrassing amount of time to realize that other people have heads, and that any one of these heads would do a better job of explaining what the purpose of my explosion might have been. This, I supposed, was why people persisted with the whole notion of friends. I seemed to have lost all mine around the time I went to prison, but I knew plenty of people who'd be prepared to tell me what they thought of me. In fact, it seemed that my propensity for letting people down and alienating them would actually serve me in good stead here. Friends and lovers might try to throw a kindly light on the episode, but because I had only ex-friends and ex-lovers, I was ideally placed. I only really knew people who would give it to me with both barrels.

I knew where to start, too. Indeed, so successful was my first phone call that I didn't really need to speak to anyone else. My ex-wife was perfect—direct, articulate, and clear-sighted—and I actually ended up feeling sorry for people living with someone who loved them, when not living with someone who loathed you was so obviously the way to go. When you have a Cindy in your life, there aren't even any pleasantries to wade through: There are only unpleasantries, and unpleasantries are an essential part of the learning process.

"Where have you been?"

"At home. Drunk."

"Have you listened to your messages?"

"No. Why?"

"Oh, I just left you a few thoughts about the other afternoon."

"Ah, now, you see, that's exactly what I wanted to talk about. What do you think it was all about?"

"Well, you're unbalanced, aren't you? Unbalanced and poisonous. An unbalanced, poisonous tosser."

This was a good start, I felt, but it lacked focus.

"Listen, I appreciate what you're saying, and I don't want to appear rude, but the 'unbalanced tosser' part I find less interesting than the 'poisonous' part. Could you talk more about that?"

"Maybe you should pay someone to do this," said Cindy.

"You mean a therapist?"

She snorted. "A therapist? No, I was thinking more of one of those women who will pee all over you if you pay her enough. Isn't that what you want?"

I thought about this. I didn't want to dismiss anything out of hand.

"I don't think so," I said. "It's never appealed before."

"I was speaking metaphorically."

"I'm sorry. I don't really understand."

"You clearly feel so awful about yourself that you don't mind being abused. Isn't that their problem?"

"Whose problem?"

"These men who need women to . . . Never mind."

I was dimly beginning to perceive what she was driving at. It was true that being called names felt good. Or rather, it felt appropriate.

"You know why you turned on that poor guy, don't you?"

"No! You see, that's precisely why I called you."

If Cindy had known how much damage she could have done by stopping right there, the temptation would have been too much for her. Luckily, though, Cindy was determined to go all the way.

"I mean, he was fifteen years younger than you, and much better-looking. But it wasn't that. He'd done more with his life that afternoon than you've ever done with yours."

Yes! Yes!

"You ponce around on television and screw schoolgirls, and he pushes disabled kids around in a wheelchair, probably for the minimum wage. It's no wonder Penny wanted to chat him up. For her, it was the moral equivalent of going from Frankenstein's monster to Brad Pitt."

"Thank you. That's great."

"Don't you dare put the phone down on me. I've only just started. I've got twelve years' worth of this stuff."

"Oh, I'll be back for more, I promise. But that's plenty to be going on with."

You see? Ex-wives: Really, everybody should have at least one.

MAUREEN

I feel a bit daft explaining what happened at the end of the intervention day, because it all sounds like too much of a coincidence. But I think it probably only sounds like a coincidence to me. I know I said before that I'm learning to feel the weight of things, which means learning what to say and what not to say in case you make people feel badly for you. So if I say that nothing happened in my life before I met the others, I don't want to make it sound as though I'm grumbling. It was just how things were. If you spend all your time in a very quiet room and someone comes up behind you and says "Boo!" you jump. If you spend all your time with short people, and you see a six-foot-tall policeman, he looks like a

DOWN

giant. And if nothing happens and then something happens, then the something seems to be peculiar, almost like an act of God. The nothingness stretches the something, the happening, out of shape.

Here's what happened. Stephen and Sean helped me get Matty home. We hailed a black cab, and the four of us just about squashed in, although the two nurses and I were pressed up against each other in the seat. And even that seemed like something. A few months ago, I'd have gone home and told Matty about that, if he hadn't been there with me. But of course if he hadn't been there with me, there'd have been nothing to tell. I wouldn't have needed Stephen and Sean, and we wouldn't have been there in a taxi. I'd have been on a bus, on my own, even supposing I'd gone anywhere. You see what I mean about something and nothing?

Once we were all settled, Stephen said to Sean, Have you got anyone else yet? And Sean said, No, and I don't think I'm going to be able to. And Stephen said, It's just the three of us, then? We'll get slaughtered. And Sean just shrugged, and we all sat looking out of the window for a little while. I didn't know what they'd been talking about.

And then Sean said, Any good at quizzes, Maureen? Fancy joining our team? It doesn't matter if you don't know anything. We're desperate.

Now, that's not the most amazing story you've ever heard, is it? I listen to Jess and JJ and Martin, and that sort of thing happens to them all the time. They meet someone in a lift or a bar, and that someone says, Would you like a drink? or even, Would you like intercourse? And perhaps they'd been thinking that they'd like intercourse, so it could seem to them that be-

A
L
O
N
G
W
A
Y

308

ing offered intercourse, just when they'd been thinking they might like it, is the most amazing coincidence. But my impression is that this isn't how they think, or how many people think. It's just life. One person bumps into another person, and that person wants something, or knows someone else who wants something, and as a result, things happen. Or, to put it another way, if you don't go out, and never meet anyone, then nothing happens. How could it? But for a moment, I could hardly talk. I'd wanted to take part in a quiz, and these people needed someone for their quiz team, and I felt a shiver go down my spine.

So instead of going home, we took Matty to the respite home. Sean and Stephen weren't working, but they were friends with all the people who were, so they just told their friends that Matty was staying there for the evening, and no one turned a hair. We arranged to meet in the pub where they do their quizzing, and I went home to get changed.

I don't know which part of the story to tell you about next. There's another coincidence involved, so I don't know whether to put it here, in the coincidences section, or later on, after I've told you about the quiz. Maybe if I separate the coincidences out, push them further apart, you might believe them more. On the other hand, I don't care whether you believe them, because they're true. And in any case, I still can't decide whether they are coincidences or not, these things: Perhaps getting something you want is never a coincidence. If you want a cheese sandwich and you get a cheese sandwich, that can't be a coincidence, can it? And by the same token, if you want a job and you get a job, that can't be a coincidence either. These things can only be coincidental if you think you have no power over your life at all. So I'll tell you here: The other person on the team was an older man called Jack, who has a newsagent's just off Archway, and he offered me a job.

It's not much of a job—three mornings a week. And it doesn't pay very well—£4.75 an hour. And he told me I'd be on probation at first. But he's getting on a bit, and he wants to go back to bed at nine, after he's opened the shop and sorted the papers and dealt with the early-morning rush. He offered me the job in the same way that Stephen and Sean had asked me whether I wanted to join the quiz team—as a joke, out of desperation. In between the TV round and the sport round, he asked me what I did, and I told him I didn't do anything much apart from look after Matty, and then he said, You don't want a job, do you? And the shiver went back up my spine.

We didn't win the quiz. We came fourth out of eleven teams, but the boys were quite pleased with that. And I knew some things that they didn't know. I knew that the name of Mary Tyler Moore's boss was Lou Grant, for example. I knew that John Major's son married Emma Noble, and I knew that Catherine Cookson had written about Tilly Trotter and Mary Ann Shaughnessy. So there were three points they wouldn't have got, right there, which might be why they said I could come again. The fourth chap is unreliable, apparently, because he's just got a girlfriend. I told them I was the most reliable person they could possibly hope to meet.

A couple of months ago, I read a library book about a girl who found herself falling in love with her long-lost brother. But of course it turned out he wasn't her long-lost brother after all, and he'd only told her that because he liked the look of her. Also it turned out that he wasn't poor. He was very rich.

And on top of that, they found out that the bone marrow of his dog matched the bone marrow of her dog, who had leukemia, so his dog saved the life of her dog.

It wasn't as good as I'm making it sound, to tell you the truth. It was a bit soppy. But the point I'm trying to make is that I'm worried I'm starting to sound like that book, what with the job, and the quiz team. And if I'm starting to sound like that to you, then I'd like to point out two things. Firstly I'd like to point out that getting care for Matty costs more than £4.75 an hour, so I'm not even as well off as I was, and a story that ends with you not as well off as you were isn't really a fairy story, is it? Secondly I'd like to point out that the fourth chap in the quiz team will turn up sometimes, so I won't be in every week.

I was drinking gin and bitter lemons in the pub, and the others wouldn't even let me buy a round; they said I was a ringer, and had to be paid for. Maybe it was the drink that left me feeling so positive, but at the end of the evening, I knew that when we met again on March 31, I wouldn't be wanting to throw myself off the roof, not for a while. And that feeling, the feeling that I could cope for now . . . I wanted to hang on to that for as long as possible. It's going all right so far.

The morning after the quiz, I went back to the church. I hadn't been to any church since we were on holiday, and I hadn't been to mine for weeks and weeks—ever since I met the others on the roof. But I could go back now because I didn't think I'd be committing the sin of despair for a while, so I could go back and ask for God's forgiveness. He can only help you if you've stopped despairing, which if you think about it . . . Well, it's not my business to think about it.

It was a quiet Friday morning, and there was hardly anybody

in. The old Italian woman who never misses a Mass was there, and there were a couple of African ladies I'd never seen before. There were no men, and there were no young people. I was nervous before I went to the confessional, but it was fine, really. I told the truth about how long it had been since my last confession, and I confessed to the sin of despair, and I was given fifteen decades of the Rosary, which I thought seemed on the steep side, even for the sin of despair, but I won't complain. Sometimes you can forget that God is infinite in His mercy. He wouldn't have been infinite if I'd jumped, mind you, but I hadn't.

And then Father Anthony said, Can we help you with anything? Can we ease your burden in any way? Because you must remember that you're part of a community here at the church, Maureen.

And I said, Thank you, Father, but I have friends who are helping. I didn't tell him what sort of community these friends belonged to, though. I didn't tell him that they were all despairing sinners.

Do you remember Psalm 50? *Call upon me in the day of trouble: I will deliver you, and you shall glorify me.* I went to Toppers' House because I had called and called and called, and there was no delivery, and my days of trouble seemed to have lasted too long, and showed no signs of ending. But He did hear me, in the end, and He sent me Martin and JJ and Jess, and then He sent me Stephen and Sean and the quiz, and then He sent me Jack and the newsagent's. In other words, He proved to me that He was listening. How could I have carried on doubting Him, with all that evidence? So I'd better glorify Him, as best I can.

JESS

So this bloke with the dog didn't have a name. I mean, he must have had one at some stage, but he told me he didn't use it anymore, because he didn't agree with names. He reckoned they stopped you from being whoever you wanted to be, and once he'd explained it to me, I could sort of see what he meant. Say you're Tony, or Joanna. Well, you were Tony or Joanna yesterday, and you'll be Tony or Joanna tomorrow. So you're fucked, really. People will always be able to say things like Oh, that's so typical of Joanna. But this geezer, he could be like a hundred different people all in one day. He told me to call him whatever came into my head, so at first he was Dog, because of the dog, and then he was Nodog, because we went for a drink in a pub and he left the dog outside. So he'd had two completely different personalities in the first hour we spent together, because Dog and Nodog are sort of opposite types, aren't they? Bloke with dog is different from bloke with no dog. Bloke with dog has a different image from bloke in pub. And you can't say, Oh, that's so typical of Nodog to let his dog shit in someone's garden. It wouldn't make sense, would it? How can Nodog have a dog that shits in someone's garden, or any dog at all, come to that? And his point is, we can all be Dogs and Nodogs in a single day. Dad, for example, could be Notdad when he's at work, because when he's at work he's not Dad. I know this is all pretty deep, but if you think about it hard, it makes sense.

And in that same day he was Flower, because he picked me a flower when we were walking through the little park down near Southwark Bridge, and then Ashtray, because he tasted like one, and Flower is the opposite of Ashtray, too. You see how it works? Human beings are millions of things in one day, and his method understands that much better than, like, the Western way of thinking about it. I only called him one more name after that, and it was dirty, so that one will have to be a secret. When I say it was dirty, I mean it will sound dirty to you out of context, sort of thing. It's only really dirty if you don't respect the male body, and that in my opinion would make you dirty, not us.

So this bloke . . . Actually, I can see one advantage to the Western way of thinking, which is that if someone has a name, you know what to call them, don't you? It's only one small advantage, and there are millions of big disadvantages, including the biggest one of all, which is that names are really fascist and don't allow us to express ourselves as human beings, and turn us into one thing. But as I'm talking about him a lot here, I think I'll call him just one name. Nodog will do, because it's more unusual, and you'll know who I'm talking about, and it's better than Dog, because you might think I'm talking about a fucking dog, which I'm not.

So Nodog took me back to his place after we'd gone for a

drink. I didn't think he'd have a place, to be honest, what with the dog and everything. He looked like the sort of bloke who might be in between places, but I obviously met him at a good time. It wasn't a normal sort of a place, though. He lived in a shop round the back of Rotherhithe station. It wasn't a converted shop, either—it was just a shop, although it didn't sell anything anymore. It used to be, like, an old-fashioned corner shop thingy, so there were shelves and counters, and there was a big shop window, which he kept covered with a sheet. Nodog's dog had his own bedroom at the back, which must have been a stockroom once upon a time. Shops are actually quite comfortable, if you can put up with a bit of discomfort. You can put your clothes up on the shelves, put your telly up on the counter where the cash register would have gone, put your mattress on the floor, and you're away. And shops have toilets and water, although they don't have baths or showers.

When we got there, we had sex straight off, to get it out of the way. I'd only had proper full-on sex with Chas before, and that wasn't any good, but it was all right with Nodog. A lot more things worked, if you know what I mean, because with Chas, his bits didn't really work and my bits didn't really work, so it was all a bit of an effort. Anyway, this time around, Nodog's bits worked fine, and so mine did, too, and it was much easier to see why anyone would want to do it again. People go on about the first time being important, but it's the second time that really matters. Or the second person, anyway.

Look at what a fool I was the first time, all cut up and sobbing and obsessed. See, if I'd been like that a second time, I'd have known I was going to have problems. But I really didn't

D

O

W

N

315

care if I saw Nodog again or not, so that's got to be progress, right? That's much more the way things should be, if you're going to get on in life.

After we'd finished, he turned his little black-and-white TV on, and we lay on his mattress watching whatever, and then we started to talk, and I ended up telling him about Jen, and Toppers' House, and the others. And he wasn't surprised, or sympathetic, or anything like that. He just nodded, and then he goes, Oh, I'm always trying to top myself. And I was like, Well, you can't be much good at it, and he went, That's not the idea, though, is it? And I was like, Isn't it? And he said that the idea was to, like, constantly offer yourself up to the gods of Life and Death, who were pagan gods, so they were nothing to do with church. And if the god of Life wanted you, then you lived, and if the god of Death wanted you, you didn't. So he reckoned that on New Year's Eve I'd been chosen by the god of Life, and that's why I never jumped. And I was like, I never jumped because people sat on my head, and he explained that the god of Life was speaking through those people, and that made perfect sense to me. Because why else would they have bothered, unless they were, like, being guided by invisible forces? And then he told me that people who were brain-dead, like George Bush and Tony Blair, and the people who judged *Pop Idol*, never offered themselves up to the gods of Life and Death at all, and therefore could never prove that they had the right to live, and we shouldn't obey their laws or recognize their decisions (like the *Pop Idol* judges). So we don't have to bomb countries if they tell us to, and if they say that Fat Michelle or whoever has won *Pop Idol*, we don't have to listen to them. We can just say, No she didn't.

And everything he said was so true that it sort of made me

regret the last few weeks, because even though JJ and Maureen and Martin had been nice to me, sort of, you wouldn't really describe them as brainy, would you? It's not like they had any answers, in the way Nodog had answers. But the other way of looking at it is that without the others, I'd never have met Nodog, because I wouldn't have bothered with the intervention, and there'd have been nothing to walk out of.

And I suppose that's the god of Life talking, too, if you think about it.

When I went home, Mum and Dad wanted to speak to me. And at first I was like, Whatever, but they were really keen, and Mum made me a cup of tea, and sat me down at the kitchen table, and then she said that she wanted to apologize to me about the earrings, and that she knew who'd pinched them. So I went, Who? And she goes, Jen. And I stared at her. And she was like, Yeah, really. Jen. So I said, So how does that work? And she went off on one about how Maureen had pointed out something that was actually blindingly obvious, if you thought about it. They were Jen's favorite earrings, and if they'd gone and nothing else had, then that couldn't be a coincidence. And at first I couldn't see what difference it made, because Jen still wasn't around. But when I saw what difference it made to her, how much calmer it made her, I didn't care why. The main thing was, she wanted to be nicer to me.

And I was even more grateful to Nodog then. Because he had taught me this deep, clear way of thinking, the way that allowed me to see things as they really were. So even though Mum wasn't seeing things the way they really were, and she didn't know that, for example, the *Pop Idol* judges couldn't prove they had the right to live, she was seeing something that could work for her and stop her from being such a bitch.

And now because of Nodog's teachings, I had, like, the wiseness to accept it, and not tell her it was stupid or pointless.

MARTIN

Who, you might want to ask, would call their child Pacino? Pacino's parents, Harry and Marcia Cox, that's who.

"May I ask how you got your name?" I asked Pacino when I first made his acquaintance.

He looked at me, baffled, although I should point out that just about any question baffled Pacino. He was large and buck-toothed, and he had a squint, so his lack of intelligence was particularly unfortunate. If anyone ever needed the compensation of charisma and good looks, it was Pacino.

"Howjer mean?"

"Where did your name come from?"

"Where did it come from?"

The idea that names came from anywhere was clearly a new one to him; I might as well have asked him where his toes came from.

"There's a famous film actor called Pacino."

He looked at me.

"Is there?"

"You hadn't heard of him?"

"Nope."

"So you don't think you were named after him?"

"Dunno."

"You never asked?"

"Nope. I don't ask about no one's name."

"Right."

"Where chorname come from?"

"Martin?"

"Yeah."

"Where did it come from?"

"Yeah."

I gaped at him for a moment. I was at a loss. Apart from the obvious answer—that it had come from my parents, just as "Pacino" had come from his (although even this piece of information might have amazed him)—I could only have told him that mine was French in origin, just as his was Italian. As a consequence, I would have found it hard to articulate why his name was comical and mine was not.

"See? It's a hard question. Don't mean I'm thick, just because I can't answer it."

"No. Of course not."

"Otherwise you're thick, too."

This was not a possibility that I felt I could rule out altogether. I was beginning to feel thick, for all sorts of reasons.

Pacino was a year eight pupil at a comprehensive school in my neighborhood, and I was supposed to be helping him with his reading. I had volunteered to do so after my conversation with Cindy, and after seeing a small advertisement in the local newspaper: Pacino was my first stop on the road toward self-respect. It's a long road, I accept that, but I had somehow hoped that Pacino might have been positioned a little further along it. If we agree that self-respect is in, say, Sydney, and I'd begun the journey at Holloway Road tube station, then I'd imagined that Pacino would be my overnight stopover, the place where my plane could refuel. I was realistic enough to see that he wasn't going to get me all the way there, but volunteering to sit down with a stupid and unattractive child for an hour represented several thousand air miles, surely? During our first session, however, as we stumbled over even the simplest words, I realized that he was more like Caledonian Road than Singapore, and it would be another twenty-odd tube stops before I even got to bloody Heathrow.

We began with an appalling book he wanted to read about football, the large-print story of how a girl with one leg overcame her handicap and her teammates' sexism to become the captain of the school team. To be fair to Pacino, once he saw which way the wind was blowing, he was suitably contemptuous.

"She's going to score the winning goal in a big match, innit?" he asked with some disgust.

"I fear that might be the case, yes."

"But she's only got one leg."

"Indeed."

"Plus she's a girl."

"She is, yes."

"What school is this, then?"

"You may well ask."

"I'm asking."

"You want to know the name of the school?"

"Yeah. I want to go up there with my mates and laugh at them for having a girl with one leg in their team."

"I'm not sure it's a real school."

"So it's not even a true story?"

"No."

"I'm not fucking bothering with this, then."

"Good. Go and choose something else."

He snuffled his way back to the library shelves, but could find nothing that might interest him.

"What are you interested in, actually?"

"Nuffink, really."

"Nothing at all?"

"I quite like fruit. My mum says I'm a champion fruit-eater."

"Right. That gives us something to work on."

There were forty-five minutes of our hour remaining.

So what would you do? How does one begin to like oneself enough to want to live a little longer? And why didn't my hour with Pacino do the trick? I blamed him, partly. He didn't *want* to learn. And he wasn't the sort of child I'd had in mind, either. I'd hoped for someone who was remarkably intelligent, but disadvantaged by home circumstance, someone who only needed an hour's extra tuition a week to become some kind of working-class prodigy. I wanted my hour a week to make the difference between a future addicted to heroin and a future studying English at Oxford. That was the sort of kid I wanted, and instead they'd given me someone whose chief interest was in eating fruit. I mean, what did he need to read for? There's an international symbol for the gents' toilets, and he could always get his mother to tell him what was on television.

Perhaps that was the point, the sheer grinding uselessness of it. Perhaps if you knew you were doing something so obviously without value, you liked yourself more than someone who was indisputably helping people. Perhaps I'd end up feeling better than the blond nurse, and I could taunt him again, but this time I would have righteousness on my side.

It's a currency like any other, self-worth. You spend years saving up, and you can blow it all in an evening if you so choose. I'd done forty-odd years' worth in the space of a few months, and now I had to save up again. I reckoned that Pacino was worth about ten pence a week, so it would be a while before I could afford another night on the town.

There you are. I can finish that sentence now: "Hard is teaching Pacino to read." Or even, "Hard is trying to rebuild yourself, piece by piece, with no instruction book, and no clue as to where all the important bits are supposed to go."

JJ

Lizzie and Ed bought me a guitar and a harp and a neck rack from one of those cool shops in Denmark Street; and when Ed and I were on the way to Heathrow, he told me he wanted to buy me a plane ticket home.

"I can't go home yet, man."

I was going along to say goodbye, but the tube journey was so fucking long that we ended up talking about something other than which crappy magazine he was going to buy from the bookstall.

"There's nothing here for you. Go home, get a band together."

"I got one here."

"Where?"

"You know. The guys."

"You think of them as a band? Those losers and fucking . . . perverts we met in Starbucks?"

"I been in a band with losers and perverts before."

"Weren't ever no perverts in my band."

"What about Dollar Bill?"

Dollar Bill was our first bass player. He was older than the rest of us, and we'd had to unload him after an incident with the high school janitor's son.

"At least Dollar Bill could fucking play. What can your buddies do?"

"It's not that kind of band."

"It's no kind of band. So, what, this is forever? You got to hang out with those guys until they die?"

"No, man. Just until everyone's OK."

"Until everyone's OK? That girl is deranged. The guy can never hold his head up in public again. And the old woman has a kid who can hardly fucking breathe. So when are they gonna be OK? You'd be better off hoping they all get worse. Then they can jump off the fucking building, and you can come home. That's the only happy ending for you."

"What about you?"

"What the fuck's any of this got to do with me?"

"What's your happy ending going to be?"

"What are you talking about?"

"I want to know what kind of happy ending is available to the rest of the population. Tell me what the gap is. 'Cause Martin and Maureen and Jess are all fucked, but you . . . you got a job hooking people up with cable TV. Where you going with that?"

"I'm going where I'm going."

"Yeah. Tell me where that is."

"Fuck you, man."

"I'm just trying to make a point."

"Yeah. I get it. I got as good a shot at a happy ending as your friends. Thanks. Do you mind if I wait until I get home before I shoot myself? Or you want me to do it here?"

"Hey, I didn't mean that."

But I did, I guess. When you get yourself in that place, the place I was in on New Year's Eve, you think people who aren't up on the roof are a million miles away, all the way across the ocean, but they're not. There is no ocean. Pretty much all of them are on dry land, in touching distance. I'm not trying to say that's how close happiness is, if we could only see it, or some bullshit like that. I'm not telling you that suicidal people aren't so far away from people who can get by; I'm telling you that people who get by aren't so far away from being suicidal. Maybe I shouldn't find that as comforting as I do.

We were coming up to the end of our ninety days, and I guess Martin's suicidologist guy knew what he was talking about. Things had changed. They hadn't changed very quickly, and they hadn't changed very dramatically, and maybe we hadn't even done much to make them change. And in my case anyway, they hadn't even changed for the better. I could honestly say that my circumstances and prospects would be even less enviable on March 31 than they had been on New Year's Eve.

"You really going through with this?" Ed asked me when we got to the airport.

"Through with what?"

"I don't know. Life."

"I don't see why not."

"Really? Shit, man. You must be the only one who doesn't. I mean, we'd all understand if you jumped. Seriously. No one would think, you know, What a waste. He threw it all away. 'Cause what are you throwing away? Nothing at all. There's no waste involved."

"Thanks, man."

"You're welcome. I just tell it like I see it."

He was smiling and I was smiling, and we were just talking to each other the way we've always talked to each other about anything that's gone wrong in our lives; it just sounded a little meaner than usual, I guess. Back in the day he'd be telling me that the girl who'd just broken my heart preferred him anyway, or I'd be telling him that the song he'd just spent months working on was a piece of shit, but the stakes were higher now. He was right, though, probably more right than he'd ever been. There would be no waste involved. The trick is to see that you're still entitled to your threescore years and ten anyway.

Busking isn't so bad. OK, it's bad, but it's not terrible. Well, OK, it's terrible, but it's not . . . I'll come back and finish that sentence with something both life-affirming and true another time. First day out it felt fucking great, because I hadn't held a guitar in so long, and second day out was pretty good, too, because the rustiness had gone a little, and I could feel stuff coming back, chords and songs and confidence. After that, I

D

O

W

N

guess it felt like busking, and busking felt better than delivering pizzas.

And people do put money on the blanket. I got about ten pounds for playing "Losing My Religion" to a whole crowd of Spanish kids outside Madame Tussaud's, and only a little less from a bunch of Swedes or whatever the next day ("William, It Was Really Nothing," Tate Modern). If I could only kill this one guy, then busking would be the best job I could hope to find. Or at least, it would be the best job that involved playing guitar on a sidewalk, anyway. This guy calls himself Jerry Lee Pavement, and his thing is that he sets up right next to you, and plays exactly the same song as you, but, like, two bars later. So I start playing "Losing My Religion," and he starts playing "Losing My Religion," and I stop, because it sounds terrible, and then he stops, and then everyone laughs, because it's so fucking funny, ha-ha-ha, and so you move to a different spot, and he moves right along with you. And it doesn't matter what song you play, which I have to admit is kind of impressive. I thought I'd throw him off with "Skyway" by the Replacements, which I worked simply to piss him off, and which maybe nineteen people in the world know, but he had it down. Oh, and everyone throws their coins at him, because he's the genius, obviously, not me. I took a pop at him once, in Leicester Square, and everyone started booing me, because they all love him.

But I guess everyone has someone at work that they don't get along with. And if you're short on walking metaphors for the stupidity and futility of your working life—and I appreciate that not everyone is—then you have to admit that Jerry Lee Pavement is pretty hard to beat.

MAUREEN

We met in the pub opposite Toppers' House for our Ninetieth Day party. The idea was to have a couple of drinks, go up onto the roof, have a little think about everything, and then go off for a curry in the Indian Ocean on Holloway Road. I wasn't sure about the curry part, but the others said they'd choose something that would agree with me.

I didn't want to go up on the roof, though.

"Why not?" said Jess.

"Because people kill themselves up there," I said.

"Der," said Jess.

"Oh, so you enjoyed it on Valentine's Day, did you?" Martin asked her.

"No, I didn't *enjoy* it, exactly. But, you know."

"No, I don't know," said Martin.

"It's all part of life, isn't it?"

"People always say that about unpleasant things. 'Oh, this film shows someone getting his eyes pulled out with a corkscrew. But it's all part of life.' I'll tell you what else is all part of life: going for a crap. No one ever wants to see that, do they? No one ever puts that in a film. Let's go and watch people taking a dump this evening."

"Who'd let us?" said Jess. "People lock the door."

"But you'd watch if they didn't."

"If they didn't, it would be more a part of life, wouldn't it? So, yes, I would."

Martin groaned and rolled his eyes. You'd have thought he'd be much cleverer than Jess, but he never seemed to win an argument with her, and now she'd got him again.

"But the reason people lock the door is, they want privacy," said JJ. "And maybe they want privacy when they're thinking of killing themselves."

"So you're saying we should just let them get on with it?" said Jess. "Because I don't think that's right. Maybe tonight we can stop someone."

"And how does that fit in with your friend's ideas? As far as I understand it, you're now of the opinion that when it comes to suicide you should let the market decide," said Martin.

We'd just been talking about a man without a name called Nodog, who told Jess that thinking about killing yourself was perfectly healthy, and everyone should do it.

"I never said anything about any of that s——."

"I'm sorry. I was paraphrasing. I thought we weren't allowed to interfere."

"No, no. We can interfere. Interfering is part of the process, see? All you have to do is think about it, and after that, whatever. If we stop someone, the gods have spoken."

"And if I were a god," said Martin, "you're exactly the sort of person I'd use as a mouthpiece."

"Are you being dirty?"

"No. I'm being complimentary."

Jess looked pleased.

"So shall we look for someone?" she said.

"How do you look for someone?" JJ asked her.

"There's probably someone in here, for a start."

We looked around the pub. It was just after seven, and there weren't many people in yet. In the corner by the gents', there were a couple of young fellas in suits looking at a mobile phone and laughing. At the table nearest the bar, there were three young women looking at photographs and laughing. At the table next to us there was a young couple laughing about nothing, and sitting at the bar there was a middle-aged guy reading a newspaper.

"Too much laughing," said Jess.

"Anyone who thinks text messages are funny isn't going to kill himself," said JJ. "There isn't enough going on internally."

"I've seen some funny text messages," said Jess.

"Yeah, well," said Martin. "I'm not sure that really disproves JJ's point."

"Shut up," said Jess. "What about the bloke reading the paper? He's on his own. He's probably the best we can do."

JJ and Martin looked at each other and laughed.

"The best we can do?" said Martin. "So what you're saying is that we have to dissuade someone in this room from killing themselves whether they were thinking of it or not?"

"Yeah, well, the laughing cretins aren't going to go up there, are they? He looks more, like, deep."

"He's reading the racing page of the f——ing *Sun*," said Martin. "In a moment his mate's going to turn up, and they'll have fifteen pints and a curry."

"Snob."

"Oh, and who's the one who thinks you have to be deep to kill yourself?"

"We all do," said JJ. "Don't we?"

We had two drinks each. Martin drank large whiskeys with water, JJ drank pints of Guinness, Jess drank Red Bull and vodka, and I drank white wine. I'd probably have been dizzy three months ago, but I seem to drink a lot now, so when we got up to walk across the road, I just felt warm and friendly. The clocks had gone forward on the previous Sunday, and even though it seemed dark when we were down on the street, up on the roof it felt as though there were some light left somewhere in the city. We leaned on the wall, right next to the place where Martin had cut through the wire, and looked south toward the river.

"So," said Jess. "Anyone up for going over?"

No one said anything, because it wasn't a serious question anymore, so we just smiled.

"It's gotta be a good thing, right? That we're still around?" said JJ.

"Der," said Jess.

"No," said JJ. "It wasn't a rhetorical question."

Jess swore at him and asked him what that was supposed to mean.

"I mean, I really do want to know," said JJ. "I really do want to know whether it's . . . I don't know."

"Better that we're here than that we're not?" said Martin.

"Yeah. That. I guess."

"It's better for your kids," said Jess.

"I suppose so," said Martin. "Not that I ever see them."

"It's better for Matty," said JJ, and I didn't say anything, which reminded everyone else that it wasn't really better for Matty at all.

"We've all got loved ones, anyway," said Martin. "And our loved ones would rather we were alive than dead. On balance."

"You reckon?" said Jess.

"Are you asking me whether I think your parents want you to live? Yes, Jess, your parents want you to live."

Jess made a face, as though she didn't believe him.

"How come we didn't think of this before?" said JJ. "On New Year's Eve? I never thought of my parents once."

"Because things were worse then, I suppose," said Martin. "Family's like, I don't know. Gravity. Stronger at some times than others."

"Yup. That's gravity for you. That's why in the morning we can, like, float, and in the evening we can't hardly lift our feet."

"Tides, then. You don't notice the pull when it's . . . Well, anyway. You know what I mean."

"If some guy came up here tonight, what would you tell him?" said JJ.

"I'd tell him about the ninety days," said Jess. "'Cause it's true, isn't it?"

"Yeah," said JJ. "It's true that none of us feel like killing ourselves tonight. But, like . . . if he asked us why? If he said to us, So tell me what great things have happened to you since you decided not to go over the edge? What would you tell him?"

"I'd tell him about my job in the newsagent's," I said. "And the quiz."

The others looked at their feet. Jess thought about saying something, but JJ caught her eye, and she changed her mind.

"Yeah, well, you, you're doing OK," said JJ after a little while. "But I'm f——ing busking, man. Sorry, Maureen."

"And I'm failing to help the dimmest child in the world with his reading," said Martin.

"Don't be so hard on yourself," said Jess. "You're failing at loads of different things. You're failing with your kids, and your relationships—"

"Oh, yes, whereas you, Jess, you're such a f——ing success. You've got it all."

"Sorry, Maureen," said JJ.

"Yes, excuse me, Maureen."

"I didn't know Nodog ninety days ago," said Jess.

"Ah, yes," said Martin. "Nodog. The one unqualified achievement any of us can boast of. Maureen's quiz team excepted, of course."

I didn't remind him about the newsagent's. I know it's not much, but it might have seemed as though I was rubbing it in a bit.

"Let's tell our suicidal friend about Nodog. 'Oh, yes. Jess here has met a man who doesn't believe in names, and thinks we should all kill ourselves all the time.' That'll cheer him up."

"That's not what he thinks. You're just taking the p——. What did you want to bring all this up for, JJ? We were going to have a good night out, and now everyone's all f——ing depressed."

"Yeah," said JJ. "I'm sorry. I was just wondering, you know. Why we're all still here."

"Thanks," said Martin. "Thanks for that."

In the distance we could see the lights on that big Ferris wheel down by the river, the London Eye.

"We don't have to decide right now anyway, do we?" said JJ.

"Course we don't," said Martin.

"So how about we give it another six months? See how we're doing?"

"Is that thing actually going round?" said Martin. "I can't tell."

We stared at it for a long time, trying to work it out. Martin was right. It didn't look as though it was moving, but it must have been, I suppose.

Nick Hornby's inimitable writing—about sports, music, family, life, or love—is original, moving, and insightful.

His first book was a breakout memoir and love letter to the greatest game. His first novel was an international bestseller about a hapless record collector and his romantic woes. His stories explore characters who are sweet, sad, funny, and flawed in a world that is filled with the complications and triumphs of everyday life. These books are remarkable for their warm sense of humor, their psychological insight, and their detailed emotional geography.

T313-0713

High Fidelity

Rob is a pop music junkie who runs his own semi-failing record store. His girlfriend, Laura, has just left him for the guy upstairs, and Rob is both miserable and relieved. Rob seeks refuge in the company of the offbeat clerks at his store, who endlessly review their top five films; top five Elvis Costello songs; top five episodes of *Cheers*.

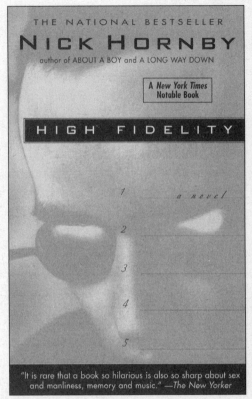

Rob tries dating a singer, but maybe it's just that he's always wanted to sleep with someone who has a record contract. Then he sees Laura again. And Rob begins to think that life with kids, marriage, barbecues, and soft rock CDs might not be so bad.

"Mr. Hornby captures the loneliness and childishness of adult life with such precision and wit that you'll find yourself nodding and smiling. *High Fidelity* fills you with the same sensation you get from hearing a debut record album that has more charm and verve and depth than anything you can recall."   **—The New York Times Book Review**

Fever Pitch

Nick Hornby has been a football fan since the moment he was conceived. Call it predestiny. Or call it preschool.

Fever Pitch, his first book, is a tribute to a life-long obsession. Part autobiography, part comedy, part incisive analysis of insanity, Hornby's award-winning memoir captures the fever pitch of fandom— its agony and its ecstasy, its community, and its defining role in thousands of coming-of-age stories.

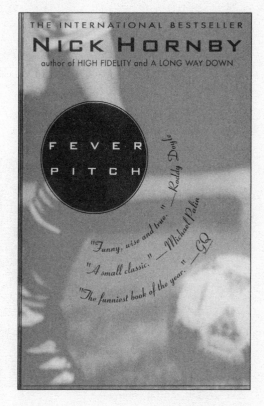

"Whether you are interested in football or not, this is tears-running-down-your-face funny, read-bits-out-loud-to-complete-strangers funny, but also highly perceptive and honest about Hornby's obsession and the state of the game. *Fever Pitch* is not only the best football book ever written, it's the funniest book of the year."   —*GQ*

About a Boy

Will Freeman may have
discovered the key to
dating success: If the
simple fact that they were
single mothers meant that
gorgeous women—women
who would not ordinarily
look twice at Will—might
not be only willing, but
enthusiastic about dating
him, then he was really onto
something. Single mothers
were all over the place. He
just had to find them.

Will wasn't going to let the
fact that he didn't have
a child himself hold him
back. A fictional two-year-
old named Ned wouldn't
be the first thing he'd
invented. And it seems to

go quite well at first, until he meets an actual twelve-year-old named
Marcus, who is more than Will bargained for.

"Hornby is a writer who dares to be witty, intelligent, and emotionally
generous all at once."   **—The New York Times Book Review**

How to Be Good

A brutally truthful, hilarious, compassionate novel about the heart, mind, and soul of a woman who, confronted by her husband's sudden and extreme spiritual conversion, is forced to learn "how to be good"—whatever that means, and for better or worse...

Katie Carr is a good person...sort of. For years her husband's been selfish, sarcastic, and underemployed.

But now David's changed. He's become a good person, too—really good. He's found a spiritual leader. He has become kind, soft-spoken, and earnest. Katie isn't sure if this is a deeply felt conversion, a brain tumor—or David's most brilliantly vicious manipulation yet. Because she's finding it more and more difficult to live with David—and with herself.

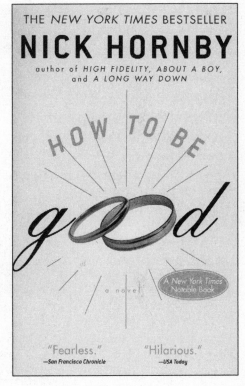

THE *NEW YORK TIMES* BESTSELLER

NICK HORNBY

author of *HIGH FIDELITY, ABOUT A BOY,* and *A LONG WAY DOWN*

HOW TO BE

good

a novel

A New York Times Notable Book

"Fearless."
—*San Francisco Chronicle*

"Hilarious."
—*USA Today*

"A darkly funny and thought-provoking ride."   —*USA Today*

Songbook

Songs, songwriters, and why and how they get under our skin...

A shrewd, funny, and completely unique collection of musings on pop music, why it's good, what makes us listen and love it, and the ways in which it attaches itself to our lives—all with the beat of a perfectly mastered mix tape.

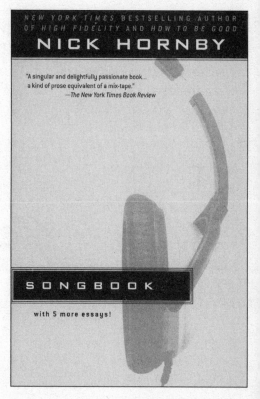

NEW YORK TIMES BESTSELLING AUTHOR
OF HIGH FIDELITY AND HOW TO BE GOOD
NICK HORNBY

"A singular and delightfully passionate book...
a kind of prose equivalent of a mix-tape."
—The New York Times Book Review

SONGBOOK

with 5 more essays!

"That whole subculture, all those mournful guys to whom the sound of record-store bin dividers clicking by is almost music enough, should love *Songbook*, yet so should anyone interested in great essays, or in the delicate art of being funny, or in how to write about one's feelings in such a way that other people will actually care." —*San Francisco Chronicle*

Slam

For sixteen-year-old Sam, life is about to get extremely complicated. He and his girlfriend— make that ex-girlfriend— Alicia, have gotten themselves into a bit of trouble. Sam is suddenly forced to grow up and struggle with the familiar fears and inclinations that haunt all adults.

Nick Hornby's poignant and witty novel *Slam* shows a rare and impressive understanding of human relationships and what it really means to grow up.

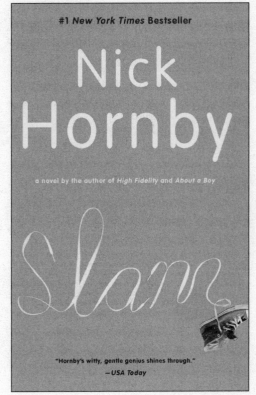

#1 *New York Times* Bestseller

Nick Hornby

a novel by the author of *High Fidelity* and *About a Boy*

Slam

"Hornby's witty, gentle genius shines through."
—*USA Today*

"We want to hear whatever this kid has got to say—the whole scary, hilarious story…Hornby just makes it look easy."　　**—*The Washington Post***

Juliet, Naked

Annie and Duncan are a mid-thirties couple who have reached a fork in the road, realizing their shared interest in the reclusive musician Tucker Crowe is not enough to hold them together anymore. When they disagree about Tucker's "new release," an acoustic version of his most famous album, it's the last straw—Duncan cheats on Annie, who promptly throws him out. Via an Internet discussion forum, Annie's harsh opinion reaches Tucker himself, who couldn't agree with her more. He and Annie start an unlikely correspondence

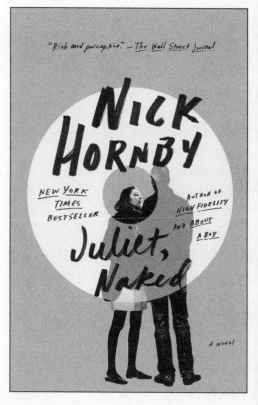

that teaches them both something about how two lonely people can gradually find each other.

Juliet, Naked is an engrossing, humorous novel about music, love, loneliness, and the struggle to live up to one's promise.

"Hornby seems, as ever, fascinated by the power of music to guide the heart, and in this very funny, very charming novel, he makes you see why it matters."

—*The New York Times Book Review*